Gentlemen in England

Gentlemen in England

A VISION

by

A. N. WILSON

VIKING

To N

VIKING
Viking Penguin Inc.
40 West 23rd Street,
New York, New York 10010, U.S.A.

First American Edition
Published in 1986

ISBN 0-670-80971-3
Library of Congress Catalog Card Number 85-40621
(CIP data available)

Printed in the United States of America by
R. R. Donnelley & Sons Company, Harrisonburg, Virginia
Set in Sabon

And gentlemen in England now a-bed
Shall think themselves accurs'd they were not here . . .

Henry V

Gentlemen in England

ONE

Maudie Nettleship

Maudie Nettleship had two letters that day, but she read them in silence over the breakfast table, and did not communicate their disturbing contents to her mother and father.

The three of them, Maudie and her parents, were seated at a heavy, round mahogany table, so highly polished that the Gothic silver toast-racks in front of each placing gleamed like little silver galleons on still brown water. Maudie, who did not feel particular hunger in the mornings, had contented herself merely with dry toast, some coffee and a fricassée of kidneys. But her father, who seldom lunched, had supplemented the fricassée with a bowl of porridge, the leg of a pheasant, somewhat congealed, and a slice or two of ham, the whole swilled down with a large cup of weak tea. He was a balding, puddingy sort of man, his remaining hairs sticking out, like a mangy ruff, greyish in tone, at the back of his head, down his cheeks and under his chin. The top of the head was strangely flat. You could have balanced, if you chose, a plate of fricasséed kidneys upon it with no risk of it slithering anywhere, particularly since, firm of jaw, the professor held himself upright. A Scotch aunt had told him at a formative age that it was injurious to the constitution if one's back touched a chair. Maudie looking at her father without meeting his gaze, thought how sad his steely grey eyes were behind their wire-framed spectacles. They were always sad. She could not bear to make him yet sadder by telling him the contents of her letters. Papa did not belong to the world of post offices and information imparted over breakfast tables. Volcanoes his expertise, he found out about the world by peering at little pieces of it through a microscope, by hammering little chunks of it, and keeping specimens of it in boxes. As it was, Maudie gathered, he had found out more than enough to account for the sad look in his eyes. Maudie did not *know* in so many words quite what her father had discovered. Her mother said it was better for them *not* to know, or they too would start to wonder if they believed any more. In a rather similar way, Maudie thought, it was certainly better for the professor not to know the news of Lionel, probably better not to know, even, the news of Mr Chatterway. He would be bound to find out soon enough.

That her mother *thought* she knew was obvious from the expression on her face as she spread quince jelly on a piece of buttered toast. Maudie's mother was extremely old, about forty, but she looked much younger than the professor. There was only a suspicion of grey in her hair which, parted in an ogee arch in the centre of her brow and drawn back into a thick chignon at the back of her head, framed her pretty face like a pair of heavy brown curtains. Her high-cheekboned countenance was pale, but the curl of her lips and the movement of her eyes were ironical. Maudie knew that her mother had identified the handwriting of *both* her correspondents. There was nothing new, besides, in her getting letters from either of them. Her brother Lionel wrote every week from the University, and, as for Mr Chatterway, his letters had been a familiar part of Mrs Nettleship's life ever since she could remember.

With its usual scraping noise, Horace Nettleship's chair was pushed back and the professor rose. His wife managed to avoid his gaze as he did so, and Maudie smiled kindly at her father, a smile inspired by the thought of how much anxiety she was sparing him by her silence.

'German today, my pretty?' asked the professor.

'No, Papa, it is Tuesday. Fräulein Schwartz comes on Mondays, Wednesdays and Fridays. On Tuesdays Mr Goe comes for Greek.'

'Oh.' The professor pursed his lips as he always did at the mention of the Reverend Field Flowers Goe. Maudie did not know why he did this. She suspected (hence her discreet silence) that any mention of the clergy pained her father since he had stopped being able to believe. But he was always 'funny' about anyone who seemed fond of her. It seemed silly to think that papa was *jealous* of Mr Goe, but that was what she did think.

'But not until half past ten, Papa. Until then I shall help Mama with embroidery, or rather, she will help me.'

'Oh.' Again, a slightly anguished expression as though an unmentionable subject had been broached. 'Oh, well then.' And, with this inarticulate valediction, the professor left the breakfast room. The shoulders of Maudie and of her mother visibly relaxed when he was gone, but it was later, in the morning room, that Mrs Nettleship raised the subject of the letters.

'What has Mr Chatterway got to write about?' she enquired.

Mother and daughter were both embroidering beaded covers for cream jugs.

'Mama, you'll never guess!'

'I certainly don't intend to, which is why I asked you to tell me.'

'Oh, but, Mama, I thought Papa would positively have a fit if I alluded to it at breakfast.'

'Hardly likely, my darling.'

'Mama, Marvo's coming back to England.'

'Dar - *ling*!'

'Mama?'

'Mr Chatterway to you.'

'Grandpapa always calls him Marvo.'

'Grandpapa is a good deal older than Mar – than Mr Chatterway, and he has known him since before I was born.'

'I know, Mama, but it surely is very exciting. Mr Chatterway is coming back to England.'

'So you said, my darling. But is there anything so extraordinary about that? After all, if not *every* year, certainly every few years, we have seen Mr Chatterway. I gathered anyway from the post mark that he was in London.'

'No, Mama, he is coming back to England *for good.*'

'Has anything Mr Chatterway ever done been, by the strictest standards, for good rather than merely for fun?'

'Would you like me to read you his letter, Mama?'

'I think we should continue with our embroidery,' said Mrs Nettleship dishonestly, 'though there is little enough light today.'

The sun had been doing its best, since dawn, to shed a little light into The Bower, Abbey Grove, but it was on the point of recognising its match in the Nettleships and going behind a thick black cloud. Earlier, from a bright cyaneous firmament, it had smiled down on St John's Wood, but it found difficulty, when it came to The Bower, in getting past the high hedges, the tall fir trees in the garden, and the laurels in the shrubbery before it got to the house. Still, the sun had done it, and made a manly show of falling upon the garish mullioned Gothic, some thirty years old, where the professor and his household chose to reside, an asymmetrical, unhappy-looking house which sprouted turrets and porches and balconies where you least expected them. Lest the sunlight thought to pierce the windows or balconies, the wary Nettleships had erected a good deal of ironwork (Fish and Co) in the way of railings, balustrades, drainpipes and lattices and then, as though faintly ashamed of the architectural exuberance of the exterior, they had trained an abundant Virginia creeper to swamp its walls from the area to the highest tower. The combination of red brick excrescences and the green of the creeper suggested that a giant piece of meat had been cast down in the garden, a raw leg of mutton perhaps, hastily covered with a liberal coating of mint sauce to disguise the fact that it had not been properly cooked.

Human entrants, no less than the sun, might find The Bower forbidding, or at any event be struck by how fiercely it hid itself from itself, how generously it was swathed. The front door itself was thickly draped with a heavy curtain, the weight and texture of a carpet, and intruders were admitted by a maid who existed beneath several layers of linen and starched muslin. In all probability there was a staircase beneath the thick carpets and the brass rods over which you would tread, just as to your right, behind a clutter of vulgar prints by Spy and the ornately floral wallpaper, there might arguably have been a wall.

Whether there were any walls left in the drawing room into which you would now be admitted is an altogether more dubious consideration, for, on all sides, there was not only a more generously entwined floral pattern – michaelmas daisies rampaging from dark brown wainscotting to fudgy ceiling – but almost every one of the little purple blooms was itself obscured by a heavy frame of gilt or walnut. There were four enormous canvases representing Scotch animals in varying degrees of decomposition. Some shaggy Highland cattle – themselves as well-swathed as The Bower – gazed, in one painting, across the room towards a stag being torn apart by hounds, Blair Atholl or Glen Somewhair or Castle Macksomething glimpsed in the background. Between these disconcerting reminders of 'nature red in tooth and claw' there were an abundance of portraits in oval frames, persons redder in cheek than in claw whom it would have been safe to conclude to be Nettleships. And those oval-framed, ill-favoured cousins, uncles, grandsires and aunts of the professor fought for space among the michaelmas daisies with views of Vesuvius, Etna, and other famous volcanoes of the world. Somewhere in the middle of it all there was a representation of Her Majesty the Queen.

Not much of this was seen by daylight. It needed the gas, as the professor said, to be seen at its best. Mere morning sunbeams could not get at it, through the creeper and the ironwork, or within the half-closed Nottingham lace curtains, and the further lined draperies of heavy green velvet which festooned the dark brown of the Gothic window frames. Such sunbeams as penetrated the swooping lace and velvet fell into a chaos of immovables and seemed to hop about as if they knew they were there under sufferance and only dared to light up one object in three. Here, as in the hallway, everything was adorned or draped or covered. The stained oak boards of the floor groaned beneath the suffocating carpet, itself darkly invisible under the sofas, chairs, occasional tables, bureaus and bookcases. Tables, chiefly octagonal in shape, were concealed with an undercloth of baize or velvet and an overcloth of cream-coloured Nottingham lace to match the curtains. A similar drapery protected the marble chimney-piece, on whose lacy and multi-levelled surfaces, as on all available table tops, there rioted an abundance of clutter, Staffordshire shepherds and shepherdesses: a bronze Laocöon, wrestling with snakes, or perhaps merely tearing at the snakes in exasperation at the sight of so many Nettleships; fans; snuff boxes, pin boxes, card boxes, a plenitude of every imaginable kind of box in gaily-coloured woods and mother of pearl. On the writing desk, as too on the chimney-piece, dozens of Nettleships, ages and genders various, closed photographic ranks and peered at the cows and the statuary from knobbly silver frames. On the wall opposite the windows, a walnut piano sprouted brass candlesticks.

In the middle of all this, Maudie sat with her mother and embroidered cream jug covers for a silent space. And then she said, 'Marv – that is, Mr Chatterway, asks me to send you his special love.'

'I wonder that Mr Chatterway spends so much of his money and energy on postage,' said Charlotte. 'Why can't he leave a card like anyone else?'

'Because, he says, he knows us too well and regards us almost as family, so that it would be too hurtful if we were to turn him away.'

'Really, Mr Chatterway is very absurd at times.' She spoke, perhaps she felt, as though she saw Mr Chatterway constantly rather than, as was the case, at intervals not much more frequent than annual or biennial. 'I have heard before of these schemes of his to return to London. They don't last because he don't settle. He can't, now, having been on the move for twenty five years.'

'I didn't think Papa would be very pleased if I had told you at breakfast that Mr Chatterway at least *intends* to make London his residence.'

'Intends. Fiddlesticks.'

'But he wouldn't, would he, Mama?'

Charlotte Nettleship laid her work on her lap for a while and stared through the gloom at her daughter. A brittle degree of understanding flowed between the two females when they were discussing Mr Chatterway, but when Maudie mentioned the professor an expression of glazed bewilderment passed over her mother's features, as though she had begun to speak in some incomprehensible tongue.

'I mean,' Maudie glossed, 'Papa does not for some reason find Mr Chatterway agreeable. I have noticed it.'

Mrs Nettleship gave out a little sigh.

'I am much more anxious,' she said, 'to know Lionel's news.'

'Oh, Mama, I couldn't tell it in front of Papa, I couldn't; and he asks me not to tell you, even, because he wants time to tell you in his own way. But Papa will be so angry with him that I shall *burst* if I don't warn you, really I shall.'

The absolute pallor of the girl's cheeks developed, in the gloomy half-light, the excitement of a pinkish ardour.

'Maudie, I *declare!*' exclaimed her mother impotently, but with a grin of girlish conspiracy. 'Either tell me or don't tell me, but don't *flirt* with my feelings in this truly exasperating manner.'

There was a pause, and then the girl blurted out, 'He wants to be a . . . ' Charlotte had somehow half-expected the revelation, half-expected the effect it would have on the teller. For, before the word *clergyman* had passed Maudie's lips, she was not as, a minute before, an undiscerning stranger would have predicted, giggling, but sobbing and sobbing in her mother's arms.

Charlotte Nettleship's elegant white little hands clutched her daughter's mane of chestnut hair and stroked it, like a cape, around her gingham shoulders. Beside her on the sofa, she rocked the girl as if she were a tiny infant. Instinct had for long informed her that any news about Lionel's future would be crushingly intolerable to his sister; why *this* news more than any other, should have made Maudie weep, her mother did not try to inquire, nor to understand. The contents of Lionel's letter were disclosed, parts of it were at length read, to the mother. He spoke of sensations to which both women were strangers: a passionate curiosity about the Arian controversy in the fourth century, a sudden sense that history, philosophy and theology had 'come alive' as a result of hearing one of the dons lecture; a growing fondness for a young man in his college called Everard Gutch; a feeling that his life would have no meaning or purpose if he were not able to serve God as a priest in the Church of England. Charlotte could have told Maudie that Lionel was not, surprisingly enough, the first man in the world to feel these things. They were all, excepting his particular fondness for Mr Gutch, commonly felt emotions; and if they were true ones, Lionel must of course be encouraged to follow his conscience. There was no good in such counsels because, as the mother was acutely and painfully aware, Maudie's heart had taken a jolt from which it would never recover. The tears were soon enough dried. Maudie retreated to her bedroom to splash about with her wash-hand basin and a towel and once more to brush her hair. At twenty-five past ten, with ludicrous predictability, Mr Goe was giving his stick and hat to the much-swathed maid in the hallway, and by half past ten Maudie was closeted with him in the dining room, construing Xenophon. From time to time, even through the thickness of doors and walls and carpets and draperies, Mr Goe's silly laugh could be heard coming up from downstairs.

Charlotte stitched silently, hearing her daughter's silence while the curate boomed and quoted and roared. All the world loved Maudie; it was her calling in life to be worshipped and adored. Mr Goe was plainly besotted with her, but so, too, was Fräulein Schwartz who taught her German and music, so too had been Miss Adeney, the unfortunate governess. Since all the grown-ups adored her, and no one who had ever met her had failed to adore her, it was quite natural that she should accept adoration as her due, poor little Maudie. But there was, as the mother observed, only one being in the universe to whom Maudie was able to give wholehearted affection in return: and that was Lionel, her brother. Perhaps none of them, six months before, had made enough allowance for the momentous transformation which was to take place in Lionel's life when he went to the University. He had, after all, gone off to Harrow term by term and returned during each vacation to his own hearth and family. Charlotte Nettleship had still not absorbed to the full the fact that her son was approaching manhood, and that however cordially he felt towards his family, the day was fast approaching when he would be ready to leave them and pursue a life of his own. To this degree, Harcourt College was quite unlike Harrow. At Harrow he had come and returned at regular intervals. At the end of his time at Oxford he would *not* return, or at least, he would not return on the same terms. His parents would *expect* him to choose some avocation befitting a gentleman of the professional class. It looked unlikely that he would be scholar enough to become a man of learning like his father: Charlotte had wondered perhaps if he would read for the Bar, and hoped, somewhat, that he would not choose to go into 'business' or the Stock-Exchange. With such a limited range of choices, it was not particularly surprising that Lionel should think of becoming a parson. Half the Harrow masters and more than half the dons at Oxford were in orders. Horace could grumble about it and doubtless would, but you could not help a young man being influenced by his surroundings and his fellows. Maudie's tears – the poor child hardly knew it herself – were not for Lionel's *choice* of profession. She wept at the half-realisation that Lionel was to have a profession at all, and was not, after Harcourt, to return to the nursery. How we assume as children, Mrs Nettleship reflected, that life will go on exactly as before. And then, with a sigh, she reflected how rarely it does, and how rarely, as grown-ups, we want it to.

TWO

Mr Waldo Chatterway

The exile was home. As Maudie had told her mother, Marvo, more properly Mr Waldo Chatterway, had been drawn back into the bricky metropolis. For weeks before the May in which he finally disembarked, his *rentrée* was heralded, in a hundred households, by the arrival of the half-legible notes of which even his most distant acquaintances could not fail, at some stage of life, to be the recipient. They had been, the notes, a self-perpetuating habit over the last two decades, enabling him, very often, to be in closer touch with the doings and habits of friends than those in the thick of the season. Even though only a handful of his correspondents replied to his scribbles, they provided him with more than enough material for his next session at the writing desk. By careful absorption and collation of the little manuscripts, usually in a female hand, which formed the subject of his matutinal perusals, Mr Chatterway was able to startle his many correspondents by knowing things about themselves almost before they had taken place. The speed and efficiency of his intelligence network had given him the reputation of a magician. Even allowing for the postal delays which were inevitable when he went much further afield than Paris, he could astound young women by congratulating them on their engagement the day *before* such an alliance was announced; or baffle hostesses by communications posted in Naples, which appeared to be fully acquainted with the composition of their last night's dinner table.

Every year or so, at irregular and unexplained little intervals, Mr Chatterway would descend on London in person, with polyglot expressions of disgust at its *mores, ton, zeitgeist* and *risorgimento*. He took it as axiomatic that the French cooked better meals, that the Italians were better musicians and architects, that the Prussians were the superiors of the English in all areas of political science. Even Mr Chatterway's voice, though betraying no continental inflexion, had developed a far-away drawl, when he spoke his own language, which suggested that he wanted to put a great distance between himself and his origins. 'How very, very *English!*' was an exclamation, on his lips, inseparable from hostility, or at best condescension or amusement.

These visits of his to London, lasting anything between six weeks and three months, would involve a carefully orchestrated social programme in which by his own account every hour of the day was crammed with society. Lord Houghton's breakfast would begin a day in which he might lunch with the Duchess of Rutland or Lady Rosebery. The evenings? It was not always apparent how Mr Chatterway spent his evenings, but sometimes he would suggest that he had attended dinners of unspeakable grandeur, or cultivated friends dwelling as he put it in unapproachable light. On the other hand, the hints given to humbler friends about the heights scaled and the slopes conquered needed to be tempered with the known historical fact that Mr Chatterway had not been received at Court for more than a quarter of a century. Nor would he ever be so received so long as (the vivid phrase was that of his friend Mr Severus Egg) 'the goody-goodies were in charge.' This hardly stopped Mr Chatterway, though approaching the age of three score and therefore old enough to know better, being the kind of man who was such a bad influence, in Paris and in London, on a very impressionable and sybaritic young man from Windsor. Some said that it was Mr Chatterway who had introduced the young man to Mrs Langtry. It was even said by those who moved in such circles that another voice in Windsor, a female one, had referred to 'that odious Mr Chatterway', a *sobriquet* on which our friend dined out for a season.

Now, however, instead of merely doing in his own fashion a season, Mr Chatterway wanted to come home. The frenetic hurry from club to lawn, from ball to house party, from race meeting to show, from wedding to funeral, was starting to tire him and, much as he liked to complain about it, he had missed, over the previous twenty-five years, the pleasure of continuous life in dear old England. The precise details of his disgrace, some twenty-five years before, had been smudged by the passage of time. Probably no one in London, except Severus Egg, knew the true story. A whole generation had grown up for whom the wronged wife, now a permanent exile, was a figure of pure legend. But legends of course are very localised affairs, and different migrant tribesmen, before the dawn of nations, developed long cycles which cast the Dark Age heroes in wildly contrasting moulds or lights. For one Germanic gleeman, Attila was a benign father of his people, while in another *comitatus,* the name of the 'little father' was synonymous with blood-curdling savagery. In the same way, Mr Waldo Chatterway's name produced startlingly different reverberations from one London drawing room to the next. For some, perhaps frivolous souls, Mr Chatterway was a gadfly, a buzzing irritant who amused them for a few months of the year but of whom they said, 'What a mercy he does not bother us all the year round.' In other households, his name could not be mentioned; it was on a level with the coarsest impropriety or profanity, words not to be heard on polite lips. Casual historians might derive the impression from such severe moralists that the hostesses who forbade him thus were thinking of his poor wife. But it was usually the case that Mr Chatterway had within, as it were, living memory been received in that very drawing room where now the mere mention of his name produced such a tight intake of breath. Perhaps for a season he had even been a favourite there before he felt the compulsion to re-enact the usual pattern of his fortunes. Something was said; something unpardonable fell from Mr Chatterway's lips. It was unknown why he did it, but presumably the excitement caused by the shocked expressions on the faces of his hostess and her friends made up for the pain when he was subsequently excluded. For sure enough when he next left his card at her ladyship's door, the footman had been instructed to announce that she was not at home to Mr Chatterway.

On being told that once again his younger friend had suffered some social débâcle; Severus Egg would always laugh that gleeful laugh of his, and say, 'Tomorrow to fresh woods and pastures new.' Mr Chatterway was as good at making new friends as he was at abusing the old. He was, after all, very charming. And his compulsive quest for society, though coloured by an unquestioned appreciation of rank, title and fashion, was not a pure *snobisme*. Many of those with whom he formed his freshest, his newest intimacies, were nothing to boast of. He had the gift of intimacy. Whether with one of his 'little friends' or with the 'taller poppies in the field' he managed to establish a playful sense that they were uniquely special to him, and when, as he always did, Mr Chatterway disappeared once more to the continent, the newly cherished 'little friend' or 'poppy' could be assured of receiving, at least once a week, some *billet* more or less *doux* throughout the drab months of winter. It was to these, the hundred and fifty or so 'intimates' with whom Mr Chatterway would communicate before making a 'flying visit' to London. And it was to them – Maudie Nettleship among their number – that he had intimated the intention, so uncharacteristic as to be to most hearers incredible, to 'settle'.

Certainly there could be no doubt that he had arrived in London. He had hardly been back three days, and already his card had been left on a hundred silver salvers in London's richer quarters; inhabitants of its further reaches, like Maudie, having to be content for the time being with notes. His arrival was very roughly contemporaneous with that of the cuckoo. An ornithologist would be puzzled were he to be informed that a bird of passage had decided to stay in these shores for ever. Observers of society were no less startled to learn of Waldo Chatterway's intention to 'settle'. It seemed a denial of nature. Yet, there were stories, and why should anyone doubt them, of rooms in Half Moon Street, and a couple of servants engaged. Perhaps a man more conscious of his dignity would have waited until the end of the season before making up his mind. What if he were not received back into the bosom of society as freely as he had hoped and expected? Would it not have been better to be able to creep off again after a month or two to Paris or Rome or Venice without making it obvious that London had rejected him? Perhaps so, but Mr Chatterway who had so much vanity had very little pride. He was not far from his sixtieth year and an inescapable and chilling meditation on his final departure repeated itself on his mind. How many of his friends were true friends? How many of them would feel anything more than a passing twinge at his last farewell? You could not write to your friends and ask them such a question, but you could write to them and say that, after many a long year abroad, you were coming home for 'good'. The lukewarmness of the replies would perhaps be a painful revelation, but it would have something of truth in it. Oddly enough, he felt confidence in almost none of his intimates. He was not sure of a single family, unless it were the Nettleships, his 'little friends' Charlotte and Maudie; but why that should be, he chose not to puzzle out. The thought was threatening to flicker through his finely handsome head when we catch our first glimpse of Mr Chatterway. Silver of hair and sombre of garb, he looks like a pillar of society; if not a lawyer or a civil servant, we might even suspect him of being a clergyman were it not for a very discreet speck of blue silk which shows above his waistcoat and beneath the sharp whiteness of his collar. The rest – the silk hat he carries in his carefully manicured hands, the coat, the trousers and the spats are all positively funereal, not to say clerical, so that his ruddy, and rather comical old face, with a lot of laughter in the lines about his bright blue eyes, comes as something of a shock at the top of it all. He is standing when we catch the first glimpse of him, on his own, at the back of the church in Hanover Square, a little despondent at its cluttered emptiness, its rows of unoccupied galleries and box pews, the lonely impression it gave out of a crowd who had all departed. The walls of its handsomely appointed aisles and galleries were adorned, not like the ecclesiastical interiors to which his continental eyes had grown accustomed, with statues or images of saints; merely with names. And they were not the names of prophets and patriarchs but of the earls and bankers and duchesses who had dutifully heard, over the previous century and a half, the words of the English prayer book read aloud in that comfortable room while they propped themselves against their red velvet cushions. It was a fine thing, the English religion, with no more of humbug in it than any other form of religion. But more than their cuisine, their democracy, their poets or their musicians, the Church of England prompted Mr Chatterway to declare, '*Que c'est très, très anglais!*'

In continental capitals, it was often his wont to stagger from the heat of a dusty pavement or piazza and penetrate the marbly cool of some interior where, blinking to adjust one's eyes to the dark, appeasing with a few *sous* the gnarled beggars who hovered as a matter of course by the reeking leather curtain at the door, one strode on into darkened aisles, where blackened and hooded figures held beads before the statuary, where pockets of flickering candlelight picked out erratic little orange haloes in the overwhelming darkness. All such churches, whether famed for their carvings and paintings or without the smallest architectural signifiance, had about them an atmosphere which was quite lacking in this ecclesiastical monument to English good sense.

Mr Chatterway took no strong theological view. This quarter-century's exposure to the externals of European religion was a matter of hanging-lamps, of muffled voices from the vast blackness of baroque confessionals, of bells rung shrilly at distant altars, of peasants queueing to kiss reliquaries. Unlike England, his beloved Europe had striven to make itself Enlightened, to organise itself along a rational pattern. But still, in all the great cities of Europe at every street corner, there lurked these temples of the irrational, these darkened hallowed halls in which no one paid a pew rent or spoke from handsome wine-glass pulpits about Paley's *Evidences,* but where anyone was allowed to stray, to mutter their secrets, to lament their sins and to confront the great mystery of things.

The seemly, square, well-painted, brightly tended box dedicated in the midst of Hanover Square to the glory of Saint George seemed designed for an altogether different purpose: without the fashionable occupants of its pews, it seemed to have no function, no reason for existing. In this place, Mr Waldo Chatterway had seen them come and seen them go. Up this very aisle his wife had walked, poor creature, some thirty years before. How many 'Te Deums' and 'Jubilates' had been trilled there since by how many dowagers. How utterly this pride of London churches lacked the *mystery* which even the most sordid fanes of Paris or Naples could provide. The English were not merely able to pretend they could get by without mystery. They appeared positively to be happier without it! The church where he was married! In an equivalent continental setting the place, which evoked such memories, might have brought back uncontrollable paroxysms of remorse, this scene of early declarations unvouchsafed and early promises unfulfilled. It was, as far as Mr Chatterway's own personal history had unfolded, a monument to human fickleness, a visible reproach. In the darkened pits of his continental city ramblings, the lessons would be driven home all too crudely, with the unavoidable statues of the most chaste San Giuseppe and the ever-virgin Genetrix. At the same time, buried in the unsalubrious shadows, was offered the most trivially easy remedy for blotting out the past; and merely to wait one's turn on the little bench beside the confessional would be to wipe out the guilt of years.

The temple of St George's offered neither the exotic pleasure of being stabbed with guilt, nor the esoteric magic by which guilt could be appeased. It brought back, merely, memories with which the intellect was fully equipped to deal. In the cities which he had made his abode for the previous quarter-century, each area of life was exotically, sometimes exaggeratedly defined. Boudoirs were definitely boudoirs. Holy places were holy. Those places given over to the vain pleasures of avarice, or of the senses, proclaimed their function with a discernible celebration of the *genius loci*. Mr Chatterway thought, as he turned away from the west door and stood in the porch, with what ease could St George's be converted into a bank, or into a ballroom, or into the coffee room of a club. On the continent of Europe, the World, the Flesh and the Devil kept up their traditional assaults upon the spirit. It was only in England, it appeared, that God and Mammon felt they should knock along together as if they were gentlemen.

It was open to question whether Mr Chatterway was a gentleman. The dubiety of his claim to the title explained why he was welcomed in some drawing rooms and banned from others. For whereas some members of the human race like to define themselves by the codes they keep, there are plenty who like to be thought daring. They would never go too far themselves but it excited them to cultivate those who would, or who had, and into this category Mr Chatterway decidedly fell. Perhaps it was possible, whatever a man's father or school or regiment, for him to forfeit the title of gentleman? If so, none would guess it from the immaculate figure who descended the steps of St George's and made his jostled progress down the blackened bricky thoroughfare of Conduit Street, and who paused by the window of Lambs to look at the kid gloves on display there. Perhaps the jaunty angle at which he wore his chimney-pot hat would have struck some observers as not altogether gentlemanlike; and by the strictest code it would have to be said that his face with brazen lack of decorum had been exposed too much to the rays of the European sun. But the most obvious fact about the man as he stood at the shop window was that, in the demotic phrase, he was at a loose end.

Mr Chatterway's end, had indeed, scarcely ever been looser. Like Noah, he had sent out a dove – nay, not one dove, but dozens, in the form of letters and *billets* and notes to his hundred and fifty friends – and the results had so far been disappointing. Few had had the courtesy to reply. The waters remained obstinately covering the sea and he had already begun to think despondently of visiting his friends in the suburbs if Mayfair should prove unresponsive to his arrival. His little friends, Charlotte and her daughter Maudie, were jollier by far than the raddled worldly dowagers who worshipped at St George's, Hanover Square.

The thought occurred to him as he meditated upon gloves. Having meditated, he entered the shop and made a purchase, and was honest enough to ask himself when he emerged from his colloquy with the glover, whether he had bought new kid gloves because he needed them, or because he would welcome the arrival of a little post at the rooms in Half Moon Street, even though it be a parcel sent round at his own request. He smiled a little at his own childish loneliness and impatience. Three days, only, and he had begun to despair of anyone still liking him. And more gloves! He had a thousand. A new pair, however, was useful, and gloves were the sort of thing at which the English excelled.

The breeze was warm, the late morning sunshine enough to revive his drooping spirits by the time he had traversed Piccadilly and progressed down Lower Regent Street in the direction of his club. Even though change was everywhere distressingly apparent in London (the crowds in Piccadilly! In his youth, the poor had simply not been *seen* there. They stayed away, or they were *kept out!*), the old place tugged at his heart strings. He abused it in the way some men grumbled good-humouredly at the women they loved for fear that too much expression of what was in their hearts would make them soft.

Turning into his club, he luxuriated in its silence. The street noise was hushed, the great clatter of wheels and shout of men and jangling of horse furniture which had bombarded his ears since quitting the church of his matrimonial indiscretion. The club brought peace, as it had done so reassuringly since he was elected thirty years before. Half the members, more than half, were unknown to him now, but the other half nodded to him in a friendly enough way. There had been those, of course, who had felt, at the time of his half-rumoured disgrace twenty-five years ago, that Mr Chatterway should have resigned his membership. The matter had been discussed in the Committee. But he had friends here and none stouter in his affections than his old comrade Severus Egg whose advice – 'Stick it out, my boy, stick it out' – had been followed punctiliously.

Mr Chatterway greeted the porter who presented him with a gratifyingly plump bundle of envelopes – ah! so his birds were all coming home to roost. Rifling through them hastily as he ascended the old staircase, he smiled again. Indeed, indeed, he had feared too soon, for he saw from the scribbled impressions on the various envelopes that Lady This and Lady That had written replies to him, and in all probability the Dowager Countess of Somewhere or Another expected him that very afternoon. A careful half-hour of research in the library would be necessary, and as he sat there with a paper-knife poised and a small engagement book open on his knee, the social calendar once more began to be populated. Hardly a lady had replied without expressing a generalised hope that he would call upon them soon, and no less than six of them had issued invitations to dinner.

There was no word of reply from *la maison* Nettleship, but then, as Mr Chatterway reflected upon it, Maudie could only have received his letter some three hours previous. The afternoon post might bring a reply, but he had rather hoped to catch up on Nettleship news from Severus Egg, who usually took his luncheon in the club at about that hour.

Severus Egg, the reader should perhaps be informed, was, in addition to being one of Waldo Chatterway's dearest and oldest friends, the father of Charlotte Nettleship. By the time Chatterway had responded to his various invitations and licked the envelopes, he had hoped and assumed that Egg's grinning countenance would appear in the library. It was two years since the friends had set eyes upon one another, though, as Chatterway often observed, there was no man in London dearer to him than Egg, no young married woman dearer than his daughter Mrs Nettleship, and no child dearer than his grand-daughter Maudie. When the afternoon was advanced to one o'clock and Egg had still not made his appearance, Mr Chatterway grew to be worried.

'Seen Egg?' he asked one of the older members who passed him on the landing, only to be informed that no one had seen Egg for a week.

'Not ill, what?' asked Mr Chatterway, to whom the old member grunted.

'How should I know, I'm not his physician, and he has not been seen for a week.'

Mr Chatterway went to lunch alone in the Coffee Room. He had been looking forward to a good bottle of Lafite '48 with his comrade while they rehearsed the doings of the Nettleships. As it was, he made do with a few glasses of the ordinary club claret and ate a chop, in a state of mounting puzzlement and anxiety. Mr Egg's appearances at the club were as regular as clockwork. He had been going there every

forenoon for as long as anyone could remember, probably longer.
Drinking a little wine, writing a few letters and playing a few rubbers
of whist were generally thought to be not merely his only respectable
pleasures, but his only activities whatsoever. To hear that Egg had not
been seen in the club for a week was like being told that another man
had not eaten for a week. A cruel thud about Mr Chatterway's heart
made him fear the worst. How old was Eggy? Seventy-five? At least.
He liked to boast in that melancholy cynical fashion of his that he was
past his prime before the death of William IV.

A waiter was at Chatterway's side. He was offering him a slice of
treacle tart, but Chatterway gestured him away with an impatient
wave of the hand. Poor Maudie, from whom he had been expecting a
note, was perhaps already grieving for the death of a grandfather?
Distracted with worry, Mr Chatterway thought that he would have a
peep into the downstairs drawing room, where the card tables were
laid out. For all he knew, Eggy was down there so absorbed in the
game that he had not noticed the hour. Perhaps he was there, in his
chair by the window, his hand clasped close to his thickly brocaded
waistcoat, saying as he said a dozen times a week (it had become a club
joke), 'I wonder when the last game of *ombre* was played in this room.'

'Hello, Chatterway,' said one of the club bores, on his appearance in
the downstairs drawing room. 'Looking for a rubber?'

'No,' said Chatterway, 'I am looking for a friend.'

'Care for a rubber while you wait?'

Only the lotus eaters played whist in the afternoons, as Severus Egg
was fond of observing. Chatterway was not in a sufficiently leisurely
mood even to contemplate a game. All he minded about now was his
old friend. He had grown perfectly convinced, during the consumption, upstairs, of the lamb chop, that Severus Egg was ailing. But
before he had the chance to inquire after his friend, the lotus eater
astonished him by placing a cigar between his whiskery lips and
lighting it with a spill from the grate. Chatterway peered at the lotus
eater incredulously. He knew him by sight, a clerk in the House of
Lords; but was he mad?

'We could play with a dummy,' he said, between puffs.

For once in a while, Mr Chatterway was speechless. He stared about
him and realised to his amazement that the lotus eater was not alone. A
dozen or so men were slouched or perched in chairs about the room
and they were all *smoking*.

'Since when did we smoke in this club, sir!' he peremptorily
inquired.

'Since last year, sir,' said the lotus eater, a little taken aback by Mr
Chatterway's tone. 'You've no objection, I hope.'

'Every objection, since you ask,' said Mr Chatterway. 'Filthy reeking habit.' But he felt ridiculous, to have been away so long that he had not caught up with it.

'Surely you have smoked yourself.'

'The point is not whether I smoked but where I smoked and when I smoked. Long before you or even, though you would find this unimaginable, I were conceived in our mother's wombs, there was a great lexicographer by the name of Samuel Johnson.'

'We've all heard of Dr Johnson, Chatterway,' said the lotus eater with a little laugh which he hoped would keep the conversation happy.

'Have we? Then you will remember what he said about cows and gardens, what?'

And with that, furious, Chatterway left the drawing room in great dudgeon, having forgotten to inquire of the lotus eater, who would almost certainly have known, the whereabouts of his old friend Severus Egg. He knew that with the young man, as with so many hostesses in the past, he had gone too far; but fear made him edgy. He almost ran down the club steps into Pall Mall, and with his hat at an even more rebellious angle than it had been before luncheon, he hailed a hansom and asked to be taken to Mr Egg's residence in Bloomsbury, convinced as he swayed about in the back of the cab, that the most he could hope to see of his old friend in this world would be a corpse. Forgotten for a moment were the dowagers to whom Mr Chatterway had written before luncheon, forgotten the cultivated witticisms of dinner parties, the excitement of balls and levées and breakfasts. Once more he was a vulnerable young man and Severus Egg his best friend in London: and he cursed himself for not having called on Egg directly he had disembarked at London docks.

'I was so sure I would meet him at the club,' he said miserably.

Pall Mall and Trafalgar Square were behind him, and their classical, though now so clouded splendours gave place, at the top of Charing Cross Road, to thicker crowds and noisome dwellings. Wheels and horses threw up billows of dust, so that Mr Chatterway passed this quarter as in a mist through which was discernible the wretched smell of the poor. Beyond the barrows in Cambridge Circus wound foetid overcrowded alleys, barefooted women with babies dangling about them like luggage and, in the ill-drained gutters, urchins staring at the passing traffic, their grey bewildered faces taut beneath their caps.

In Italy, thought Mr Chatterway, the beggars laugh. In London they look as solemn as articled clerks. But he had hardly had time to make anything of the reflection before the hansom was turning into Brunswick Square and, with a jolt of fear, he was ringing his old friend's front-door bell.

THREE

Mr Severus Egg

The door of Mr Egg's house was flung wide by a grinning, elderly negro whose curly white hair, exquisite swallow-tail coat, velvet piping and frogging, bright yellow breeches, white silk stockings and shiny black buckled shoes made a very picturesque and striking appearance.

'Ah, Bacon,' said Mr Chatterway, with the sympathetic tone one would adopt towards one recently bereaved. Mr Egg's valet had acquired his name when Mr Egg engaged him as his personal servant some forty and more years previous when sailor William was king. 'Dear Bacon.'

'Why, Mr Chatterway, sir! Only this morning Mr Egg say you was in town. Bacon, says he, why don't Mr Chatterway come up to see us? Anyone would think Bloomsbury was the North Pole – so he say, sir.'

While he spoke, Bacon's eyes laughed and his grin widened. Mr Chatterway prodded the snowy waistcoat of the butler and said, 'Has he given up all society then? What does he think his club is for? They've taken to smoking, damned filthy habit, what, in his absence. You can't get into the place to play a few rubbers without being belched at.'

'He can't go out, not this week, sir.'

'Then he *is* ill!'

'Ill, sir, why, bless me no,' and at the very suggestion of such a thing Bacon's face seemed to split in half altogether, revealing the perfection of all his ivory teeth.

'You come in here, sir, you follow me.'

This house, in Brunswick Square, was the place in which Charlotte Nettleship had grown to womanhood, a little shocked by the way in which, like her father the owner, the building had failed to move with the times. It was airy, well-proportioned, spacious. The spindly banisters swooped up the bare wooden stair in an elegant curve leading to an uncluttered landing on which stood a single Sheraton chair. The saloon into which Bacon led Mr Chatterway was full of light. No curtains obscured its tall symmetrical windows, nor carpets the polished boards of the floor. The panelled walls were a vivid apple green, the furniture, sparsely well chosen, almost all vaguely Grecian in shape and flavour and dating from the Regency. A few Italian landscapes, and a few architectural prints hung on the walls, but the main object of decoration was a large gilded looking-glass over the chimney-piece, in which the whole room was reflected.

'Chatterbox, what a lovely surprise, my dear! Bring him in, Bacon, bring him in!'

These words emanated from a figure in a bright green brocaded dressing gown and tasselated velvet smoking cap who was sitting in a cane chair by the hearth. He did not rise to greet his friend but added, 'Come and sit down, you old rascal, and tell me *all* the news. I can't get up as you see, I have been imprisoned here for a week by kind Mr Lupton who is endeavouring to capture a plausible likeness.'

'Can such vanity be matched?' asked Mr Chatterway. 'A portrait at your time of life?'

'They insisted,' said Mr Egg. 'They being the Royal Society of Literature.'

'Ah!' Mr Chatterway was genuinely impressed. Anything royal impressed him: he even looked on the scarlet livery of postmen because they delivered the *Royal* Mail with a greater deference than he would have offered to any merely republican common or garden mail.

'And this is Mr Lupton who has been commissioned by the Society to undertake the task.'

'The great Mr Lupton!' was Mr Chatterway's manner of greeting the painter. He disliked ever having to confess that he knew nothing of strangers and indeed, as it happened, the name of Lupton was not altogether unknown to him. 'A pupil of my dear old friend Alma-Tad, if I don't mistake.'

'Mr Alma-Tadema has mentioned me to you sir?' asked Lupton, very visibly surprised.

'Not in so many words,' drawled Chatterway, immediately anxious to cover his conversational traces but pleased with himself for having 'placed' Mr Lupton so quickly and readily. Much depended in the art of social history, which the vulgar called gossip, on seizing the value of coincidence. At a reception on his first evening in London Mr Chatterway had happened to run into a Varsity acquaintance who had mentioned Lupton's name as that of a 'rising' painter who was going to portray the Master of Harcourt. 'Mr Lupton, a pupil of Alma-Tadema,' the phrase had stuck in his head for some reason, and now here he was, a rather earnest-looking youth with a thick silky gold beard and penetrating dark eyes.

'Why don't you reach Tad to speak English properly?' said Chatterway. 'Ve vill all vear dogas and haf de real Roman style.'

Mr Lupton laughed at the accuracy of Mr Chatterway's parody.

'Wear what?' asked the sitter.

'Togas, Eggy. I shouldn't be surprised if our friend Mr Lupton here hasn't represented you as the Emperor Tiberius surrounded by catamites. If I'm not careful I shall end up in the corner of the canvas as a slave waving ostrich feathers, what.'

'It is not a Roman scene, sir; a perfectly straight portrait,' said the artist.

'I'm not being satirical if that's what you think. I've admired Tad for years – long ago before he ever came to this benighted island or any Englishman had ever heard of him. Saw his *Pastimes in Ancient Egypt* or some such twaddle decades ago in the Paris Salon.'

Mr Egg, who evidently liked being compared with the Emperor Tiberius, but disliked the way in which Mr Chatterway was hogging the conversation, leaving him out of it, and establishing such a distracting intimacy with the young painter, laughed a little crossly and intoned.

> This emperor hath no son, and now is old.
> Old and lascivious, and from Rome retired
> To Capreae, an island small but strong
> On the Campanian shore, with purpose there
> His horrid lusts in private to enjoy.

'Ha! ha!' And the breathy laugh, combined with the quotation, succeeded in silencing his garrulous companion. Lupton returned to his brushwork and for a moment Chatterway, looking over his shoulder, was silent, as he cast comparative glances between the canvas and the somewhat doll-like original perched opposite on his cane chair.

Severus Egg, the poet and man of letters, was quite tempting, to a painter, enough, as a visual phenomenon, without the need of dressing him up in a 'doga'. Not only were the clothes brightly well chosen, not only did the golden buttons shine on his waistcoat, and the silken cravat burst beneath his sharp little red chin like a vast overblown white peony – but the whole face, ruddy, bright-eyed, mandarin, mischievous, seemed obsolescently light-hearted. Bacon alone, his butler and valet and general factotum, knew the reason why Severus Egg's hair and whiskers retained their rich chestnutty hues, unaffected by the passing of time. Indeed to old friends such as Mr Chatterway who had grown greyer with the progress of the century, it actually seemed as though the whiskers of Severus became browner as year succeeded year, a very miracle of nature.

These years were, as the saying is, 'adding up'. Only a few malicious women in London were aware of such mathematical irrelevancies as whether Mr Egg was nearer three score years and ten or four score years in age. There was merely a generalised opinion that he carried himself well 'for his years' whatever those years might number. The expression was not inapposite since carrying himself was what he looked, much of the time, as if he were doing. He held his shoulders very high, even when sitting down, as though they bore the weight of a wooden yoke such as a milk-boy might carry from his cart. Egg had the appearance of perpetually shrugging. The resolute refusal of his shoulders to decline spoke of arrogance; or, if not arrogance, exasperation inexhaustible, at the vulgarity, the lack of *humour,* the absence of *bon ton* manifested by the times into which he survived. In fact, in his features, there was more mirth than dismay. His lips were usually wreathed in a grin, which made all the lines of his slightly creased pink old face turn upwards and gave the air less of an ancient Roman than of a courtier in some exquisite lost dynasty of old Cathay. His eyes, which darted about with nervous caprice when he spoke, were lost, when he smiled, in the hooded creases of his scornful old features.

'Tell me the news,' said the ever-allusive and polyglot Chatterway, 'of the dear Frau Professor.'

'Mrs Nettleship, you mean.' Without moving his facial muscles, almost without moving his lips, Severug Egg explained that allusion was being made to his daughter. 'I believe her to be very well, thank ye.'

'And happy in her romantic Bower, her Gothic casement.'

'Idyllically happy, yes.'

'Mrs Nettleship is one of my oldest comrades and friends,' explained Mr Chatterway for the benefit of the painter. 'If it weren't a joke my sincere friend here had heard a thousand times before I would insist that she was a very good Egg indeed, what? She lives, as her father has just informed us, a life of extraordinary serenity with a charming husband.'

'Darling old Netty,' laughed the father-in-law satirically.

'And two very handsome children – Lionel, whom I gather is doing very well at Harcourt.'

'Who do you gather that from?' inquired the grandfather incredulously. 'Really, Marvo, I know you know *every*body, but how can you possibly know how my grandson is rubbing along at the Varsity? Why, I don't even know anything of him myself.'

'Because,' Mr Chatterway was stung into revealing the sources of this piece of information, 'he happens to have made friends with

Archdeacon Gutch's boy; the archdeacon tells me they have developed
that weakness for fonts some boys go through.'

'Fonts?' asked Mr Lupton. 'Do you mean the thing in which babies
are christened?'

'That: and altars and crypts and clerestories, don't you know. The
whole caboodle.'

'Mr Chatterway means that my grandson is interested in architecture.' It seemed as though every phrase that the returning exile spoke
needed to be translated into English for the benefit of the painter. 'It is
the first I knew of it, but I see nothing wrong with such an interest.
Your calling it a weakness, makes it sound oddly improper.'

'You should have heard Archdeacon Gutch,' drawled Chatterway
darkly, but continued his description of *la famille* Nettleship, 'Lionel
who, with Master Gutch, finds piscinas and sedilias so wildly
entertaining, has a charmingly fragile and beautiful younger sister
who I should say at once is my favourite lady friend in all the *world*
and who cries *out* to be painted by your, as I now realise, very skilful
brush, Sir.'

'And how old is Miss Nettleship?' asked the painter, flattered by
Chatterway's absurdities.

'Maudie, she must be . . .'

But the grandfather interrupted with, 'Darling Maudie's still a
baby.'

'And the professor has but two children, sir.'

'But two,' said Chatterway, simultaneously with Mr Egg's repeated,
'Darling old Netty! I should explain, Mr Lupton, lest you derive an
entirely false impression from my friend Chatterway, that my
daughter's family know *nobody*. As you have already discovered
Chatterway knows everybody.'

'The Nettleships are so happy in their own society that they have no
need of anyone else's,' said Mr Chatterway. 'The professor is, besides,
too absorbed in his great work.'

'On volcanoes,' laughed Mr Egg. 'He has been working on a great
book about volcanoes ever since my daughter married him – what,
Chatterbox – twenty years ago? All their little holidays as far as I can
recollect have been spent in places of particularly volcanic interest.'

'Indeed,' confirmed the irrepressibly polysyllabic Chatterway, 'was
it not I who, on their very *lune de miel* in Napoli, tore myself away
from the dear old King and escorted them to see Vesuvius itself.'

'The professor has been to collect volcanic rocks in the Auvergne, in
the Greek Archipelago, oh, in the most surprising places. Even in
Devon.'

'Volcanoes in Devon!' The painter seemed astonished.

'A long time ago, mind you. Just rocks now, for Netty to tap away at with his darling hammers.'

'It was collecting red sandstone in Devon, I believe that *Monsieur le professeur* developed his doubts. Are you a religious man, sir?'

While the painter hummed and hawed, the sitter rescued him with, 'Take no notice of Chatterway.'

'But it is true, isn't it? Poor Nettleship began to feel that the World had not been made in seven days. Taken *le bon Dieu* a trifle longer, what, since he first said let there be *lumiére*. Million years longer. It's the sort of thing makes me glad I'm not clever, I don't have to think about such things.'

'No one is obliged to think about such things,' asserted Mr Egg.

'Unless they have the misfortune to be writing a treatise on volcanoes,' said Chatterway. 'Obviously *then* it is the sort of thing which becomes an inescapable consideration.'

' . . . and now,' chanted Egg.

> 'Led on, yet sinless, with desire to know
> What nearer might concern him, how this world
> Of heaven and earth conspicuous first began. . . .'

'Poor silent professor,' glossed Chatterway, 'he hasn't spoken since about it, has he?'

'Not much; in fact, not at all,' concluded the father-in-law with a sigh. 'But then, darling Netty was always a taciturn sort of fellow without a great deal to say for himself, don't you know.'

'At Buddleigh Salterton I believe it was, chipping with his hammer, that the doubts began.'

And rather to the young painter's astonishment the two older men, laughed, a reedy conspiratorial laughter by no means explicable in terms of what had just been said. It occurred to the painter that Severus Egg did not perhaps take his daughter's family wholly seriously, but this attitude, quite discernible, was given merely *ex cathedra* without either the justice or the malice of explanation.

In truth, explanations would have been hard enough to give. Chatterway's perhaps harmless laughter vexed old Severus in so far as it awakened a consciousness of the prosy tedium of life at The Bower. Twenty and more years before, when the professor had so unaccountably captured Charlotte's heart, Severus Egg had taken a poor view of his son-in-law. He had considered Nettleship too old, at five and thirty, to marry a girl not one and twenty. He had further thought Nettleship a very dull dog, and twenty years' acquaintance had done nothing to modify this initially harsh assessment. Doubtless Charlotte was happy enough with the man, but by the exacting standards of the poet, Netty was a sobersides, and, by marrying him, Charlotte had moved into an alien sphere.

Severus Egg had striven, throughout his youth, and early manhood, for style, amusement, *le bon ton*. Looking back with the wisdom and historical awareness which sometimes accompanies age, he recognised ruefully that he had been born some twenty or thirty years late. He had been but a lad when Byron died. But to have known Byron! As he now realised, Mr Egg had been born just early enough to see the excellence, all the light, all the fun, and just late enough to watch it all evaporate, banished by lumpishness and self-righteous mediocrity. There was a time in London when Samuel Rogers had referred to 'the sublime Egg'. The Smith of Smiths had quipped about his name and once paid him the pretty compliment of quoting, at Lady Holland's table, a whole stanza of his 'Ode on the Rising Sun', adding, 'Ah, my dear Egg, thy yoke is easy, but thy burden Light.' What days! What breakfasts! What rides in barouches, what merriment. All seemed made, mind, body and spirit, for lightness, delicacy and wit. All pleasures could combine at a breakfast in the late twenties – the stimulation of brilliant tongues and brains, the delight of the palate and the company of beautiful, funny women. And they had cultivated Egg, he had had his day, oh yes!

'*Festina lente,* don't hasten!' Rogers had urged. And there had seemed, in those leisurely days, as though there were money enough and time enough to heed his counsel. 'Egg remains unhatched' they had cruelly quipped when his thirtieth year had passed and the slimmish volume of *Verses upon several occasions* had not been followed by anything new. Perhaps the occasions which came to occupy his attention were unsuitable subjects of verse. The pentameters, for whatever cause, no longer appeared, a sort of singing inside his head, without prompting. An 'Ode to Clio' published in the *Gentleman's Magazine* had been forced and unworthy of him. Reading it in cold print he had flinched with horror and vowed never to publish a new verse until it prompted itself. 'I lisped in numbers till the numbers came.' Life, meanwhile, provided other avocations. To be a fop, a *bon viveur,* a diner-out, a flirt – these were not callings to be taken up lightly, for each required the finesse and self-application of the artist. If he were to shine in the evening, he must devote his mornings to polishing; so that while Bacon attended to his whiskers, his buttons and his cuffs, Egg himself had mended his epigrams and burnished his wit.

The century, like a young man whose features were once considered handsome, had grown thicker and more corpulently pompous once it had passed its middle thirties. At Lady Holland's table you would talk, on the one hand of Plato's philosophy and Ariosto's versifying; on the

other, you would share the momentous exchange of amorous intelli-
gences, the everlasting 'all change' of the emotional life, the sensibili-
ties and passions of his social luminaries – of who was 'in' with whom
and 'out' with whom, who up, who down, and who with whose child.
Such talk, if gaily undertaken, rapidly, mercilessly, would have no
feeling of impropriety in it. Egg looked back on the malice of the
breakfasts as on a lost Eden. Then, imperceptibly at first, the talk, with
the food and the furniture, had grown gradually heavier. When the
simpering ladies had withdrawn their ringleted locks from the glassily
gas-lit dinners you started to find yourself next to earnest-eyed young
men, green from the new-fangled flare, who prosed of the Corn Laws
or of Tracts. The divine Plato was forgotten, Tertullian and
Chrysostom were in. Less was heard of the ravishing Ariosto or the
sublime Schiller. Portentous puppies lectured you on Comte or the
school of Tübingen. London submitted, as powerless as great Rome in
vanished time, to an invasion by the Goths and Huns. The bores had
crossed its ramparts. Fervent women, their pretty hands no longer to
be held beneath the damask folds of candlelit table-cloths, recounted
how they had heard Mr Carlyle lecture and Dr Newman preach.

This was the era thirty or forty years before the commencement of
this chronicle, when the Goths crashed over the mirth of London life,
that Severus Egg had met Waldo Chatterway, at a *soirée* of one of the
last hostesses to keep the old lamps burning. Despair, some years
before, had already entered Egg's soul and he had married, but if
memory served him well he had been out alone when Chatterway was
introduced to him. Lady Caroline Jarvis, the hostess in question, was
neither a Goth, nor a Vandal. Less imaginative than Egg, with whom
she had once been on terms of very close intimacy and (just) old
enough to be his mother, she took a more optimistic view. She believed
that the lamp of hedonism and frivolity could be carried into the dark
decades ahead. When the door of her house in Stanhope Terrace was
opened, and you were admitted by a powdered flunky in wig and
breeches, there was no suspicion that the barbarians beyond the gates
had already stormed the Capitol itself. Lady Caroline behaved as if the
Decline was unheard of, the Fall an impossibility. But her salon
became increasingly the haunt of runaways. It kept up all the old
splendours – and what a contrast with your modern Howell-and-
James vulgarities they were. But for all its yellow silks and gilded
French furniture, its cane chairs, its airy, spacious light rooms, its
delicate looking-glasses, its twinkling crystal, Lady Caroline's drawing room was a catacomb where the ever diminishing faithful could
cluster. Then it was, and there it was, that the middle-aged Egg had
first encountered young Chatterway, too young to have enjoyed the

hey-day, but recognisably in kinship with it. And then it was, in a series of dizzy seasons, that Egg and Chatterway had tasted together the ever-diminishing pleasures which London provided, spiritual patricians born out of time.

Who was Chatterway? Whence had he sprung? At the time, satisfactory answers had been provided to these important questions. Purple-faced men in clubs whose wives had been grossly insulted could now be heard to protest that the man was an upstart, that he had forfeited his claim to be regarded as a gentleman. But these were the remarks made of Chatterway the silver-haired. When a man's locks are still naturally raven and his chin smooth, he is assumed to be a gentleman if enough 'people' knew his 'people'. Some of those who had known Chatterway's people had been august personages, in his own phrase tall poppies, indeed. His mother, first as an officer's wife in Seringapatam and in a subsequent incarnation as a Portuguese marchioness, had enjoyed what was called an influence over the Great Duke. Young Waldo had become the *protégé* of the old man in his dotage, and, in that extremity of youth and good looks, he had been well fitted to fulfil the role of courtier, not only at Apsley House and Stratfield Saye but also at Court in those comparatively jolly days before the death of the Prince Consort.

Severus Egg had enjoyed Chatterway's company even in those early days, though it was a pleasure marred by the ever-disconcerting sense that he was not alone in seeing Chatterway's qualities. Mr Egg disliked belonging to congregations or subscribing to creeds. Least of all he liked a *cult*. Enthusiasm lacked *ton*. There was nothing in Mr Egg's nature of the nympholept. Detachment, coolness, laughter were the best remedies the head could supply against the chaos into which the heart might always threaten to consign him. Therefore – we speak still of prehistoric time – he developed an aversion to seeing Chatterway in company. Even, once, exasperated by a cluttered crowd of worshippers at a *levée* for old King Leopold, Mr Egg had brushed them aside with the wave of a white glove. Claret-countenanced, he had *cut* the young man with the words, 'I thought of Chatterway, the marvellous *bore*.'

Oh, the furious exchanges of notes and messages when the words had, by some kindly observer, been 'passed back' to Mr Chatterway. Even in those days he was a fluent and frequent correspondent. Mr Egg received letters not merely at his house and at his club. Embarrassed flunkies would bring them to him in the middle of meals in other people's houses. He demanded apologies, he threatened a duel – Mr Egg, replying to one in three of the violent little letters, managed at length not only to pacify the young man but to become his friend. But

Chatterway remained 'the marvellous bore' – quickly shortened to Marvo – on Egg's tongue. They grew, Marvo at twenty, Mr Egg at forty-odd, into a close intimacy. Looking back, old Severus regarded that early friendship not merely a thing sweet in itself, but also a social barometer by which to gauge how much of the ancient world survived. Oh yes, he would tell himself, the Goths and the Vandals did not destroy that thing or this as early as I supposed, for I remember going there, doing that, with Marvo. Even into the sixties, for example, they had passed happy evening hours cockfighting with the Duke of Hamilton in the pits of Endell Street. And, nearer the core of civilisation, there still lingered in those days in Curzon Street and Jermyn Street, the powdered old masks of women who had known Beau Brummell. These very crones, expert in their flummery, had shewn Chatterway and Egg up the staircases of pleasure haunts long since abandoned. Now, such openly and as it were *Parisian* delights had gone underground. The bordelloes of those days, like the drawing rooms of Lady Caroline Jarvis, and the sporting pleasures of the old Duke of Hamilton, had nothing furtive about them. Now-a-days, as was widely known, London was the most virtuous of all possible Christian cities, a veritable *urbs christianissima* and thicker with whores than ever; each mud-encrusted, Jew-infested, disease-ridden street corner of its poorer quarters offering the chance of animal gratification. Mr Egg did not want what could be obtained for a few coppers by strolling out of Waterloo Station after dark. It was the same impulse which had led him into carnality as led other men into celibacy: a vision, an inviolable romanticism. Part of his vision, Marvo had come to share. They were both made unhappy by women in the same sort of way, which was what bound them together at the time of Mr Chatterway's débâcle. Some sympathised, most scoffed, but only Eggy *understood*, or so he later had been reported as saying once in a restaurant in Paris, reported back once more to Egg by a perhaps kinder Mercury than he whose services had led to that first exchange of letters. Eggy, who understood, remained, in a sense, the man dearest to Mr Chatterway in the world and his fondness for his daughter Mrs Nettleship, his interest in life in The Bower, seemed at times to equal if not to exceed the love of the phlegmatic old parent.

'I thought,' added Mr Chatterway, for silence had fallen on the room while Mr Lupton dabbed delicately at the canvas, 'of calling at The Bower this afternoon.'

'Oh did you,' said the motionless sitter, and with undisguised irony he added, 'How sad I can't join you.' (He spoke with the old voice and still said 'jine'.)

'I never heard such poppycock,' said Marvo. 'Since when were you preoccupied with anything?'

'Not all of us,' Mr Egg threw back the slur, 'have your limitless leisure to make calls. Bacon, besides, wants to take out the brougham. I thought we might take a turn round the park, and drop Mr Lupton at his home before returning.'

'Where do you live, sir? Fitzroy Square, I shouldn't wonder?'

'Indeed I do, sir' – Mr Lupton's dark eyes opened in astonishment at Marvo's wizardry.

Mr Chatterway was about to add, 'A lot of painters live there, surely?' but he merely drawled, '*Thought* so,' and took pleasure as he read in Mr Lupton's puzzled expression the signs that he was being fascinating. 'I think if you're taking out the brougham, Eggy my dear fellow, it would do you no harm to take your drive in Le Parc du Régent and call for tea with your beloved daughter. You could drop Mr Lupton off in Fitzroy Square on the way or *even*,' he smiled suddenly, rather wickedly and repeated the word as though to tease the young painter, '*even* bring him along. Not only am I sure he could do with a few portraits of the Herr Professor and his brood, but something tells me that Mr Lupton would enjoy teaching Miss Nettleship how to *draw*.'

'Marvo, you marvellous bore, you know how Bacon hates going to The Bower,' protested the unwilling grandsire. And Mr Lupton, for his part interposed, 'Really, my dear Mr Egg, I could not possibly intrude upon your . . .' But Mr Chatterway had taken charge of the situation and was pulling at the yellow bellcord which dangled by the chimney piece.

'You rang, mister Egg-suh,' observed Bacon.

'Wrong, Bacon, wrong,' said Mr Egg from his cane-chair-idleness. 'Mr Chatterway was merely playing with the bell rope.'

'You don't, I hope, dislike Mr Egg's daughter, Bacon?' asked Chatterway mercilessly, and in spite of Egg's 'Really, Marvo!' poor Bacon mumbled a truculent reply. 'No objection what, to our taking the brougham up to le Bois de Saint Jean?'

'Mr Egg normally goes to the Park for his afternoon drive,' observed Bacon, but with an air of defeat.

'But this afternoon,' said Mr Chatterway, 'he wished to introduce Mrs Nettleship to his very good friend Mr Lupton.'

FOUR

The Professor

Charlotte Nettleship ever tried to be reasonable. It troubled her therefore that she could find no good reason to justify the inner murmurings of anxiety occasioned by the return of Mr Chatterway. Without being able to explain her fears to herself, she felt that her household was vaguely threatened by the expatriate. What if he were to call too often? The professor did little to disguise his contempt for Mr Chatterway, and Charlotte dreaded the silent clashes, the need to be torn between obedience to her husband's whims and the older loyalties of childhood; for she had, indeed, known Marvo (as she thought of him, but of course never called him) all her life. The possibility, however, of his becoming a part of weekly, or even of diurnal existence at The Bower was troubling, quite apart from the fact that such an eventuality would displease her husband. In what, particularly, any danger consisted, she was too cautious, even in the secrecy of her own thoughts, to articulate. 'Danger' was probably too strong a word. She tried to tell herself that she was simply cross that the announcement of his return had been written to Maudie, rather than to herself. But it had always been Marvo's way to keep alive little friendships with children. How close she, Charlotte, had felt to him, when as a young girl, *she* had received his shower of *billets-doux*; and could she now protest if he bestowed similar kindnesses on her own daughter? She knew that Marvo had lately never posed a threat to the sturdy tranquillity of the Nettleship existence. And what made the atmosphere of perpetual machination, which surrounded even the most casual of his conversational observations, have in it something approaching pathos was the fact that he had surely never exerted his 'influence' over anyone in his life. Besides, she knew that in his own fairly vulgar way of categorising his acquaintances, the Nettleships were small beer. Mr Chatterway might, from the distance of Paris and Perugia, beguile a lonely morning in an hotel by bombarding little Maudie with a flutter of foolish letters. But if he had, as reported, retired to London, it would not be in order to bother – Charlotte plunged, to frame the thought, into an ironically demotic phrase – 'the likes of them'. He would hope, surely to resume a life discarded when he had left these shores a quarter of a century before. A geologist's family in St John's Wood could not occupy more than a fraction of the attention of a man who lived so much in the world. Charlotte tried to assure herself that Mr Chatterway would not have occasion to come north of Regent's Park more than twice in a twelvemonth. His life was dinners. His engagement book was probably full already to bursting. After all, as he had once inexcusably confessed to her husband, there were taller poppies in the field than the Nettleships.

When she was younger, and kept her silliness less fiercely in check, Charlotte Nettleship had been impressed by the poppies. A whiff of their fragrance seemed to blow into her own sedate little sphere with each reappearance of Mr Chatterway. In his presence, she had felt herself at only one remove from the Great Duke, nay from Windsor Castle itself; Belvoir, Chatsworth, Blenheim and Eaton Hall seemed but a step away from her own hearth-side as he had dropped his hints and echoes. But that was long since, before the children, and the running of the household and the melancholy heaviness of life, had come to occupy her thoughts. The older she grew – and she was but nine and thirty – the more firmly she felt herself inescapably established on the bottom of common sense. She knew herself to be altogether more *sensible* than the earlier generation. To redeem their silliness was not her concern. But she would take persistent care at least, not to imitate them, to have about her no negroes in yellow breeches, no parrot (dead now but a feature of her childhood) taught to imitate Lord Macaulay, reciting passages of *Paradise Lost*. She could moreover not simply eschew frivolity herself, she could make certain that it was not passed on to her children. Was it not the case that, as a modern poet had written,

> Not enjoyment, and not sorrow
> Is our destined end or way;
> But to act, that each to-morrow
> Find us further than today?

She believed so, in defiance of the extraordinary foppery and idleness of her parent. And she sometimes allowed herself inwardly to inquire, not without bitterness, whether she had not been first attracted to the professor because of his absolute absence of indolence, his desire, each day, to know a little more about volcanic lava, and to advance, not merely his great thesis, but the knowledge and enlightenment of the human race. Even in her moods of greatest disillusionment with her husband, she felt there was more of usefulness and, therefore, of nobility, in the professor's dogged desire to discover the truth, not only about a few rocks, but about the mystery of creation itself, than in her father, who, though perhaps a dearer man, had chosen to squander his intellect, abandon a poetic vocation, and devote his life to tomfoolery, to rubbers of whist, to bottles of Madeira, and, to what else, she did not allow herself to contemplate. She had preferred, over the years, never to heed the stories whispered into her ears by malicious cousins and family friends – particularly the Malvern relations – about the manner in which her father's life had been conducted. And what else was Marvo, with his raffish air of intrigue and scandal, his foreign phrases and his scented handkerchieves, but an emanation of her father's persistent frivolities?

The answer, and perhaps it was this which caused her bosom to flutter a little at the thought that Marvo had returned, was that Marvo had been her friend. Both he and her father were, in addition, a good deal more entertaining than the Malvern relations. She had accepted, throughout the earlier part of her life, that industry, application and seriousness, all the qualities so conspicuously lacking in her parent, as in Mr Chatterway, would, if pursued in a sufficiently single-hearted manner, leave, as her poet put it, 'footprints on the sands of time'. So, after a fashion, she still believed. Furiously busy she and the professor both had been, he with his hammers and his samples and his books, she with household management and the supervision of her daughter's education. But what crushed her spirit was the discovery that all this self-application did nothing to banish the burden of gloom which hung like a fog about her soul, whereas her father and, in his different fashion, Mr Chatterway, seemed cynically happy with the fact that they had done nothing 'with' their lives. Torn ever between these thoughts – 'he is my *father*', she had asserted to the Malvern relations in a moment of angry loyalty – the two sides of things had never been quite resolved in her heart: on the one hand, 'Life is real, life is earnest!', on the other, parlour games, laughter and frivolity; on the one hand the crushing sabbatarian silences in Malvern; on the other the mysterious and unexplained humours, presences, comings and goings of Brunswick Square, pronounced in Malvern to be an 'unsuitable place for a child. . . .' The conflict had never been resolved. For is not, in most of us, our very notion of what is right and proper synonymous with the behaviour and pattern of our parents? Charlotte had been taught, from early years, to think of her father as wicked. In many ways, he had been, perhaps. And now she would never know to what extent, in her childhood, he had neglected her, and to what extent she had been artificially 'kept from him' by the Malvern Walkers.

Mr Egg, as we have already observed, married quite late in life, nearer forty than thirty. The motives which prompted this surprising act had never been satisfactorily explained, since his wife had not been possessed of much fortune, and he had never displayed himself, either before or after his wedding day, much addicted to the domestic pleasures of constancy, or monogamy. But he was, as Charlotte noted, compulsively companionable and perhaps it was his week or two's loneliness in Malvern which had made him fall in love with her mother. Severus Egg, his constitution much undermined by a seemingly incurable addiction to late hours, to strong liquor and to tobacco, was prevailed upon to undergo a hydropathic cure at the hands of the great Doctor Gully. The water cure, which had been undertaken in a cold November a little over forty years previous, was by far the greatest physical torment that Mr Egg ever underwent in his existence: no reading by candlelight, no going near a fire, no tea, no coffee, would all have been great enough deprivations. But to be wrapped perpetually for a week in a wet sheet and plunged occasionally into a bath, now icy cold, now scalding hot, had been highly disturbing to his sybaritic metabolism. His friends said it had momentarily turned his head. But it was while recovering from the treatment, and from the intelligence, conveyed by the illustrious medic, that he would certainly be a victim of apoplexy before he was fifty, that Severus Egg had met and in a very short time married a Miss Walker, the daughter of a lawyer who lived in a well-appointed house near Malvern Priory. 'Poor dear Mary' as her family had almost immediately labelled Mrs Egg when that became her name, did not live very long with her husband in Brunswick Square. Bacon had been appalled when his master returned home with a young bride; appalled in the manner he would have adopted had Mr Egg purchased a new horse without consulting his companion and servant. Poor dear Mary did not suffer for long the indignities of being gazed upon with the uplifted brow and curled lip of a negro servant who disapproved of her existence. Not long after Charlotte's birth she had sunk into a mysterious decline. Her Malvern relations had proposed she return for a while to them. Her languid looks and morbid indolence were attributed to the unhealthy influence to which she had been subjected since her unfortunate matrimonial alliance and the Walkers paid with their own money, as they were still foolish enough to boast, as though they might have paid with anyone else's – for their darling offspring herself to undergo Doctor Gully's famous hydropathic cure.

After the affecting funeral in the Priory, Mr Egg had returned to London immediately on the train with the child and her nurse, and Bacon whose presence, though sombrely clad, at the obsequies had been pronounced by the Walkers to be the final insult. Charlotte's had henceforth been a London childhood, and her father, by his own lights, made great effort to engage a succession of nurses and governesses until the child reached the age of discretion. Even before she arrived at that momentous turning point in life, her Walker relations had intimated, in a manner calculated to terrify the little girl, that some of these nurses and governesses had been 'insulted' by her father. She did not know at the time what they meant by this phrase; nor, now, could she have any specific certainty about why, for instance, Mollie or Flossie or even the unfortunate Miss Jakes had left so hurriedly.

After the Miss Jakes incident her aunt Walker had called at Brunswick Square and insisted that 'the child' be put into her care. Mr Egg had pointed out – the story was repeated to Charlotte more than once in adult life, never more cheerfully than at that lady's funeral – that he, and not Aunt Walker was the child's parent. Aunt Walker had dabbed her eyes and asked if he had no sensitivity. Was she not the sister of poor dear Mary? On this occasion, she had been sent packing.

But when, a year or two later, her father had made a journey to the Bahamas, both to negotiate the sale of some inherited property there, and to allow Bacon to visit his old mother, little Charlotte, then aged twelve, had been left in Malvern for nearly a year.

It was at that age that she had been introduced to her future husband, Horace Nettleship, the former college friend of some Walker relation or another, who was taking a walking tour, hammer and chisel and specimen boxes in a knapsack, over the Malvern hills as far as Ledbury or Hereford. Nettleship, not quite then a professor, had been a somewhat heavy young man of twenty-eight winters, when this encounter had taken place. Charlotte, an obedient and biddable girl, was one of those sponge-like, chameleon characters who absorb with ease the quality of her surroundings. At home – Brunswick Square and never Malvern was 'home' in her vocabulary – she might tease Macaulay the parrot, learn, from her father, to read Ariosto, or make, with Mr Chatterway on his irregular visits to the capital, exciting expeditions to the zoological gardens or the waxworks. At Malvern, however, she did not pine for these things and learnt to adapt herself to the stiller routines, the strict sabbatarian calm, the wholesome hill walks in heavy boots and Mr Walker's tedious insistence that she 'get on' with her mathematics. It was therefore, a serious, demure little girl that captured the attention of the suet-featured Nettleship, a girl who accepted the rebukes of her aunt Walker in silence ('affected hussy' if she quoted from the Italian poets) and was happy to recite to the visitor, her future lord, multiplication tables. She had in her nature the quality of acceptance. It was not the same – as a woman she knew the distinction very clearly – as the virtue of patience. She was simply able,

by temperament, to accept her immediate surroundings as the normal
ones and not be discontented with her lot.

In time, of course, she returned to London, to the gayer life of
Brunswick Square. But it was, if more carefree, also lonelier. Now,
often enough, she would eat her meals with her father, which
frequently meant sitting alone in the dining room of Brunswick Square
while her father dined at his club. She would meet his 'jolly friends' —
but to glimpse them only for half an hour in an evening, when she
might be asked to play an air of Donizetti on the clavichord before
being packed off, in the best humour imaginable, to her own rooms
and her books. Marvo alone, of all her father's friends, had treated her
singly, given her the impression that he would call at the house to see
her, even had he never known her father; larded her with presents, and
with ironically expressed but warm-hearted flattery. He stood out
from the run, but he was hardly ever there; and though, in these days,
she often received a letter from her 'very affectionate friend Waldo
Chatterway', she might pass several years at a stretch without seeing
him.

Life in what Mr Chatterway called '*la casa* Walker' might be as
funny as her sophisticated old friend implied, but it was a good deal
more companionable than the solitudes of Brunswick Square. It was
the callous truth, she sometimes believed, that she had married Mr
Nettleship because her father spent so much of his time at the club. It
was not until several years after this union had been contracted that
she learnt, from her husband's lips, that he had conceived the notion of
marrying her from the moment she was able correctly to recite the nine
times table to him all those years before. Certainly whenever during
girlhood she went to Malvern (often for extended periods) there was a
likelihood that Mr Nettleship would be there for at least part of the
time. Aunt Walker, it appeared, had more or less promised the little
girl to Nettleship from that first 'twelve nines are one hundred and
eight'. In the six years that slipped past after that, she matured into
young womanhood, and he acquired, as well as a balder head and a
plumper stomach, a chair of geology at one of the colleges of London
University.

It was indolence, she believed, which allowed her father to draw up
the marriage settlement. Rudimentary inquiries were made into
Nettleship's family and affairs. His father, who had been a headmaster, was thought to be a gentleman. The professor was neither
vulgarly rich nor grotesquely poor. He seemed earnest in his desire to
marry Charlotte and, as she now saw, putting herself into her father's
shoes, there had been no obvious objection to the match, beyond the
difference in age between the bride and groom. She was honoured by

the attentions of Nettleship. All the Walkers said that he was a very
eminent scientist, and she felt a little awed by his knowledge, as though
Galileo or Sir Isaac Newton had invited her to share her life with them.
Mr Nettleship was very kind. Since he was such a close family friend of
the Walkers there would have been, unquestionably, offence taken if
she had rejected his kind propoal. Perhaps she had been frightened, a
little, by the loneliness of her life in Brunswick Square. And perhaps
she had been simply flattered that anyone liked her enough to marry
her: it was a fact worth advertising to the world by solemnising it.

Looking back to her eighteen-year-old self from the perspectives of
maturity, Mrs Nettleship could not, in honesty, remember what it felt
like to be acquiescent in the notion of loving Mr Nettleship. It had
happened. No one had stopped her, and, now that her own children
had reached or were approaching the age at which she had made her
decision she found herself horrified by their, by her, innocence and
smooth-faced simplicity. How could such creatures know anything?
How could they be allowed to entangle themselves for life with
someone they scarcely knew?

Charlotte's matrimonial experience had not been a happy one. Mr
Nettleship was, as she repeated to herself, a perfectly good man, a
worthy man, an honest man. He had never betrayed her or dis-
honoured her. He had provided for her, after his own fashion,
handsomely. The only disadvantage of the whole arrangement was
that she did not very much like him. She discovered this gradually and
she only admitted it to herself after the birth of Maudie. There had
been no more children. Charlotte would not have breathed a syllable
of her feelings to anyone, but she found, unhappily, that it was
increasingly difficult, in consequence, to breath a syllable at all.
Converse with her spouse became, in fact, impossible.

He accepted it with the same slow hurtful doggedness with which he
accepted everything. 'Some years ago,' his manner seemed to suggest,
'you spoke to me. Now you do not. Very well. This is a misfortune but
it is not something which need interrupt the harmony of the Nettleship
home.' He had himself, besides, become increasingly taciturn since the
great crisis of his life at Buddleigh Salterton when, chipping away at a
piece of volcanic lava, he had finally shed the last vestiges of credence
in Archbishop Ussher's theory that the world had been fashioned at a
precise date in 4004 BC followed about a fortnight later by the Fall of
Man. Charlotte knew that two courses opened themselves to a dutiful
wife when confronted with this threat to her husband's spiritual
tranquillity. She could have followed Horace on his spiritual pilgrimage, acknowledged his superior knowledge and experience, and
even joined him on his occasional visits, in place of church, to the

meetings of the Ethical Society in Red Lion Square. Or, recognising the
supreme seriousness of what it was he cast aside, she could, like a good
Christian woman, have pleaded with him, wept at his apostasy,
soothed his worries with a soft hand on his troubled brow and finally
inspired him by her cheerful example to lift up his heart from the
trough of doubt and despondency into which it had fallen. But she had
done neither thing. She still continued to pay her guinea a year for their
pew in St John's Wood parish church. Now she took Maudie (and
Lionel when he was at home) without their father, to hear the fatuous
Mr Goe. It was, alas, a welcome opportunity to have an hour into
which the professor could be guaranteed not to intrude. As month
succeeded month the husband and wife spoke to each other less and
less. No agreement was ever made between them that they should
continue living together for the sake of mere appearances. They did
not say, 'Love has died between us, but let us spare our children this
knowledge' – but there was an accepted, wholly unspoken agreement
between them that no one should be made privy to the true state of
things. Charlotte, and for all she knew, her husband, were under the
impression that no one had noticed the silence between them. She had
become so habituated to it that many of its automatic conventions no
longer struck her as odd: for instance, the fact that she could speak
quite animatedly to Maudie, and Maudie to her father while the three
sat together of an evening without a single word passing between the
husband and wife. In front of her own children, without the least
intention of doing so, Charlotte thus let her guard slip. In front of
strangers, she was more careful, Horace yet more so, to preserve the
veneer of visible marital intercourse. On these occasions – how she
winced always at it – he laced his talk to her with endearments and
even – most horrible of all – made love to her publicly! He would hold
her hand or stroke her shoulders in the presence of strangers and call
her the light of his life. But how rapidly they both snuffed out the light
again when the servants had shown the company to the front door;
how rapidly, and in Charlotte's case with what anguish of guilt. She
hated being made to nurse feelings of anger. She hated the abandonment of good manners which this grave emotional subsidence had
occasioned. She hated herself also, inescapably, and with less justice
than her other hatreds, she hated Horace for having led her into all this
indignity. Thus they had gone on, from week to week, from month to
month, from year to year, both secret victims of a daily humiliation
and torture. She was silenced by now almost altogether by self-disgust
that she could so recklessly and without thought have so unsuitably
thrown away her life at the age of eighteen. But the silence was not one
of calm, rather one of churning, scorching anger – anger with life that

could be cast aside with such ease, anger with all the Malvern Walkers
who had imprisoned her in this inescapable hell, and anger with her
father who could, all those years ago, have forbidden the match and
told her (oh, she would believe it if he told her now!) that she did not
properly know her own mind.

The anger she felt with Mr Chatterway was different in kind. He
had been there, after all, from the beginning. He had known the
comparatively carefree life of Brunswick Square; he had seen the
encroachment of Malvern with all that it implied. He had seen it all –
from a distance certainly – and it was only when she grew to maturity
that she understood how he had warned her. But, oh, so obliquely!
Long before her wedding, indeed so shortly after the announcement of
her engagement that it was amazing he should have heard of it so soon,
he had written her a congratulatory note from Rome, where he then
resided.

'*I hope you will regard the period of your engagement as a time of
testing – for this is what it is meant, on both sides to be*' had been one
of the surprising sentences in a polysyllabic epistle bestowing ironically beneficent epithets upon the head of her 'brilliantly oblique and
handsomely-provided-for geological genius'. True, Horace was what
the vulgar called 'comfortable'. Mr Chatterway had been right there –
but right, too, to express good humoured surprise that '*so youthful
and innocent a vestal as my ever-beloved Charlotte should find as her
soulmate an avuncular investigator into vanished volcanoes*'. Oh, but
she had been too innocent to see all this as a warning. Marvo had,
whatever sins he had committed, discovered with pain the hazard of
the matrimonial course. If only he had been explicit! If only he had told
her that she *must* not marry the professor. But even as she articulated
the thought, it became necessary to confess to herself that she would
never have heeded the advice. She knew that he had never forgotten
giving it, one and twenty years before. By some arcane fancy, an
unacknowledged telepathy, she knew that he was aware of the
condition of her heart. And it was this, more than her fear that he
woud flirt with her daughter or irritate her husband which made Mrs
Nettleship dread the arrival of Mr Chatterway at The Bower. What
she could not have known was that, even as she had the fancy, Mr
Chatterway was speeding towards St John's Wood in her father's
brougham – Mr Timothy Lupton at his side. It was with a flustery
astonishment that she heard Maudie excitedly shouting in the hall:
'Grandpapa, *I declare!* and Mr Bacon.' At first, indeed, although she
had been meditating upon Mr Chatterway for a full hour and a half
she could not understand when she heard her daughter's voice, why
her father and his servant should have called upon her unannounced.

'Mama, Mama!' Maudie plunged into the drawing room flushed and over-excited, a very slight touch of pink in her pallid freckled features. 'Guess who has *arrived*.'

'I can hear that it is your grandfather,' said Mrs Nettleship with a quietness calculated to put her daughter *down*. 'It seems no reason for becoming so excessively shrill.'

'And Marvo!' shouted the girl.

'Maudie, how many times have I told you that you *must* not refer to Mr Chatterway . . . ' but the rebuke died on her lips, for at that moment the servant showed in her dear old friend, a little plumper than on his previous visit.

'My dear little Maudie is excited to see a traveller from the continent of Europe in much the same way that her very aptly firm mother used to be in the Brunswick Square days. What?' And he kissed her forehead. 'Now *listen!*' – a habitual punctuation to his speech, as he prodded Maudie a little in the stomach and with his other hand shook Mrs Nettleship's fingertips as though to alert her attention, 'I've brought to see you in addition to your distinguished and poetical father the, in his field, no less distinguished painter who is engaged in capturing your father's likeness.'

'I fear that this is an intrusion,' said Mr Lupton as he took Charlotte's hand. She saw his great dark eyes, his thick blonde hair and whiskers, she felt the firmness of the painter's grip as he squeezed, and then released, her fingers.

'Not in the least,' said she.

'Mr Lupton is painting my portrait,' said Severus Egg, who never came into his daughter's drawing room without a feeling of awkwardness. His shoulders were even more hunched, his mandarin smile more fixed, than when we first introduced him to the reader. 'For the Royal Society of Literature which is rather flattering.'

'Only proper,' said the daughter with pride.

'You should get him to paint you, Charlotte,' shouted Chatterway, 'only he'd probably want to do you as the sister of Moses in the court of Pharoah, or the wife of Socrates pleading with Alcibiades for the body of her husband.'

'*Basta, basta,* Marvo,' murmured Mr Egg.

'Mr Chatterway means that I also paint historical and classical scenes,' glossed Charlotte's laughing cavalier.

'Great friends with Alma-Tad,' butted Chatterway in. 'Neighbour of yours, Charlotte, what?'

'I have had the pleasure of meeting Mr Alma-Tadema once or twice,' said Mrs Nettleship. 'He lives a little further nearer the Park than we do. I am a great admirer of his works.'

'It is some years now since,' the young man paused and, again, their eyes met, his and Charlotte's, 'since I was on my own. But of course I revere Mr Alma-Tadema as my master.'

'You ought to get him to paint Maudie here,' said Mr Chatterway, 'or to give her drawing lessons. Who gives you drawing lessons, my sweet?'

'Oh, Mama, wouldn't that be *wonderful!*' She was wide-eyed with excitement, almost, her mother thought, like some infinitely vulnerable wild beast, a deer or gazelle, scampering involuntarily from the brake into the jaws of a predator. 'Please let me.'

'You speak as if Mr Lupton were for hire,' laughed Charlotte primly – yes, laughed so as to show her teeth. Already, she felt her eyes meeting those of the painter with devastating familiarity. 'He's much too busy to paint you, my child. He is used to painting portraits of great and famous men like your grandfather.'

Uncut by the edge of these epithets, the old man did protest ('I say!') when Maudie riposted, 'Grandpapa isn't *that* famous!'

'I shall be when Mr Lupton has finished his painting.'

'I would be honoured to paint Miss Nettleship,' said the young man with a little bow.

The sights and faces which were so familiar to all others present in the room were new to him and he stared upon them with particular freshness, like Adam on the first day of creation. The Nettleship parlour was, perhaps, scarcely the garden of Eden. Mr Lupton was not immediately enamoured of the imitations of Landseer which covered the walls, nor yet of its general air of anti-macassared, antipathetic and anti-cultural comfort. But his eyes were not dwelling, much, upon artifacts. He looked from the figure of Mr Egg in its doll-like stiffness to the demure sorrows of the daughter, her brow already prematurely worn with an unburiable sorrow. He looked from the smiling brown-faced Mr Chatterway, who threw out his chest as he spoke and balanced both hands on his hips, to the pale frenzy of Maudie Nettleship. The older men, in the brougham which had conveyed them to St John's Wood, had spoken of 'the child', the 'girl' and 'little Maudie'. These phrases had not prepared Mr Lupton for the figure who now stood before him. At sixteen, Maudie had grown to her full height – some five foot six inches – and was, in feature and form, already a beautiful young woman, though one so freshly youthful in appearance that the word woman did not, upon surveying her, come to mind. She was clad however, still, to advertise her youthfulness. The gingham dress trimmed with lace, though obviously expensive and from some shop like Lewes and Allenby's, was tight waisted, and stopped short at her black-stockinged calves. And her abundant chestnut hair was not piled on her head in the style of her mother but was allowed by virtue of her tender years to flow loosely over her shoulders. Looking at Maudie's rich brown eyes, Mr Lupton was reminded, as her mother had been, of fragile nature, fawns or does scampering to their doom in mountain rocks. The girl's perfectly snowy brow was high, the nose narrow and straight, the white cheeks dappled with a faint band of freckles, and now and again, flushed with an excited rose. Her lips very slightly pouted, but opened, when excitement made her jabber, to reveal a lot of gum above her perfectly straight teeth. For some reason the gumminess of her smile also increased her air of vulnerability. And from the first Mr Lupton rejoiced in the technical imperfections of her smile: without them Maudie's beauty would have been too chilly and perfect.

'Would you truly like to paint me, sir?'

'Very much.

'And teach me drawing? I have lessons in music and languages but I have not had instruction in drawing since Miss Adeney.' Again a display of teeth, as though Maudie were letting him into a forbidden and hilarious secret. Happy at the flattering conspiracy, he inquired, 'Who was Miss Adeney?' at which she laughed openly. With delicate lily fingers Maudie tapped the side of her temples.

'A mad woman?' laughed Mr Lupton. 'You were taught to draw by a lunatic?'

'Maudie!' exclaimed her mother crossly. 'What *are* you saying?'

'I never said anything, Mama, did I, Mr Lupton?'

'No, no, nothing at all.

'Miss Adeney is better not talked about,' said Charlotte.

'She was the governess who went off her head,' said Mr Chatterway who had never met the unfortunate but spoke with more authority on the subject than all those in the room who had.

'Extraordinary memory you have, Marvo, my dear,' said Severus Egg. 'It is more than I can do to remember my own servants' names, let alone other people's. The chief reason I made darling old Bacon change his name was so that I could remember it. Deuced awkward if you ring for your own butler and you can't remember what to call him.'

'Didn't she do something peculiar at Brighton?'

'Bacon? Hasn't been to Brighton since King George died, I shouldn't wonder.'

'No, no, the unfortunate Miss Adeney.'

As the two old gentlemen collogued about the lost governess, Maudie whooped with merriment, the infection of which was caught by Mr Timothy Lupton. For Charlotte, it was unseemly to laugh at the poor wretch, but if there was something a little too shrill in Maudie's laughter it was preferable to the sobs of the morning.

A letter which made Maudie weep might well inspire a volcanic eruption in the professor.

Charlotte was often in the habit of telling herself that it was impossible for a household to be more unhappy than her own. And then something new happened, in this case the letter from Lionel, which threatened the whole tranquillity of existence. And with what dread she recognised that it would inevitably involve some form of verbal communication with her husband.

So, as Maudie giggled and shrieked and the older men, led from the mention of Brighton to recall the early decades of the century, Charlotte smiled tolerantly on the scene, and allowed her eyes to repose on the whiskery charm of Mr Lupton, his fine tall figure in its frock coat and check trowsers. How kind he was being in cheering Maudie along. Maudie was repeating the legendary Miss Adeney's views on mashed potatoes; they were very funny, and Mr Lupton at the same time was carried away to the point where he remembered something a nanny of *his* had believed concerning calves' foot jelly. Mr Egg was trying to recall a visit to Brighton with the famed Mrs Piozzi, Dr Johnson's friend, and Mr Chatterway, not to be outdone, had started to allude to last year's season at Baden-Baden and his close intimacy with the house of Saxe-Coburg.

This part of the conversation was interrupted by the intrusion of a lugubrious maid who covered the already swathed moroccan tables with a further layer of Nottingham lace and then staggered into the room with a cake-rack and large tray of comestibles.

'Are you *frightfully* famous?' Maudie was asking Mr Lupton. 'You see, we have never heard of anyone in this house.'

The question was met with laughter. Old Severus Egg asserted that Mr Lupton was extremely famous and the young man blushingly denied any such fancy. Charlotte was making the tea, and Mr Chatterway was assisting her with the required dispensation of cream jug and sugar tongs when he called across the room, 'If you are going to persuade Mr Lupton to be your *Meister,* my girl, you had better show him your sketchbooks. No, no, I protest, modesty is too absurd in one of your years – only the old need to be modest, and they so rarely are. I assure you, Mr Lupton, that Miss Nettleship is a most accomplished draughtswoman.' One of Maudie's sketch books, as it happened, was easily reached down from the top of the pianoforte and she was able to sit with it open on her billowing gingham lap while Mr Lupton stood beside her and watched her turn the pages, becoming increasingly extravagant in his praise at the revelation of each commonplace watercolour. Mr Chatterway spoke the while in a low murmur to Mrs Nettleship, who had abandoned her protest that poor Mr Lupton should not be made to look at *all* the sketches; and grandpapa Egg sat a little apart and watched the house-martins twittering against the grey sky. By the time the sketch book had been thoroughly mulled over, and each person in the room had consumed scones, quince jam, brown bread and butter, potted meat, baps and cakes (both of seed and of Dundee) the afternoon had worn on. When at last the door opened, and the professor of geology appeared, a strange chill descended upon the atmosphere as though a stern schoolmaster had entered a room full of unruly children.

Nettleship, bald and grey and quiet, stared about at the picture of satiety and contentment from which he had been excluded. The tea things were discarded. The room was dotted here and there with shining blue tea plates and jam-stained dainty bone-handled knives. Worship, evidently, was in progress.

As chief hierophant in the cult of Maudie, Mr Nettleship strode forward to raise her from her chair and hold her in his arms, placing his grey whiskers on top of her chestnut crown and clasping her velvet trimmed bodice to his own large buttoned black coat.

'Oh, Papa, look what you've done!' said the girl crossly as she disengaged herself – the sketch book had tumbled from her lap and a saucer and teacup, happily empty, had tinkled to the floor giving a momentary impression of anarchy outburst.

So this, the father's hurt eyes seemed to say, was what he had *done*, this dog-eared sketch book, these scattered tea-leaves, this – oh dear – this handleless cup. A young man whose acquaintance the professor had not yet made was grovelling at Maudie's feet like a spaniel, retrieving first the sketch book, which he was dabbing with a pocket handkerchief, and then the handle, then the saucer, then the cup.

'My darling love,' said the professor turning to Charlotte and switching on an awkward smile, 'you should have rung. I did not know that tea was ready. I would certainly have come up at once if I had known we had company. And by the sound of laughter earlier, convivial company.'

'I am sorry if we disturbed your work,' were the words she regretted allowing to escape from her lips, for they inspired him to abandon his daughter and blunder across the carpet to his spouse whom he now addressed.

'Light of my life! You failed to catch my tone! I am only too happy for you to,' he paused and surveyed the company with gritted teeth, 'to entertain your friends.' And he picked up one of his wife's limp white hands and caressed it as though it were a little *objet d'art* of his own acquisition.

'Papa, Mr Lupton is going to teach me to draw – isn't it champion?'

'We have not been introduced, sir,' said Nettleship. Charlotte wondered what it was about her husband's tone which placed one in the wrong even when it was not heavily reproachful. She introduced Mr Lupton to the professor and added gently, 'Mr Chatterway of course.'

'I see that, angel sweet,' said the grinning geologist, whose caress had extended to her forearm. By now his smile was positively glacial. Even in early days, when talk had still happened between them, Horace had conveyed to Charlotte that he 'drew the line' at Mr Chatterway. She had, in this matter, persistently defied him, and there she now sat, brazenly, with the ruddy-faced mischief-maker swaggering in the middle of *his* drawing room, surfeited with scones and bannocks which the cook had prepared for his refreshment. No wonder that Nettleship's, 'Good afternoon, Chatterway, Egg' was a little perfunctory. He sensed that they were all finding him amusing and that, in this amusement, there lurked some element of unpleasantness or corruption, but he would not understand what it was. He only knew that it made him angry that his father-in-law had been entertained 'behind his back' – bringing with him the undesirable Chatterway and a blonde painter who was manifestly flirting with Maudie and crawling about on his carpet.

'Did I not hear your name praised only weeks ago at Baden-Baden, sir' was Chatterway's rhetorical question, 'by a German professor of geology whose name was Kunz?'

'Ah, indeed. Kunz is a great name – though in a very different field. He is limestone and I. . . . '

'Quite so, sir, quite so you are, as the generous Kunz conceded, the very *dernier cri*, when it comes to volcanic lava. Indeed he would have given me quite a lecture on the subject had I not been accompanied by the two very deafest descendants of George III. . . .'

'Indeed sir, and are you in London for long?'

'Papa, Marvo, I mean Mr Chatterway, is in London for *ever* isn't that *thrilling*?'

'D.v. child, d.v.' drawled Chatterway.

'Is this true sir?' Horace Nettleship's outraged expression suggested that he ought to have been informed (perhaps his permission sought) before anyone chose to reside in London.

'As I said to your delightful daughter, if Allah intends it.'

This light tone when referring to the deity was to Horace Nettleship in the highest degree disgusting. Mr Chatterway's smile either suggested that he did not notice how little pleasure his company was giving to Nettleship or, more mysteriously, that he positively wanted to bait and enrage his host. Afterwards, when the shock had been created, they imagined that Mr Chatterway had led up to this catechism with deliberate malice, but at the time it seemed like the mere chaos of what passed for a social butterfly's mind, for he fired off a salvo of questions. How's the election going to turn out? Why do they allow that scoundrel Hutton to write such balderdash in *The Spectator*? Who's this man Bradlaugh? When did they last dine with the Dean of Westminster?

'London gone to sleep or something?' he asked, which made Mr Egg laugh and declare that 'all that mighty heart is lying still'.

'You fail to understand, sir,' said Nettleship, 'that my life does not take me into the great world. We do not, if I may say so, sir, *aspire* so high.'

'Hoity-toity!' exclaimed Marvo, delighted with the insult. 'I thought at least you knew the Stanleys.'

'I am acquainted with the Dean of Westminster, sir, of course. But he has his work to pursue and I have mine.'

'. . . Met' – Chatterway ignored Nettleship's spluttering self justifications – 'Archdeacon Gutch there the other evening.'

Charlotte's heart missed a beat at the mention of the word Gutch. There could not be two Gutch families. Her son's letters were full of the presence of Master Gutch at Oxford, and now her old friend introduced the name of Gutch into the conversation.

'I have not had the pleasure of making the archdeacon's acquaintance,' said Nettleship.

'Even though the Reverend Lionel sees so much of the heir.'

'I am afraid that remark is lost on me.'

'You don't get what the dear Duke of Connaught has taken to calling my drift.'

'I don't, sir. If you are talking about *my* Lionel, my son. . . .'

'Dear Father Lionel. Mrs Gutch was telling Lady Augusta that they're almost papist; more Puseyite than the learned Dr Pusey himself, Everard and Lionel.'

'My *son*, sir, a papist?'

'*Almost,* was what she said, Mr Nettleship. I dare say that they will grow out of it but at present they both pine to be curates in a Puseyite parish in the slums.'

Charlotte was chiefly anxious during this most unexpected conversational development, that Maudie should not burst into tears or, if she did so, that she should be allowed to weep discreetly. She looked up at the girl, for Maudie, too, was staring in astonishment at Mr Chatterway. It was only that morning that Lionel had announced his intention of taking orders to Maudie, his closest confidant. And yet it now appeared that it was the talk of London – and Mrs Gutch, and Lady Augusta Stanley and Mr Chatterway had been discussing it freely the previous evening.

'I can almost see darling Lionel as a parson, yes,' said the boy's grandfather tactlessly. 'Isn't it odd that there used to be so many funny parsons about?'

'Our dear friend the Smith of Smiths. . . .'

'Him of course, Marvo, but there were others. And now they are all so *solemn*.'

'The Gutches are prodigiously rich,' added Marvo as though Lionel had engaged himself to be married into that family. 'Own half Herefordshire. Mrs Gutch is the sister of Lady Wisbeach.'

'Be that as it may, sir,' insisted Nettleship.

'Oh, but she is. Did I not go to her wedding in '57 or '58 – on which occasion *all eight* sisters, many of whom pined to marry me themselves, were present, the elder of whom, Dolly, became Lady Wisbeach. . . .'

'I do not dispute the relationship between Lady Wisbeach, sir, and Mrs Gutch. You bow to me in the knowledge of volcanoes. I bow to you in the knowledge of the genealogy of the upper classes. But I fail to understand how you can have heard something about my *own son* which is strange news to all close members of his family.'

'I expect they both knew but were too shy to tell you,' said Marvo unhelpfully.

Nettleship looked at his wife quizzically. Her gaze fell to the floor.

'I see,' said the professor. 'Everyone knew of this but I. My son thinks to throw away his life in the grossest form of superstition and nobody appears to think I will be interested?'

'Oh Papa, don't be like that.'

'*Darling*' (he had a particularly cross way of saying this word) 'I can be "like" whatever I choose without your instructions.'

Mr Egg's, 'Calm down Netty, my dear,' was said with a grin and the certainty that this was the opposite of what Mr Nettleship would do.

What had happened to the scene? A moment earlier there had been such happiness in the room. Maudie surveyed it all through a tearful haze. How could Mr Chatterway have known that his innocent reflections upon Lionel's choice of career would produce such an effect of tortured horror? She hoped that no one would see the moisture of her eyes. She felt so tremblingly ashamed of them all. A moment earlier, Mr Lupton had been offering to teach her to draw. What would he think of them now? He would never wish to come near The Bower again, Papa so stiff, pompous and angry, Mama inscrutably silent and staring somehow so as not to seem to focus.

He was taking her hand now, Mr Lupton Maudie's.

'I shall call soon, if I may, to see the rest of your sketches,' he said.

Maudie was too overwhelmed with embarrassment to reply properly and had to leave it to Mama to say, 'Nothing could be kinder Mr Lupton, we would *always* be glad to see you,' which was anyway drowned by Grandpapa patting Mr Chatterway's shoulder and saying, 'Come on, Marvo, you've done enough damage for one day.'

There was a distinct feeling, from the way Mr Nettleship stood by the chimney-piece, that all three visitors were being turned out of the house. Maudie did not return to the drawing room. She went to her own room and cried until it was time for dinner, unconscious that not a word had passed between her parents since the three men evaporated from The Bower.

Charlotte, for her part, was severely knocked up by the afternoon. She felt that she had been carrying all its weight, and suffering as no one else in the drawing room had suffered, from all its nuances. She had known that the return of Mr Chatterway would be accompanied by its tremors. But who would have thought that he would have heard about Lionel? As soon as the word *Gutch* was past Marvo's lips, Charlotte had been torn by a sense (less trouble) that Horace must be *spared* the ensuing anguish, and an angry, rather new, questioning spirit which asked her by what strange scale of values she placed her unloved husband's sensitivities above the dictates of good manners or above the happiness of Lionel? Why *should* Horace's mood have been allowed to descend on the room like a Homeric mist and envelop them all? She knew of the pains he had endured over geology and the book of Genesis, which had left him 'peculiar' about religion. He could not even be civil to Mr Goe. But her pity for him; the last vestige of emotion in her bosom which Horace Nettleship was capable of inspiring, had diminished that afternoon. Her father's scornful smile had seemed so sane and, irrelevant as that was to the general matter under meditation, Mr Lupton's beauty was so astonishing. At the time, Charlotte had felt there was something positively blatant about the way he had looked at her and allowed their eyes to meet for a full five or six seconds. She knew, already, that his desire to teach Maudie to draw was the merest 'excuse'. Normally so sane, normally so bustlingly anxious to leave footsteps on the sands of time by embroidering cream-jug covers or writing letters, or managing the servants, Charlotte felt on this occasion a resurrection of almost silliness. Anger with her husband had perhaps inspired a propensity to silliness closer than any she had permitted herself before. But by the irrational laws which govern these things, Mr Lupton's beauty of countenance made her even angrier with her husband and even more inclined, if need be, to take Lionel's side.

She had changed. She liked to change early each evening and sit for a while of contemplation beside the hearth in her own room. Sometimes at that hour she would read a novel, but this evening she merely, her maid dismissed, sat staring out of the window at the twiggy skyline and the bleak April sky. It was while she was so engaged in private musings that her maid reappeared and placed an envelope into her hand. Mr Nettleship had asked her to deliver this.

'Thank you, Aggie, you may go.' The girl was hovering inquisitively and Charlotte felt no desire to gratify her curiosity by reading the letter in anyone's presence. It began with no salutation and started peremptorily in:

There was manifestly a conspiracy to keep me in ignorance of Lionel's behaviour, but I am sorry that it is a conspiracy you have seen fit to join. When I desire Mr Chatterway's opinion of the best manner in which to educate my children, I shall ask for it. Until then I must ask you not to entertain either Mr Chatterway or Mr Lipton who was behaving in a frankly improper manner when I entered my own drawing room.

H.N.

Each word of the epistle stabbed into Charlotte as she read it, tormenting her with a mixture of fury and embarrassment. The silence which normally existed between herself and her consort had allowed her to build up the pleasing illusion, not quite so much that he had no inner life, but that she need never be made privy to it. She did not bother him with *her* thoughts. Why should he parade his, so raw and savage and painful, emotions on paper to her? It further angered her that the letter, so full of falsehood and injustice, demanded an answer. She went immediately to her bureau and dipped a furious pen in the ink.

A quarter of an hour later, in the voiceless misery of his own apartments, Horace Nettleship requested the maid to wait while he read his wife's scrawled response.

It is ludicrous to speak of a conspiracy and merely insulting to suggest that I would join one. How *can* you think that? I knew absolutely nothing about Lionel's plans until after breakfast this morning. You were already in your study and Maudie told me that she had heard of them in a letter. We both agreed that we could not spring the news on you since you would be bound to make such a fuss about it.

Mr Chatterway knows everything; how, I do not know, but he is a wizard. He is my oldest family friend and it is simply out of the question that we should cease to receive him merely because he heard from Mrs Gutch that Lionel wants to be ordained.

As for Mr *Lupton* (not Lipton) he is an artist of rising eminence who does us great honour by suggesting that he will help Maudie. I was with him throughout his visit and was not a witness to the impropriety to which you allude. I think it was the product of a fevered imagination.

Five minutes later a flustered maid was handing her mistress a single sheet of paper folded in the middle. Charlotte could hardly believe that her husband could be so ungoverned, so simply crude, as to reveal their disquietudes in this manner to the servants.

Am I to understand that you disobey my specific instructions? I have forbidden you to receive either Mr Lupton or Mr Chatterway. Do you intend wilfully to disobey me? H.N.

Her instinct was to scrumple this missive, which the maid had certainly read, into the grate, but instead she took it to her bureau and inscribed the single and angry word, YES.

'Please take this piece of paper back to Mr Nettleship,' she managed to say, adding with a crossness which implied that the maid had been wilfully delaying the hour of repast by flitting about landings with messages. 'It is already past dinner time.'

A bell in the hall confirmed this observation, and Charlotte repaired almost at once to the dining room. Maudie joined her and, after they had sat together for five minutes, the professor entered and rang the small handbell at his sideplate. Soup, sole, shoulder of mutton, carrots, boiled potatoes, and marmalade suet were brought in and out. The professor consumed a good quantity of each course, not appearing to notice the absence of appetite in his womenfolk. He did not exchange a glance with his wife. No allusion was made to the tea party, still less to Lionel's chosen vocation. Most of the meal was silent save for Nettleship's chewings and slurpings, but he managed to keep up a few observations to Maudie whenever a servant came in to clear the things, about the progress of her German lessons. It was only over the marmalade pudding that Maudie, who knew nothing of the pre-prandial correspondence which had engaged her parents, let fall a remark about her Cumberland sketchbook, filled during a holiday the previous year.

'It has my best sketches. D'you think it would be better to show the best ones to Mr Lupton or the worst? Do you see what I mean? He might think I was simply bragging, or worse, that I was better than I really was. And then everything I did after that would disappoint him.'

'I'm sure it wouldn't. Do show Mr Lupton the ones you did in Windermere. They are pretty.'

Charlotte spoke the words with careful deliberation, which struck her daughter as a little odd. Moreover, she said the words looking, not at Maudie, but at her husband. He refused however to meet her gaze.

'I should so hate to disappoint him,' said Maudie.

'Some imperfection can be discovered even in the best ones,' added her mother. 'Remember he has offered to teach you, not merely to praise you. It is inevitable that he should find some fault or there would be nothing to teach.'

Horace Nettleship discarded a spoon sticky with marmalade sauce so that it clattered on his pudding plate.

'I shall admit to Mr Lupton that I had luck in the Lakes,' answered Maudie. 'Perhaps it is easier to do mountains than the things I have been attempting to draw during the last winter.'

'You will admit to Mr Lupton nothing,' announced her father curtly.

'I should show him all your recent work, dear,' said her mother, not acknowledging by the flicker of one facial muscle that her husband had spoken.

Maudie looked desperately from left to right at one parent and then at another.

'Mr Lupton is not to teach you drawing. Mr Lupton is never going to call at this house again.'

'But, Papa, *why?*'

'I thought you might have your lessons with him,' continued Charlotte firmly, 'in the conservatory. There is much more light there.'

'But if Papa. . . .'

'Mr Lupton *will* be teaching you, of course,' said Charlotte, angered into admitting, though tacitly, that a voice had thrown doubt on the matter.

'He behaved in an unseemly fashion this afternoon. . . .'

'Of course, if you preferred to do your sketching in the day nursery that would be equally suitable.'

Maudie's eyes now darted from father to mother in fear. There had never been such a confrontation. She had never seen her mother so tight lipped, so dogged.

'Papa, I don't understand. . . .'

'I am very happy to hear it, Maudie my dear. I hope you never will

understand. Suffice it to say that when I came into the drawing room
this afternoon, Mr Lupton behaved disgracefully.'

'But, Papa.'

'There are no buts. . . .'

'You knocked a cup off the table and he stooped to pick it up. He is a
famous painter, a pupil of Mr Alma-Tadema.'

'I am not surprised to hear it.'

There was an agonised silence. Then Charlotte said, 'Of course, if
after a few visits he finds the house unsuitable, you could visit him for
your lessons in his studio. I presume that all artists have a studio. It
would be extremely interesting to see Mr Lupton's.'

'Oh,' exclaimed Maudie after another painful little jab of silence. 'I
think you are both being horrid. I don't *understand* you!' And,
ignoring her father's observation that there was no need to raise her
voice, she got up from the table and slammed the dining-room door
behind her.

Charlotte listened for a space to her husband breathing, to the air
battling its way in and out of the bushy entrances of his nostrils. A
sentence half-came to her, but until she had honed its cruelty, she
remained silent lest by the faintest incoherence she suggested that she
was disconcerted by her husband's behaviour. She looked down at the
table, casting furtive glances in his direction, happy to discover that he
was afraid as she of their glances meeting. There was a moment when
he opened his mouth, but by a cruel matrimonial telepathy she read his
thought process – 'If I speak, she *must* reply. But no, she might brave
out the silence, and win this little battle of nerves.' So his lips, too, set
firmly.

Braving out the silence became a battle in its own way. They sat
there long after the hour at which dinner usually ended. The servant's
'I thought you had forgotten to ring, sir' was greeted with a false
jocularity which seemed of operatic loudness. Some strange looks they
received, the husband and wife, as the last dishes were put on the
trolley, and the servant came round with a crumb-tray.

'Is everything all right, sir?'

Nettleship looked up at his servant. Everything was all wrong.
Perhaps it had been for years, but he had never felt it so keenly as
tonight. His wife was prepared to humiliate him before his own
domestics. Very well. He conceded defeat and, with a scrape of his
chair legs on the dining-room boards, he arose, stalked off to his own
apartments, and left Charlotte upright and stony in the ghoulish gaslit
room.

Perhaps now, as he stalks pompously across the hall and into his
study, is a poor moment to try to enlist the reader's sympathy with

him. After all, he has been behaving like an ass. But the painful thing, if we knew Horace Nettleship better, is to recognise that he *knows* he is behaving like an ass.

He sat before the study fire consumed with a twisted mixture of wounded pride and self-hatred. His thoughts were no longer coherent, but he was unable to banish them from his mind. Phrases and images, all painful, clanged insensitively about his brain. In my own house! My own drawing room! My own son! Superstition! Impropriety! Oh, Charlotte, how could you! Oh – this addressed to himself – for whom he had no name – how could *you!* And by this he meant how could the thirty-five-year-old Horace Nettleship have so mismanaged twenty-one subsequent years of life that he now sat like a prisoner in his own house – mocked by his servants, railed at by his daughter, defied by his wife and overwhelmed with his own misery.

His feelings towards the little Charlotte had been, all those years ago, so extremely tender. How much he had wanted his child-paramour to be happy. Setting up house together had had something of the quality of nursery play. How bright the red pinnacles had been of their villa, how happily they had filled it with furniture and pictures, how young had seemed the housemaids and the garden evergreens. Now those hopeful stripling firs which the previous owner had planted too near the house blackened the Nettleship windows. And how thick the laurels were in the shrubbery, and how high the hedges. Here Lionel had been born when a little light still reached the ground floor of the house. The next two had been lost – one stillborn and another dying in infancy. Percival. His tiny coffin was a perpetual grating memory in his father's brain. And then, into all this darkness and death, little Maudie had been born, her existence bringing such light and strength and joy to both parents. Maudie her father had loved in a fashion which was quite new to him. He knew from the child's earliest years not merely that he loved her, but that she had a power over his happiness which was greater than any living mortal. At a much later date he reframed the thought and wondered whether he did not love his daughter more than his wife. Honesty compelled him to admit that he did, but he could not help wondering what had gone wrong. The love he had felt for Charlotte when he first saw her in Malvern, reciting her mathematical tables, seemed only a foreshadowing of the love he was to feel for a daughter. Well and good. How could marital love be separable from the emotions and responsibilities of bringing offspring into the world? But between himself and his wife there had been a failure of sympathies, and for this he could isolate no discernible reason.

He had come to the unhappy conclusion that his wife was a

somewhat foolish, thin-natured individual, more heavily imbued with her father's dandified ways than with the solid morality of the Walkers. Charlotte made a show of believing that life was real and life was earnest, but her response to the great tragedy of her husband's life suggested on her part an almost mind-boggling superficiality of temperament. The tragedy was of course his loss of faith. When they had married, Horace Nettleship was not merely a practising member of the Church of England. He was a man of devout and prayerful habit. Each day of their early married life began with a private prayer; and after breakfast a Scripture reading and family prayer in front of the servants. In the evening, likewise, short but fervent orisons were offered up from The Bower, while, throughout the day, as he pursued his scientific researches, the professor had felt he could echo the *Christian Year*.

> When round thy wondrous works below
> My searching rapturous glance I throw,
> Tracing out wisdom, power and love,
> In earth or sky, in stream or grove.

The Doubts began, certainly, because of his geological researches. The professor's hammerings and samples, his chippings at lava, cold a thousand ages, his periodic distraction by fossils, all told him that Creation had been a more ponderously slow and haphazard process than was suggested by the opening chapters of the Book of Genesis. At first, his brain had resisted all the knowledge which it was accumulating in libraries, fieldwork or laboratory. The implications were too tremendous. Then he had hoped that it might be possible to dismiss merely the Creation story as mythological, while clinging to his other beliefs in the religion which gave him not merely his salvation, but his whole comfort and joy. But it was not possible to stop the Doubts once they had besieged his mind. If he disregarded the Book of Genesis as myth, did he not also have to discard his belief in the divine inspiration of Holy Scripture itself? By what canon of reason or theology could he believe that one book and not another of the Bible was so inspired? If Genesis were full of scientific falsehoods, what of Leviticus, what of Chronicles, what of Malachi? What of the Gospels themselves? With his brain, his heart, with every sinew of his being, he had fought back the Doubts, but with furious and blasphemous insistence they had returned. If these writings which he had read aloud every morning to his wife, children, servants, had *not* been divinely inspired, was it not fair and just to assess them with the same intellectual impartiality to which any other ancient text might be submitted to academic scrutiny?

Would the author of Genesis have written his book had he been in possession of modern geological and scientific evidences? Would, for the matter of that, the authors of the Gospels have so written? Was it not obvious that they were men conditioned entirely by the primitive and superstitious thought processes of their own day? Trembling from the profanity of it, his scientific mind had led him on further, and further. Was it not obvious that parthenogenesis was a biological improbability and that the Gospel writers themselves had doubts about it since they had traced Our Lord's ancestry back to King David *via* Saint Joseph? Was it possible or even helpful to believe that water could be turned into wine, that human bodies could walk on water, or that, having undergone a painful death, they would be resurrected from a tomb after three days? And was it further possible, knowing all that we now know about the composition of the firmament, that He had, as the thirty-nine articles put it, ascended to Heaven 'with flesh, bones and all things appertaining to the perfection of Man's nature'? In a post-Copernican age, was not one bound to ask the question: Where *was* this body, and how, through the infinite skies and numberless stars, could it have found its way to a place called Heaven?

Horace Nettleship had been collecting mineral samples in Buddleigh Salterton when these momentous questions finally accumulated in his mind to the point that he could resist them no longer. There was no trace of the hypocrite in his nature. Once the Doubts had become inescapable, he felt bound to confess them to his family and to reorder in consequence his life. He had lost infinitely more than a set of childish and anti-scientific opinions. He had lost his hopes and his inspiration for existence. Gone were not merely the aspirations to meet his master in a future life, to be reconciled to lost loved ones and to dry the tears from every eye. Gone too was the sense of the Universe as God's beautiful plaything, created for His pleasure and that of His favourite creation, Man. Instead, the universe now seemed like an infinitely empty, infinitely extensible accident. The warm comfort which for all his life he had derived from prayer, and the close consciousness of his Saviour's love, now seemed like the most hollow self-delusion. As well as being intensely ashamed of his own earlier naïvety, Horace Nettleship also felt completely bereft. It was impossible, of course, to continue going to Church, although his Saviour's love was something which he missed as intensely as if it had been that of an earthly father, brother or companion. Now, simply, the sun of his soul was blotted out and Keble's words, still inevitably retained in the memory, mocked the loneliness of his spiritual quest:

In darkness and in weariness
The traveller on his way must press,
No gleam to watch on tree or tower,
Whiling away the lonesome hour.

But if the heavens were empty of their God, and there rested no possibility of knitting up the broken threads of old amity in a future state, how much the more should the intimacies and loyalties of this transitory life have meant to him! After the blow had fallen, after Buddleigh Salterton, Horace Nettleship had turned to his wife, not only for support in his hour of tribulation, but with a renewed sense of love's importance. His love for his wife and family had seemed then the one discernible incentive for living in a manifestly futile universe. He had turned then to Charlotte, but he had turned in vain. He had hoped for comfort and understanding. It was hard for him to articulate the grandeur of his sufferings, harder still to explain the awful implications of our state. But she had made no effort to draw out his words, and expressed in his doubts, no particular interest. Could anybody *be* so trivial? She had accepted his stumbling efforts to explain why he did not want to continue family prayers, why he could not accompany them to the parish church, why he believed in fine that there was no God, with calm and even bored detachment! He might have been telling her that there was no longer a greengrocer in St John's Wood High Street, but even *that* would have evinced more interest. She continued to go to Church, to express, publicly, her belief in a final judgment. She was therefore presumably of the opinion that his infidelity put him in peril of eternal perdition. But she had raised no objections whatever to his lapse from faith. Did she not care either that she was expressing belief in the most absurd and superstitious fairy tales or (if that were not true) that her husband was going to hell? Did she not care?

Horace Nettleship was unable to escape the obvious fact that she did not care in the least. Uncaring indifference had marred her demeanour towards him for a dozen years or more. Little by little they had drifted apart and, too distraught and shy to ask her the nature of his offence (for she seemed always a little cross), he had retreated into the embarrassed silence from which it now seemed impossible to emerge. The more silent they grew with one another, the stranger became the whole texture of life at The Bower. He toiled at his treatise on volcanoes. In his youth he had explored the earth's surfaces and seen the eruptions of Iceland and Mexico. It was the experience of twenty or thirty years which he poured into his three-volume monograph, so that there was no temptation to idleness when his study door closed behind him. But the silence had made him into a stranger – not merely to his wife and servants, but also to his children. Maudie, his younger child, had been, by her careless and affectionate little nature, the person who had saved him from absolute despair. Perhaps she was, after all his sufferings and many years, what the twelve-year-old Charlotte had merely foreshadowed as she recited her multiplication tables at Malvern. Maudie saved him, and Maudie was his reason for existence. But it was the elder child Lionel towards whom he owed a greater responsibility. Lionel was after all a boy, and as a man he would have to make his way in the world. Mr Nettleship felt it was his duty as a father to bring Lionel up with no false illusions. The boy should at least be spared the torments of disappointment which assailed a soul who lost its faith. He should be given no faith to lose in the first place. It was impossible, while he was at Harrow, to hope that he would avoid the conventional attendance at daily scenes of Christian worship. When that time came to an end, Mr Nettleship had rather hoped that Lionel would go to London University, where it was not necessary to subscribe to the orthodoxies of the National Church. But the lad had been passably good at Greek and Latin and implored his father to send him to Oxford to read Greats. Six months earlier, therefore, he had gone up to Harcourt, and his father had discussed with him the perils of intellectual dishonesty. It was necessary, for an Oxford undergraduate, to attend chapel, as he had attended the chapel at Harrow. If he intended to take a degree, it would be necessary to do so in the name of the Holy and Undivided Trinity. A measure of compromise was in the nature of the case unavoidable. Perhaps influenced by his mother the boy had blushingly confessed that this chapel attendance, this Trinitarianism, would cause him 'no difficulties'. Mr Nettleship knew that there were many Oxford men, such as Mark Pattison the old Rector of Lincoln, who pretended to no Christian faith whatever, but were willing to go through the forms of the thing to avoid trouble. Lionel must search his own conscience. He had promised that he would. If necessary he could make an inner proviso that, while *assenting* to the Christian religion as the prevailing one at Oxford, he did not commit himself intellectually to any of its wilder claims. It had made the father unhappy giving this casuistical counsel to his son. He felt as though he were an early Christian urging his progeny, for form's sake, to sprinkle a little incense on the altar of Caesar. Lionel had grown distant from his father during his schooldays. Mr Nettleship had no idea at all what his beliefs, if any, were. He no longer believed that a youth of eighteen years or nineteen, was in a position to entertain any opinions

whatever. But he wanted to spare Lionel disillusionment and he
wanted to be loyal to the Truth. It was perfectly obvious to all his
household how Mr Nettleship felt about the matter. Perhaps (it was
too late now to ask) Charlotte did in fact deeply disapprove of his loss
of faith. Perhaps Lionel had never fully shared it; and never seen why,
for instance, his father found the very sight of a clergyman so heartily
disagreeable. But in the matter of family loyalty there could be no
doubt about where the duties of his family lay. He had, after all, been
into the matter more deeply than they had. He knew as a scholar and a
scientist that there was no greater evil than to deny the truth and that
to assert that the world was made in six days, or that five loaves could
feed five thousand people was simply a denial of the truth. He had seen
that, clearly and unambiguously: it was the duty of his family to follow
him.

But now, this afternoon, that coxcomb Chatterway had come
strutting into his drawing room. Mr Nettleship had always felt
rebuked by his father-in-law. He knew that by the standards of Mr Egg
and his entourage he was perhaps dowdy, serious, and a little
ridiculous. Egg himself never said so, but his friend Chatterway, who
had always pretended to far too close an intimacy with Charlotte,
made it plain by every word and gesture that he despised Mr Nettleship. Now he had the infernal cheek to bring some grovelling painter
into the house and announce that the young man was to teach Maudie!
And not content with this insolence, Chatterway had then come out
with this extraordinary story about his son taking holy orders. The
Reverend Lionel, he had called him! The words had stung Mr
Nettleship, but this pain had been nothing to the discovery that his
wife had been in the conspiracy all along, and that she had contrived to
use the incident to turn Maudie against her own father! Mr Nettleship's anguish was terribly acute. The world saw only a stolid
overweight bald man with greying whiskers and not much to say for
himself. But behind this unprepossessing exterior was an anguished
human soul, who had lost his faith, who was heartbroken at having
lost the love of his wife and who now gazed on helplessly while corrupt
and foolish people tried to rob him of his own children. Maudie,
Maudie, Maudie, his little Maudie. If the child knew what pain she
had inflicted by her two words: You're horrid! He smarted from them
as if he had been thrashed with scalding rods. Chatterway was the very
devil, but Charlotte, too, must take her share of the blame.

He groaned, as he sat in his study chair. He almost wept. He said
aloud in a low growling agony, 'Oh, oh, if *only*, if only . . .!' He spoke
to no one, so he did not need to expound what he meant by the words.
But if only Charlotte had been kind to him. . . . If only Lionel had never

gone to Harcourt. . . . If only Mr Waldo Chatterway had never been born.

Opening his ink-well, Mr Nettleship penned a letter to his son.

FIVE

Lionel Nettleship

It was a miscellaneous assembly, college men heavily outnumbered by townsfolk. Although Lionel could see, dotted about in the shilling seats, some undergraduates of his acquaintance, all the persons in his immediate vicinity of threepennies were of the roughest class and type. A red-faced woman, almost a gypsy, was joking with her man, a tall, rugged, ill-shaven brute in mud-bespattered leggings and a coat of greasy worsted.

"'E say to me, you minds as how you cover your arms with a shawl moi dearie if you's as a-coming in 'ere,' she cackled.

It was indeed the case that stewards, collecting the shillings and sixpences at the doors, had forbidden entry to any woman whose dress could be considered immodest. Hands and face were the only part of the female anatomy allowed exposure in that provincial hall. Elbows had to be swathed in a sleeve or draped with a shawl and throats were to be hidden with mufflers or chokers. Few women's dress had needed to be adjusted to admit entry, and those who had been asked to cover their arms, like the woman in front of Lionel, seemed to take it in good part, since this was part of the conventional procedure of Father Cuthbert's meetings. (Not to have been asked to cover their arms would have been to miss part of the distinctive experience.)

The atmosphere was a mixture of church and a fairground. The density of the crowd added to the excitement and expectancy of the scene. Lionel knew that in large measure he had been led to the Town Hall that night by pure curiosity. Father Cuthbert was a famous, not to say notorious, itinerant preacher who was said to draw crowds of over 50,000 when he spoke in London or Birmingham. Ever since this eccentric Anglican deacon had declared his resolution to revive the monkish life in the Church of England, his name had been blazoned with notoriety. No bishop seemed willing to ordain him priest. There had been various lawsuits over property and the vulgar newspapers periodically accused him of kidnapping young people and walling them up in the cells of his monastery in the Black Mountains of Wales. Gutch said that most of these stories were probably exaggerated. Gutch, who had introduced Lionel to so many exciting aspects of life in the Church of England, would not accompany his friend to the Town Hall. Fastidiously High Church, Gutch had dismissed Father Cuthbert as 'a ritualist or Upper Class Moody'.

The appellation of 'upper class' could certainly never have been applied to all the crowds gathered in the Town Hall to see this famous phenomenon. Lionel had never in his life been so close to so ragged an assembly. The very quality of their skin, the stubbliness of the men, the shining redness of the women – was different from the human beings with whom Lionel was used to consorting. And the odours produced by over a thousand people closely packed in a small Town Hall had something of the farmyard.

The expectant chatter and excited murmuring died down when, on the stage, a tall, etiolated young man with shaven head and monkish habit emerged from the wings and sat himself at a harmonium.

'That be the Holy Father,' whispered Lionel's neighbour, immediately rebuked by her spouse who said, correctly, 'It bain't.' The young monk at the harmonium had started to play a hymn tune, unfamiliar to Lionel, and those members of the audience, or congregation, who could read were rustling their 'service sheet' and singing to the lilting rhythm of the Father's own composing, one of the famous Llangenedd hymns.

> Jesus! let thy Presence
>   Breathe a sense of rest
> O'er our tired spirits
>   By Life's toil oppress'd.

Swayed by the faintly hypnotic melody, the crowd gave themselves up to its power, and all eyes strained towards an elevated stage where, besides the gangling shaven youth at the keyboard, there was a table groaning with a potted aspidistra, a lectern, and a vast white banner, proclaiming in scarlet letters the device JESUS ONLY.

> Jesus! Sweet Refreshment
>   When our spirits faint,
> Flashing forth sweet visions
>   Love alone can paint.

Lionel was then aware of heads turning away from the stage towards the back of the hall. Instead of his expected entrance from the wings of the stage, the Monk of Llangenedd was making his entrance down the central aisle. There were so many heads and shoulders and bonnets in the way that he was unable to see anything as the music and voices swirled and soared. Then the little procession, for such it was, arrived at the stage and climbed up the steps. Two nuns, in elaborate neo-medieval habits, led the way, their arms folded demurely beneath their scapulars, their eyes cast downwards so that to the watchful audience it was if they had their eyes shut. Next came a little boy, not above nine years of age, still with his childish shock of hair, but clad otherwise as a monk. Over his little black habit, knotted at the waist with rope and dangling with an elaborate rosary, the child had cast a lacey surplice or cotta, embroidered with emblems of the Sacred Heart. He was followed by the monk himself, his habit billowing about him like a vast black balloon and the dramatic quality of his appearance greatly enhanced by the fact that he wore his hood up, thus covering almost all his face. It might have been the entrance of a pantomime ghost or the most vulgar and ghoulish product of a popular novelist's imagination. But almost immediately, as this strange figure assumed the rostrum, the crowd succumbed to his charm or power. When he reached the lectern, he cast back his hood and revealed his features.

Lionel could now see him very clearly. He was surprised by how small the monk was (no more perhaps than five foot six in height) and he bridled, prepared to resist his hypnotic spell. He suddenly felt that Gutch had been right to warn him against coming and that there was something theatrical, if not downright unseemly, about the little man. The face, however, had an undeniable attractiveness and animation. Tonsured, like the young monk at the piano, Father Cuthbert, with his monastic coiffure, had something of the look of a Roman emperor. Markedly angular eyebrows ensured that his face would always wear an expression of surprise. On either side of his sharp nose beady eyes now in this, now in that direction stared about. They were the liveliest eyes that Lionel had seen in his life. Even from where he stood in the hall he could see them gleaming, darting about, and fixing individuals in the body of the auditorium. The music died away, and from the abundant folds of his habit, the monk produced an elongated lily white hand which he raised towards his listeners.

'Oh *Jesus!*' were his opening words. 'O my beloved Jesus, Thou art here with us at this evening hour. Abide with us, dear Lord Jesus, for the night of our lives is far spent, the night of sin, the night of death, and the Day, O Precious Jesus, the Day is at hand, when Thou wilt judge the sins of the world. O dearest Shepherd of thy sheep, be near to Thy flock tonight. Come after Thy lost sheep, Lord Jesus, Thy dear lost sheep for whom Thou didst shed Thy most precious blood. O Jesus! O Jesus! We love you, Lord Jesus! Come now into our hearts and fill us with the radiant vision of Thy glory and Thy love!'

The voice which spoke these words was a high contralto; if one closed one's eyes it would be assumed to be the voice of a maidenly old woman. But it was impossible to close your eyes. Father Cuthbert held them. Each eye in the hall was irresistibly fixed upon him, and within quarter of an hour, many of those eyes were streaming with tears. His text was simple: *Christ died for our Sins.*

'Perhaps there are few in this great company who understand the value of these five short syllables. Yea, there was a time when I myself did not do so. But now God has opened my eyes' – and as he said these words, his fiery beady eyes seemed to open yet further, and to be ablaze – 'so that now, today, I am the possessor of the Gift of God – that gift which is within the reach of all who will accept Jesus, from the Rich Man to the "King of shreds and patches", from the white-haired Patriarch, to the tiny child who can scarcely lisp the Holy Name.'

Then Father Cuthbert told them 'the old old story of Jesus and his love', but here was preaching with a difference. Many there were who confessed and called themselves Christians who believed that Our Lord performed miracles eighteen hundred years ago. 'But go, and shew John again the things which ye do hear and see in this reign of Queen Victoria – how the blind receive their sight, and the lame walk, the deaf hear, the dead' – he gulped and his high voice rose yet higher and then broke into a sob – 'the dead are raised up. And the *dear* poor have the gospel preached to them.'

Some of these modern miracles were then related. He told how he had himself raised up the dead, restored sight to the blind and hearing to the deaf. And then his tone changed to one of irony and mock-humour. For there were those learned men who would deny that Our Lord had performed miracles, either in the first or the nineteenth century. There were those who were so imbued in the pernicious plague pits of Plato that they no longer believed God's plain word written. And, somewhat to his astonishment, Lionel heard the monk mount a furious attack on Doctor Jenkinson, the Master of his own College. Doctor Jenkinson's translation of the Dialogues of this pagan monster were an open invitation to sin; a book in which sins were held up not as crimes, but as ideals to be admired and emulated by the youth-student of the day. Why were not the Master of Harcourt and all the disseminators of this Platonic Civilisation liable to the inquisition of the Penal British Law?

It is to be doubted whether, at this point of his discourse, many of his audience knew what Father Cuthbert was talking about, but sensing that 'gown' was being attacked, 'town' murmured in agreement. Shop boys and soldiers, labourers and serving wenches felt for a moment fervent in their disapproval of the Dialogues of Plato. And this same Doctor Jenkinson and other learned men said there was no miracle!

But it was another learned Doctor and oh! a dear, most dear friend of
Father Cuthbert, no less a man than Doctor Pusey who had said that if
there was any truth in the Master of Harcourt's teachings, there was
nothing left for Christians to believe.

'Nothing! But we who had been saved by the shedding of the
precious Blood of Jesus knew that there was everything! Yes! Yes! For
He had died for us all, while we were yet sinners, and loved us.'

Lionel's emotions were as yet seemingly detached from the speaker.
He was able to register mild surprise at the inclusion, in a passage of
popular oratory, of so esoteric a matter as an attack on Plato. He even
wondered whether he believed in the monk's miracles. But then,
would a man dare to get up in public and claim to have raised the dead
if he had not? And was it not true that if our Lord was indeed divine,
that he would continue to perform miracles through his chosen
ministers? And then had come the revelation that the monk was a dear
friend of Gutch's hero, old Doctor Pusey of Christ Church. Lionel
afterwards would say that it was enough to make a man think. But he
was at that moment doing much more than thinking. His whole being
was in ferment when the music began and they were invited to
punctuate the Monk's discourse with some more sacred song of his
own composing.

> Called to leave father, mother,
> And worldly wealth or fame,
> To give up all for Jesus
> And glorify His name.

In his fervour and excitement, the little monk ran over to the
harmonium and took the place of the novice who played there. Even
above the roar of voices which filled the packed assembly one could
hear his own high trilling

> Yes! like a fountain, precious Jesu
> Make me and let me be,
> Keep me and use me daily, Jesus,
> For Thee, for only Thee.

Lionel found, during this singing, that he was completely carried away
by the excitement of the moment. There were some occasions, he
knew, when Father Cuthbert met with violent opposition from roughs
and rowdies and from Protestants genuinely shocked by his attempt to
revive the monastic superstitions of the Middle Ages. But tonight,
Lionel felt the strange power and thrill of a whole crowd moved to one

thought and one mood. The great stubbly brute at his side who, half an hour before had seemed such a rough diamond – not the sort you would care to meet in a dark alley late at night – was now sobbing like a baby. He was not alone in his tears. Many wept as they sang. Lionel found that he wept too. It had been a principle of his schooling that blubbing was unmanly and he had always before sought, when tears came upon him, to conceal them. But now he wept openly, freely and felt his heart almost literally lift up. He would not have been surprised then if his body had risen with his heart to the roof, and he had performed a miracle of levitation. He felt so heady, so happy, so much at peace. Furthermore, he felt the Presence. There could be no doubt at all that Jesus was present at that hour, as close and as real as when he had walked the earth. Lionel had known for the previous six months, the comfort and delight to be derived from the *practice* of the Christian religion in its outward forms and ceremonies. He had learnt from Gutch much more than just the technical architectural terms, the difference between a *gradine* and a *piscina,* or the function of the lavabo. He had learnt that the Church of England was not an historical accident nor a mere department of state – a religious Post Office – but a part of Christ's Holy and Apostolic Church. He had learnt to revere the Church as the bride of Christ, and order his life by Christ's sacraments.

But in the crowded Town Hall that evening, he realised that he had never accepted Jesus Christ, God and Man, as his personal saviour. He had never opened his heart to Jesus and let him in, to change and purify his whole life. And now during the singing of the hymn he did so, and he felt his whole being suffused with a glow which he knew to be the sure token of Our Lord's presence with him. He wanted no sign, no proof, no outward assurance.

For Thee, for only Thee!

When, after a silence, the monk rose from the harmonium and led them all in prayer, Lionel realised that Father Cuthbert was the chosen vessel of God's grace for his, for Lionel's salvation. The words which proceeded from the mouth of the monk spoke so completely to Lionel that he knew them to come from God himself. He said, Father Cuthbert, that the Shepherd was calling to the sheep. Even at that very hour he had retrieved one of his lost lambs and placed it in his everlasting arms. . . . The words were no longer the sound to which Lionel was listening, nor to which with his conscious brain, he was attaching 'a meaning'. Rather the Holy Spirit of God spoke with a language too deep for utterance so that the monk's words and his own inner joy sang together in one inexpressible harmony. Jesus only! And Jesus had come into his heart that night.

Soon, all too soon, the meeting was over. The monk, the two nuns, the novice and the little boy (the Infant Samuel) were jostling their way down the aisle and trying to make their way to a four-wheeler which waited to take them to the station. Lionel longed to get near the Father, but it seemed impossible. Indeed the monk was so small that he soon became completely lost in the writhing jostling mass of people. But Lionel prayed, 'Dear Lord Jesu, my saviour, if it be Thy holy will, let me touch the hem of his garment,' and he was pushed or carried as if by the spirit out through the press and the squash so that he was standing on the steps *outside* the Town Hall.

In the lamplight the crowds gathered about to catch the last glimpse of the neo-medieval phenomenon on the pavement. Many who had nothing to do with the meeting and had never heard of Father Cuthbert hovered about as if a spectacle were about to occur. Little boys with no shoes loitered, the stub of cheroots retrieved from a gutter and stuck smouldering between their lips.

''Ere 'e be,' shouted one voice.

For the first time that evening someone shouted, 'No popery!' but Protestant fervour was in suspension that evening. Suddenly, there they were on the steps, Father Cuthbert and his entourage. Outside and in the lamplight he seemed even smaller than on the podium. But Lionel's prayer was to be granted, for he knelt down at the Father's feet and felt that long gentle white hand rest momentarily on his head.

'Oh Father . . . ' he could not speak for the emotion which choked him. But Father Cuthbert smiled at him with his firm rat-trap mouth and said in his piping tones, 'We will meet again. Until then, may God's blessing be upon you, my son.'

And with that, the vision faded, and the monk with his novice, his sisters and his infant oblate had been bundled into the four-wheeler and were clattering away over cobbles past the brash new Gothic of the Post Office towards the railway.

Lionel himself turned away and walked back towards his college. The church tower at Carfax, the base of which was a common meeting ground for ruffians and low types of all sorts, struck nine as he passed into the gabled haven of Cornmarket Street. He felt a little conspicuous in his cap and scholar's gown and tried to ignore the shouts of the loiterers whose unspecified abusiveness was not necessarily directed at him. Above the shambling old roofs of the Cornmarket the clear stars shone benignly in an April sky. At his back he heard the great boom of Tom Tower at Christ Church tolling out its hundred and one, a little behind Carfax; and ahead, the clocks of St Michael at the

Northgate and St Mary Magdalen were chiming the hour and it was as though the night air was full of bells.

His college porter nodded to him as he signed himself in: fierce old man, he was almost as much an 'institution' as the Master himself and he had been in that porter's lodge for longer than anyone could remember. He perhaps believes, thought Lionel, that I have merely been out to the meeting of some Society – perhaps to a debate at the Union. He cannot know that I have been to meet Jesus, and that Our Lord has come into my heart.

There was a lightness and spring in Lionel's step as he bounded up his staircase. He had never known that joy could be so intense, and when he found that his room was occupied, and his best friend and confidant making cocoa on the gas-ring, he wanted to burst out at once with the joyous news of his salvation.

Gutch, who knelt by the grate with the saucepan of cocoa in one hand, and a scarlet volume indented with gold called *The Ritual Reason Why* in the other, was a boyish young man, two years older than Lionel. He wore only his shirt-sleeves – a coat and gown were slung over the back of a sofa – but his whole appearance, from his black boots, dark trowsers, high black waistcoat and stiff white collar, had a clerical air, which was increased by the fact that his pale whiskerless face was crowned with a black smoking cap, which he called his *zucchetto*, an object which he wore in imitation of the great Doctor Pusey.

'It says here,' he said, without looking up from his book, 'that the priest uses two stoles in administering Baptism, the first violet and the second white. I'm not sure that's right, are you?'

'I don't know,' said Lionel truthfully.

'My father would never wear two stoles, but then I doubt whether he would ever wear *one*. Someone told me the other day that the holy Doctor' (by which Gutch meant doctor Pusey) 'wears a stole *under* his surplice scarf and hood when he celebrates. Quite possible I should think. How was the mad monk of Llangenedd?'

'Wonderful!' Lionel blurted out. 'It was the most wonderful experience of . . . my life!'

Gutch did not withdraw the epithet 'mad' but he said quietly, 'I'm told he can be very impressive,' as he poured the cocoa out into cups.

'The whole crowd were *held* by him.'

'Did they shout back? He normally gets some antis.'

'Oh Gutch, I *wish* you had been – I wish you had. I realised that I had never before accepted. . . .' He hesitated and drank his cocoa. A curtain of embarrassment had fallen between the two friends, but Gutch said, 'Go on. . . .'

'Well, I didn't have a *personal* knowledge and love of Our Lord until now. And He really has come into my heart. It wasn't the monk of Llangenedd I was hearing, you see, it was . . . it was Our *Lord*.'

Gutch paused and ate the cocoa skin off his teaspoon with some relish. Then he said a little ambiguously, 'I believe he's some sort of cousin of mine. You know the way mother is related to everybody. He *may* or may not be a cousin. It is possible he is only a connection. But he is a cousin of the Dean's who is a cousin of mother's.' The Dean was always, in Gutch's vocabulary, Dean Stanley. Normally Lionel found Gutch's two chief topics of conversation – Church ornaments and his own relations – very restful and interesting. Gutch knew a lot about the former and had endless numbers of the latter. But the present seemed hardly the moment to discuss either.

'What was he wearing?'

'A simple habit.'

'Simple? Are you sure it was him?'

'It was a flowing, unadorned habit.'

'That sounds more like the monk. I am told he wears a knotted girdle which is of course quite un-Benedictine. I am sorry I called him the mad monk, Nettleship old boy, I'm sure he really was top hole. The Dean always says that he is the one primitive Christian still living, but I think he only says that to annoy cousin Augusta.'

SIX

Mr Timothy Lupton

'Do you mean to say that you were simply turned away at the door?'

'The servant –.'

'Aggie, I expect –.'

'Very naturally I got no inkling of the servant's name.'

'Aggie has a never to be forgotten and not unwinning, *comment dit-on en anglais,* glide.' And Mr Chatterway managed, for a moment, to induce into his own brightly normal eyes something of Aggie's irregular stare.

'But I saw her at the window. I saw her looking down from the room where we were.'

'You mean the room where we all went for tea?'

'I do. I could swear it was that room. I saw her sad face peering down. She had drawn aside the lace curtains and was peeping over the window box and the petunias.'

'By her do you mean the little girl?'

'No. It was Mrs Nettleship, you see, that I asked to see. I felt I could not call . . . on the *child.*'

'Even though, if I suspect rightly. . . .'

'You don't suspect, sir, anything. But dash it, why should Mrs Nettleship say she was out and then *allow* herself to be seen at the window?'

'Mysterious, I grant you. Nor is it like my ever beloved Mrs Nettleship to be lacking in *politesse.* You didn't insult her, did you, while the rest of our backs were turned? I suspect you of being a dark horse.'

Already there had grown up between the two friends the possibility of such badinage. Mr Chatterway perhaps had more the gift of intimacy than of friendship. They had met quite by chance changing their books at Mudie's library and strolled out together with apparent purposelessness into the sunshiny King's Road, Holborn.

Whether or not Mr Lupton was a dark horse in any sense of the words he felt flattered by the suggestion, and said, 'You saw me – you introduced me, indeed, into the household. It was *their* suggestion that I should call again and teach the child to draw. I would have been happy to do so.'

'And I would have been happy for you too,' said he who ten days before, had known nothing of Lupton's existence. 'An unattached and artistic young man needs the stability of some nice bourgeois family who can feel a bit adventurous by patronising him, what?'

'I'm not sure that would have been necessary. . . .'

'Even though the great surgeon of Guy's takes so very dim a view of his son's artistic endeavours.'

Lupton greeted this reference to his father with silence. It showed beyond question that Chatterway had been doing his homework. The older man took his arm as they ambled, their two hats bobbing on that pavement in a multitude of chimneypots. Chatterway added, 'Mr Nettleship is not the only man in the world whose son appears to have chosen a profession deliberately to disoblige his father.'

'The governor is perfectly happy for me to be an artist,' said Lupton nonchalantly.

'It's not what one *hears,* dear boy, it's not what one *hears.*'

Certainly, the surgeon of Guy's had been angry enough when, a dozen years earlier, Timothy Lupton had declared his painterly ambitions. It was one thing at Charterhouse to flirt with the Muses, to prefer sketching and painting to construing Cicero. But, when all his contemporaries had pursued the careers of gentlemen, and gone to the University, or got themselves commissions or entered one of the learned professions, it seemed embarrassing that young Timothy should have continued his dalliance with art. Old Doctor Lupton seemed to his colleagues and friends at the club to be a crusty old gentleman of the old school. But in reality he was perhaps only three quarters a gentleman. When he had railed at Timothy for his Bohemian ambitions, he had done so as one who had risen from obscurity. The doctor's father had been an apothecary in Chelmsford, and his grandfather on the edge of the Essex marshes in Napoleon's time a peasant farmer. Timothy by his rashness had threatened to cast himself back into the primeval slime. But that had been long ago. And if the young man thought of it sometimes during his somewhat sordid matutinal routines and rituals – the heating of his own shaving water in a kettle somewhat rusty, the blowing of dust off the butter kept for convenience under the wash-stand, the impaling of a slightly stale bun on a button-hook which also served as a toasting fork – he thought that on the whole he had made the right decision, and that, by some people's standards, he was doing well.

After school, he had been fortunate enough to learn his craft in the studio of the celebrated Mr Alma-Tadema, newly arrived in England, and to watch the master cover canvas after canvas with figures from the ancient world, lolling on marble. After a year or two of the discipline, Mr Lupton was a perfectly competent craftsman. Indeed, if what you wanted was a marble pillar, or a reverend senator pensive at some pool's edge, or the daughter of a Pharaoh with her scantily-clad handmaids finding Moses among the bullrushes, there were few young men in London who would supply them with more professional skill than he. Had the surgeon of Guy's been more encouraging, Timothy Lupton would have liked to concentrate all his expertise on such productions, but the necessity of earning a living made any such indulgence impossible. He had taken on too much. He had illustrated magazines and three-volume novels, and he had lived beyond his means, and, living beyond his means, he had found himself mixing with company who mysteriously diluted his artistic fervour.

He had turned aside, some years ago, from the straight and stony pathway of pure art. He told himself that he could only paint great pictures if he had the leisure and the means, and in order to achieve these elusive prizes, he had become a portrait painter. Plenty of his school friends, now rising merchants or legislators, felt rather flattered in having a 'Bohemian' friend in old Timmy Lupton. It was easy to tell himself that he spent too much on hats, clubs, cards and drink solely because he wanted to put 'his best foot forward'. He could barely afford the grandeur of the studio which he rented (eschewing the vogue for Chelsea) in Fitzroy Square, and none of his friends knew of the dusty little attic, round the corner in Charlotte Street, where he laid his head each night. Socially, it was 'paying off'. Old Doctor Lupton had felt almost reconciled to the youth when he heard he was painting the portraits of dowagers, bankers and archdeacons. To that degree, Chatterway was a little out of date with his information, as young Mr Lupton tried to explain.

'I knew of course that you had painted Archdeacon Gutch, and that you are doing my dear friend Mr Egg. Who else have you lined up?'

'The Master of Harcourt.'

'Have you indeed, the poppies getting taller all the time. No wonder there should be some rapprochement between you and your chirurgically manipulative parent.'

'Really, you exaggerate the differences between the governor and myself. We've always knocked along together perfectly well. My only regret. . . .'

'Not enough time for what you want to do?'

'Precisely. It all seems a little like a betrayal of trust, as though I had failed in a vow.'

He hesitated, wondering whether to tell Mr Chatterway, who had the curious power of sympathy and who, for all his obvious habits of indiscretion, had a power to elicit confidences, about his dream of the previous night, but it was hard to do so without the implication of impropriety.

He had been lying in a thickly wooded coppice. Parting the bushy boughs which concealed him he had glimpsed a party of fair-tressed maidens by a river bank, washing rich stuffs on the even whitish stones there. He had rushed from the brake and in doing so caused whoops of anguish to arise from the snowy armed nymphs – for he was naked. And all the girls ran away save one, Maudie Nettleship, whose white body seemed as if it had been fashioned out of Parian china and whose long brown hair was framed with a garland of white flowers and olive leaves.

'Goodly Odysseus,' the child had called out. 'Let us give you meat and drink and shelter.' But as she had led him away he found that he was in the coffee room at Boodles, and after a passage of the dream which he did not remember, he had woken up.

The dream had been more than the usual nightly book of nonsense written by nature in our brain. It had been a great imaginative experience and, indiscreet as it appeared, he half wanted to share it with Mr Chatterway, because it was the beginning or background of his subsequent visit to the Bower. Although he had read as much Homer as the next man at Charterhouse, it had been chiefly in the *Iliad* and it had never made much mark. Then, about six months before he met the Nettleships, Mr Lupton had read Andrew Lang's new English translation of the *Odyssey*. It had been one of the most inspiring few weeks of his life as he read and re-read the great book and cursed himself, after something like eight years at school learning the subject, that he did not have adequate Greek to read the poem fluently in its Attic original. But ever since reading Lang's prose poem he had been guiltily aware that he wanted to settle (if only the demands of his hack work would allow him) to a series of canvasses illustrating the *Odyssey*. With portraits to paint and the novels of Hesba Stretton and Rowland Grey to illustrate he had put the great notion from his mind. He had even begun to wonder whether his artistic energies had not been altogether sapped, whether the imagination itself might not be dead within him. But his dream recalled a favourite scene of the arrival of Odysseus in Phaeacia, where, after weary toil, he finds rest, and the beautiful princess Nausicaa entertains him in the house of her father, Alcinous high of heart. The mingling of Nausicaa with Maudie Nettleship sparked off in his head a high imaginative excitement. He had felt once more that he could *paint*. The dream, and all that it awoke in his heart, had momentarily conquered the triviality of existence. And it had therefore been in no mere spirit of social politeness or curiosity that he had boarded the omnibus that morning and made the pilgrimage to St John's Wood.

'I wonder if Eggy would have light to shed on the matter,' said Chatterway, to whom, in the event, Mr Lupton felt capable of explaining nothing. 'Let's stretch our legs a little and walk towards Brunswick Square.'

'I could even give him a sitting.'

'And Bacon could cook us a muffin.'

The two men traversed at leisurely speed the orderly squares and thoroughfares of Bloomsbury, while Mr Chatterway, in explanation of the fact that he had been 'out of touch' with *la casa* Nettleship for a full ten days, rehearsed an extravagant catalogue of social activity, interspersed with scurrilous reflexions on the marital history of Mrs John Millais. His dedication to the intimate analysis of every private life in London was in itself almost artistic, as though he were peopling an enormous frieze or painting an allegorical ceiling crowded with figures.

At Mr Egg's front door, they enjoyed the usual ritual, the grinning and bowing of the negro in yellow breeches.

'Is your master in, Bacon?'

As on his previous visit, Mr Chatterway saw concealed in the attendant's smile a secret which amused him.

'Big trouble, sir,' he said, as he admitted them into the drawing room.

Mr Egg reclined there on an old chaise longue, wearing a dressing gown of turquoise silk and a smoking cap, of identical hue, from which a golden tassle was suspended. His daughter, Charlotte Nettleship, sat beside him, pale and tense, and upon the entrance of the two visitors she started as though discovered in some illicit activity.

'Speak of the devil,' groaned Severus Egg.

'Father, *please!*' Mrs Nettleship's anguish seemed almost tearful, but Mr Egg in a languid good-humoured way would not be discouraged.

'We've got to *tell* them, dear child. They will think it so highly mysterious if they keep toiling up to St John's Wood and finding you not at home.'

Mr Lupton's eyes met those of Mrs Nettleship. He felt he might be blushing and he could see that she most certainly was.

'Are you going away?' asked Mr Chatterway bluntly.

'I wish I was,' she said crossly, and then, with another meaningful look at Mr Lupton, she cut herself short.

'It's darling Netty,' said Mr Egg. 'He took frightful exception to your both gobbling up his tea the other day and he doesn't want you to call there again.'

'Oh, father, it *isn't* an occasion for flippancy.'

Mr Egg pursed his mandarin lips and his eyes smiled behind their creased lids as if he were asking himself whether there was ever a moment in his life which was not an occasion for flippancy.

'The truth is,' said Charlotte Nettleship quietly, 'that my husband. . . .'

'What about him?' asked Mr Chatterway.

'My husband has been suffering of late from considerable anxiety.'

'He thinks because he don't believe in God nobody else should,' said Chatterway. 'Lionel isn't the only one who does, you know. I mean, there's the Queen, and the Archbishop of Canterbury and the Pope and a few others.'

'But you put your foot in it there, Marvo. How on earth could *you* know that Lionel had got it into his head to be a parson? He hadn't told anyone else.'

'I told you – Mrs Gutch was talking about it. Her husband the archdeacon is as you probably know one of our young friend's illustrious subjects' – he bowed to Mr Lupton – 'and the Gutch boy is up at Harcourt with Lionel. In your day, Eggy, it was probably racing with phaetons, but your modern undergraduate gets very excited about ritualism and all that.'

'It seems very rum to me,' said the grandfather. 'But instead of letting well – or at any event not ill – alone – darling Netty wrote off to the boy telling him he mustn't become a parson.'

'What did the boy say to that?'

'He sent back the most charming and *enthusiastic* epistle which would really have been better addressed to a Colossian or a Thessalonian. Have you got it, my darling?'

'I don't want to read Lionel's letter as if it were some kind of joke,' said Charlotte coldly. 'It *is* very worrying. I share my husband's anxiety.'

'I wish you would read it, but so be it. The most uplifting thing outside the bible you ever read in your life.'

'You remember Miss Williams?' asked Chatterway.

'No. Was she a friend of mine?' asked Eggy.

'You must remember *Williams*. She tried to convert the Duke. And d'you remember she was in the middle of some pious sentence.'

'I do!' laughed Eggy. 'And he chased her round the room crying *I love you, I love you!*'

Mrs Nettleship looked at Mr Lupton in anguish as the two older men shared their little memories.

'It is, naturally, to you that I feel most awkward,' she said quickly. 'I believe you know how very grateful I was to you for expressing such interest in Maudie's sketch books. As for your offer to help her with her work. . . .'

'It was made most sincerely, Mrs Nettleship.'

'I know that,' she said. She did not remove her gaze from him for an instant as she spoke. He felt as though he were being scrutinised by her gaze. 'I felt very acutely embarrassed, therefore, when I was obliged to turn you away this morning without a word when you must have been very fully aware that I was in fact at home.' The words were starting to flow now in a bitter little stream.

'I saw you,' said Lupton gently, 'at the window.'

Her blush now become total, but her reply surprised him.

'I meant you to see me,' she said. 'The embarrassing fact is that I must ask you never to call at my house again.'

'What!' called out Chatterway, ignoring Mr Egg's automatic 'Darling old Netty!' – 'You've never met Mr Lupton before the other day. What possible reason can you give?'

'The ban applies equally to you, Marvo, my dear,' said Mr Egg. 'Darling old Netty really means business.'

'It is,' added Charlotte, 'very unfortunate, and no one regrets it more than I do. But in the circumstances. . . . I think I ought to leave you, gentlemen.' And, planting a very formal kiss on her father's head, she hurried out of the room. Presently they heard Bacon showing her out, and then the domestic brought in the tea.

'Can anyone possibly explain to me what the deuce is going on?' asked Chatterway, who obviously found the whole matter much less amusing than Egg did. 'And if you say "Darling old Netty" again I shall, in spite of your years and seniority, be tempted to strike you.'

'I don't understand it myself, Marvo, my dear. It must be more than baffling to you, Lupton.'

'What did we do wrong?' asked the young painter.

'That,' said Mr Chatterway, 'is what I have been asking myself all my life.'

SEVEN

Charlotte

Over the watery broth, the herrings in mustard sauce, the chicken pie and the spotted dick which constituted dinner, Charlotte Nettleship cast frequent glances at her husband. She wanted to convey to him that the matter was finished, and done with. She had acquiesced. But it had been so long since she had ever attempted to catch his gaze, that he did not apprehend her attempt. His habit was to keep, from an ocular point of view, himself to himself.

'Mr Goe wishes us to start the *Odyssey*,' was Maudie's announcement as she dabbed at some of the mustard sauce (a little lumpy but irresistibly piquant) with a piece of bread.

Her mother: 'That would be very nice, darling.'

Maudie: 'We are going to start in the middle, with his getting past the sirens – Ulysses, I mean, not Mr Goe.'

Her father (interrupting her snigger): 'Odysseus, Odysseus. Ulysses is his Latin name, not used by Homer.'

Maudie: 'But you know what I mean, and Mr Goe read me Lord Tennyson's poem, and I was so moved I could choke.'

Her father: 'I am very gratified, of course, that you should take such pleasure in your reading, though I really have no confidence in a tutor who can allow you to speak of *Ulysses,* when. . . .'

Her mother: 'Do we have all the right books, darling? We must not let Mr Goe provide both the books as he did with the Xenophon.'

Maudie: 'Oh Mama, Xenophon was so boring that I thought I would die.'

Her father: 'But I would be equally happy for you to discuss your German work. Miss Schwartz has given me to understand' – and here his lips quivered into the hint of a smile – 'she has given me to *understand* that you are doing so much better.'

Oh, the treachery of that half-smile! Charlotte and he, by the same tacit agreement which made all enterprises at The Bower possible, simply did not make secret assignations with Maudie's teachers to discuss the child's work. Were it not for Horace Nettleship's anti-clerical bias, he could have heard the testimonials of Mr Goe two or three times a week in the drawing room or at the bottom of the stairs.

There was nothing furtive about this. But Fräulein Schwartz. It was not for Fräulein Schwartz to express opinions to one Nettleship only.

Maudie: 'I so much prefer my Greek to my German, even though I know that German is such a *lovely* language. Oh Papa, please don't tell me that Fräulein Schwartz is a brilliant tutor, for I simply couldn't bear it.'

Her father: 'There is much that I notice you can not bear, that would make you choke; and you are afraid you are going to die. You must learn, Maudie, that intelligent people do not use immoderate language of this kind.'

Maudie: 'Sorry, Papa.'

Her father: 'It is something which you would learn if you enjoyed more society. The fault in part lies with your mother and myself.'

Charlotte Nettleship's anger shot silently across the condiments and the epergne which gleamed dully on the mahogany surface of the dining table. How dare he, how *dare* he, include her in his fault. The absence of society in that household was not of her choosing.

She had come to dinner with a small envelope, which at the end of the meal, she had intended to place into her husband's hand. It said, *I visited my father this afternoon and asked him to convey to Mr Chatterway and Mr Lupton that they are not to call here any more.* She had written the card in fact, that morning, before her visit to Brunswick Square, and before her encounter with the two gentlemen named in her assertion.

'Now that Mr Chatterway is back, I am sure that we shall not lack for society in any sense of the term,' said Maudie breezily.

Her Father: 'Mr Chatterway is. . . .'

Maudie: 'Quite fantastically gregarious.'

Her father: 'Maudie, I have warned you.'

Maudie: 'Sorry, Papa, I mean that he is very gregarious.'

Her father: 'That is better. But remember that it is almost never necessary to qualify an adjective.'

Her mother: 'Put your hand in front of your mouth when you cough, Maudie.'

Maudie: 'Sorry, Mama.'

Charlotte looked down the table. In the small pocket of her gown was contained a card which would put his mind at rest. She now regretted most bitterly the illogic which had allowed her to submit to his tyrannies. She would not have done so if the varieties of guilt awakened by Mr Chatterway and Mr Lupton had not combined in her bosom with embarrassed rage against Lionel.

When Mr Chatterway had called and passed on the relatively harmless news that Lionel wished to become a clergyman, she had felt that her husband's over-reaction was absurd. But in the silent hours of evening, and the sleepless hours on her solitary pillow, she had come to share what she knew were the professor's misgivings. There was something indescribably hurtful about being told news of one's own child from the lips of a comparative stranger. It did not matter if the news was less dire than Horace pretended. The sensation was an unpleasant one. It was impossible to avoid *pique*. She knew, in a way that Horace Nettleship almost certainly did not, that Mr Chatterway's utterance was made with mischief, not malice. But, once the pain had been caused, one involuntarily associated it with him.

The guilt was the stronger because she had found his young companion, Mr Lupton, so altogether charming. She was prepared to concede that her father had brought the young painter to The Bower under sufferance. Perhaps Mr Lupton did not want to come at all. Perhaps it had all happened *by chance*. But Mr Chatterway was not a man who left things, particularly things so likely to cause disturbance and turmoil as human relations, to chance.

Charlotte had always prided herself on the absence of vulgarity with which she conducted her marital relations. To give her husband cause for jealousy would most certainly have been vulgar and she had always done her best to avoid doing so. Anything which concentrated his attention more firmly upon her was to be avoided and eschewed, for she sometimes felt scorched by his attention, or by the mere awareness that he was in the house. The troubles, the dangers with Mr Chatterway were long past; and then no jealousy, because no suspicion, had ever been felt. Her husband's displeasure at Mr Lupton's appearance had been instantaneous, obvious. She did not choose to play the game so much in Horace's way that he would find in the young a cause for reproaching *her*.

And then, after a week's silent meditation on the subject, they had received another appalling epistle of Lionel. Her husband's unreason on the subject of religion was not sympathetic to Charlotte. There was something ill-mannered, almost a little mad, about the way in which he could not be civil about Homer because of the blind poet's connection, *via* Mr Goe, with the Established Church. But when she had read Lionel's letter, she had felt, for the first time in years, a dart of fellow-feeling with her husband. For, she was not a Colossian or an Ephesian and she would *not* be written to by her own son as if she were one. The embarrassingness of the boy's piety had stabbed her, word by word, so that the letter was still intolerable to remember. There was no logic at all in her response. But she was angered and at the same time made awkward by Lionel's letter. She felt, moreover, on her husband's behalf *awkward* in relation to Mr Lupton and because she remained *piqued* that Mr Chatterway should have known before her of Lionel's religious mania, she resolved to obey her husband's desire. She *would* banish Mr Lupton and Mr Chatterway from her drawing room. She would at least convey to her father that they must not be brought near The Bower for *a bit*. She would write on a card that she had done so and give it to her lord and master at the hour of dinner. That had been her resolve. Then they had assembled in the dining room, and he had, as usual pulled out his chair, before sitting down, in a manner which made a scraping noise on the wooden floor. By the time that pieces of chicken pie were by the forkful being hidden behind the white whiskered cheeks, Mrs Nettleship no longer felt the desire to reassure her husband. And when, over the spotted dick, he had registered his disapproval of Mr Chatterway, she felt a great surge of loyalty to her old friend which made her regret most bitterly having met him that afternoon and forbidden him her house. She despised particularly the way in which Horace Nettleship did not quite dare to say out to his daughter that he disapproved of Mr Chatterway. 'It is almost never necessary to qualify an adjective.' Nothing about his wish that she should never see the gentleman again: her own godfather! The professor was too cowardly, simply, to explain to his daughter that her godfather would no longer be received if he called at the house. He was too cowardly to say it, Charlotte realised, when the chair scraped and they all rose to their feet, because he did not have the confidence that he would be obeyed. In his own house! No, she realised with glee that he was still, after more than a week, uncertain. He did not trust his wife to obey his instructions. When they parted after dinner, therefore, she did not give her husband her card, or his satisfaction. Let him writhe in his own uncertainty, as he did, throughout the evening of his study-solitude, while melancholy through the house the picked-out airs of Mendelssohn and Maudie's maddening cough, drifted from the child's piano practice, and silent, silent upstairs in her own room, Charlotte sat miserably. She wished she could unsay the words spoken that afternoon to Mr Chatterway, to Mr Lupton, in her father's house. She wished that she could remember how to weep, for tears, if they knew how, should have come now to her dry eyes and washed away some of the immovable miseries of life.

EIGHT

At the Zoo

'Anyone can find out the rules after they have been broken. The important thing is to know the rules first and *then* to break them.'

'But if you don't know what the rules are! They simply won't *say*, you see'

'Saying!'

'How else is one supposed to know them?'

'When I was your age, my almost Prussian and never to be satisfied parents and schoolmasters made it all too peevishly obvious what was and was not *verboten*.'

'But why should it always be they who make the rules?'

'Because, childie, it always is they. Always, always.'

A koala bear, the first in England, had that spring been presented to the Zoological Gardens. Mr Chatterway naturally pined to catch an early view, for his social appetite extended beyond human society to the lesser mammals, and he would hate to have dined out that week without being able to claim acquaintance with the diminutive antipodean dendrophile. A letter had been dispatched to The Bower, proclaiming for Maudie's eyes only (eyes not capable of deciphering every word of the scrawl) that, in the words of the music hall song, 'Walking in the Zoo is the okay thing to do.' It was perhaps inevitable that much of their too short space together should be devoted to a discussion of these sentiments from their moral viewpoint.

'Mama's reasons for being cross would be different from Papa's.'

'Of course.'

'Mama would be cross that I had come out without permission.' This was Maudie's way of saying that she had given her mother the impression that she would 'walk to the corner', after a German lesson with Fräulein Schwartz. 'Papa on the other hand would be cross. . . .'

'Papa would be cross because it was you,' she got out. And it was obvious in a queer way that her getting it out gave pleasure to them both.

'I'm not so sure I agree with your analysis.'

'Why not?'

'And I'm less sure that I agree with the propriety of our discussion. It

is the *maleducata* who talks about her parents before they are dead –
you should watch that cough – and you seem to forget that in this
particular case your doubtless exasperating and allegedly censorious
mother and father are almost my oldest friends.'

'You mean grandpapa is.'

'He too. But also your parents.'

'And Mama.' She was embarrassed to go further and say that she
somehow knew that her godfather was forbidden the house.

'Cinnamon cures it,' he alluded to the suppressed barking which she
smothered with her glove, but which had startled the wide-eyed koala,
peering at them pathetically from a branch in his cage.

'What is he eating, olive leaves?' she asked when she had recovered
from the latest most tiresome bout of coughing.

'Eucalyptus, the old gum tree. Up a gum tree are you, old friend?' he
called to the koala bear, and Maudie half-wondered if he would boast
to the creature of his acquaintance with the best-bred kangaroos in
Queensland, or with the Governor of New South Wales. 'Like the rest
of us,' he instead added. 'And do we know any more (you see what a
good godfather I am because I can take you to the Zoo to make sure
that the sight of all these steadily evolving creatures don't make you
lose your faith, what) about the sainted monk of Harcourt?'

'Lionel?'

She would not be drawn, but her pursed lips told him that she was
quite as annoyed as her parents.

'Anyone would think he had become a Mahommedan. He gets sent
to an ancient and Christian foundation and becomes a Christian, and
the poor boy's family want to disown him.'

Struggling not to show how much it hurt to talk about Lionel – for if
she let it show, Mr Chatterway would certainly pursue the subject
relentlessly until the last syllable of recorded time, the child was glad
that a cough made an immediate reply unnecessary. Then she said,
'We are all to go down for Show Sunday, since it was arranged. I was
to have been taken to the Commem. with Lionel's friend Mr Gutch.'

'Your first ball.'

'But now, perhaps. . . .'

'Have I not known the Gutch family almost as long as I have known
the Nettleships? You will find Everard Gutch a most attentive and
attractive partner.'

'Papa now thinks I am too young for a Commem.'

'But think of the difficulty they have in procuring enough young
ladies. And think of your promise made to Mr Gutch. You *can't* back
out now. I have already told his mother. . . .'

'Oh, Mr Chatterway, you *haven't*. Tell me you haven't, please!' She could not tell from his laughing features whether this were all a tease.

'He has been led to expect Dante's Beatrice and the Homeric syrens and Alice in Wonderland all rolled into one.'

'Please don't, please.'

'It looks to me as if young Gutch is going to break the heart of your devoted and Homerically-minded painter friend.'

'Painter . . .?'

'Come, come, missy, there are not so many famous painters in your entourage of admirers.'

She sniggered and showed her gums, for the entourage undeniably and gratifyingly did exist, even if she would not choose to 'gas on about it' in quite Mr Chatterway's fashion. She had felt, in fact, a little disappointed that Mr Lupton had not acted upon his professed desire to return to The Bower. There had been talk of his teaching her to draw. She wondered now if it had not been a mistake to blurt out, to Mr Lupton, her accustomed reflections on Mr Goe. Her Greek tutor *was* very funny, his adoration as pleasing as it was hilarious. But it had been perhaps a little blatant to *tell* the painter about it so immediately. 'I am so frightened that he will make me recite all the principal parts of ἵστημι that I simply . . .' and she had lowered her eyes, and the painter had supplied the word 'flirt'. And she had said, 'Not flirt, no', and laughed, and then said, 'Oh, Miss Nettleship!' in her Mr Goe voice. Perhaps Mr Lupton had gone away thinking that she intended to make a similar monkey out of him. She had meant to say at once that she regarded him as *different* from Mr Goe, or else why should she have taken him into her confidence? That it would not have been true would hardly matter, she loved Mr Goe's attentions, and she equally loved the pleasure of mocking them, to Mr Goe, Fräulein Schwartz, Mr Bacon, and Aggie. Doubtless, if he had been admitted to the house, Mr Lupton would have joined the *galère* with which the curate allowed her to punctuate her Greek lessons. But he had not returned. Papa had been furious with him for retrieving the cup which fell to the ground at tea, furious that his own clumsiness had been thus exposed by a visitor. But Mr Lupton could not have perceived how furious Papa was made by this.

'I think,' Mr Chatterway continued, 'that since Mr Lupton is forbidden to visit you in The Bower, we should arrange some meetings at the house of your venerable grandfather before the much vaunted and spoken of portrait is complete.'

'I don't understand, sir, what you mean by forbidden.'

'What the majority of other English speaking people mean by the word. *Vietato,* if you prefer.'

'But who has forbidden it?'

'Not Aggie.'

'But. . . .'

'And scarcely the Master of Harcourt, what?'

'But why should Papa . . .?'

'And not the erudite exponent on volcanic eruptions. It was your mother who has forbidden Mr Lupton to visit your house.'

'I don't believe you,' she said abruptly. 'You are just making it up.'

'Frightened perhaps by his desire to depict you as the semi-decent attendant of Pharaoh's daughter on the banks of old Nile. My serpent of old Nile, what?'

'I don't understand what you mean, sir.'

'Very likely not,' he said, having lost interest in his new Australian acquaintance and turned his back on the koala. 'Very likely not.'

And they walked for a moment of silence out into the shaded suburban street, and back in the direction of Abbey Grove.

NINE

Epiphany

Maudie often referred in her mind to this conversation, as the extent of the mystery began to unfold like a rising mist over everything in the days which followed. The more impenetrable the mystery grew, the more impossible it became to speak of it openly to her mother. Perhaps Mr Chatterway was simply mistaken. Perhaps it was all a singular example of his notorious desire to 'make trouble'. He himself was not seen again for a fortnight, and there was no reason to doubt, from the professor's demeanour, that the mischievous exile had been made unwelcome at The Bower. But by *Mrs* Nettleship? This Maudie found not only hard to believe but impossible to understand. Was there, after all, such a moral gulf between Abbey Grove and Brunswick Square?

The truth was, they had seen Mr Lupton so repeatedly at her grandfather's house that any visit of the painter's to The Bower would have been superfluous. Maudie wondered somewhat whether quite so many drawing lessons were, strictly, required. She had, after all, got by for over a year without any such supervision. Fräulein Schwartz and Mr Goe each came twice a week. It was necessary to keep German and Greek constantly burnished. Music, too, needed to be practised regularly. But now she had drawing lessons almost more frequently than she had Greek, German and Music put together.

It had been accidental, when the first time, she and her mother had called at Brunswick Square. Mama had seemed markedly discomposed to find grandpapa's portrait *still* in progress. But with considerable nonchalance they had all accepted one another's presence there and the instruction in perspective had begun. Mama had not bristled or bridled at the suggestion, after half an hour or so, that the lesson should be repeated, or continued, on the morrow.

And so the matter had continued. Maudie sometimes asked herself, as her instructions progressed, why it was that she needed a chaperone during her drawing lessons but not for the *Odyssey*. It had something to do with silly-billy Goe being in holy orders; something, more bluntly, to do with Mr Lupton being 'a proper man' and not, perhaps, (who knew?) quite the proper gentleman. It was a mysterious area of reflection to which she often returned in her mind.

With Mr Chatterway she had been one of the first Londoners to see a Koala bear, such a dear thing that she wanted to hug its heavenly little furry body to herself and keep a koala of her own. It was alien and strange and at the same time wholly sympathetic. It seemed as though one could dominate and possess it. Perhaps when one was wholly a woman, married and with a household, one felt in this way about men. Maudie was yet to do so. They seemed to her, men, if anything, more mysteriously alien than koala bears, and infinitely less sympathetic. One would not want to squeeze a man, as one would squeeze a dear little bear.

Mr Lupton, as a physical phenomenon, was by now highly familiar to Maudie. Since he often sat quite close to her and even, on occasion, guided her hand, as it held a brush or pencil, across the paper, she had become extremely aware of him. But his fine nose, his bright blue eyes, his broad shoulders or his silky blonde hair and beard fascinated her less as an example of any supposed singularity of physique than as a specimen of the generalised masculine phenomenon. She had seen it before in the hairy ears and bald pate of her father, in Mr Goe's red cheeks and cheery whiskers, and in the various male visitors and domestics to be seen in the drawing room at The Bower. To a lesser extent it was to be seen in her grandfather and Mr Bacon. Only in Mr Chatterway, strangely enough, was it not at all a disagreeable phenomenon.

She could not find a word in her head for what she meant by 'it': merely that it was observable. And here was Mr Lupton full of it. Even if one quite ignored all the other considerations, how truly extraordinary it was, this *hair* growing out of their faces. Not only did it mark them out as a quite different species, at one with the koalas and (for all Maudie knew of Darwin) the apes. But it marked them as a different category of creation whom it was impossible to take quite seriously. Everyone laughed at Mr Goe's mutton chop whiskers and curled moustachios. But in their way, the scrubs of white whiskers framing Papa's cheeks and chin were just as comical, and the mane of golden hair which sprouted so profusely from Mr Lupton. Several times, home after an afternoon in his company, Maudie had gone to her room and surveyed the looking glass with wonder, run her delicate white fingers over her upper lip, her chin, her jaws, and been captivated by the softness of her own skin as if it were an artifact quite separate from herself. If her own pale freckled features were suddenly to be deformed with the growth of a coarse thick growth of hair, she would feel that life had become unendurable. How did poor dearest Lionel face the prospect? Though she knew that he needed to resort to the razor, his face was as yet comparatively smooth and human.

Perhaps it would never be so hard and rough as some of the more bear-like individuals who haunted her life. Some men were spared the worst indignities. Mr Chatterway, for instance, either by magic or design, was quite wonderfully smooth of countenance and if, when parting, he embraced her, she felt no more roughness to her cheek than if she had been kissed by a woman. To be kissed by Mr Lupton was happily an event which was out of the question but it would be like having one's face rubbed mercilessly with a clothes brush.

Naturally acquiescent and passive, Maudie now took it for granted that she was, most flatteringly, taught to draw by a rising artist. She knew that it was her own flirtations, in the first instance, her breathless bright-eyed excitement which had brought all this about, and if she now found it all a little less exciting than it had appeared in prospect, she did not find it wearisome. The soon-to-be famous (so they all believed) painter could merely join the tribe of worshippers. It was easy to fit him into the scheme of things and devote very little thought to any of the implications which might result from her drawing lessons. Papa, she told herself, did not really like anyone to be fond of her except himself. He was in a perpetual fury with Mr Goe. It was no wonder that he had not taken well to Mr Lupton. It seemed almost natural not to mention to him that she was, in defiance of his whims, receiving lessons in drawings and painting from the new *bête noire,* or *bête blonde.* Yet, and this was where the whole thing seemed quite clouded in mystery, she had the sense that a particular wrong was being committed with Mr Lupton. Only when 'it' had been 'going on' for about a fortnight did the obviousness of her wrong-doing become apparent to her.

The three of them, the professor, Mrs Nettleship and Maudie were assembled over the curried eggs at the time of this moral epiphany. Maudie, who liked curry exceedingly, was helping herself to more of the gravy, even though she knew that there was all the heartiness to follow of bread sauce, mashed potato and roast capons, and so completely was she forced by gluttonous appetite to concentrate on her food that she did not listen very attentively to her father's monologue.

'Lionel's University is in the grip,' he spoke religiously, 'of indif-ferentism. Professor Mosely for instance, when teaching natural science, allows the religious among his audience to make up their own mind over such questions as evolution and Creation. Their own minds! Where is the scientific principle in that? He should tell them outright the truth.'

'Yes, Papa.'

'I shall look forward on our visit to Lionel to seeing old Mosely again, nevertheless.'

'Yes, Papa.'

'Please Maudie,' her mother interupted, 'please stop coughing.'

'Sorry, Mama.'

'Such spluttering.'

'I believe all the arrangements are now made. It is a great honour actually to be dining with the Master of Harcourt,' said Mr Nettleship.

'I thought he was such terrific friends with grandpapa or used to be,' said Maudie.

The professor frowned. It was true that the Master of Harcourt, like Severus Egg, belonged to that select group of persons who 'knew everybody' and that he, the professor, did not. It was unlikely in fact that they would all have been invited to dine with the Master on Show Sunday if Mrs Nettleship had not been paternally connected with the illustrious past.

'I hope,' Maudie prattled on, 'that I shall like this dreadful-sounding Mr Gutch.'

'For my part I feel you are still too young for the ball,' said the professor.

'It won't really matter whether you like Mr Gutch or not,' said Charlotte. 'After all there will be quite a party. I think it very nice that your partner at your first ball should be such a friend of Lionel's.'

'Papa, you should *see* the gown Mama has bought for me at Lewes and Allenby's. I am so excited. I think I shall burst.'

'Much will depend upon your cough being better,' said her father, as though he had thought of it that moment for himself.

'Do you think Mr Gutch will be *very* parsonical?' asked the girl. 'I couldn't bear it if. . . .' And when she laughed, if not when she coughed, she *did* put her hand to her mouth and held her fingers in front of her ivory teeth and her wide gums.

'There is no reason to suppose that Mr Gutch will be remotely like Mr Goe,' said her mother. One did not need to be *clairvoyante* to see whom or who was making the child laugh, and it was always pleasant to mention Mr Goe in the dining room, since it produced such sharp intakes of breath, such disapproval from the bald freethinker.

'Can you imagine dancing a . . .' her laughter turned once more to a hacking cough but she could not stop herself pressing on with the joke, '*polka* with Mr Goe?'

'It is rather foolish,' said her father, 'to spend so much time thinking about your teachers.'

Charlotte Nettleship shot a glance across the greasy remains of the capons to test out her spouse's features. In the last few weeks, since his embargo on Messrs Chatterway and Lupton, she had come to believe

that no utterance in the dining room was made without the intention
of wounding her. His curiously impassive pasty face could quite
conceivably have concealed a knowledge of their surreptitious
encounters with the young painter. It would, she reflected, be *like
Horace* to try to make a scene about them before the child.

Horace Nettleship for his part with the cruelly automatic telepathy
of marriage recognised at once that his wife had registered annoyance
at his inquiry. A little surge of wrath prompted him to ask why a father
was not entitled to make a reflection about his daughter's tutors. But
he repressed the sarcasm and said instead, 'You seem to be taking a
great interest in sketching once more. You had rather abandoned it
after. . . .'

'Miss Adeney,' said the girl quietly, earning from both parents a
stern look which seemed to remind her that there was no need to be
vulgar.

'And to what can we attribute this suddden revival in the graphic
craft?'

'I am sorry, Papa?'

Charlotte Nettleship, as she watched her husband ask Maudie the
question, and saw the tensing of his lips, the nervous crinkling of the
skin about his eyes, the furrowing of his brow as he waited for the
answer, was reminded forcefully of her first encounter with the man,
when he stood over her and asked for her nine times table. But much
more hung, as both females silently recognised, upon Maudie's answer
than proof of arithmetic competence. Suspense suddenly filled the
atmosphere, punctuated by the removal of the capon carcases, the
plates with their stains of congealed gravy, their little traces of bread
sauce hardening on the pattern of rampaging floral borders which
adorned their porcelain Worcester dinner service. While the servants
clattered with the plates and a cherry tart was conveyed to the table,
sugar gleaming like frost on its thick short crust, the three diners sat in
awkward silence.

Mrs Nettleship opened her lips, but could not quite speak. Had she
done so, she would have had to say so much. She would have had to
say, rather brutally, that she would no longer endure her husband's
habit of *using* Maudie as an instrument against her, that she found
these sessions of dining-room torture intolerable, and that she would
not, in future, allow him to inflict them. But there was much more to
say than that and Charlotte, radiantly beautiful in her vulnerable
statuesque fashion by gaslight, at last felt foolish or courageous
enough almost to say them. She wanted to say – for the child was most
surely going to be engineered into admitting the truth, that they had
seen Mr Lupton almost every day since the embargo – that she no

longer cared for her husband's injunctions. He had forbidden Mr Chatterway and Mr Lupton the house, and in a moment of madness which she had at once and most bitterly regretted, she had passed on to those two gentlemen the embarrassing intelligence that they were to visit her no more. It would not have been possible to articulate what surges of wrath and guilt and self-reproach, and simple feelings of foolishness, overtook her whenever she recalled this episode. How could she have submitted to her husband's madness?

All this she opened her lips and prepared to say. But there was more, more to say than this. And she no longer cared whether she said it in front of Maudie, in front of the servants, or in front of all the world. Horace Nettleship had forced her to marry him. He had borne down upon her when she was a child of twelve and all the family elders, who should have protected her, handed her with alacrity into his maw. She had not loved him on her wedding day. She had not grown to love him. The words of the marriage ceremony about loving and cherishing, sickness and health, and the rest, were a mockery and a torture to her. For more years than she could count, particularly more years than she could feel – for all the Horace-blighted years – she had probably hated her husband. And none of this mattered because she blamed herself for her foolish mistake, and there was no route back through the tangle of wasted years which would enable her to undo all her girl-follies. She had even taken a briskly cynical delight in the knowledge that her life was to be thrown away. Its few consolations were to be found in an inner consciousness of her domestic efficiency, and in the occasional intrusion, into her domestic miseries, of friends. Mr Chatterway, she realised since his banishment, was infinitely dearer, by his close ties of funny intimacy with her family, to her than her husband. But at the same time she was so cross with Mr Chatterway for his foolish and wounding revelation about Lionel's ecclesiastical ambitions, since confirmed by the Colossian epistles, that she had done not much about seeing Mr Chatterway in order to undo his banishment. In fact, she had half-enjoyed it, felt it safer altogether in the *circumstances*. Mr Chatterway and she were able to conduct their relations on a long time-scale. Intervals of three years had passed before now in which they did not see each other. It would surely be possible to sustain three weeks of a London summer without a cheerily mischievous visit from her old friend.

Her time-scale, however – this she opened her mouth and was less able to say to the pudding-face of Horace – was altogether different when it came to Mr Lupton. About the painter she would *not* allow Maudie to be interrogated. In fact, Mr Lupton was sacrosanct.

At thirty-nine years old she had been overwhelmed with sensations hitherto only read about in novels and the works of the poets. She was now able to speak with a new authority when, unspeaking, she communed silently with herself. She said that she did not love her husband. For crude as all the initial symptoms of the thing were perhaps bound to be, she at last knew what it was to be in love. Her brittleness, her cynicism, were cracked and dry and ready to fall away. She was, at last, *in love*! She was in love, simply and passionately, with Mr Lupton.

All this, she opened her lips and would have liked to say as she watched her husband cut the cherry tart and put a slice of it on her plate which seemed larger, at that moment, than she required. It was impossible to say so. One of the most tedious features of their conversational non-communication was that, when he carved or served at table, she was never able to specify (nor of course was she ever asked) what size of portion she would like. When, sadistically, he had passed her plate, and donated some of the tart to Maudie and a somewhat grosser proportion of the thing to himself, the professor resumed his inquiry. Charlotte's heart was, as the saying goes, in her mouth.

'You were about to tell me, Maudie, why you had developed this sudden and passionate interest in drawing. I hope it isn't because that charlatan-chappy suggested you should go to him for lessons.'

Maudie saw her mother glaring. A momentary glance flickered between mother and daughter.

'Of course not, Papa,' said Maudie automatically. She knew at once that this was what she must say. She could not tell whether she said it because her mother willed her to say it, or because she herself willed her mother not to make a scene over the matter. She wanted both her parents to go away to their separate rooms – Papa to his study and Mama to the drawing room – and simply leave her alone with her cough and her thoughts. The cough dominated her thoughts at that second almost as much as her embarrassment concerning the drawing lessons. For its sudden heaving irritations in her chest made it hard to eat; and she knew that if a cough came suddenly while she had a mouthful of cherry pie, it might be difficult to avoid spraying the table with pastry crumbs. Besides, her parent found the noise of it tedious, and she did not want to annoy them in that particular way.

'I am not spending any time on drawing which could have been spent on the *Odyssey*,' she said.

'I am not concerned with the *Odyssey*,' he said with a brief irritability, as if to remind her by this frightening tone that for all conversational purposes in The Bower, Homer was a clergyman of the Established Church, and therefore to be slapped down and kept in his place.

'I have practised just as much at the piano,' she insisted. 'I now play that Mendelssohn minuet to perfection. . . .'

'I do not doubt,' said the professor.

'Papa, how can you doubt or not doubt when you haven't *heard* me play the piece through?'

'One catches the noise of your practising. It comes,' he said self-pityingly, 'down through the study ceiling.'

'Oh, Papa, you are mean. I know that you are a musical ignoramus. . . .' Why should she not fight back? She grinned and left a large slice of pie on the side of her plate as it was taken from her.

Silence fell once more during the clearing away. Professor Nettleship glanced suspiciously between mother and daughter.

'And my German . . .' the girl was trying to blurt out, while Hopkins brought in the tray with the Welsh rarebits and the mustard.

The professor held up a hand. 'I am not conducting an enquiry into all your lessons,' he said. 'I am merely observing that you have devoted a lot of time to sketching, if the results all over the drawing room are something to judge by. A drawing room indeed.' He hoped for some response from this pleasantry, but Maudie only said:

'I wanted to do them.'

'At your grandfather's house?'

'Not all.'

'But when, the other day, you and your mother encountered me in the hall, and told me that you were going to see your grandfather. . . .'

'So?'

'There is nothing to be gained by impertinence, Maudie.' He put down his knife and fork with a clatter and savoured his toasted cheese. 'Maudie darling,' he added, for she saw in his besotted and hang-dog expression that he was still, even in his wrath, the chief hierophant in her cult, 'I would merely wonder why,' he said, 'you had suddenly taken to visiting your grandfather so often. And with a portfolio. For you were, I think, the other day in the hall, carrying your portfolio.'

'Oh, Papa, really, I can't remember whether I took my portfolio or not. Perhaps I thought grandpapa would be interested. He has known so many of the great painters. You know, he remembers Northcote, and Etty and . . .'

'And subsequently, this ruffian.'

'You only call Mr Lupton a ruffian,' said his daughter, 'because you broke a teacup and he stooped to pick it up.'

'You are telling me that you have not seen Mr Lupton at your grandfather's house – even though he is painting your grandfather's portrait?'

'The portrait was finished some weeks ago, Papa.'

Charlotte Nettleship looked at her daughter in astonishment. The girl was, after all, a most practised and accomplished liar. It obviously suited her – for what reason Charlotte found it impossible to guess – not to answer Horace's questions. Maudie was, it now emerged, a tough little combatant, with less innocence than her childishly abundant hair, and her wide eyes, would suggest. Perhaps, her mother thought sadly, she had lost her innocence that very evening over the dinner table.

The servants hovered during this last course. There was the opportunity for more cheese on toast, a chance which Charlotte seized, for her appetite had returned and the cook made this simple dish so particularly well. But Maudie refused more. It was as much as she could do to eat what she had on her plate.

'It is so salty,' she said. 'I wish I could eat some fruit to take away the taste.'

'You ate very little of your cherry tart,' said her father. 'I think that children would, if left to themselves, eat nothing but fruit, having little sense of how injurious it is to the constitution.'

'I could eat an orange now.'

In reply, her father said, 'An orange would be very bad for you.'

But her mother, who came perilously close to recognising that her husband had been speaking, cut across his bows, and said, unable to be silent for much longer and desiring to provoke, 'Your fondness for oranges exceeds all bounds. We are told that even the queen eats one each day.'

Maudie laughed. 'By whom are we told.'

In The Bower, the Royal Family were indelibly associated with Mr Chatterway. It was he who gave them their little tit-bits of information.

'She has a hole cut in the middle of her orange and a lump of sugar placed in the middle. Then she sucks the good of it,' said Charlotte. 'A very messy way of eating, Marvo says.'

The laughter of mother and daughter was interrupted by the desired effect of this calculatedly painful observation, the scraping of the professor's chair. He rose with an attempt at dignity and, still masticating the last of the cheese on toast, he clumped across the parquet and, without acknowledging the servant who opened for him the dark shining stained oak door, he disappeared into his study.

'Oh,' exclaimed Maudie, 'what more does he want? He has excluded Mr Chatterway from his house. Are we not even to mention him at the table?'

Her mother smiled at her, sadly. Neither woman – Maudie had left childhood behind in the course of the meal, and was now, only too clearly, a daughter of Eve – needed to allude to their shared secrets, nor to their unshared secrets. There had been, in the routing of Horace Nettleship after the Welsh rarebit, a peculiar joint satisfaction. They could sit for a short moment basking in it, without Maudie having to find out what was so special about Mr Lupton that her drawing lessons be kept a secret, nor having to disclose that she had, on her zoo walks, seen the forbidden Chatterway. For a moment the two women were united in their common enmity of the man who had just left them and to whom, by the laws of God and men, they owed such unquestioning obedience.

'Oh *darling*,' said the mother, 'you must *do* something about that cough.'

TEN

St Thomas the Martyr

Scroggs, the shrivelled old scout, felt things had come to a pretty pass when the young 'gentlemen' were up betimes afore of him. He was used to having to shake the young men, bellowing in their ears, or threatening to dowse them with water before they got out of bed. In the old days of the daring young blades, when the gentlemen *was* gentlemen, he had more than once flung open the door of the bedroom to find the bed stuffed with a bolster. Scions of several noble houses had been sent down from Harcourt because of what Scroggs had discovered, or not discovered, in those bedrooms; such as the night when the Marquess of Malmesbury's boy, Lord Edward Buxton, had failed to get back from the Derby, a secret which, for a sum, had been locked in Scroggs's bosom ever since. A proper gentleman, Lord Edward had been, who kept a four-in-hand coach, and, for the summer months, a pinnace on the river.

Into the very set of rooms where Lord Edward had so rarely slept, a score of years since, the aged servant now tottered. The air was as clean as a whistle, no whiff of a segar, no signs of previous nocturnal dissipation, no broken glass, no spilt wine. He drew back the shutters to let in the bright rays of May sunshine, and then seeing that there was little enough for him to do in the sitting room, all neat as a pin, he rapped on the inner bedroom door.

'Half past seven, sir. Do you breakfast in?'

Lionel Nettleship, instead of letting out a semi-somnolent groan from the bedclothes, opened his door and stood there, fully dressed and (as if that were necessary) shaved. He smiled and nodded at the scout.

'Well, sir, do you or don't you breakfast in?'

The boy nodded like a loon but would not utter. Then, brushing past the old man, he went to the writing desk and, dipping his pen in the inkwell, he wrote on a piece of paper, *I shall breakfast in with Mr Gutch. Two eggs each please.*'

'Very good, sir. Lost your voice have you?'

Young Nettleship blushed and shook his head, but no sound proceeded from his mouth.

'Lot of young gentlemen have a sore throat from the moment they matriculate. It's the river air, you know, sir. Brandy is the cure for it. Drink a little drop of brandy with your breakfast is my advice. Oh, and speaking of Mr Gutch and breakfast, I believe that he has ordered up some bacon and kidneys from the kitchen. Would you like that as well, sir?'

Lionel Nettleship, again blushing and silent, shook his head.

'Very good, sir. Now, have you finished in the bedroom or shall I come back later and do it?'

Without replying to this perfectly courteous request, Nettleship stalked out of the room and left Scroggs staring after him with disapproval and bewilderment. The young man himself was crimson to the very roots of his hair. It was excessively embarrassing that he could not reply to these simple requests from his staircase scout. But he had recently made a vow that he should abstain from speech, as well as food or drink, before receiving the Holy Sacrament. And, it being Sunday, the service in the college chapel was to be a Celebration.

A Celebration of *what*, Lionel was not quite ready to articulate. Like the young man in the poem, he was 'wandering between two worlds, one dead, the other powerless to be born'. He had learnt from Gutch that to say 'I am going to Communion', meaning 'I am going to attend the Celebration', was improper, since it was perfectly possible to attend without receiving Holy Communion; indeed this was the custom in the greater part of Christendom. He thought to himself that he was attending 'the Holy Eucharist', but, except between friends such as himself and Gutch this uncolloquial expression did not have a very plausible parlance. And he did not dare to say, as Gutch had been heard to do, that he was going to 'Mass'.

Whatever he called it, Lionel Nettleship had discovered since his conversion, a deeper sense of Christ's presence in the Sacrament than formerly he would have conceived possible. It was as though his being was fused totally, body and soul, with that of the Godhead. The knowledge that he was to receive the Sacrament filled him with awe and happiness and excitement all through the previous day. He had broken off the conversations of the previous evening with Gutch and his cronies, and taken himself back to the solitude of his room. There, in silence and stillness, he had knelt for over an hour, examining his conscience for any failures in the previous week, and preparing his heart for the reception of his great Guest on the morrow. When that morrow had dawned, he had woken early, before light, and it had been, as each Sunday morning was now, infinitely more exciting than any Christmas morning as a child. For he knew that he would return from the chapel, bearing in his own person the Godhead, the Word

which had been made flesh once more, not in the body of Our Ladye St
Marie in Nazareth, but on the altar of the church.

The altar in question was, in fact, a dark oak Georgian communion
table which stood up at the east end of the building, quite unadorned,
an arrangement which Gutch said was utterly out of keeping with the
modern Gothic of Mr Butterfield's stripy brick chapel. Lionel found it
hard to keep up with all the 'rights' and 'wrongs' of liturgical practice
and aesthetic judgement which fell from Gutch's lips. He himself, for
instance, was a devotee of the Gothic style and thought the college
chapel one of the most beautiful he had ever seen. But Gutch, in spite
of believing the pointed arches and the oak table to be 'laughably
incompatible', professed to dislike the 'northern barbarism' of the
Gothic style and to prefer to his own college of Harcourt the Renaissance splendours of Trinity and Queen's. This apparently had something to do with things he had learnt in the course of conversations
with his Greek tutor at Brazen Nose.

Lionel tried not to think of these trivialities as he took his place in
chapel. He was very early – the first member of the congregation to
arrive. The pews were arranged from north to south, facing one
another, like the stalls of an ancient monastic foundation, and he felt
himself as he gathered the scant folds of his commoner's gown about
him, as though he were the member of some antique religious order.
Discreetly, since there was no one yet about, except for the chapel
scout fussing with flagons and linen, Lionel made the sign of the cross
and closed his eyes. Even as he did so, the distractions and cares of the
modern world, worries about Little-go and Responsions and all the
petty annoyances and troubles of life were lifted from him; he felt the
warm and certain glow of the Presence which made it possible to pray
without words. While he knelt there, dissolving into ecstasies, the
chapel scout laid a fair linen cloth on the altar, and opened the prayer
book, which was balanced on a red velvet cushion, at the north end of
the Holy table. Then he draped the altar rails with a long white
'houselling cloth' and with loud clearings of his throat, he retreated to
the back of the chapel to hand out surplices to the fellows and scholars
as they came in. Gutch, who was a scholar, wore a surplice, and took
his place next to the ecstatic Lionel about ten minutes later. Although
the chapel was now quite full, Gutch evidently felt no fear at all about
making the sign of the cross. Indeed, he had often said to Lionel that it
was more important to make this sacred action in public than in
private. 'Party badge, my father calls it. Makes him furious.'

When the chapel was more or less full (most of the figures in dark
gowns, and some in surplices), a silence fell. The murmurings and the
shuffling which inevitably preceded services became subdued, and the

master, rubicund and surpliced, took his place in his stall just as the clock was striking eight. Once in a blue moon the Magger celebrated himself. But this morning it was not Jenkers – as they called Dr Jenkinson, nor Chapper, but the mathematical fellow, McCabe, who, wearing a surplice (beneath which one could see several inches of trowsers) and a red MA hood, celebrated. He read the service in a clear, unimpassioned voice:

Honour thy father and thy mother; that thy days may be long in the land which the Lord thy God has given thee.

At this phrase in the commandments, Lionel replied, like everyone else in the chapel, *Lord have mercy upon us and incline our hearts to keep this law.* But it jolted him out of his purely spiritual reverie to an acute twinge of conscience. His mother, of course, he honoured; more than honoured, worshipped and loved. She was, next to Maudie, the dearest person to him in the world; the funniest, the cleverest and the most beautiful. His days would indeed be long in the land if all it depended upon were the honouring of his mother. Towards his father, however, he felt very differently. He honoured him in a purely formal sense. But he felt no natural filial sympathy for Mr Nettleship. And since his conversion, Lionel felt even more strongly that he had a duty to withhold, in part, any natural feelings of loyalty which he might possess for the professor. His father had, after all, made it very clear that he did not want him to come to the University at all, if that meant assenting to the Articles. He was overt in his unbelief, outspoken and crude in his blasphemous inability to accept the very truth by which the human race was saved. In a dispute between his Lord and his father, Lionel had no doubt where his loyalty must lie. For had it not been written, *I am wiser than the aged: because I keep thy command-ments.* And again, *If any man come to me and hate not his father and mother, and wife, and children, and sisters, yea and his own life, also, he cannot be my disciple.* There was no doubt in Lionel's mind that so long as his father persisted in strident unbelief, it was necessary, quite simply, to hate him. And yet he was only bidden to receive the holy sacrament if he truly and earnestly repented him of his sins and was in love and charity with his neighbours.

He had come into the chapel intent on a complete and spiritual self-forgetting, a union between himself and Christ which was unsullied by any purely human consideration. And yet he found, for the duration of the service, that he was nagged and distracted by thoughts of his father; and when he finally came to troop, with the others, out of his stall, and up to the altar rail to receive the body and blood of his

Saviour, he was in a torment of pure irritation with his father. He hated his father for his atheism. He hated him for the domestic misery which he inflicted on them all in The Bower. And he hated him because they were all coming to stay and to go to the Commemoration Ball in only a few weeks. He returned to his stall, therefore, not glowing with the warm sense of Christ's presence, but furious that his Holy Communion had been spoilt by these terribly mundane considerations and aching with the knowledge that he *did* love his father as well as hating him.

During the concluding prayers, he was able, a little, to compose himself. *And although we be unworthy through our manifold sins to offer unto thee any sacrifice, yet we beseech thee to accept, this, our bounden duty and service. ...* With these words, some warmth returned to comfort him, some of the 'glow' which he associated with the Real Presence of Jesus Christ. He remembered that it was only through Christ's Grace that he was saved, and that he should not think, even after a thorough examination of his conscience and confessions of his sins, to present himself faultless at the altar rails. For we have all fallen short, and we all need the redeeming love and grace of Christ.

He therefore felt chastened and uplifted as he joined in the recitation of the *Gloria in excelsis,* and felt indeed, at the blessing, a little of 'the peace of God, which passeth all understanding.'

'Mine was rather stale,' said Gutch crossly as he walked out of the chapel, tossing his surplice over the arm of the chapel scout who waited at the door.

Lionel thought that he must have misheard.

'What was?'

'It wouldn't happen if they used wafers and kept them tightly boxed in a tin. But that would be far too romish for their tastes.' He smirked a little at Lionel, who felt unable to respond. It seemed wrong to be making a joke of the service so soon after they had received the Holy Sacrament. And the profanity of commenting on the staleness of the bread seemed unbelievably shocking. 'All those crumbs,' Gutch continued. 'I think it highly unlikely that McCabe ate them all when he tawped. Probably the fair linen is still littered with particles of Our Dear Lord.'

'What's tawping?' ask Lionel.

'Taking the Ablutions at the Wrong Place. Surely you know that. Almost all our priests do it. Instead of taking them immediately after the last person has been communicated, as in the Latin rite, they leave Our Lord unconsumed on the Holy Table until after the blessing. Of course, some people think that means that the prayer book justifies extra eucharistic devotions, but I am not so sure.'

When they got back to Lionel's room, they found that the scout had put on water for the eggs. It was merely left to the young men to boil them, and to make their own tea and toast by the fire. While Lionel was so engaged and Gutch lolled languidly on the window-seat, a servant brought over his 'kitchen order' of kidneys and bacon.

'Poor Scroggs,' said Gutch. 'We don't leave him many eggs, do we?'

'We pay for them,' said Lionel.

This was true. All undergraduates automatically paid, as part of their battels, for a 'foundation breakfast', consisting of tea, bread, butter, milk and eggs. Two eggs each was the allowance; but on staircases where the young men were extravagant, and breakfasted off 'kitchen orders' (for which extra was charged) they frequently forgot to eat their two eggs. The scout on such a staircase could hope to take home sixteen free eggs a day, and many of them did a brisk trade out of them.

'The question really is,' added Gutch, 'where we go *after* breakfast.'

'Won't we go to Saint Barnabas?' asked Lionel in surprise. On most Sundays that term – except for the memorable day when Doctor Pusey was preaching at Matins in Christ Church – they had made their way to the ritualist church in the depths of the town's 'base and brickish skirt' enjoying what Gutch called the 'rare atmosphere of purest *trecento*.'

'Habit,' said Gutch, tut-tutting. 'Habit is relative to the stereotyped world. Failure is to form habits.'

'Yes, but if we like going to St Barnabas's . . .'

'It's time you saw a shrine which was a little more . . .'

'You don't mean?' For an agitated moment, part horror and part rapture, Lionel thought that Gutch was proposing to take him to the Catholic chapel in St Clement's.

'No,' said Gutch, reading his thoughts, 'I do *not*.'

'We don't want to get proctorised.'

'Dear child, we are not living in penal times. Or rather, our Roman brethren are not. We Catholics within the bosom of the Established Church suffer, I fancy, rather more. When one *thinks* what poor Father Lowder has endured at London Dock; and Father Mackonochie at St Alban's in Holborn. . . . These Protestants, I tell you, will stop at nothing.'

Whenever Gutch spoke about the famous ritualist slum priests of London, Lionel's bosom thrilled with excitement and he longed to work with them, bringing the Gospel to Christ's poor and perhaps nursing them during a cholera epidemic or something of the kind.

'It is necessary to see these things' – kidneys and bacon were now being consumed, with the eggs, and with relish. Lionel accepted, gratefully, a rasher from Gutch's plate – 'from a firm historical perspective. The roughs might try to smash the windows of Father Lowder's church, but those churches are there and the work they are doing among the poor is something which the bishops can't gainsay.'

'*They shall lay hands on you and persecute you, being brought before kings and rulers for my sake,*' said Lionel. 'It is astonishing that, in our day, a man like Father Tooth can be sent to prison simply for wearing eucharistic vestments.'

'Ah, poor man.'

They spoke of these ritualistic heroes as familiars, though they had never met any of them, but Gutch had it in mind to go to work in a London slum during the 'Long' after their reading party in Monmouthshire.

The two young men consumed a great deal of toast, liberally buttered. Their talk continued to ramble over the great ritualistic question. Gutch reminded Lionel how much, in how short a time, had already been accomplished. Twenty-five years had not passed since the first Anglican clergyman had dared to don the vestments which were now, since the Public Worship Regulation Act of 1874, illegal. He had frequently been set upon by gangs of rapscallions in the street, and many of his parishioners had refused to come to church since these 'popish' advances of the churchmanship. But he had stood firm. Through two violent cholera epidemics he had fearlessly nursed the sick, aided by the sisters of the convent he had founded and by volunteers, such as Doctor Pusey himself, who had supported his championship of Catholic truth. And all these things had happened, not in the slums of London, but in a church not a quarter of an hour's walk from where they sat in the austere comfort of Lionel's room in Harcourt.

It was to see this hero of the Catholic revival, Canon Chamberlain, that Gutch proposed this morning, and Lionel eagerly agreed. When their toast was exhausted, and they had sat an hour or two over the cooling teapot, they donned their caps and gowns and sauntered out into the sunny air. The Broad seemed to shout with the joyous sound of bells: the whole air was full of it, a poignant music hypnotic to them both. From all quarters, the sound of ringing wafted through the warm May. St Michael at the Northgate sang to St Mary Magdalen. And as they walked down George Street they caught the tolling of St Peter-the-Bailey, the jangling of St George's on Gloucester Green, and the distant high-pitched tinkling of Worcester. Barges drowsed on the canal by Hythe Bridge. In Upper Fisher Row, children played among the osiers, bound and stacked by the huts in the sunlight.

They entered a quarter that was both slummy and rustic. To their right, the Great Western Railway station sprawled in its ugliness, but they turned left through the mean houses of Hollybush Row. To one side, the overpopulated yards and rows of St Thomas's High Street were brimful of an alarming and alien vigour and life. Young bonneted women lolled in doorways with their babies, and in the straw-strewn streets where chickens waddled, and boys brawled in the dust, collarless workmen, filthy and unshaven smoked their sabbath pipes, while only a little way beyond all this thick congestion, the cattle grazed on open fields.

Now the chaos of bells was left behind them, and the music of one tower predominated. It was, as Lionel thought, countrified and ancient, a square medieval tower of grey stone. The fane itself was set in a lush churchyard, well planted with yews. It seemed in spirit a hundred miles from Harcourt and the other colleges, a Cotswoldy sort of place where everything had gone on unchanged for centuries.

'Anatomy of Melancholy Burton was the vicar here two hundred and fifty years ago,' said Gutch. 'He was the last priest in the Church of England after the Reformation to use wafers for the Holy Eucharist.'

They entered by the south porch, adorned with the arms of Democritus Junior, and, within, their eyes still accustomed to the bright sunlight, found all dark and mysterious. The dark oak pews were already quite full, the first rows being occupied by the dark-veiled sisterhood of St Thomas the Martyr. Before taking their places, Gutch took Lionel over to see the north aisle and showed him the newly-installed window which depicted a fully-vested priest at the altar, elevating the chalice. Saints, angels and patriarchs knelt around in adoration above his head, the Lamb of God was enthroned, the Precious Blood gushing from his breast into a cup on the celestial altar. It was an awesome sight, a depiction in brightly coloured glass of the very essence of their creed. But to see it quite newly placed in an old Church of England setting was somehow doubly remarkable, and brought home how God had indeed, within the last generation, done marvellous things.

They took their places at the back of the Church and fell to their knees. As Lionel's eyes became accustomed to the darkness, he could see that the walls were all brightly painted, as in medieval fashion, with floral emblems, and above the flickering candelabra, in ancient Gothic script, were painted legends from the psalms: *Non moriar, sed vivam; Et narrabo opera Domini.*

The psalmist's words were the first they heard, too, when the bell stopped ringing and, after a short pause, the procession of priest and server came up the aisle.

A quavery voice from the darkness at the back gave out, *Who shall ascend into the hill of the Lord, and who shall rise up in his Holy place?*

Choir and people responded, in the ancient Gregorian chant, *Even he that hath clean hands and a pure heart.*

The quavery voice struck up again. *This is the generation of them that seek him; even of them that seek thy face, O Jacob.*

The procession which made its slow progress towards the altar, where two candles burnt on the gradine, graced with flower vases, was led by a young man in cassock and surplice who gently swung a thurible, filling the thronged air with its enchanting vapours. Two servers followed, each bearing lights; after them a priest in surplice, stole and biretta; and after him, three ministers vested, two curates in tunicle and dalmatic, and last, Canon Chamberlain himself. They passed so slowly that Lionel was able to study his face – the deep-set, weary eyes, the sharp aquiline nose, on the end of which was balanced a small *pince-nez*, and the silver hair brushed back from a squarish forehead. He looked tired, and worn down by age, and took no notice whatsoever of the crowds who thronged the pews on either side. When, the psalm finished, they reached the sanctuary, the servers divested him of his cope and he cast over his head a full golden chasuble of thick damask.

The rite which ensued used exactly the same words as the service the young men had already heard that morning at eight in Harcourt Chapel. But the contrast between the two services was considerable. The Ten Commandments and the collects, as well as the reading from the Epistle, were all chanted with high ceremony. The Gospel was sung to the accompaniment of lights and incense and the tune to which they sang the creed was that same *Missa de Angelis* whose tones were being heard in churches at that moment all over Catholic Christendom. There could be no more eloquent assertion of the belief that the Prayer Book Communion Service was in all essentials the ancient Mass.

When the creed had been sung, the three sacred ministers sat down on chairs to the south of the sanctuary, and the bald priest in the stole and the biretta advanced into the pulpit. In a breathless rapid voice, he announced his text from the sixth chapter of Nehemiah: *And it came to pass, that when all our enemies heard thereof, and all the heathen that were about us saw these things, they were much cast down in their own eyes: for they perceived that this work was wrought of our God.*

Briefly, at first, he expounded the history of the Jews at the time of Ezra and Nehemiah. He told how the people of God returned from their Babylonian exile to find the religion of their fathers discarded, the

Temple in ruins, the very walls of Jerusalem a heap of rubble. It had been Nehemiah's task to purge and reform these abuses and to rebuild the walls of Jerusalem. The obstacles to completing the wall were many and various. The sloth of the inhabitants, the dread of external enemies and the extortion of usurers had all hindered the task. But Nehemiah had rebuilt the wall, and attributed, as was most justly due, the completing of the work to Almighty God.

'Oh, my brethren! We, too, have seen the hand of God at work, in our own land and in our own church. For our fathers came out of exile and found it a heap of rubble. And by faith they were given, as we have been given, the grace to rebuild the walls of Jerusalem. How can I fail to give thanks to God in this dear place? The late Bishop of Brechin, Bishop Forbes, always used to say of St Thomas's that it held the first place in his prayers. And so it must be in the prayers of all those who hold and teach the Catholic faith and who are called to work in the dark mission fields of our English cities. Yes! Mission fields, brethren, as dark as any in Africa.

'When I was first led by Divine Providence, to establish, some twenty-five years ago, a Mission church in Wapping – the mission of St George – there were, I should calculate, thousands of poor benighted heathens living there. English heathens, brethren, who had not so much as heard the Holy name of Our Most Blessed Lord. I can simply testify that I claim nothing – *nothing* – for myself. I felt, as all my fellow priests in this dark mission-field have felt, simply as though we were instruments of the Lord's salvation. And there is still so much to be done. But, when I reiterate that twenty-five years ago in that place there was *nothing*, is it not a very remarkable thing that we now have a thriving church – built some fourteen years ago, and now attracting some four hundred and fifty communicants each Sunday. We have schools for some 600 children – would that we had schools for 6,000! We have a hostel for the aged and a Club, or Dining room where, for a moderate cost, working men and their families can eat. We have night-schools and infant schools and playgrounds. . . . Oh, perhaps you will think these things are little enough. But you will all have read what Wapping is like, what dirt and vice and pure enmity to the Gospel of Our Lord has flourished there. And can any of us doubt that in Wapping, as in other parts of benighted London, as in this University, and in the towns and cities of our land, throughout our church, God is rebuilding the walls of Jerusalem and breathing new life into old bones. . . .'

This was none other than Lowder himself, the man about whom Lionel and Gutch had been so animatedly speaking over their break-fast, the ritualist hero who, in defiance of mobs, policemen and bishops had brought the Catholic religion to the poor of Dockland. There was an awed hush as the priest returned to his stall. Here the congregation was mixed. Perhaps the preponderance were poor people of the parish, but there was also a high proportion of Varsity men, both dons and undergraduates, genteel folk from the northern suburbs who had come down in their carriages to witness the *outré* ceremonial, and pious black-bonneted ladies who clustered, rather in the manner of Belgian *béguines*, around the sisterhood.

A burst of music, after the Offertory, proclaimed the advent of the high point of the rite. Then, after the solemn singing of the *Sanctus*, silence broken only by Canon Chamberlain's quiet voice reciting the Prayer of Consecration. When the most solemn words were spoken, the church bells were tolled three times, and during the priest's communion, the congregation, none of whom made their communion at this late hour, sang a eucharistic hymn of St Thomas Aquinas:

> Thee we adore, O hidden Saviour, Thee,
> Who in thy sacrament art pleased to be.
> Both flesh and spirit at Thy presence fail,
> Yet here Thy presence we devoutly hail.

After the service was over, all the clergy processed, with their expressionless faces, to the sacristy at the back of the church and were not seen again. Lionel had hoped that they would meet Father Lowder, that, perhaps, he might have been seen mingling with the crowds assembled on the path outside the south porch.

'Pity that Chamberlain tawps just like everyone else,' said Gutch. 'Otherwise it was most impressive. Hullo, there's m'tutor.'

A prematurely antique forty-year-old shuffled, almost limped, towards them. He wore a coat and trowsers of darkest coal-black, but his neck tie was a bright apple green. He had a heavy, pasty complexion and a thick moustache which gave him the look of a retired military man.

'Very touching and attractive,' he said, 'most *winning*, I thought.'

'Nettleship, you have never met my tutor from Brazen Nose, Mr Pater.'

'How d'ye do, sir?'

Lionel had wanted to linger by the yew trees and catch a glimpse of some of the other members of the congregation. The clergyman in a frock coat looked like Liddon, and the old lady in the black bonnet, retrieving her dog from a footman at the West door of the church, was Miss Skene, heroine of the last dangerous cholera outbreak in the town, and a famous philanthropist. The sight of the nuns, trooping back to their convent in a gaggle, all eyes down, also fascinated Lionel, and the well-scrubbed respectable rustics who made up the great part of the assembly. But, instead, Gutch's tutor had taken him by the elbow and they were walking decidedly away.

'A pity to spoil the illusion,' he drawled in rather a deep voice, 'by seeing too many of them at close hand. Particularly, I think, the' – he paused and twinkled at Lionel to catch, as it happened unsuccessfully, some gleam of comprehension in his eyes – 'the *acolytes*.'

'I'm not sure it's correct to raise and lower their candles in that manner at the consecration,' said Gutch.

'Now, now!' Mr Pater wagged a delighted finger at Gutch and, still not releasing Lionel's elbow, he fixed his grey-green eyes upon the lad and said, 'He likes to miss the essence. He does it, do you not suppose, to vex us? Just a little? You and I, Mr Nettleship, sensed surely the *medieval* atmosphere here. Is it not a place where exotic flowers of sentiment might expand, among people of a remote and unaccustomed beauty, somnambulistic, frail, androgynous. . . .'

As if himself sleepwalking, Mr Pater, who had relinquished Lionel's sleeve, raised an arm in benediction and clambered into a waiting fly.

ELEVEN

Koalas Revisited

'Everyone's in such a sulk that they wouldn't notice whether I was there or not. Papa sits in the library *perpetually*. Mama takes me off to grandpapa's every day, almost, only not today because it's Sunday. . . .'

'So we *gather*.'

'And then, of course, Sundays put Papa in an even worse fuming fury than usual because of the Book of Genesis or whatever it is.'

'It isn't a matter of flippancy.'

'Oh, honestly Marvo – allow me to call you Marvo, I implore?'

'It seems as though you have already decided upon it. I would take exception to your doing so in *company*, but you may when we are alone together. As things stand, if it is possible to forecast such matters, we are very unlikely to be in company together again.'

'Mama loves you, I know she does.'

It was hard to tell whether the groaning noise which he emitted at this juncture was intended to suggest incredulity, love-lorn anguish, or merely an impatience at discussing the intimacies.

'I think she's trying to please Papa, however strict he may be. You see, they are both fearfully miffed – well, we all are, really, about Lionel turning out so dashed holy.'

'Marvo I can tolerate on your lips, my pretty one. Dashed I can not.'

'Not deuced?'

'Certainly not deuced.'

Spontaneously, she took his arm and hugged herself a moment against his stiff old shoulder.

'And please, Marvo, tell me I a'n't selfish, but don't you think I am now receiving rather too many drawing lessons?'

'And you blame me for introducing you to our amorous Mr Lupton?'

'I don't, I don't.'

Again, the growling and groaning, which Maudie began to think might be directed not towards her, but towards the encaged koalas at which, while they conversed, they both continued to stare.

'Only,' she continued, 'I can't devote the whole of every afternoon to draughtsmanship, can I? It is an impossibility. My German is starting to relapse and Fräulein Schwartz was so angry with me the other day.' To judge from the display of teeth and the mockery in Maudie's eyes, the wrath of the Fräulein had been sufficiently amusing. 'And I'm getting nowhere with the *Odyssey*. It's partly because Mr Goe will *do* it all for me. When I get stuck on a word, he just won't be all stern and cross like Papa would be, or Fräulein Schwartz. He says the answer straight out, just like that. It's hopeless, isn't it? I shall never learn Greek at all that way. Then there's my music, how can I hope to practise a new piece by Mendelssohn if Mama expects me to be drawing for Mr Lupton each day? It is insufferable. Oh, tell me I don't speak about myself all the time, but truly it *is* very hard to know what to do.'

'We all speak about ourselves most of the time. The only things which distinguish you are that you are honest enough to own it, and that your self-prattle is charming. In the case of most human beings it is repulsive, what?'

'Then there's the whole business of the Commem. Oh Marvo, I was so much looking forward to it all, *so* much.'

'And now you are afraid that you won't be able to fall in love with young Gutch? He's a good enough egg, I do assure you. His mother used to be a very good chum of mine.'

'You really *are* a magician. How did you know I was going to the ball with Mr Gutch?'

'Oh, simple magic. But, one hears these things, you know, dear girl.'

'From whom, I should like to know.'

'From your own prattling lips, about four times in the last ten days. You forget the half of what you say.'

'I suppose. . . .'

She simply turned to stare at him. He sensed that she was daring herself to say something, to make, perhaps, a little confession or declaration.

'I do not talk so much as I once did to Mama,' she said. 'I am sorry if it means that I talk too much to you. And then, Mama is being so unkind she says that if my cough isn't better I simply *can't* go to the Commem., that there is no arguing about it. Did you ever hear anything so cruel?'

'I had made up my mind that you were practising an imitation of a sea-lion. It is certainly unpretty.'

'I cannot help. . . .'

'There you go. Take a pastille.' As so often, their colloquy was interrupted by a hopeless fit of coughing.

'There are my gowns and dresses – we have only, so far, bought two outfits, and I am already disillusioned with the one and bored by the other. Men are so highly fortunate. It doesn't matter what they wear. . .'

'Already so *blasé*. You haven't been to your first ball and you are finding it a *bore*.'

'I'm not. You're cruel. You know precisely what I mean. It's because it's not boring that I mind so much. It's because I want it to be *all* so special that I don't want to spend a whole evening talking about church things with Lionel's friend Mr Gutch.'

'I can't imagine Sybil Gutch's boy being so uncivil, I do assure you. You will have a heavenly time.'

'That is what I somewhat dread. The pleasures of a ball should be, surely, terrestrial.'

'Little Miss Sharpe.'

'But I don't want to be bored. Oh, Marvo, I so don't want to be bored.'

'If so, I fear you came to the wrong place, my angel of another planet. This earth was a funny place to alight if your desire is not to be bored.'

'I don't believe you are ever bored. You manage to find out so much.'

'Find out?'

'About other people, their lives, what they are going to be thinking tomorrow, who they will marry. It is all your magic, is it not?'

'I fear that Marvo's magic may be wearing a little thin. I could never have predicted that your mother would behave with this stubbornness, this unmannerly stubbornness. She will see Lupton – who has also been banished, placed under the incomprehensible interdict of the eminent geologist, Lupton, whom she has known two minutes, she consents to see. And Chatterway, we are to take it, is a wretched creature.'

With unabashed vulgarity Maudie said, 'You know how Mama can never resist an easy bargain. Who could have thought that a famous young painter would want to teach me to draw for nothing?'

'Don't flatter yourself, childie, he is only famous nor-nor-west.'

'I scarcely need to flatter myself. Mr Lupton flatters me ceaselessly.'

'Which is difficult to find unattractive. I see that. It has, of course, its dangers.'

'Mama sees none whatsoever.'

'You see them, however?'

'Oh, I see dangers everywhere. I am composed of fear.'

He took a stare at her – the wild eyes, the pink flush, the tiny hat perched a little absurdly just above her brow, her entanglements of hair cascading down the back of her left, the front of her right, shoulder.

'I believe you speak the truth,' he said, hushed and pained. 'But Maudie, darling, don't fear. Don't fear.'

'But I do. Everything makes me a little afraid at the moment.'

'What most? Not the flattering of, let us be frank, Alma-Tadema's least accomplished, though perhaps most charming disciple?'

'Oh, *everything!*' She turned to Mr Chatterway now in a high flush. 'Everything and everyone.'

'Even me?'

'Especially you.' She laughed and made a joke.

'Only I think,' she said, suddenly changing her tone and clutching his arm. 'I think you would protect me, wouldn't you, Marvo?'

'Against what assaults? It's a long time since I left m' regiment.'

'You know what I *mean*.'

'For the first time in my life, I am not sure that I do.'

'Then again,' she said, dismissing whatever the unspoken subject had been, and resuming another. 'I am frightened of going to stay for the Commem. and finding that Lionel has *changed*. He has changed, don't you think?'

'You forget that it is some years since I so much as set eyes upon your ecclesiastically-minded and. . . .'

'No, but you *feel* things. Is it just Mama and Papa being foolish; or has he really changed, really and truly?'

'My dear, how *can* I know?'

'That frightens me more than anything.'

'You expect a monkish spectre? Don't be ridiculous. Plenty of young men take it into their heads to be parsons. Why not? If he gets a good living which, with his connections should not be. . . .'

'What connections are those, pray?'

That was a little too pert for him, and he pursed his lips crossly. She, rallying, saw his sympathy ebbing away and assumed a tone of pathos.

'But I am frightened, truly. Lionel was all to me, all in all. I could not endure it if he went away and became, well, I know this sounds an *awful* thing to say, but, well, *too* religious and holy.'

'You mean,' said Chatterway mercilessly, 'that you do not want to live on your own with Mama and Papa. . . .'

'I do that already,' she said quietly.

'And does that frighten you?'

There was a pause while they stared away from each other and towards the encaged koala. Then she managed her answer.

'It is *coming* to frighten me.'

'As you come to understand, what?'

'I don't understand anything. I am simply frightened, and I think that you will protect me. Oh, Marvo,' and all at once she took both his hands, as though they had been those of a young lover, and she looked into his laughing, bright blue eyes. 'You will look after me, won't you?'

'You're losing me,' he said, genuinely puzzled.

'If I ask you, you would look after me, wouldn't you?'

'Of course.'

'I am starting to feel – oh it is such a terrible admission – that I cannot trust quite *everyone*.'

'Darling Maudie, isn't that the beginning of wisdom?'

'If so, wisdom makes you no happier.'

'Decidedly – I speak as the wisest man in the world, a miraculous magus – most decidedly *not*.'

They paced away from the bear cage, the koala on its branch, for that part of the Zoological Gardens was starting to fill up. On the path, with her arms enclasped in his, she could to all outward appearance have been his daughter.

'Do you sometimes see something really really *terrible* about to happen? I mean, people behaving so stupidly and foolishly . . . and there is nothing you can do about it? Is that what it is like being a magician?'

'I think it is a very long time since I ever wanted to "do" anything about anything. It very rarely "does" to "do" things, you know.'

'But, for me, there is nothing that I *can* do. I simply have to sit and watch.' She coughed, but not melodramatically, and looked at Marvo with an air of desperation, *hoping* he understood, that he would rescue her, that it would not be necessary to spell out the nature of her fears.

'Watch what, my pretty?'

'Why, don't be so obtuse! Watch Mr Lupton making love to Mama, and her *letting* him.'

TWELVE

Youth and Art

Sun, a few days later, burst in generous and exaggerated rays upon Mr Lupton's apartments in Charlotte Street, but they failed to wake him. He looked like Abu Ben Adhem, as though he had been dreaming a deep dream of peace. When the sharp sunlight assailed his eyelids and the dream began to fade, he was not sure whether the dream had been peaceful or not. He assumed, for thought of her was habitual, that he had been dreaming of Maudie. But whether it was Maudie as Nausicaa, or Maudie dancing in the garden of the Hesperides (gouache studies in the studio soon to be painted *up*, properly, on canvas) or Maudie merely as she *was*, he could not recall.

He knew, as he lifted his head from the pillow and the room focussed, that he had consumed too much brandy on the previous evening; and the recollection disturbed him, for Chatterway had blown in and out of the club and said to him something incomprehensible about 'dallying with the Frau Professor'. Chatterway disturbed life, certainly; it was his function in the scheme of things, like some gaseous exhalation at the bottom of a pond, without which the other forms of aquatic life would never respond each to the other. But he was not quite sure, were it not for the fact that Severus Egg seemed so tolerant of the man, that he would, left to himself, altogether cultivate 'Marvo'. Old Eggy, as he had become since the completion of the (very passable) portrait was quite a different 'proposition'. In Mr Lupton's charitable perspectives, Egg was an old stager, one of the Olympians, the last, perhaps, of the true stylists.

By style, Mr Lupton thought more of a generalized brilliance in the management of life rather than any simple accomplishment of penmanship. It was *something*, Lupton had told himself often lately, to play a rubber with a man who had once partnered Sydney Smith at the game, or to hear by oral succession the reminiscences of a man who had heard from Northcote's own lips his memories of Sir Joshua Reynolds. Eggy was a bridge to the past. That was the beginning of his charm. He was more: he set an example. The moralists told us that there could only be a disastrous conclusion to a career in which a man esteemed the pleasures of the senses more highly than the dictates of duty. Eggy's triumphant survival into his seventy-sixth year defied their wisdom. He had never *made* money; spent it a good deal, and never saved it, so that it was a mystery to Mr Lupton how Eggy 'lived'. Such a prosy consideration had probably never crossed the old poet's mind. He had an income, and that was that. Perhaps, if it were money that needed to be 'handled', he left the whole tedious business to an adviser, to, who knew, 'darling Netty'?

Mr Lupton recognised that, without the catalytic intervention of Mr Chatterway, he would almost certainly never have met his sitter's family from St John's Wood. Since getting to know Mr Egg, some months before the execution of the portrait, there had been little enough allusion to The Bower. The old man's talk had been almost exclusively of the *past*, descending only occasionally to gossip of contemporary interest, or to surprising and vivid little bursts of bawdry. This had little enough, Lupton saw, to do with darling Netty. But Mr Chatterway, from long residence abroad, had numbed his sense of the proprieties and the boundaries. When, initially, he had suggested their all 'blowing in' at The Bower, Mr Lupton had experienced, from the first, a chilly sense that the alien camp was to be penetrated. It was as though, all talk of the Wooden Horse abandoned, Agamemnon had suggested a quiet drive in a brougham across the plains of Troy to hobnob with the sons of Priam.

A gulf, undoubtedly, that day at tea, had been momentarily transcended: pioneers on a perilous rope bridge, they had swung heroically across the gorge, the foaming rapids beneath their feet could at any moment have swallowed them and dashed their bloodied limbs against the harsh pebbles.

'Darling Netty' had shewn himself to be a more ferocious adversary than any of them had dared to hope. Like a performing dog, the professor had leapt through Chatterway's hoop – or so it now seemed to Lupton. He did not understand what Chatterway was 'up to'. He had come to feel, rather, that his own destinies were to be mysteriously linked with those of the Nettleships. Mr Chatterway had merely thrust his needle into the bare outlines of linen gauze: already, the furies were embroidering images upon it in which Mr Lupton and Maudie were indelibly entwined. Maudie from whose head hung those thick chestnutty tresses, abundant ropes of hair in which Mr Lupton was spiritually entangled; Maudie, whose bright hazel eyes seemed to be staring at him, wherever he went, and in whatever company he happened to find himself. If he shut his eyes, he saw her all the time, staring, staring, staring, and at the same time mocking him. But it was delicious to be mocked by such a beauty. In his inner heart, Maudie, too, was of all ages: a tiny child sometimes, little more than an urchin;

at others, she seemed like a goddess, and in his reveries, she towered over him. Sometimes, he thought intently of one tiny feature of Maudie's appearance, such as the very delicate shape of her chin, or the way in which, when you glimpsed the stocking at her ankles, the white wool was very slightly crinkled on the left leg. These things could absorb Lupton for hours. He had forgotten, in fact, how his inner, casual thoughts, passed before he had met Maudie. Presumably, he had had daydreams, carnal or spiritual, still did, but they were always overlaid and interwoven with Maudie-thoughts. The pretty model who came to his studio, some mornings and evenings, for his studies of *Nausicaa and her Maidens* was distracting enough after her own fashion: a thing of pale shoulders, white arms, a waist which was limp rather than slender in its nakedness. In spite of the intimacy he shared with her, it was not in the least difficult, both on the canvas and off it, to transpose upon this slip of a creature, the features and attributes of Maudie. Likewise in conversation with his peers, where he was unable to make his friends unconsciously echo Maudie's talk, he could derive exquisite satisfaction merely by raising a subject which had, at their last encounter, been on her lips. No one would know why, at the club, he had suddenly started to discuss the arrival at the Zoo of a koala bear from Australia; nor would many eyebrows be raised if he were to say to a crony, 'What's this Divvers the young chaps have to take at the Varsity?' or 'You're a Varsity man – are Commem. balls like any other; like London balls I mean? How young are the girls there would you say? Is sixteen too young to go to a Commem?'

If anyone remarked his sudden interest in University affairs, they almost certainly attributed it to the fact that he was painting the portrait of the Master of Harcourt. But in fact, no one *did* remark it. For when your head and heart churn with love, there is nothing to shew for it in outward appearance.

Such daydreaming would not, Mr Lupton decided, do. A busy forenoon stretched ahead, and already, the dusty green marble clock on his chimney-piece announced with its habitual exaggeration that it was five and twenty minutes past nine. This meant that it was, at least, past nine o'clock, and, casting back the bed-covers, he arose. Clothes from the previous evening's revellings were scattered hither and thither on the carpet. His wardrobe for daily wear was in a heap by the washstand, and he rummaged about in it for his check trowsers, a pair of almost-matching socks, a shirt which, with shaking, could decently be imagined to have another day's life in it, a waistcoat and spats. Drumming about, next, on the chest of drawers which also served as a dressing table, he happened upon a sugared bun, not wholly obsolete, which served as breakfast while he searched for collar studs. After some splashing at the washstand, and some combing and preening in front of the faded looking-glass, his hair and beard were ready for day. His cravat pin was fixed, his clean collar shone briefly beneath the yellow expanses of his beard, his black coat, with some rubbing, looked almost clean. With only a few crumbs and granules of sugar still clinging to his moustaches, he imprisoned the secret squalor of his solitude behind the splintered door and locked it. Out in the street, he was once more three quarters a gentleman.

'Always pay, my dear, for *ton*. You are so right.' The counsel had been Eggy's; needless as it happened, for Mr Lupton had already, some years before, seen the truth of it, when he started to pay rent for the splendours of his studio in Fitzroy Square. Doubtless the illustrations for popular novels which had formed the staple income for the first few struggling years could have been accomplished easily enough in the garret in Charlotte Street. But if remuneration for one set of illustrations of a story by Maxwell Gray 'kept him going' for a week, his payment for a 'society' portrait could sustain him for some months. The commissions now flowed steadily in. The 'capturing' both in the visual and monetary senses of the idiom, of the bishop-elect of Calcutta had been the beginning of his good fortune. Since then, there had been the Dowager Countess of Bayswater, Lord Wisbeach, the Dean of Selchester and Mr Severus Egg. Now he was to depict the Master of Harcourt. This was to be an easier commission than the others, since the Master had declared himself too busy, when in London, for sittings. Having borrowed the robes of a Doctor of Divinity, Mr Lupton had been able to do all but the face with the aid of a tailor's dummy; and Eggy had even asked him why it was necessary to stop short at the face.

The answer was that he had been asked down to finish the portrait *in situ* and to stay in the Master's lodgings. He dreamed of the look of happy surprise which would light up Maudie's face when she arrived at the ball and found him there. He had already danced, in his imagination, countless waltzes with her, and strolled, when tired with dancing, through ancient cloisters and over velvety lawns beneath a starry night, with Maudie on his arm, felt her loose shocks of hair entangle themselves in his own beard, felt her tiny fingers clasp his own, and her bird-like little body heave devotedly against his breast.

When he arrived at the studio, into which the sunlight poured in straight golden horizontal rays, he smiled at the tailor's dummy, arrayed as the Master, and thought with joy of all the romance which would attach to the finishing of this portrait in the University town. At the opposite end of the large studio, the easel bore witness to his efforts of the previous evening, before dinner and cards had distracted him:

Nausicaa and her maidens, less well accomplished, in the daylight, than he remembered. The two images facing each other – the half-finished naked girl, and the dummy in the doctor's robes – in themselves a 'still life' emblematic of the early antithesis of his ambitions. His father had been outraged that he had not pursued the normal career of a gentleman and gone to the University. But Timothy Lupton had no regrets about his refusal of the scholar's life. He had had only one great ambition in his life: to be a painter. In early days, this had been a much loftier thing than his present prosaic desire to make ends meet by producing here a set of novel-illustrations, there a likeness of some pompous dignitary. It seemed symbolised by the daub of the maidens which the tailor's dummy faced with such resolute disapproval. Now that he was past his thirtieth birthday, it perhaps seemed that his ambitions were misplaced. He was quite a passable draughtsman, he could produce with confident success, portraits to please his customers. But when he tried to produce 'pure art', the result seemed almost childishly unsuccessful. Still, as he often told himself, a man's reach should exceed his grasp or what's a heaven for?

What, Eggy might have added with a sigh, indeed. In his 'serious work' it was by no means clear in which direction Timothy was reaching or grasping. He regretted in many ways, his tutelage under the great 'Alma-Tad', for, popular as these scenes of the ancient world undoubtedly were in the galleries, Mr Lupton knew that he was striving towards something much more fundamental than a summoning up of spurious images of antiquity when he held a brush in his hands. Almost all his contemporaries saw the universe as riven with practical and moral mysteries which failed to engage his attention. He was indifferent to the question of Irish Home Rule, felt no curiosity about our imperial triumphs abroad, and had never devoted his mind to Suffrage, Free Trade, the price of Consols, or the legality or otherwise of remarrying one's deceased wife's sister. All the things which seemed to occupy the great world passed him by, as in a dream. He was interested chiefly in Light, and he wished there could be a way in which he could learn his craft all over again. He would like to experiment in the way of the young American visitors to Europe such as Sargent and Whistler. The painters he had come most to admire were Turner and Rembrandt. Abroad, particularly in France, the mysteries which these masters had commanded were once more being reopened. In too-brief visits to Paris he had been fascinated by the work of the Barbizon School, and seen the 'Impressionists' which were such a joke to the philistines. Timothy had felt reproached by their canvases. For they seemed to have realised what, when he began to paint, he had half-felt, but never understood, to be his vocation: to capture the very qualities of light itself. All things, he was convinced, were physically relative. All images of shapes and colour come into our heads through arrangements of the optic nerve, itself shaped by the peculiar chemistry of our own bodies and by our imaginations. Things do not possess the properties of colour, however rigidly Ruskin might have claimed they do, in *Modern Painters*. Each individual set of human eyes rearranges the kaleidoscope of visual impression into its own image, its own picture of the world.

The great painters were the ones who seemed to penetrate this very process of arrangement while it was happening, and to capture the particles of the light itself and reassemble them on to their canvas. Turner's landscapes – Corot's too, to a lesser extent – did not *represent* light so much as they seemed to *be* light: so too, a gleaming helmet in Rembrandt had as much the quality of light as a burning candle. It was what Coleridge called the repetition in the finite mind of the eternal act of creation in the infinite I AM. As a physical embodiment in the mind of the painter, it seemed more remarkable to Timothy than do the purely ethereal eruptions of primary creativity in the mind of the writer. In either case, however, it gave to his idle air and bohemian carelessness an underlying core of seriousness, which would be irritated, ruffled or shaken by his more truly cynical companions. The surgeon of Guy's had intended him for the Bar, a career, perhaps, in Parliament. Even the fact that he had abandoned these tedious goals so early in life did not entirely debar him from membership of the *beau monde:* a handful of drawing rooms received him, and he belonged to a couple of goodish clubs, so that the dressed tailor's dummy continued to stare at the naked maidens, and the dream of capturing light itself in paint was always threatened by the relaxations of the gentlemen, one of whom, it will be remembered, exercised a traditional jurisdiction over the realms of darkness. Claret, whisky and seegaws are not catalogued by Vasari in his *Lives of the Painters* as having been indispensable adjuncts to the nurturing of Raphael's genius, nor that of Michelangelo. But then, had either of these celebrated painters had the privilege of mixing with English gentlemen? It was not an absurd question, for Timothy. He valued his recent friendship with Severus Egg almost as highly as he valued his artistic vocation.

Eggy had brought two profound reassurances. In what might be deemed moral areas, he presented the grinning impression that he had long ago given up trying; an abandonment which, however reprehensible in absolute terms, or wearisome to his immediate intimates or contemporaries, made him, as an old man, a very restful companion. With Eggy, whatever one's own failures or misdemeanours, there was no competition. He had long ago outgrown an inverted desire to excel in violations of the moral code and make of his 'lapses' a matter of brag. His smile suggested that 'morals' need never 'come up': a level of detachment shocking to the scrupulous (doubtless especially shocking to 'darling Netty') but reassuring to the aspirant *mondain*. It was something in his moistish grin, straight and soulless. Timothy Lupton had come to love it.

The level on which this abandonment was achieved, was of course, wholly conversational, but since it was on this level that both men chose to live their lives, it would not dull its keener edge to call it superficial. Surfaces are important, few more so than those superficial impressions of our person formed on the optic nerves of friends and loved ones, impressions as arbitrary as those of colour.

This being so, Lupton's second debt to his friend was perhaps deeper than that of moral release. Eggy's smile, his laugh, his old cane (it had belonged to Leigh Hunt, a present to Eggy forty-five years since), his weary exclamations that he had lived too long in the world ('I have survived into the era of the goody-goodies') were all likely enough to relax the moral fibre of his hearer. This aspect of his friendship had the qualities of wine, an impression strengthened by the fact that, at whatever hour one saw him, some vinous refreshment would ever be insisted upon. But the second debt owed by the younger to the older man was something much richer and more exacting. It was hard to put it into a word, but Timothy supposed that it enveloped the notion of 'standards', a feeling that in artistic and intellectual terms, it was always necessary to be on one's toes. With this side of Eggy's tutelage, Lupton associated the glazing eyes, the lofty old vowels (no distinction between loins and lines), the stiff soldierly neck and shoulder and the whiteness of his knuckles as he clutched and fingered his stick. It seemed paradoxical, and even a little pathetic, that a hack illustrator turned society portrait painter should have been able to nurse ambitions of artistic excellence without giving himself whole-heartedly to a pursuit of form, colour and light. There was nothing which forced him to dine out, to have the studio in Fitzroy Square, to keep up membership of his clubs. A garret in Paris would doubtless have given him greater opportunities to advance than the garret on the fringes of Soho. But Eggy's purism was of no such romantic kind. He abominated incompetence. It was said of him in old time (it was Thackeray's friend Brookfield who made the quip) that Egg took ten years to write a couplet. His rate of production, even in the days when his odes and verse tales were being written, was prodigiously slow. But he had confidence in the good sense of artistic agonising.

'Nothing else is *worth* our agonising,' opined the perfectionist.

Trapped in the limitations of words, Egg had eventually been locked altogether in their paralysing discomfiture, their crude immalleability. If *Tuscany* had taken ten years, *Benvenuto Cellini* had taken yet longer, remained, indeed, to this hour unfinished. Unable to achieve perfection, he had laid down his golden pen (the gift of Joseph Severn, it had been held in the hands of Keats). The passion for perfection survived, however, in the simplest epistolary exercises. He had been known to screw a dozen pieces of paper into balls, and to discard half-finished as many sentences, when composing the most humdrum responses to the requests and demands of tradespeople or hostesses: and the letter could not be released until the formula of Mr Egg's thanks to Lady ———— for her kind invitation had been pondered, reworked, adorned with the stamp of his humour, without the perilous and ever to be avoided descent into whimsy.

The drying up, first of the well of poetry, at last of all written fluency, Egg's fastidiousness, his reluctance to write anything which was second best, made him a by-word long before he had fallen in at the club with his young friend the painter. Lupton, who could turn out ten illustrations a week, a portrait a month, felt, in his wholly workday visual medium unfettered by any such mandarin distaste for what came easily and ran freely. But, if not hampered by conscience in the matter, he knew Eggy's predicament to be, in its fashion, a reproach to the hidden wells within. There had been not merely a failure of scruple, but of courage. Since he had defied the father and not, as was expected, pursued a life in the world through the familiar channels of the University or the Inns of Court, he might have felt liberated to go 'the whole hog': to pursue art alone for its own sake. Mercenary strictures forbade the Muse. An easy pencil produced, through a modest remuneration, enough to maintain the innocent façades of gentility which he was still able to assume when he stepped down to Pall Mall or Piccadilly. 'Lupton lives in lodgings' was a carefully sustained joke over which he exercised certain though delicate control. In cruder minds, the implications of the domestic arrangement even suggested a bohemian *ménage* into which demure respectability would not probe: 'These artists.' His association with the old Regency *roué* lent weight to these largely false surmises.

But beneath the diurnal surfaces of meals and whist in clubs, of dinners in the houses of his married friends, and of mornings and afternoons in the studio, the spiritual reserves, the desire for the Light, remained untapped.

He knew them to be there, as he stood before starting work, staring out over the trees and house-fronts of Fitzroy Square. The calling could be held back, but he knew that he was merely waiting for its inner clarion sound; that he was not smothering the gift so much as keeping it safe. The morning sunlight of May caught windows in splashes of intolerable brilliance so that the blinking eye, dazzled by their irregular sharp gleams made of all the scene – houses, trees, pavements, clopping drays of milk-carts, the silhouetted figures beyond the nearest sun-rays, a whole smudgy haze, shimmering iridescent and perpetually changing. No colour remained constant; all was an arrangement of fluctuating hues. One day, he knew, the hour would come when, at the risk of all commercial disaster, it would become his sole business to catch that light, to gaze towards it, encapsulate it, repeat it in exercise after exercise; not to explain but to record; to surrender himself to the eternal act of creation; to become its minister and its vessel. Then, with the submissive readiness of the neophyte, he would be ready for the sacrifices which the quest demanded. This certainty of a vocation was a quiet secret. Erring towards *gravitas,* it of course lacked *ton.* But it glowed within him there as he stood by the window, one arm on the dummy Master of Harcourt, the fleeting light-patterns of the square mingling with a never-far-absent visual preoccupation with Maudie Nettleship.

The daydream had made him neglect to shift through the modest pile of envelopes left by the postman, mostly composed, as a casual glance assured him, of requests from the more optimistic traders, for prompt payment of overdue accounts. One small envelope, however, inscribed with a neat calligraphy half-familiar to him, a woman's hand, arrested his attention, and he slit it open with a palette knife. For all his complete besottedness, his adoration of Maudie, Timothy Lupton was still young enough to feel a flutter of excitement at the sight of his name in *any* female hand. To open such a letter – though it turned out to be from the most raddled old crone requesting a portrait, brought with it the possibility of new adventure, a shimmering of romance. Who was this from? *Dear Mr Lupton,* he read – it was a short enough epistle, written neatly, but he suspected hurriedly, on a piece of blank paper, no date. *Explanations are in order I know, and we must meet. But where can we find 'neutral ground'? Might I suggest, though it sounds a trifle foolish, that we encounter one another 'by chance' at the haberdashery counter of Peter Robinson, Regent Street, tomorrow morning between the hours of ten and half past? C.N.*

THIRTEEN

La Gioconda

Charlotte Nettleship did not know what she should say to Mr Lupton when they met alone for the first time in shop-anonymity. She had written to him in the hope that the decisiveness of the action – the very appending of a red penny stamp to the envelope, the dispatch of it, with some ceremony, from the Post Office in St John's Wood High Street – might clear the mists. She could not *go on* expecting him to put up with Maudie's giggling egotism; and even if he were agreeable, there had become something absurd about the frequency with which 'drawing lessons' were arranged at Brunswick Square. Her old father was far too cynical to complain. And he was not so obtuse as to ignore the probability that the lessons caused Horace Nettleship discomfiture. Therefore, they were encouraged to the full, and Mr Bacon had borne to the table where the young lady sat with the painter, untold lemonade jugs, biscuit plates, and fingers of cinnamon toast, while the lessons were in progress and Charlotte sat, a little apart, witnessing each movement of the pair and, in the intervals when Maudie was silent with her pencils, conversing with Mr Lupton.

Horace, of course, *knew*. Of this, Charlotte had convinced herself. There could be no other explanation for his supper-outburst some nights before. How pompously he had looked as he said it. 'I am not conducting an enquiry into all your lessons.' Of course he was, and he was, inevitably, already aware through marriage-telepathy of what was afoot. It was mere boorishness to have bullied Maudie about it. But since he could not assail Charlotte in person, what else could he have done but make 'comments' at meals?

Well, Charlotte was *glad* he knew. She had begun to scent liberty and to feel that, somehow, she would escape with her . . . lover. At first, when she heard from Mr Chatterway, that it was being 'talked about', she had felt smartingly furious. How dare they? What business was it, if they had a business, of *theirs* (whoever *they* were)? But in fact, the letter from Mr Chatterway had been thrilling. It was the receipt of this little communication which had made her so anxious to see Mr Lupton on her own. It was necessary to establish that he knew as much as she did about their notoriety.

These thoughts she articulated to herself by frequent expressions of anger with Mr Chatterway. It was, she said several times that morning to herself before setting out from the house, *just as well* that she was no longer receiving Mr Chatterway; else *it* would be 'all over London'. There was, moreover, something of malice in his too-knowing tone, and in his embittered desire to laugh at the most ennobling and elevating of all the passions. Whatever had inspired Dante to write his *Commedia*, Shakespeare and Mrs Browning their sonnets, now coursed and charged through Charlotte's being. What, conceivably, could be found to laugh at? But this could not stop Mr Chatterway writing to her in the vein of the previous morning:

Carissima Carlotta, or should one say Gioconda, since you now seem to mix with painters? You know you are, as in the surely-much-over-esteemed monograph on Mona Lisa by (I believe) young Gutch's in more senses than are wholesome, Greek tutor, 'older than the rocks', or in this case painterly admirers, among whom you sit? And how does Herr Professor bring himself to tolerate this daily lovemaking under the roof if not always the eye of your poetical and himself never wholly unamorous parent? You are presumably much too busy being talked about to spare the time for your old and still, though banished and insulted, lieber Kamarad. . . .

Such a letter was an insult, of course, and one successful in its obvious calculation: it threw her into alarm. Into so few polysyllabic and semi-comprehensible phrases, so much poisonous insult was crammed that she felt at first weak, quivering, with rage. The fact that he had been her acquaintance ever since she was born did *not* entitle him to comment on her age! She did not understand the references to Gutch. She had not heard he had a tutor, nor why it should matter if he were a Greek. In another sense, the letter was 'Greek' to her. But she knew that, exaggerated and malicious as Waldo Chatterway's epistle had been, it did represent what London was starting to *say*. If London did not say it before he wrote, they would most certainly be saying it *after*. Her own father, she knew, would never gossip openly about her. Bacon had, perhaps, said something to a servant who had passed it back to master or mistress. This person would perhaps have asked Mr Chatterway about it the next time he strutted into their drawing room. How dispassionately we exchange news about the emotional lives of strangers: this girl is engaged, that old man widowed, this pair in and that out of love. For the participants this is the most absorbing area of human elation or torment but we can pass from it as a subject of conversational trifling when it does not immediately touch ourselves with as much indifference as we abandon a discussion of the weather. Charlotte had a thousand times done it herself. And she had laughed at Chatterway's chronicles of London absurdity as they unfolded each year or so. Now, with scalding embarrassment, she realised that her name would be recited with the rest of the canon. 'My little friend Mrs Nettleship, so amorously entangled with Alma-Tadema's disciple Lupton' – some such phrase would drop from his lips, Chatterway's, and women who had never met either Charlotte or Mr Lupton would drop their forks and beg to be told more and vulgar more. But it was impossible not to feel, too, excited by all this, just a little. *Who* had told Marvo did not much matter. It was material, merely, that he had been told and with him, therefore, half London. To tell Chatterway a secret was cheaper and undoubtedly more effective than advertising it on the front page of the *Morning Post*. And this, distressing as in some respects it might be, would be least puncture the atmosphere of heart-breaking ambiguity which engulfed her relationship with Mr Lupton. Because they had always met in Brunswick Square, under the gaze of the little girl and, oftener than not, that of Severus Egg and the butler, there had been no possibility of Mr Lupton speaking out. Charlotte had been obliged to catch all his meaning from the coded emphasis of quite innocuous phrases.

'I do not know when you will be available for another lesson, Mr Lupton.'

'I am, my dear Mrs Nettleship, at your *disposal*.'

'You must be so busy.'

'Not so busy that I would not drop everything at your command.'

What could have been more specific than that exchange, which had happened only on their second or third encounter? Then again, in another interview, Maudie had infuriatingly and, with such impertinence, said that she thought she was having almost too many drawing lessons. To which he had replied, 'Not too many, if your mother will allow me to say so, for my tastes, Miss Nettleship. I secretly believe your mother to be a great lover . . .' and there had been such a pause, such an ocean of silence, before he added . . . 'of your drawings.'

While the child scribbled and sketched, the lovers had talked. It did not matter that so frequently the subjects discussed were in themselves prosaic. Charlotte's father had upbraided them with being tedious when he had pottered, velvet-slippered, into his own saloon one afternoon and heard Mr Lupton trying to explain to her why Mr Bradlaugh would not take his oath and be sworn in as the member for Northampton in the new House of Commons. 'Very elevating to the spirits,' Eggy had exclaimed. 'Thank the Gods! I have never had the very smallest interest in politics.'

Mr Lupton was, she had come to suspect from several of his observations, something of a radical, and this excited her enormously, almost as much as his sheer and dazzling beauty of person. When she had timidly ridden her own little 'radical' hobby-horse and alluded to her dream of Women's Suffrage, the painter had not dismissed such chat with the scornful smiles of most of the men of her acquaintance. He had nodded sagely, and with the air of a pensive young prophet, in Maudie's direction and asserted that by the time the child's daughters were grown to womanhood they would probably be sitting in the House of Commons.

Bacon had grinned so stupidly when his master had said, 'We shan't live to see it, Bacon – *Laus Deis!* What nonsense you do talk, Lupton my dear. As bad as Tennyson in his younger days. *"Let the great world ring forever down the ringing groove of change."* Tosh, balderdash and bunkum.'

It had been the closest that her hurtfully indifferent parent had come to expressing disapproval of the lovers and their trysts in the drawing room at Brunswick Square. The trysts, as she recognised, placed her father in a position of embarrassment. If, as now seemed inevitable, 'it' went further, and 'something were to come' of her dangerous attachment, it would appear, at the least, her father had done nothing to stifle the affair in its formative phase.

Her mind would not rest with a contemplation of the past weeks. It raced ahead to the imagined future. Though she had only just penetrated the foothills, she already saw herself in possession of the mountainous heights. In moments of wool-gathering, she allowed her mind to form pictures of herself and Mr Lupton so vivid that it was impossible, once the day-dreams had evaporated, not to believe that they had not in truth taken place. They had already strolled together by the shores of the Mediterranean, picnicked in an olive grove in Thermopylae, and enjoyed, with what ecstasies of rapture, all the connubial intimacies. Sometimes, when recovering from these reveries, she told herself that it was 'not like her' to be so fanciful. But the very implication of the phrase inspired a new spirit of defiance. Who was she, or who was anybody, to say that there was a fixed and immutable Charlotte who could not be changed, and refashioned anew by experience? She felt dangerously capable of adventure. A former self would have advanced so many arguments of common sense, and reminded her of her domestic responsibilities. She had the servants and the meals to think of; she had the moral tutelage of an impressionable and highly-strung daughter; she had, oh, how she hated the fact, a husband! But the more clearly she saw that an outburst of bad behaviour would wound her husband, the more passionately she grew attached to the notion. Why, she might even find herself being divorced by him!

Whether or not she looked like the kind of woman who might one day be divorced, it would be generally conceded that Charlotte, on the morning of her shop-tryst with Mr Lupton, looked formidably handsome. Her dress was a blue watered silk, tightly waisted, with a bodice of white. Delicate blue buttons swooped in a perfect curve from her pale throat to her tiny feet. Her snowy powdered face, which had grown more angular of late, was crowned with a neat little blue hat, beneath which her hair was thickly piled. Aggy, opening the front door for her to step into the waiting hansom, had stared to see her mistress so extravagantly arrayed. The disapproval on the servant's face had given a little lift to Charlotte's spirits as the cab clattered off across Regent's Park, for in the fantasy of the moment, her face had, she knew, acquired a desperate beauty.

She wished now that she had chosen a *rendezvous* a little less prosaic than a haberdashery counter. Why not throw caution to the winds and meet at an hotel? As the journey progressed, she became as agitated as a girl. The stories in her head raced faster and faster. He would perhaps take her hand and suggest that they elope at once. What then? She would go, of course. She would go to the ends of the world. What if he made some more fundamentally farm-yard proposal for the here and now, that morning in London? To that, too, she felt equal.

By the time she had reached Oxford Circus, however, her courage was failing. She had half a mind to ask the hansom to drive past the shop altogether and leave her instead in some neutral place, such as the National Gallery, where she could collect her thoughts again in peace. A vestige of her former self rose up to reproach her, and, as the horse slowed down to a halt, she felt very foolish.

Mr Lupton was standing outside the shop, endeavouring to find the contents of the window interesting enough to justify a ten-minute perusal. He saw her, unfortunately, at once, so that she had no time to compose her countenance. In fact, as he raised his hat and their eyes met, she felt herself blushing deeply.

'Are you keeping the hansom or should I perhaps . . .' he volunteered. And in her confusion, she realised that she had not paid the cabby, and was only able to utter incoherent protests as the young painter fished in his trowsers pockets for change.

'I insist upon paying you back.'

'I should not hear of it.'

'But it is so *silly*.'

'*Please.*'

In full view of the passers-by, he rested a gloved hand upon her mittened wrist. She trembled with the touch.

'What was it,' he continued, 'that you wanted me to see in the haberdashery department?'

'Oh, oh, nothing at all,' she laughed. 'I merely thought that it would be a convenient place for us to meet.'

'Would you like us to repair there or should we stroll?'

'Do let's walk. It is such a nice day.'

It was, in fact, no longer a particularly nice day. The sunshine of the early morning had been overcast with dull clouds of a whitish grey. There was even a slight nip in the air. No one could think that it was going to do anything so interesting as rain; but then, nor was anyone going to see their shadows on the pavement that morning.

'It saves me from a perusal of the Master of Harcourt's features,' he said, in reply to her hope that she was not wasting his time.

'You do not mean that Dr Jenkinson is waiting in your studio?'

'Lord lumme no, I do it nearly all with photographs. I shall only need the Master *in propria persona* for the last sitting or two. I have his robes on a valet and a face on photographic plates. I fancy that when we meet, he will seem a little superfluous.'

'He is a most amusing man, though very shy,' she said.

'A friend of your husband's I suppose? Is that why your son chose to go to Harcourt?'

'Dr Jenkinson is an old friend of my father's,' she said abruptly, unable to respond to these allusions to her own hearth, as she took his arm and they wandered down towards Piccadilly Circus.

'I have been struggling with his latest Platonic dialogue. A little above me, I'm afraid. It almost makes me wish I'd been to the Varsity and read up all that philosophy – Kant and Hume and Aristotle, don't you know. Now, Homer. . . .'

'I too, lack an analytic intelligence. But I am sure,' she added hastily lest it be thought that he take his own modest estimate of himself at face value, 'that you are concealing your true. . . .'

'On the contrary.'

'Concealment is very necessary sometimes. Without it perhaps we. . . .'

They walked for quite five minutes in silence, and found themselves crossing Leicester Square. It was quite evident to him that she had something important to say, but what it was, he was dashed if he now knew. From time to time, he felt a flush of embarrassed hope that she did know of his love for Maudie and sympathise with it. At other times, his certainty faded like a phantom. He decided to sail close to the winds and test her.

'Maudie I believe, is quite an Homeric scholar,' he said.

'Yes, she is, though I don't believe she really has much aptitude,' said the mother. 'What I mean by concealment is that sometimes we feel things too deeply to be able to say them.'

'We are afraid,' he said. 'Afraid that if we do reveal them, everything we most hoped for might be lost.'

'Afraid,' she agreed, 'that we have been living in a dream and that our declaration will force another to shatter that dream.'

'But sometimes, it might not be a dream,' he said, 'it might be a glimpse of reality.'

'Our only glimpse,' she agreed. 'Do you remember that poem of Browning's, "Youth and Art"?'

'I can't say that I do.'

She paused under the plane trees and looked intently into his eyes as she quoted:

> Each life unfulfilled, you see;
>   It hangs still, patchy and scrappy;
> We have not sighed deep, laughed free
>   Starved, feasted, despaired, – been happy.
>
> And nobody calls you a dunce,
>   And people suppose me clever:
> This could but have happened once,
>   And we missed it, lost it for ever.

There seemed nothing to say to this, or if there were, he kept it to himself. There was a funny sort of deliberation in her voice as she spoke. She did not herself sound passionate. Only at the words *been happy* did her tone acquire a bleak pathos.

'Mrs Nettleship,' he tried to begin.

'Yes, Mr Lupton?'

'I am sure that you must have wondered why, at your father's house. . . .'

'Yes?'

'In recent weeks, that is to say, since you so very kindly had us to tea – your father that is, and me, and Mr Chatterway. . . .'

'Wondered what, Mr Lupton?'

'Well, to be candid, wondered at the frequency with which I have sought out the possibility of drawing lessons – giving them, that is, even though in the circumstances it is all highly embarrassing.'

'Why?' she asked with sudden passion. 'Why is it embarrassing?'

'Because I have it from your own lips and in your own hand that I am not welcome at your husband's house.'

'You would be more than welcome. You know that.'

'An opposite impression – forgive me, Mrs Nettleship, but not three weeks. . . .'

'I spoke for my husband on that occasion, it is true,' she conceded. 'But that is not to say that my husband has any right whatsoever to speak for me.'

There was anger in her tone, and Mr Lupton feared to intrude upon its cause. It disconcerted him acutely to believe that husbands and wives, whatever disputes they might have privately, would choose to make their differences known to others.

'I know it is not at all for me to say this, Mrs Nettleship . . .' he hesitated.

'You may say anything, Mr Lupton, to me.'

'Your friend Mr Chatterway. At the same time as you wrote to me originally expressing your displeasure, your husband's displeasure, in my society, you also indicated to Mr Chatterway that he too was to be no longer received at your house.'

'Yes, I did.'

'I am constrained to admit to you, Mrs Nettleship, that Mr Chatterway is very deeply hurt by this exclusion. He finds it, I know, incomprehensible.'

'He has been gossiping to you about it, I suppose?' She laughed, suddenly. Could the simple explanation of Marvo's extraordinary letter be that Mr Lupton was already *speaking* of her as his beloved? Could such a thing be credited or believed? She knew that she should have been outraged by the insult to her good name, but her heart became light with it. 'And it was you, I suppose, who christened me the Mona Lisa?'

'I?'

It was not at all clear whether she had heard this monosyllabic rejoinder, for he spoke quietly, and the clatter of wheels in Charing Cross Road was thunderous.

'Mr Chatterway likes to make mischief,' she said.

'He is one of your oldest and dearest friends. He has told me how deeply he values your friendship.'

'You and he appear to have become very intimately acquainted.'

'In a manner, perhaps we have.'

'I too have treasured Mr Chatterway's companionship in the past,' she said.

'Mrs Nettleship, you will think me very impertinent.'

'Why?'

'I am fully sensible that you may entertain whom you choose in your own house. It is simply that I do not like to see a man *pining*.'

'Come, Mr Lupton, that is strong language.'

'It is strange.' He smiled to himself.

'What is?'

'But three months since, and I did not know any of you. I knew your father of course. I have been fortunate enough to be acquainted with him for a number of years. Then, when the Royal Society of Literature asked if they could have a portrait of him for their walls, he was kind enough to propose my name as the artist. I know they wanted a bigger name, but I suspect that he persuaded them that 'a Lupton' is considerably cheaper these days than 'a Watts' or 'a Millais.''

'It will not always be so.'

'I fear it will be.'

'I am entitled to my own view.' There was coquettishness in her tones.

'I came to know your father much better in the course of painting his portrait. I am now, almost, truly, an intimate.'

'That has never been quite my privilege. I envy you.'

'Since then: Mr Chatterway, and the tea party, and then. . . . What developments!'

'Are they developments which please you, Mr Lupton?'

'Like the lines you quoted, "This could have happened but once".'

'And it has' – was she sensible of a tightening of his hold on her arm? – 'happened to you?'

'Mrs Nettleship, these are very dangerous waters.'

'For me, as much as for you, remember.'

By now they had wandered to Trafalgar Square, and stood on the corner by the National Gallery looking down into Whitehall. Her observations seemed to him merely quaint. She obviously wanted a confession out of him before the morning was through. He had heard of such mothers. But could he really claim that a mother, launching a daughter upon the world, sailed in more dangerous waters than the man whose heart could be reduced to torment by a mere flicker of that daughter's eyelashes?

'I understand from what Maudie was saying,' he resumed in a lighter tone, 'during yesterday's lesson, that you will all be going to the Commemoration Ball at Harcourt.'

'We are to dine with your subject,' said Charlotte. 'Papa was asked, but he has little taste for travel these days.'

'He once told me that he had never been on the railway.'

'The untruth was typical.'

'I wondered, merely,' coyness entered his voice and threatened to melt her, 'whether there would be a chance, perhaps, of our meeting one another, when you are staying with Dr Jenkinson.'

'We are not staying with him, merely dining. My husband prefers an independent existence,' she said with an attempted ambiguity to which Mr Lupton was quite deaf. 'There are scientists whom he will wish to see. While he talks of his lavas and his granites, we can perhaps see the colleges together.'

'And this means, that for the time being, there shall be no more drawing lessons?' he asked.

'They are surely very wearisome to you?'

'Not in the least.'

'You are cursed with the inheritance of politeness, Mr Lupton. I can tell that they bore you, and embarrass you.'

'But, Mrs Nettleship. . . .'

'I will be frank with you. It is the least we can do to be, from the very first, truthful with one another, come what may.'

His heart missed a beat. As the moment of frankness approached, he was not altogether confident that he would be strong enough for it. He preferred the ambiguities of the previous weeks to the harsh reality of being *told* not to flirt with her daughter. He could not speak. It was now she who had taken command of their colloquy.

'You are perfectly right to extract from me the embarrassing fact that my husband did not wish me to receive either you or Mr Chatterway at The Bower. But this is not something which can go on *forever*. In the *changed* circumstances, I do not pretend that he would be the more ready to receive you. In fact, it goes without saying that he would think his first instincts had been right. What those instincts exactly were, I do not quite know. But what the circumstances *now* are, we both know – you and I.'

His 'Yes' was hoarse.

'My husband belongs to a different moral universe from my father. But I am caught between the two, you see.'

'It is awkward for you.' It was hard not to make the sentence, considering they were discussing his entire future happiness, seem flat.

'Quite *entre nous*. I do not worry about either of them. Not from a moral point of view. That shocks you, perhaps?'

'Not at all.'

'I can tell that it does, a little. When you know me better and understand my history, you will know why I say that. Oh, *Timothy*, it is the child who wrings my heart.'

The use of his Christian name was altogether startling. He wanted to assure her that he loved her daughter, and that his intentions were wholly honourable; but he could not Charlotte her, and his self-justification, rising to his lips prefixed with a Mrs Nettleship, died before he could speak it.

'We can not *use* the girl.'

'Of course not.'

'I do not deceive myself. She is not wholly innocent of what is taking place. It would merely compromise her intolerably with her father if we presumed upon her innocence any longer. Before I set out to see you, I was not sure what I would say, or what I would have the courage to say. But at least I have said that. I receive letters. I have made my position shockingly, ignominiously plain to you. Now, the decision here rests with you.'

'The decision? It has to *be* a decision?'

'Do not let us spoil things by rushing them.'

It had become apparent that the elopement would not happen that morning. She felt by now that she had said enough, and that, by walking him into a public spot he could scarcely be expected, there on the gallery steps, to make any very demonstrative declaration. But she had had her say!

'Do I take it,' he asked, a mixture of bafflement and distress, 'that we are to meet neither at your own house, nor at Brunswick Square?'

'I leave it to you when we should meet,' she said simply. 'And you know that I hope it is soon.'

A stronger clasp of his arm before she released it was her valediction. He stood staring down the steps after her, as, without looking back, she made her way to the stand outside the gallery and was helped into a cab.

'If that's being shockingly plain,' he said aloud. 'Blow me!'

FOURTEEN

At The Athenaeum

Even Horace Nettleship, who prided himself on not being over-sensitive to atmosphere, had begun to find The Bower oppressive. His Maudie was becoming a stranger to him. The girl passed him now and edged away if he reached out to caress or embrace her on a landing. At meals, if not wholly taciturn like her mother, she had begun to be 'short' in her replies. She no longer seemed, and this was the part that baffled him, to accept him as the chief hierophant in her cult. Indeed, she seemed to bridle at being noticed, let alone, loved by him. The transformation in his daughter had taken place so gradually that he had not noticed it happening. He had tried to persuade himself that she was out of sorts, and troubled by coughing; or that she was merely consumed by those little clouds of melancholy which from time to time descend upon the young. But she was the reverse of baleful. Perkiness, if not a positively cruel brightness, characterised her manner. Affectations had crept into her speech. She seemed to have developed all her mother's harsh cynicism without the weariness of soul which gave to Charlotte's *contemptus mundi* the occasional appearance of moral weight.

The professor did not suspect anything so crude as a conspiracy between the two women – for, yes, now they were two women with whom he shared his silences. He could not be certain that Charlotte had not complained about him to their daughter. But he thought it would be uncharacteristic. To complain of someone suggests that you mind about them. Studied indifference had, for the last fifteen years or so, been Charlotte's demeanour towards him. She was now capable, almost all the time, of behaving as if he were not in the room. She could eat, as she had done that morning, a bowl of bottled plums, a plate of kedgeree, a slice of cold ham and a few pieces of toast while seated nearly opposite her spouse in the dining room, but pay no more attention to him than if he had been a toast rack. His daughter, on the other hand, registered impatience with him. As she made her more modest breakfast, and gasped with disappointment as she lifted each silver cover on the sideboard, he had felt as though it were he, and not the kedgeree, that was failing to satisfy Maudie's exacting standards.

'Why can't she' (she being Mrs Reynolds) 'provide coffee for our *petit déjeuner?*' the child had embarrassingly inquired.

'Because you have never asked for it,' said the father.

'There should be a choice each morning – coffee, chocolate or tea. Why must it always be tea? In *civilised* countries, tea is hardly drunk.'

'I don't know to which countries you refer.'

Now, what had been funny about that sentence? But it had sent Maudie into a peal of silly giggles. When, having consumed almost nothing, the girl had left the table, it would have been natural for the parents to talk about her; for one to lament the way in which the child was 'turning out'; for the other to reassure and assert that she was passing through what is known as an awkward age. But they were unable to indulge in any such little talk. A syllable passing his wife's lips would, in some insane way which he perfectly understood, have been a concession of defeat. They must not speak to each other. Looking was, by the rules he played, allowable. But Charlotte did not concede him so much as a glance. He had gazed across the breakfast table at the wife he had married and seen a figure of extraordinary poise, over-touched beauty. His only revenge had been the reflexion that she was not quite so clever either as she or as others supposed. To hear her inane prattle to Maudie about books or about subjects of the hour was to receive the hideous impression that she considered herself well-informed. Afghanistan, Ireland, Mr Gladstone and Mr Bradlaugh were names which passed between the two females, not a little to the professor's almost-amusement. It certainly almost-amused him that his wife, whom he had thought pious enough to pay pew-rents, should apparently support the embarrassing actions of Mr Bradlaugh who, after the late election, had refused to take his oath in the House of Commons on the grounds of atheism. The MP for Northampton's request to affirm his loyalty rather than swear it in the presence of God apparently touched a chord in Mrs Nettleship. A sensible Liberal could not approve of all Bradlaugh's ranting radicalism, but as an ardent atheist who had more than once heard Bradlaugh speak, most persuasively, at the Hall of Science in Old Street, the professor had sympathised with the Commons outburst. Why his wife should have done so was a mystery. He had assumed her in theological matters to share the opinions of the prime minister, who had written a pamphlet on the literal, scientific and historical truth of the Garden of Eden and Adam and Eve.

Maudie's reaction to the Commons brawl with which the newspapers were full had been equally surprising to her father. She had decreed that Mr Bradlaugh was *maleducato;* a gutter-snipe, a man who in atheistic fervour was incomparable with 'dear Diderot' and who was scarcely, as a radical, your Danton, or your Garibaldi. How did women learn to speak or *think* in this way? It was all part of the process, the professor felt, of freezing him out; freezing him out, indeed, of his own house. The letters, largely unnecessary, which he wrote and read each morning, and which used to keep him, with his books, in his study until luncheon, now drew him instead to the library of the Athenaeum. After the agonies of the kedgeree conference, he arose and announced to the empty air (for though his wife was still in the room she was not listening) that he would perhaps lunch in his club.

Aggy, hovering by the sideboard with the crumb-tray, inquired if this was definite only as how if it was she should go to Mrs Reynolds and tell her not to peel so many potatoes. When this imporant injunction had been communicated to the cook, the professor set out by foot and by omnibus, for that haven of learning in Pall Mall. The servants might treat him like a foolish schoolboy. His wife might ignore him, and his daughter cough and snigger and now cheek him with pert and macaronic expressions of her own superiority to the rest of the universe. But at the Athenaeum he was somebody. Walking up the huge stairs of the Athenaeum everyone would feel, and to an extent was, a somebody. The figures who sat about the library were all manifestly stiff-collaredly, frock-coatedly or gaiteredly eminent somebodies. Myopic, bald and whiskery old Trollope sat scribbling at the table at the far end. The mournful countenance of the Bishop of Bath and Wells drooped, by the fireplace, over that morning's *Times*. The snowy beard of Charles Darwin was spread over the notebooks on one of the library tables. Opposite, the pen of James Froude scratched its frantic and rather angry passage across blank leaves. Others, less celebrated, but no less whiskery, pored over their lamps and their pages. A provincial stranger who had read only the romances of Mr Morris, coming upon these bearded ruminants and not knowing himself to be in the library of the Athenaeum, might have supposed himself to be in a spacious cavern full of elves or wizards, as they silently scratched and wheezed. Here, at least, the professor was among his peers. No one here scoffed at him, and if they met outside the silence room, they even grunted their greetings or spoke to him with whatever cordiality they could muster.

Froude nodded to him across the table as he sat down. Absently, he wrote a letter or two; a brief note to one or two scientists whom he hoped to visit before the Commemoration ball next week; a letter to the Master of Harcourt, confirming that he, his wife and his daughter looked forward to dining with the master before the ball; a curt note to the boy ignoring the embarrassing effusions of his last *Kolossian-*

epistel. But, even at these mundane tasks, Horace Nettleship found it hard to *settle*. The gradual alienation of spirit which was taking place between himself and his daughter was, combined with so much else, gradually breaking his heart. He now felt that he could almost accept the fact that the religion by which he had tried to govern the first forty years of his existence was a falsehood and a sham. He could have accepted the terrible disillusion which this loss of faith had occasioned, and gazed stoically, like Titus at Jerusalem, at vacant seats and empty halls, at a sanctuary with no presence to hallow it and heaven left empty of its God. He could have borne all these things, he told himself, had he had a sympathetic help-meet and spouse. But, life brings forth from its store strange consolations for many of our inconsolables. And he had found it possible to live without the two props of his existence – the knowledge of God and the love of his wife. His childen had enabled him to do it: his son Lionel in whom he took such pride, his daughter Maudie with whom, simply and besottedly, he was in love. The estrangement with Lionel was, he had assured himself, only of that temporary and inescapable kind which divides fathers and sons when sons reach a certain age. All this neo-medieval hocus-pocus would one day be abandoned, and they would be reconciled. The father would, he had decided, proceed gently with the boy, introduce him, perhaps, to some of Huxley's writings, or even take him to meetings, during the Long Vacation, at the Hall of Science.

What Mr Nettleship enjoyed with his daughter was something quite other, an intimacy bordering on romance. With each loss and estrangement, he had been like an acrobatic artist whose fall, though alarming at the second he dropped from the trapeze, was never fatally scaring. He knew, always, that a net was being held beneath him. He fell from faith into the net of marital reassurance. The 'net' provided by his wife was not, in the event, there, but he had tumbled and cascaded on downwards, confident that he would be consoled by his son. The companionship of Lionel had, over a few school holidays, been enough to give the father confidence to resume his position at the top of the circus tent. But, since Lionel's matriculation at Harcourt, there had been little support from *that* net. Still, the acrobat had fallen on, happy, even in his fall, knowing that the last net was the securest of all, and the place where he most, in any case, wanted to be. But the last net was weakening. Maudie had started to use foreign phrases. To be coquettish. To be impatient – was it possible? – of her own father.

He looked about him at the old men bent over their scribbling pens. To an outward observer, he too, perhaps was as old as they; his whiskers were as white, his head quite as bald. And yet he felt all the agony and awkwardness of youth. It was almost as if he were a young swain and Maudie a maiden repelling his advances. He wished that he could dismiss the conclusion that the girl was using her pertness to be deliberately hurtful. He wished, more fundamentally, that her innocence might be taken for granted. Oh, and a thousand times more than her innocence, her love!

He knew that his misery was irrational, but, sitting there in the library, it swept over him in waves. He had intended, after his few necessary letters, to settle down to another chapter in his volcanic survey of the world. It was a work to which he was always adding. Two hours in the Athenaeum, with a number of necessary open books in front of him, would have added a thousand words to the world's knowledge of lava. But he could not settle to it. He was too tormented. And the antique scribblers all round him did nothing to lighten his spirits. He was neither so vain nor so unimaginative as to suppose that they had not, in their lives, suffered as much as he. One scriptural adage which kept its truth whether or not there was a deity, was the certainty that this world was a vale of misery and tears. But the knowledge as he looked at the grey elves of the Athenaeum, that they too had broken their hearts, they too had known the anguish and misery of hearts once warm to them and now grown cold; they too had known the isolated bleakness of intellectual adventure and the stultifying greyness of dead desires, did nothing to console Mr Nettleship. It increased, rather than diminished his suffering, to know that almost all his torments were self-indulgent and, by the strictest practical standards, 'unnecessary'. He had never known want or physical hardship; he had never slept on straw, or watched a starving family rot and fade before his eyes. He had never even, beyond the diurnal threats of toothache and dyspepsia, known anything which could be dignified by the denomination of great physical pain. And yet, his mind was oppressed and clouded to the point where each breath he took was an unendurable agony. At the prospect of losing Maudie's affection, the father realised that he would prefer to lose consciousness itself. Searching in those mental clouds, he could discern no firm reason why he should not do away with himself. It was only, after all, the mummery of the Christians, with their invented hells and purgatories, which suggested anything so improbable as punishment in a future state. Nor was it merely crabbed old eccentrics like Doctor Pusey who insisted upon the truth of this palpable fiction. Intelligent members of the Athenaeum, and subscribers to the London Library, and otherwise intellectually respectable members of civilised society, assented to this hell-belief. The Prime Minister was addicted to it. Had they ever paused to contemplate the *implications* of their creed? The most curmudgeonly of human superiors – the cruellest headmaster, the most extortionate of mill owners, the vilest proprietor of a Stepney sweat-shop, the most relentless litigant in the High Courts would all, at some stage of life, be capable of relenting towards their victims. If they did not forgive their debtors, their pupils, their miserable employees, these savage-breasted human monsters would probably tire of persecuting. For even the most insensitive human spirit can conceive the possibility of forgiveness for even the most heinous of offences. It was only the God of the Christians, the God of Abraham and Isaac and of Jacob, the God of Pusey and Gladstone and Lionel Nettleship, who could not find it in His heart to forgive errant sinners, and who went on for all eternity punishing His victims in a Hell which He had especially constructed for the purpose.

Considering this scheme of things superficially and logically improbable, Mr Horace Nettleship had very few qualms in dismissing it. He could not believe that we did survive the decay and corruption of our mortality, still less in any moral accountability beyond the grave. And, although he believed quite passionately in moral accountability – to all that is strongest and noblest in ourselves – on this side of Death, he still found it impossible to condemn what was, in the ancient civilisations of Rome and Japan, to cite but two examples, considered noble and even necessary. And yet, from day to miserable and tear-drenched day, he stayed alive, hoping against hope that he might regain the love of his daughter. On some days, he even hoped that he might regain the love of his wife; that he would wake and find all the gloom of the previous fifteen years had been but as a dream, and that reconciliation, peace and joy, as in the conclusion of some Dickensian romance, would bless his hearth and glow over his declining years. He knew, truly, that this was an unlikely enough eventuality. He knew, too, that the only major justification for his existence was in the great volcanic treatise. It was in good measure because the book was so important to him that he felt uncertain about its likely completion. If *Nettleship on Volcanoes* were to be finished, then Nettleship himself would probably be finished. But while he could vex himself with reworkings of earlier drafts and chapters, and the knowledge that it could never be a survey as encyclopaedic as his imagination would require, he could brave the heart-struggles of life with a doughtier courage.

Poor Nettleship, the book-lined cavern where he had ensconced himself with the bearded scribblers was no place for a melancholy man. He rose, and paced for a while about the long drawing room. Then he walked down the enormous sweep of stairs once more, and thought that he would read the newspapers in the morning room.

'It is Nettleship, isn't it?' asked a gaitered figure by the chimney-piece. The agnostic started at being addressed by a member of the clerical profession; hardly a reasonable reaction since a good half of the club's members must have been bishops, deans, or, like his present interlocutor, archdeacons.

'It is,' he replied suspiciously.

'How fortunate. I have known you by sight for some time, though my visits to London are perforce all too rare. Gutch is my name. Our boys are great friends together at Harcourt. Indeed, I believe we are all to form a party together. . . .'

'Indeed,' said Horace, wishing heartily it were not so.

'My daughter, Hypatia, and your daughter – I forget Miss Nettleship's name, sir.'

Horace felt no obligation to disclose it, but conceded at length that it was Maud.

From a neighbouring cluster of gentlemen came the roar of unrestrained gossip about George Eliot who, the previous week, had been married to a young man twenty-five years her junior. Since Nettleship and Gutch seemed unable to think of conversational topics of their own, the archdeacon borrowed the theme, snatched it as it were from the air, and said, 'I have never had the pleasure of meeting the lady, nor can I say that I very much admire her books.'

'There, sir, we differ,' said the professor stiffly.

'I am sure she is in every way admirable. . . .'

'She is, sir. It distresses me to hear her made the subject of mere tittle-tattle. She is a neighbour and friend of twenty years' standing, and, surely, though I am no judge of these matters, one of our finest romancers.'

'To tell you the truth, I so much prefer Scott,' said the archdeacon. 'Indeed, in my admiration for Sir Walter I come close to committing the sin of idolatry. If I can not read a novel by Scott, I rarely see the point of reading one at all, though Harrison Ainsworth and Bulwer Lytton can always be read with pleasure.'

Horace was on the point of dissenting from this preposterous assertion when he realised that, if he did so, he would have been 'drawn in' to a conversation with the amiable archdeacon.

'We will meet soon enough with the Master of Harcourt,' he said, managing a rather ghastly smile. 'I unfortunately have a number of engagements before luncheon which compel attention. . . .'

'My dear Nettleship, do not let me delay you a moment longer. Merely to have encountered you,' he added with florid hyperbole, 'is to have made my morning. Until our meeting with the Master of Harcourt, I bid you farewell.' And with a theatrical bow, the archdeacon, who was rather tall, and handsome and bespectacled, made a stately procession in the direction of a side table where he began to peruse the *Pall Mall Gazette*. Having announced that he was in a hurry and implied that he was engaged until the hour of luncheon, the professor had effectually banished himself from the Athenaeum for the rest of the day. Almost certainly, the relentless Gutch would still be sitting there at whatever hour he returned and press his unwelcome attention upon him, with all its reminders of Lionel's lapse into superstition. The fact that Gutch himself looked reassuringly unspiritual did little to compose Nettleship's rumpled humour. There was nothing for it but to retrieve his hat from the palatial hall and walk out into the streets.

Motion, in any case, was said to alleviate melancholy, and for this cause, the professor was given to frequent perambulations. It annoyed him that Gutch had approached. It annoyed him that he had been so gracious and handsome. It annoyed him that he had raised the subject of George Eliot. The lady married? It was the first that Horace Nettleship had known of the matter, and he reckoned himself to be, or to have been, an intimate at the Priory. He did not wish to expose his own ignorance, and he was aware that he had been 'dead to the world' for weeks. Normally, once or twice a month, notes would pass between himself and Charlotte and a rudimentary dinner would be arranged. The Leweses – as they called George Eliot and her former partner – had, on occasion, been privileged to join these parties. If not strictly fashionable, there had been, in Horace Nettleship's belief, an interesting, if unglittering circle of persons entertained at The Bower. While the meals were in progress, his wife responded to him with studied solicitude. Her performances were so successful that sometimes, when a dinner party came to a close, he had believed her attitude towards him to have changed. She had, while the guests were there, allowed him to express endearments to her, to hold her hand, to treat her as any husband might want to treat the wife of his bosom. But, when the last guest had departed, the iciness and the silence would all descend again.

Over the years, very gradually, he thought that perhaps these dinners had become less frequent, and less extensive in their range. George Eliot had not been to the house, now that he considered the matter, for years; not since George Lewes died, which was a year or two since. The Hopkinsons had not been to see them either – a very nice banking family opposite. Indeed, as he paced along, he wondered if the Hopkinsons had been in some way offended by their evening *chez* Nettleship, for they had never asked them back.

Pacing along Pall Mall towards Trafalgar Square, he found his mind suddenly consumed with the question of his social desirability. It had been those fellows in the club talking of George Eliot which started it. Charlotte, he thought, perhaps quoted too much poetry and showed off her 'literary' knowledge. This was not always appreciated. There had been something relentless, some months ago, about the way that she insisted upon telling the doctor's wife about George Meredith's *Modern Love*. She seemed incapable of leaving the subject alone. Horace himself, thinking to widen the discussion so that it might appeal to some of the other guests – a fellow-geologist called Donald- son and the Bursar of University College – had attempted to change the subject, but his wife had been unstoppable. Afterwards, he realised that his guests had not liked it. Nor had he, when he felt, without comprehension, that she was trying to tell him something across the heads of the Donaldsons, something hidden in the poet's lines.

> Warm-lighted looks, Love's ephemerioe,
> Shoot gaily o'er the dishes and the wine.
> We waken envy of our happy lot
> Fast, sweet and golden, shows the marriage lot.
> Dear guests, you have now seen Love's corpse-light shine.

There had been something ostentatious about quoting the poetry, quite above the level of the Bursar's wife. As he contemplated the scene, it seemed to him certain that perhaps they were not asked out with the frequency he would have expected because of this habit of quoting to which his wife was addicted. It was not impossible.

He did not know, because his wife had become in the most absolute sense strange to him. He had slept under the same roof and shared the same board as Charlotte for over twenty years. But for fifteen of those years, since the commencement of the Ice Age, all intercourse between them had been curtailed; weeks could pass, not merely in which they did not speak, but also in which they barely looked at each other. When, like the sudden lifting of Ramadan, the ice was officially melted for guests, and the Nettleships found themselves in society, Horace looked upon Charlotte as an old acquaintance, not seen for many weeks, months or years. The clues and data which she offered were no more than those given by any other animated, well-governed stranger at a dinner party. At the same time, he went on considering this glacial personage as the same little girl he had met, the same maidenly young person he had married in Malvern all those many years previously. He knew, as a matter of scientific observation, that the stranger bore no resemblance to the bride of yore. Who the stranger was, what she was, the icy one, who had come like a supernatural presence to inhabit the body of *his* Charlote, he knew not. Clues were given him, and he darted after the paths they appeared to point down, only to come to a muddle. In the assembly of information required for anything so confident as knowledge of another human soul so much memory was required. In the baffling case of Charlotte, Horace both forgot and remembered too much. He remembered the obsolete evidences of Malvern days. He forgot the clashing and incomprehensible fragments of recent tradition. What or who it was, in short, signified these days by the words Charlotte Nettleship he was in no wise sure. He did not know whether her behaviour might be thought charming, repulsive, intelligent or tedious. He did not know, even, by what standards one might start to assess her physical beauties. There was nothing markedly rational, after all, about considering one arrangement of human features more charming than another. Anthropological scientists had, in any case, made it perfectly clear wildly divergent standards of 'beauty' were applied in different societies: that the stretching of the female neck with rings, or the perforation of the nose was, in primitive cultures considered as becoming as in polite society it would be held revolting. This tribesman thinks to beautify himself by scarring his cheeks or decorating his naked torso with gaudy pigmentation. That foppish European, no less absurdly perhaps, considers his beauty to be enhanced by the cultivation of mutton-chop whiskers or the application of unguents to his carefully crimped and parted hair.

It was not merely the Gods in whom Horace had ceased to believe. He had developed habits of scepticism which applied to all judgments of which his mind was capable. He could no longer muster intellectual arguments to condemn suicide, nor could he find any rational justification for considering one woman more beautiful than the next. This was not to say, however, that the instincts of nature were wholly defunct in him. Even now, this morning, as he advanced into Trafalgar Square, he felt his spirits lift a little. The greybeards of the Athenaeum with their depressing talk were behind him, and it was possible, in the morning air, to forget himself momentarily, to forget the pressing demands of the volcanoes and the domestic tortures of The Bower, as, with something in his step approaching a spring he *could* notice, indeed, could not escape noticing, the charms and attractions of the sex. That beauty over there, for instance, arrested his gaze quite inevitably. A young woman, evidently in love, pawed the arms and shoulders of her husband or fiancé, nuzzling against him in a moment of farewell which revealed without shame to any observer the extent to which she was his slavish adorer. She was a handsome, sprightly young woman in green silk, even from across the road Horace Nettleship could see the pure quality of her complexion and read passion in her high flush and bright glance.

But to describe this process of observation in anything so cumbrous or extended as a sentence is to obscure its momentariness. His glimpse of the pair was for a second or two obscured by a passing omnibus, but before they came back into view, he had recognised his wife with Timothy Lupton. The brief half-moment allowed his heart to heave through three quite distinct sharp experiences. It began as a happy impulse of thinking the woman on the gallery steps very fine and very beautiful. It continued into a felicitous pride, this epiphany, when he discovered that the woman he had so spontaneously admired was the wife of his twenty years' sharing. But this half- or quarter-second of elation was itself shot through with simple, horrified amazement. For there, brazenly, she stood, the adulteress, on the gallery steps with the artist. And there, defying every standard of decency and public morality, the fellow remained, cocksure in his profligacy, as Charlotte hurried down the steps at whose base, at the rank, she was handed by a cabby into an attendant hansom.

FIFTEEN

Commemoration

Maudie had expected to be startled by the strength of over-drawn mannerisms and cultivated eccentricities, by posturing men and affectedly crabby dons. Though these filled the girl with terror in anticipation, she was so certain that they would provide her with dominant impressions over the week in the Clarendon that she had not allowed herself to imagine that she was visiting a place. In fact, Maudie had had no sense of place at all until this visit; and it was the *place* which had overwhelmed her. Even from their first taciturn station-departure from Paddingon the outing had the promised feel of a pilgrimage. They had set out, for trivial reasons effected by the professor's everlasting 'arrangements', in the late afternoon, and journeyed therefore into the gold haze of the westering sun. The very glass and steam and light gold of Paddington had foretold a revelation, but of what kind she could not guess since topopathy had been hitherto dead in her, as in almost all children. True, sense had occasionally demonstrated to her the difference between the sea-shore at Westgate with its sounds and smells and the clatter of St John's Wood High Street. It has been a thing almost entirely of physical sensation and individual *aperçus:* sea-weed, not flower-stalls; nebulously fishy smell and not one of horse-dung; a certain cold dampness in the breeze even on the hottest day. But she had not entertained any particular sense of Westgate, nor of London. She therefore had foretold to herself no imagined sense of this other magic city where brother Lionel had for six months been enchantingly immured.

But even in that steamy golden dream-laden hour from London, the place seemed to be calling her, for she forgot her parents, she forgot the war of silence which they both with such brilliance kept going in their first-class compartment; nor did she even think particularly of the inner dramas which had shaken existence so in former weeks. Mr Chatterway, and grandpapa, and Mr Lupton were all for a moment lost in her stunned appreciation of this miracle. Their first glimpse from the fly that bore them from the station, had been enough to capture her, and to assure her that she was entering upon new experiential territories. The warm air had drowned in bells. A countrified slum had quickly given way to streets and buildings which were not merely of overwhelming beauty, but also which came at you, all of a piece, coherent and complete.

Her father, with a rare piece of consideration, had suggested that the fly drive about the place a little before alighting at the hotel, to 'give Maudie a feel of the place'. So it had done, and she had glimpsed, with choking wonder, the soft stones of churches, libraries and halls, seen, flashing past, crumbling gothic tracery behind the generous profusion of herbaceous borders, seen young men in gowns, lolling beside ancient archways, and tottering clergymen black against the purple abundance of wisteria. Everywhere, bells. The place seemed drunk, crazy with them. And when the little fly had turned into the very sanctum, where university spire and library's dome were formed into a tiny square of warm stone, the cobbles roared with bell-echoes, casting the sounds back from wall to wall to honey-coloured crumbling wall.

There had been many of the things she had dreaded, in the ensuing days. Hotel life with the parents had been brittle, particularly since, on their very first evening, Mr Lupton of all people should have called there to leave his card. He was there to paint the Master of Harcourt's portrait. Papa had received his card without a word; handed it to Mama with absolute silence; and, leaving his two womenfolk to their own devices for the evening, he had strode forth to make his own visits to luminaries of the geological world. Mr Lupton had not, Maudie was happy to own, repeated his call to the hotel. Whether either of her parents had met the painter in the course of this visit she did not much care. Her chief preoccupation had been with Lionel, combined as it was with this dizzy discovery of *place*.

'This is Addison's Walk,' he informed her as they walked down the straight avenue of trees with the thickness of June meadow abundant on either side. He liked to tell her all the particularities of form and nomenclature. She was already, after only two days, the mistress of them – scouts, the Giler, the Maggers Memugger, Responsions, Little-go, the High and the Broad, Schools, the Jenker (already the Jenker to her though still to the mater and pater 'the Master of Harcourt'), Jaggers, Tom and his hundred and one, the Plain, Port Meadow, Jericho – all this esoteric terminology now conveyed something to her. Lionel, moreover, though unquestionably an enthusiast, had not, as she had dreaded, been lost to her by his spiritual and academical transmogrifications. He was still the same dear boy, with his thick, springy curly hair, his pale face, his waxy nose and ears tending to redness. She was proud to take his arm as, blazered and straw-hatted, he prosed to her about the essayist and hymn-writer who gave the place its name.

'And all that is Magdalen?' she asked. 'How different the New Buildings' (she learnt fast!) 'are from the old tower and cloisters. They seem like my picture of a French *château*.'

'I'm afraid they have all the wordly qualities of the so-called enlightenment which created that style of architecture. There's nothing in it to *uplift* you. Gutch sneers at the Gothic – his tutor at Brazen Nose has taught him to, don't you know. But you can't deny that it tries to drag us all heavenwards. . . .'

'Darling Lionel. I'm *so* fond of you.'

'Of course I owe everything to Gutch. He taught me the outlines of the faith. But I am coming to feel that it might be left to me to give it *back* to him one day when he has come down out of his aesthetic cloud. Does it sound to you very self-righteous to speak in that way?'

'I think Mr Gutch is most amusing,' she said, a trifle guardedly. 'I have been afraid, well, that he would want me to talk just about church-things. And instead he was such a fund of stories yesterday when he came to dine at the hotel.'

She repeated the insolence of a waiter, once, to an uncle of Gutch's at Goodwood. Strange, both their hearts were swollen with the importance of the previous few months. Lionel had received his Lord and Saviour into his life. The joy and peace which had followed were of a kind which words could barely describe: but he knew that it must be his life's work to describe them, and to pass on to others the wonderful tidings of salvation. Even if the unspeakable heights could not be put into conversation, he could at least have told Maudie of the books he had read, the sermons he had heard. Above all, he could have described the evening in the town hall when Father Cuthbert, the mission preacher, had held the crowds spellbound. But instead, they repeated to one another stories of Gutch's relations.

Maudie for her part had tales to convey which alike eluded articulation. She wanted to say what had happened in St John's Wood, but she became aware as the words fluttered to her brain and died on her lips that she equally wanted to say what had happened to *her*. The stodgy meals had continued to be absorbed in silence. The lessons in German and Greek had proceeded. But, ah! the lessons. There was grandfather. There was the return of Mr Chatterway. There was the sudden and highly embarrassing spurt of drawing lessons with Mr Lupton. There had been all his beard-closeness, the coming-near of his large square fingers as her own tiny white hands clutched the pencil, the smell of brandy on his sensual lips. These things could not quite be told. Earlier, they would have been things like Mr Goe's adoring foolishness, about which the two of them, Lionel and she, would have shrieked and giggled. But now there was something different. Mr Goe had created his own minor dramas, it was true. There were the sharp intakings of papa's breath whenever the clergyman was mentioned, and her mother's dismissal of the curate as 'an idiot, but an amiable idiot'. But Greek was one of life's necessaries. Of this there was complete agreement in The Bower. Drawing was a different matter, a superfluity. And from Mr Lupton's first carpet-crawling and her father's first sight of the painter as he retrieved the handle-less cup at the tea party, Maudie had been aware that the age of innocence was over. The intrusion, almost the explosion, of Mr Lupton into the secret life of herself and her mother had somehow changed everything. She did not know what had happened, she only knew that it was all so dangerous that she had had to lie about it to her father and (her own guilty secret) gossiped about it to the banished exile of Half Moon Street.

When the story of Gutch's uncle was done and they had laughed, they paced for a little while without speaking. The fresh new moist green leaves danced high above their heads, bright against the clear blue sky. The water meadows to the right and left were specked with yellow flowers in the long grasses.

'When you come home,' she tried, 'you'll find things different.'

'Don't say the mater's redecorated the parlour.'

'It's not wallpaper.'

'But I liked the wallpaper. You mean she's painted it?'

'No.' Again a laugh and a squeeze of his arm. She wanted to say how reassuring it was to have someone to squeeze after so many weeks of no affection at all.

'That's a relief.'

'I mean. . . .'

'Oh, Maudie, I'm sure Mama's right, and you shouldn't be out with that cough.'

'It's. . . .' When the fit had subsided, she could say, 'It's all right. I am *determined* to go to the ball.'

'She seemed quite as determined to stop you.'

'It isn't because of my cough'. This was blurted out. It was the beginning of the declaration. With Lionel, it would be possible to explore the truth. For all his astounding self-absorption, he knew enough of their mother to be able to grasp, surely, what she was trying to say without a cascade into explanations. 'Lionel, other people's parents aren't like ours. They're *not*.'

'I dare say they aren't.' There was a hint of hurt in his tone.

'The Bower's been so miserable since you went up to the Varsity, it has really. I'm so looking forward to your coming home for the holidays.'

'I'm not sure how I'm going to spend the Long,' he said loftily.

'Oh, but you don't mean you won't be coming home? That would be too beastly of you.'

'Of course I'm coming home for some of the time. But one of the tutors at Harcourt is having a reading party in August and I really ought to join that. And then Gutch. . . .'

'Gutch!'

'As you know, he's taken Schools now so he'll be going down. I shall miss him next year when he's gone.'

'Just as we have missed you at home *this* year.'

'He's going to be ordained at Christmas. His pater has given him permission to go and live at the clergy house in Holborn with Father Mackonochie and Father Stanton. It's dashed decent of the arch-deacon, 'cause it's not his sort of religion at all. I dare say he hopes that Gutch will get all that sort of thing out of his system in a few months. Certainly there's no hope for preferment if you serve your title at such a place.'

'I suppose not'. She was not sure what a title was, nor what it was that made Holborn, from a theological point of view, so different from anywhere else in England.

'I might even go down and help him a bit during this Long. I dare say there is always work to do there. Those men like Stanton work without ceasing among the poor.'

After a little silence she said, 'Lionel, you know how upsetting Papa finds all this.'

'Is that what's made everything so different? At home, I mean? I suppose he *was* pretty cut up about it when I wrote to tell him that I want to be ordained. I don't expect *him* to understand. I'm sorry if it's made life tough for you too, Maudie.'

'Oh, Lionel, I'm so frightened.'

'You're as bad as the pater. Anyone would think I'd said I was going to live in a leper colony.'

'No, it isn't that. I will be truthful and say that I was upset when I thought you wanted to be a clergyman. Darling, I know it all *matters* to you so. But you can't imagine how *foolish* the clergy seem to the rest of us.'

Something came to the lips of Lionel about the wisdom of this world being made foolish and the foolish things wise. But his sister had now darted tangentially away from the subject.

'But, you old silly, I'll love you *always*, whether or not you wear a white linen night-shirt and spend your life giving soup to the poor.'

'Maudie it *isn't*. . . .'

Her words continued and drowned his. 'You don't understand what frightens me. It isn't you as a parson. It's me, on my own with *them* when you've gone for a parson.'

'With the mater and the pater.'

'With *them*. Oh, it has become simply horrid. Why are they so beastly to each other, and so sort of mad? It is as if they hate each other.'

'Maudie, you can't *mean.* . . .'

'I think mama would be happy if papa died tonight.'

She announced it calmly, stilly. They heard their own footsteps on the gravel of the path. Suddenly the trilling birds in the trees overhead seemed callous in their jabberings. The two held to each other a little more closely so that an observer might have taken them for sweethearts. With something of the furtiveness of lovers, they now looked downwards as they strode. They were not lovers walking in Eden in all the innocence of early joy, but possessed of the guilty knowledge and certain that paradise, such as it had been, was lost. In Maudie's bosom there was a gush of pain which was almost like relief, even though she was aware that what she had said had wounded her brother and shot through all the sunny confidence of his high spiritual serenity.

It was appropriate that, as they parted from the happy garden, some angel with a flaming sword should have been there to preside over their banishment. But as they rounded the corner, having finished the circuit of the meadow, and made over the little bridge to re-enter the college through the high wrought-iron gates, they did not expect to meet Mr Chatterway. Used to him as a black-garmented figure, Maudie did not at first recognise the grey-hatted, grey-coated, white-spatted embodiment of summer elegance who grinned at them.

'There is a lazy but far from foolish pike lolling down there under the stone,' he drawled, leaning on the parapet of the bridge and waving a silver-knobbed cane in the direction of the water. 'Like you two, avoiding the eights.'

'Marvo!'

'We *agreed*,' he reproached her.

'Mr Chatterway, then.'

'Why, good afternoon, sir,' said Lionel raising his straw boater. 'My sister had told me that you were in England, but I had no idea. . . .'

'Like to come down for the eights, invited by my old chum the Rector of Lincoln, no less, whose wife is one of my very *oldest* friends, and whose household, as you may imagine, buzzes with a certain subject not for ears either as juvenile or as censorious as your own.'

'Is Pattison resigning?' asked Lionel.

'No fear. And he shows no signs of dying either, which would be more to the point. As full of acid as ever about your own revered

Master, dear boy. Positively spits poison at the very mention of the name Jenkinson.'

'Which guarantees that you name him as often as possible,' said Maudie.

'Little Miss Pert.'

'I know no one at Lincoln,' said Lionel, as though that finished the matter of the Pattisons. But Maudie was a natural gossip and wanted to know what the 'news' was with which the sour old Rector's lodgings 'buzzed.'

'Suffice it for your tender if not as innocent as you would like us all to believe ears that they know rather more than should be known about poor old Charles Dilke.'

'Really?'

'Crawford, apparently the woman's called. . . .' His voice trailed off into an almost inaudible groan. 'What is it that that book you're so fond of says, Lionel? "How are the mighty fallen," what. There'll be trouble in that quarter, mark my words. You aren't quite a papist yet I gather?'

'Oh, Lionel!' Maudie, genuinely shocked, turned to her brother as though there was something he should have told her.

'No, sir.' He blushed badly.

'Otherwise you might have heard from Dr Manning, perhaps. I believe he has Dilke's *ear*, or Dilke has his. Rum business, very. But *anyway*,' the word declared the subject closed, and his conversational pace quickening, he hurried on to the next subject of moment, 'your father has been round seeing professors of science. Didn't know there were so many myself. Lunched in Merton, I believe, and spending the afternoon in the labs peering at some stones some tomfool character has been collecting in South Parks Road.'

'Really, sir. Did he tell you that was how he was passing his day?' asked Lionel. As it happened, the boy knew that it was true, but he wondered who had informed Mr Chatterway.

'No, no. Just something one *gathered*. And the beautiful Mrs Nettleship, what of her? Mrs Pattison sent messages to you all saying that you were welcome to join them on the Lincoln barge. I felt sure that you, Lionel, would feel that your college loyalty was as threatened by appearing on the barge of an aquatic rival, just as your theological principles would be compromised, what, but taking a cucumber sandwich off a self-confessed infidel like Pattison. Am I right, sir?' He did not stay for an answer, but continued, 'while you, Maudie, were so anxious to be alone with your brother that you would be shameless in your neglect of all social duties. It was left, I fancy, to your mother alone to go to tea with the Pattisons. They are old friends of Eggy, of course, so they would have much to talk about even if they weren't entertaining our brilliant young friend.'

'And who might that be?' asked Lionel. Maudie, who had not released her brother's arm, once more squeezed it tightly to avoid the painful revelation, but there was no stopping Marvo's desire to impart wounding information.

'There's considerable anxiety in the Pattison camp that he should paint Jenkinson with rather more warts than he has and rather more all. I shouldn't be surprised if Mark were not bribing our young Michelangelo to make the famous portrait as ugly as possible.'

'Really, Mr Chatterway. That's quite enough,' said Maudie.

'But since you are all on your own and a mile from the barge in question where your mother doubtless sits Cleopoatra-like though surrounded by poops of the nincom rather than gilded variety, perhaps I can persuade you to take counsel and or tay with me?'

'It is for me,' said Lionel, who had understood not one word in ten of Mr Chatterway's conversation, 'to offer tea to you.'

'Then let us stroll,' said the old gentleman, 'in the direction of Harcourt, and shun the overwhelming temptation of walking back through New College whose verbally infelicitous Warden has quite a party, including his pretty niece Kitty, and a young man who, if all impressions and accounts are to be believed, makes one think that not every parson in the world is a bonehead. Name of Inge, I believe. Perhaps there's hope for the Reverend Lionel yet, what?'

SIXTEEN

A Lamb for the Sacrifice

'There is more faith in honest doubt, doesn't dear Tennyson say?' The high-pitched squeaky voice of the Master of Harcourt rang out in reply to some observation of Nettleship's. But in spite of the import-ance of the subject under discussion, Dr Jenkinson had his eye on all his company and did not conceal his anxiety that dinner should start late. His pink face and round cheeks seemed particularly florid above the high white collar and white tie. He fidgeted nervously with the swallow-tails of his coat as though his fingers were accustomed to feeling an academical gown about his shoulders and now, in the wider conviviality of the social gathering before him, he felt bereft.

'But why is it *faith*, that is what I cannot understand,' persisted Horace Nettleship. All the indications were that the Master did not wish to plunge into these profundities five minutes before dining. But the professor was one of those, evidently, who felt that if faith *were* possible, it could only be possible on the honest and intellectually respectable terms of the Master of Harcourt.

'The truth – devotion to the truth – passing into a knowledge of the True,' squeaked the Jenker without quite looking at Nettleship. 'Ah, *dear* Lady Bayswater.' And with the arrival of this considerable dowager, the party was complete.

This was no college dinner but a private affair got up by Jenker for some of the grander folks from London and the shires. Some thirty people were to eat together before going on to the ball. The young had made their own arrangements. Lionel and Maudie were dining with Gutch and his sisters at the Clarendon and trying to pass as jolly an hour as possible in the circumstances. The outburst of their mother had been so uncharacteristic that they were all shaken, disgusted. She herself, now splendid in her swooping evening gown in the Master's lodgings at Harcourt, was still frozen and appalled with herself.

Archdeacon Gutch, an amiable man whose chief subject of conver-sation seemed to be standing stone circles or henges, had taken her arm and was leading her into dinner. Charlotte nodded, smiled, agreed. Nothing could be more certain than that men once worshipped the sun. Its very rarity value in Wiltshire would be enough to explain the existence of Stonehenge or the circle at Avebury. A polite laugh at the Archdeacon's pleasantry; but her mind churned and heaved with self-loathing. How *could* she? How *could* she, on the very day of the ball, have tried to prevent Maudie from attending it? It was true that there was something very tiresome about the dreadful sea-lion bark which the child seemed unable to control. But had she really believed Maudie to be unequal to the evening she would have insisted that she remained behind in London – perhaps that the whole expedition be cancelled. There was really no need, after all, for the Nettleships to make so much of Everard Gutch's university career coming to an end. Neither Horace nor Charlotte had met the boy until this week. Doubtless he was pleasant enough, though she continued to blame him for Lionel's latest fever of enthusiasm. And was it not irregular for a young man in his first year, as Lionel was, to be attending a Commem. at all? It was meant for old stagers.

'I should dearly love to visit the *Orcadian* sites,' continued the Archdeacon, 'but I daresay I never shall. The belief that these ancient places of worship are merely circular cattle-pens is one which I most *emphatically* reject. . . .'

But how, once the thing had been set up and begun and allowed to continue, could she have sunk to such peevishness? It was extraordinary. Horace had spent the day in his laboratory-perambulations. Lionel and Maudie had slipped off on their own. This had caused her a momentary pang of distress, it is true, but she was always glad to see the Pattisons, and the river had been enchantingly pretty, with the barges all fluttering with banners and bunting, and everyone dressed in summer finery. Much compensation here for the loss of her children's company for a couple of hours. Indeed – such was the muddle in her heart at the moment, she had felt maternal gladness to see Lionel and Maudie so happy together, so eager to be alone, so unaffected, it would seem, by Lionel's Damascene transformation.

Then! Even as vile old Mr Pattison was passing the little plates of shrimps, her Adonis had appeared on top of the barge. She had known he was in the town, and half-expected him to be glimpsed later at the Master of Harcourt's dinner. But his appearance in the enemy camp was enough to unbalance all her composure over the tea tables. There could be no doubt either that he was equally surprised to see her there, for a blush – what exquisite guilt there had been in that blush – hurried through all his features and glowed even through the thick silky softness of the golden beard. He had looked, in honesty, such a perfection of beauty that she had been afraid, at his sudden white flannel apparition, the ruddy health of the neck swathed in white silk, the very abundance of his blonde hair springing from a sunburnt brow, the virility of his hands clutching his straw hat, of fainting into an ecstasy. Manners had somehow rescued her. A full eight days – strictly accurate it was more like nine – had passed since their first serious tryst outside the Regent Street emporium, their wild farewell on the gallery steps. It would have been possible, since then, surely to meet. She had gone through many violent changes of mood in the period – fury with him for his timidity, pity for his innocence, simple crossness a million times intensified with *Horace*.

She had felt twinges of worry about Maudie's cough. But with a large part of herself she had been 'dead to the world'. *Blasée*, Maudie had (a little surprisingly – where did she pick up her vocabulary?) called it when her mother had refused to gasp and shriek at each spire and the chime of each bell as they arrived in the 'home of lost causes'. Somnambulistic, had been her demeanour until the electrifying beauty of the white-flannel God shot into view at the Pattisons' tea table. It is hardly worthy of remark that, at that moment, she had been thinking about him but it is perhaps pertinent to say that she had been thinking about him in a particular way. For an undercurrent of talk at the Pattisons', when open malice against other dons was momentarily discarded, was the marital unhappiness of a certain Mrs Crawford and . . . Sir Charles Dilke! The thing was only alluded to; it was covert, it was not even clear what line, if any, was taken, except in so far as Mrs Pattison made clear that she thought this woman was a liar and, if women could be so described, a scoundrel. But the hints and murmurings were in themselves disquieting enough. On the one hand there was the thrilling suggestion behind much that was not said, that even though this irregularity were perhaps the product of a wicked woman's fancy, such extra-marital unions were far from uncommon. Charlotte felt as she captured the nuances of the shrimp-symposium, the moral gulf which divided her own household in St John's Wood from the decadent sophistication of the Pattisons' friends in Mayfair or Chelsea. Her own thoughts, cravings, longings and passionate desires over the previous weeks had thrilled her in part because of their complete outrageousness, their near-unattainability. But here, while the boats glided by and the coloured pinnaces fluttered over the river barges and boathouses and the dons munched brown bread rolls and butter, it was apparently accepted as a normal part of the human predicament. There was prurience in their tut-tutting. But – she noticed it at once – there was an absence of real *shock*, or rather there was a studied attempt in all the talk to adopt an attitude of unshockability. Very strange, this, in a seat of godliness and good learning! She was not such a fool – indeed, she was no kind of fool – as to suppose that this impermeability was not cultivated. The Pattisons were different, determinedly so, from the others. Free thought might lead readily enough to free love – though love in such a quarter seemed a queer word to be using. But even the knowledge that this *acceptance* of what had, or had not, passed between Sir Charles Dilke and Mrs Crawford was in itself a contrivance *pour épater les autres* did not release Charlotte Nettleship from its hold. She departed from the tea barge *corrupted*. She had departed, moreover, not unaccompanied, for Mr White-flannels Lupton scampered along at her side and insisted that they walked a couple of times up and down the Long Walk together until their few hours' separation before dinner at Harcourt. Her awareness of him during this *display* (how else could one describe a walk with a married woman in a public place?) was of an uncompromising and physical kind – the glistening of a sunburnt face, the very lightness of white flannel against thighs – and the whole walk produced in her a new temptation, something wildly anarchic and surprising. In all the Dilke conversation she realised that she had not been scorning the guilty pair whose most intimate doings were now the conversational property of strangers, nor had she been pitying them though that would have been a reaction natural enough. It was envy that Charlotte Nettleship had felt; simple envy, of those who were beyond the pale. Was it not in its fashion, a way of escape: not to be obliged any longer to pretend; not to be imprisoned in the round of conventions and obligations, dinners and cards. That had been, as she now understood, Mr Chatterway's freedom, and his tragedy. He was, if not beyond it, as close to the pale as anyone she knew; had been this quarter century. But there was no one of her acquaintance (herein the tragedy) with a more devoted knowledge of the pale, a more encyclopaedic sense of its vagaries, a more eager nose pressed against its glass. Strangers and exiles; perhaps she was about to join them. Although she felt, welling within her, a great *crossness* with Mr Lupton for his failure to materialise in London in the previous three weeks, her momentary happiness in his physical presence was so intense that all other emotion passed out of her. She would, during these moments in the dusty Long Walk, its torrid heat and maddening warm breeze, have been prepared to yield herself totally to whatever he proposed. Nature had made them, this was what she felt, Nature had forced them into this position. The enraging wind and the scorching summer sun poured out benediction on their bodies and made them man and wife. Yes, made them so!

But he had talked so shyly, demurely as a parlour-maid.

'I have naturally . . . thought *much* about our last. . . .'

'Encounter,' she had had to help him. 'It was for you to suggest another.' No names now. No 'Mr Luptons' or 'Mrs Nettleships'.

'And above all, your sense that Maudie' – he had been hardly able to say the word – 'Maudie should not be, I forget quite how you expressed it, but. . . .'

'Manipulation was implied.'

'There was something which was never spelt out clearly between us. I mean in our last talk in London. I feel that I owe it to myself, as well as to you and your family to set the matter straight in my mind.'

'Say on.' She was now shamelessly kittenish, for she had felt in that minute that she had power over him, a power which would outlast the conventional mouthings which he so childishly felt the need to utter.

'Does your husband, does Mr Nettleship, that is, the professor, does *he*. . . .'

He stumbled. She helped him.

'Not for many years,' she said. 'If you speak of the affections, perhaps never. Not in the sense you are asking about. Does that answer your question, my tender-hearted searcher?'

There had been a shocked silence.

'I had meant, Mrs Nettleship, does your husband know that I have been teaching Maudie to draw?'

Why had he chosen to wound her with this gratuitous *cruel* teasing? He had drawn out of her the most intimate information which a woman could ever give another; that he had done so deliberately there could be absolutely no question. But then, cautious as a ballet dancer, he had skipped away from the implications of his discovery and asked only of the drawing lessons and, odious phrase, her *husband*. She had been, in consequence, on her return to the Clarendon, in a state of taut weariness. But, for the first time since the whole business had begun, she felt her anger directed not against her lord and gaoler, but against Maudie. It was one thing, during the drawing lessons themselves, and even during their first independent tryst in the London streets, for Mr Lupton to keep up the fiction between them that they were chiefly concerned with protecting the child. It was another, altogether, to intrude references to her into a discussion such as *theirs* in the Long Walk. The mother, during her indignant walk back to the hotel, had suddenly begun to view her pathetic over-excitable daughter in a different regard. There had been the matter, referred to with such giggling frequency of the insane governess, Miss Adeney. There was the abject doting of Professor Nettleship himself. In the mood which then overtook her, Charlotte had told herself that her husband's affections had been alienated by the *child,* and felt as though she, to whom those affections were most repulsive, minded the alienation. The mother was shocked to find in herself such wells of resentment against the beloved daughter. How could she mind old Nettleship's pathetic fondling of the child, his rubbing of stubby white fingers through her chestnutty hair? But she did, Charlotte did. It was now, she said, *all of a piece*. The absurd devotion, the simpleton's laughter, of the curate. The intense gleam in Fräulein Schwartz's eyes as she discussed Maudie's progress in strong verbs. . . . It was all a repetition of the same story, the child's power to bewitch. Not the least tiresome example of it, from Charlotte's point of view, had been the way, doubtless through her own clumsiness, she seemed to have *lost* Mr Chatterway altogether. She did not suppose that Maudie actually saw the old man. But she was not blind. She saw the notes brought hither and thither by postmen. And now, at this stage of her inner drama, Charlotte, who was so alone in her journey beyond the pale, felt that she would have valued the company of a man who had done the pilgrimage and returned, more or less alive. Maudie had taken that, too. She was emotionally greedy, the child. That was how the mother saw it. She wanted to snatch all the cream cakes, and all the cherry tarts and, not content with such triumphs, she wanted to wolf down all the bread and butter too. She was not content until the whole world bowed the knee to her in adoration: parlourmaids, professors, exiled roués . . . it was of its essence unthinkable that Mr Lupton should subscribe to the cult in quite the manner of Fräulein Schwartz or Mr Goe. There was surely enough understanding between intelligent persons of mature years to avoid any such confusion. But Charlotte felt angered almost to madness by the fact that even in this sacred area of life, the first sacred area she had penetrated in nigh on forty years, the name of Maudie should be raised; and that even Love might itself be interrupted, if not squashed, by the infant's confounded lessons and arrangements! Such, more or less, had been Charlotte's frame of mind when she returned to the Clarendon. In the hotel yard Mr Gutch stood, an innocent, grinning, lofty young man, who said, 'Good afternoon, Mrs Nettleship. We quite thought you had all got lost.'

'All, Mr Gutch?' Why was he speaking as though Commemoration were his own private house party and all the visitors to the town his guests?

'Professor Nettleship was accounted for. He had calls to make. But I am sorry to have missed you at the eights. As for Lionel and Maudie, well – as you can see.' He grinned. He spoke of the brother and sister as if they were a happy pair who had just announced their intention of getting married. How dare he? How dare, for that matter, Maudie behave in this way, and *monopolise* Lionel? It was unhealthy. Hot, tired, confused, Charlotte had felt anger welling inside her. And there they had been, standing by the stable doors with the ostler, another triumph for Maudie, for the knock-kneed old man in his shirt sleeves had doffed his cap and was grinning with toothless devotion towards the girl.

'Oh, Mama, isn't Mr Atwood an *angel*.' This individual, to signify that he was the angelic Atwood, touched his forelock to Mrs Nettleship. 'He says the day after tomorrow we can have a wagonette and go out to *explore*. Woodstock, Lionel says, but Mr Gutch thinks, where was it?'

'Kingston Bagpuize. I just thought you might be amused because one of my great aunts was married there.'

Well, perhaps they were no longer quite children, but she could not tolerate them making arrangements behind her back. There was little doubt that the expedition with the wagonette included her. Soon young Gutch would be absorbed into the circle of worshippers. There was no rational explanation for her outburst. 'I never heard of such a suggestion,' was all she had said before sweeping into the hotel. But, once in their rooms the fur had flown. Maudie had an infuriating tendency to burst into tears without provocation. There were tears soon enough on that occasion. Then, more coughing. 'It is out of the question that you should go galloping around the county with strange young men whom you have never met.' 'But Mama, Lionel would be with us. Mr Gutch is not strange. We are supposed to be having a party with the Gutches this very evening.' 'If you think you are going to the ball, you are much mistaken.' 'Mama!' 'Your terrible cough forbids it. You know that your attendance at the ball was conditional upon your *resting* during the afternoon. We now gather that you have spent the entire day gallivanting.'

Charlotte hated herself for allowing the conversation to become so uncontrolled. It was, she knew as soon as she issued the ultimatum, ridiculous to have made this journey for the Commem. if they were not to attend it. Whoever heard of not doing something because of a cough? But the injunction was made. She had heard it flying from her lips. *Maudie was not to go to the ball.* Lionel had protested. He had done so on the feeblest possible grounds. Who would Everard (Mr Gutch apparently) have to dance with? And, he would *go to Papa*. Well, let him. The young people, were in any case, with proctorial dispensation, supping together at a private room hired by Gutch at the Clarendon before joining their elders in the hall of Harcourt for the dancing. Horace, who, since his arrival in the town had been keeping up a lugubrious grin, did not reveal, in the hansom which conveyed them from the hotel to the college, whether he had been *gone to*, and if so, what his judgment had been. The grin, partly Charlotte supposed for appearance's sake, was also inspired by his inner confidence that here, among intellectual folk, he was being a conspicuous social success. The talk in the northern suburbs of the town, of Lava, had evidently been rewarding. The chats, on the border of the Parks, about Limestone, had been distinctly jolly. But he was not so hilariously dislodged from convention that he would attempt to address a word to his wife in private. As soon as they reached the Master's lodgings, it was all, 'My darling, may I present you to Doctor Jenkinson', an absurd solecism, since the Master had known her since she was a little girl, and had even met the professor a number of times before. Adding blunder to ineptitude, Horace had started to talk about religion and challenge even the slender threads of faith to which the Jenker was alleged to cling. Charlotte, drifting through the politenesses, and led into dinner by Archdeacon Gutch, was in a sea of misery. The day thus spent passed and repassed before her as the churchman discussed standing stones and slurped his turtle soup. She agonised about her daughter. If Maudie did not come to the ball, all pleasure in it would be ruined for Charlotte. She had so looked forward to helping the child with her dress, perfecting her hair, lending her jewellery. Her first ball! Forbidden at the last moment! Charlotte wanted almost to send a message back to the Clarendon to insist that the child be brought along by Lionel and his friends. But there was a strange stubbornness still in the mother's heart. She knew that if Maudie *did* appear, and looking a terrible frump with no one to dress her or groom her, it would be in direct defiance of her mother's expressed wishes, so the child's chaotic and unkempt appearance later in the evening would, if it happened, be not only a public reproach to the mother but a private victory. It would mean that she had been to Horace and that the professor had overruled his wife.

'Such a happy conjunction,' the archdeacon was saying. He had abandoned the henges. 'My son Everard is not, I should have guessed, very much of an adept at the dance. But I know that he has been looking forward *intensely*. . . .'

'Oh, indeed.' This was worse torture. Should she warn him that Maudie was unlikely to appear?

'And what very handsome children, Mrs Nettleship, you have. It is kind of you all to come and make up our party. In my day at the Varsity we never made so much of Commem. I had heard from various cousins that it was now, as they say, the thing, so I naturally was highly delighted when Dr Jenkinson suggested we all came.'

'It was a very happy idea.'

She could almost weep when she said it. Her son, thanks to the idiot-influence of the archdeacon's child, had almost broken his father's heart by becoming a church mouse. That father, Horace, there he was, further down the table, waxy and pale, a stranger to her though twenty years and more her husband; a man whom she had hated, but also the individual in the world whom she most pitied. Maudie, who had been looking forward to this evening for several months, and prided herself on the excellence of gown, hair, ribbons, shoes, was sobbing and coughing in some lonely hotel room. And she, Charlotte, heaved and tossed on the seas of lust for the man she could glimpse at the far end of Dr Jenkinson's table. Yes, he was there! And in the weakness of her desire for him she could almost have cried out with longing, though with each breath she took, she felt the full torture and farce of the thing; she, a mother and a wife, she, the matriarch of a family! Yes, it was a happy idea.

'Everard has been, well, I would not say difficult because he has not. But his mother and I have sometimes felt him to be too solitary. He has a most singular fascination with the *church*.'

'I should have thought that would please you, archdeacon.'

'Pray don't mistake me, dear lady. Nothing could please me more than the flourishing of a healthy, a *manly* religion. But I am sure that you would agree with Doctor Jenkinson that not all the developments in modern religion have been, shall we say, *wholesome?*'

'I know very little, archdeacon, beyond what goes on in St John's Wood parish church. And that seems to me wholesome enough.'

'Indeed, indeed. But there are *excesses*. Much of the so-called religious revival in recent years, is not I regret to say, to be welcomed. It has been superstitious. We must all, surely, contrive to use the intellects which the Almighty gave us. I do not feel that all the movements in the church at the moment are very interested in the God-given power of *mind*.'

'Perhaps not.' She thought of how Maudie's tear-stained face would be unfitting her for the ball, even if the child could be rescued and brought along, after all. She caught the eyes, far away, beyond the polished mahogany and the rows of glasses, knives and forks and plates, of Timothy Lupton, his golden beard like a lion's mane falling into the stiff white of his shirt-front.

'I do not know if Lionel has apprised you of Everard's plans?'

'No, no, he has not.'

'His mother and I are *distraught*. He proposes to spend the summer, if you please, in the ritualist church at Holborn. Now I am sure that these clergymen in their way mean very well. But I have three very grave objections to them. First, what they are teaching is erroneous and grossly superstitious. Secondly the rituals which they perform are completely illegal. Why, they wear Roman Catholic costumes, they make no secret of the fact that they encourage their people to use the confessional. It is not often a word I use. But Mackonochie and his men are *papists*.'

'I do so hope Lionel won't get interested', said Charlotte. This was all rather worse than she had feared since the first coming-in of the Ephesian-epistles.

'My third objection to that church in Holborn outweighs the other two and is very important indeed,' said the archdeacon. 'It is this. I have not the smallest doubt that those men are socialists.'

'You can't be serious, archdeacon. Whatever else you may say about them they are, I take it, clergymen of the Church of England.'

'I wish I shared your confidence, Mrs Nettleship. There is, moreover, no excuse for it. They are gentlemen, or *were* until they forfeited any claim to be so regarded. They have a curate there by the name of Stanton. His family and mine, as it happens, are not merely acquainted but actually related by marriage. He was educated, as I was myself, at Rugby, and he went on to Balliol, I believe. There was absolutely nothing to stop him having a useful and decent career in the Church if he felt that this was the way his talents could best be exercised. But, against all advice, and with the greatest stubbornness, he went and attached himself to this infernal place. That part of London is infested with crime and disease, and 'undesirable elements' of every kind. Why Fagin's lair is in the very parish. And can one doubt where it will end if gentlemen go to live in such a place and put it about in the heads of the foolish and disgruntled poor that they are prepared to live on the same level as themselves? Why, it is revolutionary. It is *disgusting*. My only prayer is that Everard, after a few months of it, sees the error of his ways. I feel that to speak too harshly about it to the lad would only inflame his misplaced enthusiasm. 'Let him go', that was my cousin Hypatia's advice. I turn to her when in difficulties. 'Let him go and smell the poor. It will soon have him running back to you.' I have fixed the matter with the bishop. He will be made deacon at Michaelmas if things go according to plan and I do not have the smallest doubt that I can ease him into the living of Willerton Magna by next Christmas at the latest.'

'I hope, archdeacon, that you will be successful.'

'I mention these things, Mrs Nettleship, lest you had *wondered*.'

'It is all very interesting.' She had not wondered at all about Everard Gutch. In fact, the *égoisme à la famille* of the Gutches had only lately begun to impinge on her consciousness.

'A handsome parsonage house in one of the richest parts of Herefordshire. It would, you see, be an altogether pleasant place in which to exercise his ministry. His mother is so anxious that he should. . . .'

But with a forkful of turbot in mid-air, even the archdeacon held back from the ultimate vulgarity of explaining the exact nature of Mrs Gutch's anxiety. Charlotte began to divine it very clearly. They were afraid that Everard Gutch, being a shy young man of monkish disposition, would be so swept along by the tide of ritualism that he would not *settle* to the infinitely important task of peopling the world with more Gutches. Maudie, apparently, after a couple of days' acquaintance, had passed whatever test the archdeacon and his wife applied to the eligible maidens whom they chanced to encounter.

'I hope he will be very happy,' she said vacantly, thinking with horror of how she, as a child, had been sacrificed in a doubtless similar way. She gazed down the table once more, and down the wrecked vista of all the wasted years in which she had been Mrs Nettleship. She tried to gaze towards Mr Lupton, but she caught only her husband's eye and turned quickly again to her own place, where a hot plate had been laid. The atmosphere gently filled with the ancient sacrificial odour of cooked lamb, as waiters bore that delicacy to the table, with steaming tureens of new potatoes and glistening little mountains of bright green peas.

SEVENTEEN

Slices of Cucumber

Not since childhood, if, as we are agreed, that now, properly speaking was over, not at any rate for a number of years, had Maudie Nettleship been seized with such a wild hysteria of grief. She was sixteen, very nearly *seventeen* years old! To be sent to bed with no supper was an ignominious enough nursery-punishment when she was a shrimp of but ten. To be humiliated in front of the young gentlemen, and in the hotel yard with servants and Mr Atwood and other guests looking on: this had been past enduring. And then, the scene which followed in the bedroom.

Maudie had, it may be thought, quite enough people in the world to love her. She had always assumed that her mother was one of them. In the ridiculous colloquy which they had had a few hours since, however, the child had seen nothing but rage and hatred in her parent's face. Whence it sprang was not a question which came naturally to mind. She was not concerned to explain her mother's behaviour. She reeled, merely, from the cruelty of it; she sobbed beneath its shock. How long the sobbing had gone on, she did not know. She was so convulsed and absorbed by it that the crying had taken on its own momentum and driven out rational thought of anything else. People had come and gone. Mr Gutch, untroubled but unshakably flippant, had hovered in the background at one point as Lionel tried to comfort her. She had not wanted comfort. She had not wanted to soothe the darting stabs of agony which were the only feelings appropriate to the occasion. Her mother had intended her to suffer. She was suffering.

That mother had been in, and out, and in. She had, Maudie thought, held her hand, and stroked her forehead and said something about the heat and too much activity. A maid had appeared, and been dismissed, suggesting that she get the young lady 'ready for bed'. Maudie could not allow her mother the satisfaction of knowing she was in night clothes before they all set off for the ball. She would lie there, simply, and suffer.

Her father had appeared: poor Papa. He had been so hopeless, and so full of a desire to comfort. He had clearly wanted to reverse

Charlotte's decision. Even though he, all along, had been saying that Maudie was too young for such an evening, it really seemed as if he had wanted his little Cinderella to get to the ball. Cowardice and muddle had shown on his features. For him, for her own darling papa whom irrationally she had at that moment wanted to love more than anyone in the world, though she actually failed, quite, to do so, she sat up on the bed. She flung her arms round his greasy old bald head and hugged him and stared into his bewildered eyes. Through her tears he was a vague blur, like an out-of-focus photograph of a steak and kidney pudding.

'My darling, I don't *like* to see you like this', had been his contribution to the Maudie debate. But after the hugging, and the dribbling on his scurfy shoulder, he had shuffled out of the bedroom and she had watched him go, a faintly risible creature in his swallow-tail.

Sitting at the dressing table and surveying the damage already done to her features, Maudie saw that attendance at the boys' supper-party downstairs was unthinkable. Her eyes were swollen, sore and salmony. Her cheeks were blotched and smeared, here red, here grey, here ashen white. The whole face was a mixture of desolation and sweat and she knew it would be hours before it was *right* again. Moreover, when she coughed, her very eyeballs seemed to shake and she felt sure that it was the coughing as much as the weeping which had made them bloodshot.

Lionel had come in again while she sat there. Really, having hysterics insured that one would enjoy a constant stream of visitors.

'They've gone now,' he had said timidly, as if, at the sight of her more composed, he feared that any conversation would once again provoke an outburst.

'Yes,' she said, 'I know.'

'Maudie, I'm sure Mama didn't mean it. And even if she did. . . .'

'Mama was right, Lionel. I am too ill to go to the ball.'

'You'll feel better after supper. We are all waiting for you – Everard and his sisters and the other fellows. Do come down Maudie, there's a good sport.'

'I couldn't eat. What would be the point of my coming to supper?' This strange calm came over her, so that it sounded as though she were trying to snub Lionel. He obviously took it that way, to judge from the hurt, troubled expression in his eyes, and his faintly trembling lip as he left the room for *his* attempt at conviviality. Pity for him made her break down again, when he had gone. And she was still crying a little, though upright on her stool by the dressing table, when the door of her chamber opened yet again. She saw it do so in the glass before her, so she did not need to turn to identify the intruder. It seemed, nevertheless, altogether astonishing that it *should* be he. Anticipating her objections to his presence, he appeared to be in mid-sentence before turning the door-knob.

'And just as doctors are allowed in the bedrooms of young ladies in cases of illness, the old heart-doctor *Monsieur le Médecin* Chatterway claims an absolute right to penetrate the chambers of his unhappy friends of whatever gender they may purport to be. Though errant, this particular knight doesn't like to see a damsel in such torrents of distress.'

'Marvo, this is so naughty.' Her whimper was mumbled through the involuntary flood of tears which his appearance occasioned and partly through a strange little laugh which gulped its way up through all the misery.

'Don't rub, you'll make stains, or should I say more stains.'

'What are you *doing* here?'

'I've got a cucumber here. Let's try a few slices over your eyes.' It was no vain boast. Removing a pocket knife, he sliced two wafer-thin portions from the vegetable and, ignoring protests, came behind her and held each disc over her throbbing sore eyelids. 'Augusta Stanley says it's something they have to do with You-know-who when she gets into a tantrum: got through half the vegetable patch, what, in the week she discovered about Bertie and the * * * * * * woman, coming hot foot upon the news that the far from lonesome Marquess of Lorne was playing fast and in a moral sense loose to the considerable consternation of Her by no means temperamentally equable, though to me always perfectly charming daughter.'

'That's lovely, so cool.' She felt his large silky hands cover the whole of her face. There was complete gentleness in finger-tips, holding the cool slices of cucumber to her sore eyes. It was infinitely reassuring to smell his soap at such close quarters. 'It still doesn't explain what you're doing here.'

'*Herr Doktor* Chatterstein. I told you.'

'But how did you know?'

'I know everything. Never heard of a know-all?'

'Your omniscience is. . . .'

'Perhaps your mother was right and your cough *is* too bad for the ball. Oh don't be ill, angel-girl.'

'Silly cough. I'm not ill and I shall refuse to believe ever again that mama could be right about anything. What can have got *into* her?'

'I thought you had already come close to making a diagnosis during our koala-spotting.'

'Our conversations at the zoo have always been so rushed, so, in a way, difficult. I've been trying to tell you things and half-wishing I wasn't saying them; and half-not knowing, either, what it was that I was trying to say.'

'But the drift was clear enough to both of us, what? About Lupton?'

'You would think me so conceited if I said what I really thought.'

'I would think you worse than conceited. I would think you a fool, which you are not. Only a fool says what she *really* thinks. It is only by insincerity that we can hope to arrive at the truth, for it is only when we are *not* being ourselves that we can rise above the distractions and prejudices of our own personality.'

After a silence, she asked, 'Why did you come? And where are the others?'

'You could, if you liked, remove the cucumbers now.'

For a while, since he released his hold on her eyelids, she had continued to press the little green slices to her face, looking comically as if she were adorned with a species of vegetable *pince-nez*.

'They really are most soothing.'

'The young' – his phrase conveyed at once the miscellany below – 'were almost at the conclusion of their jolly little supper downstairs when I arrived. I had hoped to surprise you all before you set out for the ball.'

'My capacity for surprise has been dulled since you began. . . .'

'To what, pretty?'

'To pester us all!' She laughed at the crestfallen expression which this savagery engendered. 'But what of *les jeunes?*' she asked dreamily.

'Maudie's first ball, what? The Gutch family, one with whom I have been connected as long, though not as intimately, as I have with Eggs and Nettleships.'

'You *did* want to interfere. . . .'

'If a joint party were being formed, not to mention an alliance, it was natural that one party who had known the two houses. . . .'

'Both alike in dignity,' she quoted portentously.

'Wrong there, *ma petite*. I think the Gutches will be found to have rather more escutcheon to blot than the yeoman-ancestry of the high-minded geologist.'

'You are a beast.'

'Your father knows the history of rocks. I interest myself more in the evolution of social and human *strata*. If that reduces me to the level of the animals. . . .'

'Who are themselves our cousins if all *they* say is true.'

'Talking beasts, what?'

'Papa and his friends.'

'Oh.' He mused and then laughed. 'Silly little Ponsonby got into fearful hot water for not shutting me up the other night for saying, within *earshot* of the Duke of Connaught, that I didn't know which was more troubling, the knowledge that some of us descended from apes, or the *certainty* that some of us descended from George III.'

'I don't believe you said it. You thought of it afterwards and wished you had said it. Besides you are always saying what a good man George III was.'

'Thackeray got him completely wrong of course, but then Thackeray hated the last century almost as much as your sainted and ever-to-be-cherished grandpapa loves, and has taught me, to love it. I remember your grandfather, one evening at the Brookfields', telling Thackeray that that month's issue of the *Cornhill* – was it? – simply wouldn't do – *The Virginians*, what? Forget my own name. . . .'

'Are you yourself invited to the ball?' The question, as posed, seemed suddenly to be crude and naïve. She felt herself blushing, both at its terrible clumsiness, and at the simplicity which asking it had revealed. Seeing the extent of her self-reproach, he drawled, 'Don't *try* and be clever. You are clever already. Don't try to be weary with life or *above it all*. That will come with the years, that will come. I had come because I hoped to see you in the ball-dress. The young told me that you were ill, but since there was an empty place at the supper table, I was asked, all unworthy, to fill it. Jolly crowd, your bro's friends. The real difficulty – that you had a tantrum.'

'I *didn't!*' Indignation once more welled into her face, but it was of a different order from her quarrel with her mother.

'Gutch, a little ungallantly, in your noble partner, wanted to be prompt at the ball. Lionel the mad monk I suspect did not enjoy the prospect of going at all to dance with Fräulein Gutch in the hall at Harcourt. But, they went, and, presuming upon my kindness, they asked if I would look after you.'

'I don't believe Lionel asked you to stay here and look after me.'

'Not quite in the way you suggest, no.'

'I believe that he would not have gone to the ball if he thought you would have remained behind with me.'

'Possibly.'

'In fact, you are fibbing, Marvo.'

'In a manner of speaking.'

'A liar.'

'Yes.'

After the very long silence, the girl said, 'I can't believe that I am not going to the ball. I've been preparing for it – for so long, I have been preparing. The dress, the dance steps: I have been practising for weeks, and looking forward to it all. Of course, if I had been truly ill. . . .' She was not speaking brokenly, or with obvious distress. She was not spitting out the words in anger. There was almost an absence of modulation in her tones. She spoke like one who was recovering, very slowly, from shock.

'Commem. balls are very sorry affairs – hardly, if we are using language strictly, balls at all. When one thinks of the Jenker treading a measure with the not inconsiderable form of Augusta Gutch, one realises that it is scarcely the *dernier cri* as far as this world's *bon ton* is concerned. I would like your first ball to be a more. . . .'

'Something glittery? You want princesses always in tiaras.'

'*Some* princesses.'

'Papa would be very angry with you for being here.'

'I am aware that there is nothing more vexing to a parent than a stranger who is capable of cheering his children up.'

'He would think it wasn't the thing.'

'He would be right.'

With delicacy, he removed the cucumber slices which were still poised between the other's thumbs and forefingers. They moistly settled on the lace coverlet of the dressing table at which she still sat. He raised her to her feet and she realised that the low growling in his voice had ceased to be conversational and made some approximation to the air of a waltz.

In stocking feet, she hardly reached above his waist, so that her head was pressed against the stiff white of his shirt front, and his arms, when they folded about her, enclosed her shoulders and the tangles of her tormented hair. There was a feeling of repose, of curling safely back into the nest, in thus allowing herself to be wrapped in his embrace. He, speaking no more, directed their dance steps about the bedroom, in a waltz which became livelier and yet livelier. And thus, for half an hour Maudie danced with Mr Chatterway, to the accompaniment of his half-tuneless renderings of old German music.

EIGHTEEN

The Scarlet Thread

The glow of candles, the glare of gas, the brightness of silver reflected in the high polish of walnut veneer, the irritating movement, first of Mrs Gutch's earrings, then of her ears, finally of four of her ears and two of her heads: these were some of the smudgy impressions upon which Mr Timothy Lupton tried to focus as he sipped Dr Jenkinson's uncommonly good Sauternes and nodded, with implausible enthusiasm, at an animated but earnest young woman on his right discoursing first of Spanish history, then of the spread of doubt, which she seemed to link up in some way with her own family, the see of Hereford, the sea of faith, her uncles, her grandfather, her kinship with Archdeacon Gutch, with Matthew Arnold, with, for all Mr Lupton knew, everyone in creation from Dean Stanley down to the orang-outangs. He listened with only half an ear. There were blank spots in his literary knowledge. This lady seemed to be nothing but an emanation of literature and theology.

It had all been, for him, rather a disappointment, this Varsity lark. Other fellows spoke about the place as if it were a combination between the hanging gardens of Babylon and the Garden of Eden before the gate was shut. Mr Lupton felt it had not been all that it was cracked up to be. Not one of the rooms in Doctor Jenkinson's house, for instance, could compare with the coffee room of Lupton's club for elegance, or for comfort. He had expected the college chapels to be little gems of ecclesiological brilliance, but they did not, in his rough and dismissive idiolect, hold a candle to half Wren's churches in the City. As for the walks and gardens, perhaps they had a certain provincial quaintness, but where were the vistas of Cliveden, the rich herbaceous borders he had seen at Leeds Castle or Belvoir, the sheer size and romance and surprisingness of the gardens at Matchingham? This place would *do*, Mr Lupton supposed. But what it would do for, he left to others to discover. He felt no pang of regret that his own artistic and unconventional promptings had denied him the chance of savouring three years – the stultification! – in this torrid valley-town.

The Master of Harcourt had been a surprising old bird, too. Sharp-tongued and more like a woman than a man. There had been two sittings so far and the portrait was now all but complete. Mr Lupton had never had such a 'difficult customer'. Archdeacons, dowagers, ambassadors, had all yielded to the young man's charm and been happy to talk to him throughout his sessions. Not so Dr Jenkinson, who sat with a suppressed amusement on his face which was most malicious. It seemed as though the old man were expecting you to make an ass of yourself and was inwardly rehearsing the number of ways that you could do it. After they had sat in total silence for three quarters of an hour on the first day, the Master had asked his portraitist, 'How do you like our new chapel?' It seemed a clear case of a trap question. The thought had passed through Lupton's head that Doctor Jenkinson had had the new chapel built for the discomfiture of visitors. Were they to speak what was the undeniable truth, and risk arousing the Master's wrath? Or were they to pretend to like the place and thus earn his scorn? Lupton had only given the building a cursory glance in the morning, and could remember very little about it.

'I don't awfully like the painting behind the altar,' he eventually volunteered. It was not as cretinous a reply as the Master had been hoping for, but it was evidently good enough; for the tight, womanish lips suddenly wreathed themselves into a prim smile.

'Do you have to say *awfully?* This isn't a girl's school. And it isn't a painting. It's alabaster. Surprising that you in your profession should not have a better visual memory.'

In later years, those who gazed at Mr Lupton's portrait were to remark, with distaste or admiration, that he had captured a quality of *superciliousness* in the Master's expression. Silence had dominated the rest of the sitting.

Nevertheless, as he was doing now after something like a week in the Master's lodgings, these old dons feasted like kings. He was grateful to a man beyond the young woman on his right, for drawing her away and discussing, by the sound of it, George Eliot. The lady on his left was also engaged in conversation, and with his head spinning no more than was pleasant, he was able to look down the swaying table and catch, from time to time, the eyes of Mrs Nettleship. Now that she knew his secret, and seemed positively to encourage his besotted devotion to Maudie, Mrs Nettleship's mysteriousness had become the subject of some of his most fascinated meditations. It had puzzled him throughout many of the silences of the Master of Harcourt. It recurred to him now, as he watched her down the table. He had forgotten why it was the case that young men such as he regarded all potential mothers-in-law as enemies. They thought perhaps only of the risks involved, the possibility that the young men might not be very *good* men, in the Shylock sense of the word if in no other. He had felt, when the mother of any young object of his devotion had been known to him, that she would disapprove: distaste for his Bohemian manner of life, his dusty rented rooms, his late hours, his absence of much by way of people. He had never come across a mother who seemed positively to like the idea of him, and who even, in a way which made him red to think about it, seemed to approve not merely of the fact that he had a fondness for her daughter but that he had a passion for her. It was, taken all in all, deuced rum. More, if he knew his way round it, he would have been able to say what there was in it which he found more than rum: beguiling. The heart, if it is to survive unbroken in the world, or if broken, broken decorously, must frequently ignore the evidence of the senses. The signals were of their nature too simple, and too shatteringly crude, like one of the bawdier substitution-narratives of the Arabian nights. It was not, that, discerning a meaning in Mrs Nettleship's thousand glances and half-finished sentences, he had been shocked enough to banish such allurements from his fancy. It was rather that the allurement was so unthinkable that it did not come to him as an allurement; that the bargain, if it were ever to be struck by him, had not formed clearly in his mind. Its very baseness, its positive orientalism, obscured it as a possibility!

The water-ices which accompanied the Sauternes were consumed with long silver spoons, calling to mind, by a process of irrational association, the possibility of diabolical partners at a supper table. Absent from any of the conversations, all of which bored him very considerably, he was enjoying that haven of non-communication which can sometimes be found in the very midst of dinner conversation, a vacancy of mood in the thickest of crowds which seems as self-contradictory as the notion of a city-hermitage, or an anchorite at a levée. Nevertheless, in the precious silence such moments allow, the man lost in thought at a dinner table is as solitary as Moses on the mountain-tops. Charlotte Nettleship was therefore able to occupy all his attention and he could see many beauties in her this evening which the brisk common sense of her day-clothes perhaps contrived to disguise. He was, for instance, extremely aware, even at a distance of perhaps ten yards, of the quality of her skin, of shoulders and throat. The pale shoulder skin was in the most delicate and subtle manner lightly freckled; but to say that suggests a combination of whites and browns which should be banished at once from the palette. The hues involved were all infinitely pale and well-diluted versions of mushroom pink. What browns and whites there were were subsumed in a pallor of great subtlety. Charlotte's flesh had an extraordinary quality of its own: one was interested in it, that is, as flesh, one could gaze at any particular area of it with almost equal interest – the elbow, the upper arm, or the throat, where the skin was more marbly, rising, in the nape of her neck, as he saw when her head turned to catch some well-turned malice of the Master's, into a haze of just governed downy straggles, the foothills as it were of the great mountain, the line where her hair began. Tonight, there was almost a 'sweet disorder' in the way that Charlotte had done her hair. A few loose tresses dangled enchantingly beneath the thick chignon at her head's back, giving a little vision of what it would be like loose, thick and full about her bare shoulders. Mrs Nettleship's hair was less crimped, less curly, and less glossy than her daughter's. Where the brown was on the point of turning grey there was a sort of ambiguous duskiness in it; and it was straight. If unwound, however, it might half-cover the naked form which the shoulders very naturally suggested, suggesting even in its bare unadornment much of the woman herself. If she were to stand, thus naked, and to pose for one of his historical scenes, Mr Lupton could not translate Mrs Nettleship into an Egyptian empress or a wife of a Caesar. 'Boadicea' was a suggested title which came to mind at once. A British warrior queen, bleeding from the Roman rods, as in the *Reciter?* There was something undeniably defiant about her; and yet, it was a sufferer's face, 'full of rage and full of grief'. The contract which he now more than half discerned to have been on offer in their two perambulatory colloquies was too bizarre to be absorbed all at once, but this evening at the Jenker's table it was far from uninviting. He thought of the Shakespearean obviousness of the young person calling up the lovely April of the mother's prime. Here was the greater wonder of seeing lovely July echo what had already become hauntingly familiar in the buds of March. The face of Charlotte was the face of Maudie. But it was Maudie chastened, Maudie grief-stricken, Maudie uncertain. Then again, in the mockery of Charlotte's eyes and the faint delicacy with which her face was lined, there was a sense that the face of the almost forty-year-old woman was more interesting than the unformed softness of the girl. There was something odder about the reveries that now possessed him. If it were necessary for the achieving of the ultimate goal, the conquest of his promised land, to take refuge in the household of the scarlet thread, then assuredly he would do so. Such was what, with inebriated concentration, he discerned as the most distinct of post-prandial possibilities.

Perhaps, if one had met her independently for the first time on such an evening as this, one might have supposed her to be younger than she was; perhaps, he reflected without much mercy, almost of an age with himself. But the mother was inseparable from the daughter. He both loved and feared her for *producing* Maudie, for having been the agent of the child's advent into consciousness. That latest business, if he got it right, was what the popular imagination might consider *desperately wicked;* if pondered sufficiently, a good enough term since the unquestioned wickedness of Mr Lupton's thoughts at that moment were occasioned by a blankness, and by a surrender to animal impulse, which were in all respects very similar to despair. Maudie – the very thought of her reduced him to a state where he might have wept openly. The mother was beginning to have a similar ability to touch his heart and more than his heart, as appeared to be mutually recognised when, gazing up over the fruits and glasses, the moist red faces in the candlelight, she smiled at him with the confidence of a coquette.

'The Master,' said his earnest young neighbour – did she say her name was Mrs Wardle? – 'the Master was telling my husband and myself that your portrait makes him look grossly conceited. I suppressed the thought at the time, but I can express it to you, Mr Lupton, that if that were the case, then you have assuredly caught Doctor Jenkinson's likeness.'

'He was a difficult subject.'

Was his speech slurred? Lupton devoutly hoped that he had not said *shubject* to this brilliant young woman and that there was nothing in his bearing which made her switch the subject of talk so abruptly to the drunkenness of the London poor. He was rather glad when the ladies withdrew, leaving perhaps fifteen, perhaps twenty men in the long panelled room to drink more wine and to relax themselves somewhat before the ensuing rigours of the ball. He discovered from his neighbour that the young woman to whom he had been speaking was called Ward – 'Tom Arnold's girl' – and that her husband was at the other end of the table talking to Professor Nettleship and the Master. The pleasant glow of inebriation lost its anxiety with the women gone. He no longer cared whether he was repeating himself, nor did it much worry him if he stumbled over the sibilants in pronouncing the name of the Marquess of Salisbury, who was, for some reason, mentioned. By the time that the wine had done its rounds twice or thrice more, Mr Lupton felt that he had dined very well, and he staggered into the quadrangle to commune with himself, to light a cigar in the moonlight before deciding to rejoin the ladies. The Master's party were going to go over to the Hall, where the dancing would happen, *en masse.* The dancing would require, as the inebriated Lupton saw it, a considerable finesse. He must not be seen to dance exclusively with Maudie; he knew that. But the very thought of her flitting about the hall in the arms of anyone else filled him with the most exquisite loathing, as though he were being flayed. At the same time, in his new perception of things, there was the mother, and she must be, not merely placated, to be given the first dance, but also *conspired with*. They must not be seen to mutter together as they waltzed; but mutter they must. And, the cigar discarded, the room resumed, the lawn crossed, the politeness with the other guests exchanged, the banter received from the Master himself, it was the muttering, and the conspiracy, on which Mr Lupton focussed his fullest, fuzziest attentions.

NINETEEN

At the Ball

The cold fowl, meringues, cherries and fizzy wine had been shaken up considerably by the time Lionel Nettleship had been dancing for three quarters of an hour. He felt the worse for it. Not drunk, not as though he were about to suffer the ultimate gastric calamity, but simply the worse. He had danced with several members of the party, including Gutch's mother, Gutch's cousin Phyllis, Gutch's elder sister Dorothea; and now he was dancing with Gutch's younger sister Hypatia. All these females bore a resemblance, more or less strong, to Gutch himself, so that when, as it was apt to do during dances, his mind strayed into vacancy, Lionel was half under the impression that he was waltzing round the Hall at Harcourt with Gutch in a species of absurd pantomime costumes.

Lionel would have exchanged any one of these partners for a glimpse of Maudie. He had been so much looking forward to treading a measure with his sister, and, more than that, to seeing her in her ball finery. It pleased and excited him very much that they were to be grown-up together, he and Maudie. He could not articulate quite why this gave so much pleasure, but he knew that, grown up, they would have achieved a degree of the independence of the parents which was necessary if sanity were to be maintained. This afternoon in the meadows around Addison's Walk, he knew that there were a thousand exciting things that they could have been doing. The opportunity, for instance, for tea with the Pattisons was not to be missed. But both Maudie and he had missed it, because they were so happy in one another's company. What fun the ball would have been, if she had been there. How dreary and unprofitable seemed all its uses without her.

'I feel sure Mr Chatterway will bring Maud along to the ball as he promised,' lisped Miss Hypatia Gutch, as she and Lionel took their seats once more at the side of the hall. Lionel had said, in view of his sister's non-appearance, that he could not stay long. Miss Hypatia Gutch's conversation, for the previous quarter of an hour, had been in a high degree comparable, not to say identical, with her sister Miss Gutch in the quarter of an hour previous to that. There were even areas

of conversational overlap between what the two Miss Gutches chose
to discuss and the subjects favoured by their mother and their cousin
Phyllis. Lionel now felt very fully acquainted with the doings, sayings,
illnesses and marriages of all the Gutches' nearest Herefordshire
neighbours and relations. He felt richly familiar with the seasonal and
social cycle of Willerton Magna. Three times he had expressed
astonishment at the extent of the equipage of Lady Wisbeach, the local
grandee. Three times he had confessed that he did not hunt. Three
times, he had managed to steer the talk to the novels of Miss Yonge;
three times he had discovered that his interlocutress was an enthusiast
for *The Pillars of the House* and unacquainted with *The Trial* or *The
Daisy Chain*. Reading, though it suggested an area of common
experience, was not apparently something you talked about. Friends
and relations, though your hearer had no more met them than he had
made the acquaintance of Adam and Eve, were apparently something
you could talk about all evening.

'I do not think Maudie will be coming to the party now,' said Gutch,
who had come up to join them. 'Mama has just told me that she thinks
Mackonochie is a devil and his curate Mr Stanton even worse!'

'Are these the clergymen in the church where you are spending the
summer, dear?' This from Miss Hypatia.

'Papa says they are clergymen of the Church of England, and in so
far as they are loyal churchmen he cannot see any objection to my
working there.'

It was odd that Gutch could keep up this relentless flow of
ecclesiastical chit-chat even through the strains of German dance-
music which emanated from the little orchestra. To Lionel, all this
reduction of the things of God to the level of gossip was beginning to
fray his nerves, to emphasise with some violence the dislocation
which, on such occasions, appeared to be happening in his life. He
had, at that moment, no desire to be at the ball at all. Two inner
dreams, two visions of romance separated him completely from his
surroundings. On the one hand, the peace which passes understanding
tugged at his heart and made the music, and the ball-gowns, and the
red faces of the men in their swallow-tails seem pathetically unreal,
insubstantial. How could anyone care about a *ball* when they had
received into their heart Him who was the King of Kings and Lord of
Lords? In so far as he did have strong impulses of human caring, Lionel
longed to be with his sister. His love of her, and his love of God,
seemed alike to draw him away from his company, into an interior
mood of vacancy. Gutch seemed to have no such difficulties. Perhaps it
was because he was older. He, after all, had now become a Bachelor of
Arts. Perhaps it was a sign of his deeper maturity that he could sit with

his sisters, dressed in a stiff white shirt, sipping lemonade and
discussing with one breath the local Master of Foxhounds, and with
the next such esoterically liturgical questions as whether Mister
Mackonochie of Holborn practised something known as 'The Little
Elevation'.

'Wasn't it funny,' said Miss Gutch, 'Mr Chatterway arriving at the
hotel just as we were finishing our supper? Do you suppose that we did
right to leave them together?'

'What else could we have done?' Gutch asked.

'I still wish I had stayed with her,' said Lionel. 'It seems such jolly
rotten luck, her first ball and all that. Old Chatterway's practically an
uncle to us, don't you know. But all the same.' He twisted and
retwisted the lemonade glass in his hands with an agony of
awkwardness.

'You said just now she liked Mr Chatterway,' said Gutch.

'Oh, she does. I think he'll have cheered her up, I do really. All the
same,' he blushed deeply, 'its *rotten*.' Doubtless, rottenness was at the
core and there was putrefaction, moral and physical, everywhere.
They did not ask him to elaborate on what, specifically, was rotten,
though it was generally understood that Lionel was about to refer to
the conduct of his parents. He fell silent, for he had caught sight of his
mother on the dance floor; and all the young people stared at her with
a mute admiration. She seemed, rather than dancing, to be gliding, or
dancing about the floor even though her partner was by no means
steady on his feet. She seemed, too, to be quite ageless. Lionel at first
stared at her, not as his mother, but as a vision of delight and loveliness
skimming past. She radiated joy and something which he was too
young to recognise, but which was youth, so that in after years, when
the scene returned as it so often did to his memory, he thought of the
phrase in the old minstrel about being made young and lusty as an
eagle. The psalmist spoke of the revivification of the soul by a celestial
power. No less, Lionel could feel in that instant, his mother was visited
by something celestial, not by the God who had invaded *his* heart but
by another, no less voracious and all-consuming. She and the painter
had, as the saying is, eyes for no one but themselves. They glided about
the floor in a conspicuous trance. Mrs Nettleship seemed actually to
hang from her young consort, her delicate white hand never leaving his
shoulder for an instant, and her eyes never removed from his gaze.
They danced through the crowds, ignoring everyone about them.

Lionel did not know if others saw what he saw. In every corner of
the hall, things appeared to be continuing much as before. Somewhat
absurdly, the Master was dancing with some wobbling dowager, if
dancing was the correct term for such restrained and almost motion-

less shuffling. Those who were not dancing – and this now seemed to include most of the younger Gutch party – were drifting out into the hall and towards one of the rooms where lemonade was spread out for the refreshment of the more ardent revellers. But had they seen? Had Gutch seen? Seen, moreover, *what?* His mind could not accept what it had witnessed, so that he was not forming sentences in his head, nor describing *to himself*, what he had seen. He knew merely that Gutch's mother, the wife of the archdeacon, the aunt of Gutch's cousin Phyllis and the sister of Lady Wisbeach of Willerton Magna, would not have danced with Mr Lupton in that *way*, with that *abandonment*. Lionel, who had begun the evening as Laertes, was in danger of ending it as Hamlet.

Gutch got his mood, for he asked, without introducing the topic artificially, 'Have you seen that painter fellow's portrait of the Magger? Cousin Phyllis says it's blotchy, but I am a poor judge of these matters.'

TWENTY

Conjugal

This town, even in a mild and dry June, exhaled river vapours, so that the pavements outside Harcourt at one in the morning (the hour of carriages) had an almost autumn mystery. Lionel had been sent to bed. The farewells had been made. The Master had been finally saluted. Hopes had been expressed on all sides that Gutches and Nettleships, in a variety of permutations, would see one another, in a different place, in the course of the remaining season. Charlotte had even had her hand pressed warmly by the archdeacon. And now, for the first time that evening, she and her husband stood alone on the misty pavement awaiting their brougham. Never in fifteen years had they spoken to one another in private. Not a syllable, not a breath, had passed between them. All their talk had been for show; and it was surprising how little of *that* could, in Charlotte's still schoolgirlish manner of expressing it to herself, be *got away with*. Ye gods! When the estrangement had begun, she was perhaps little more than two or three and twenty. No wonder the locution was juvenile. For all those years, she had felt the weight of Nettleship's personality hovering at the border of her own. For weeks, for months, she had managed to *get by*, another getting, without ever focussing her eyes upon him, without, strictly, looking at him at all. But with the marriage telepathy of which mention has already been made, she knew that tonight the silence of fifteen years was going to be broken. She dreaded the words which would pass between them. There had been something about the great unspokenness of all her miseries which had been oddly comforting to her. Perhaps she had always dreaded saying what she felt, for fear that she would be unable to feel what she said. It was not that she feared recrimination, on the contrary. She had often wished that quarrelling – no other form of communication – had been possible to her and Horace. She had envisaged a formalised hostility, limited, like the terms of a mediaeval *disputacio* to a set time and place, but which would give vent to some of the unuttered, and now perhaps unutterable anger, of the years. It would have helped. No, it was not anger, or the expression of it, which she now dreaded. It was the knowledge that if they spoke, something would happen to both of them from which it would be impossible to retreat. She did not know what this was, but she dreaded it with the instinct which made her shrink from, and at the same moment thrill to, all things new.

She looked at her husband now, in the lamplight at the college gate, and he, with unaccustomed candour, looked back at her. She saw lips drawn downwards like those of a boy trying not to weep. She saw appalling disappointment in his dull yellowing eyes and she glanced away again at once, fearing to pity those eyes. But as she glanced away, she carried with her the memory of his expression: anger, grief, and something like madness all present, almost grandly, in the suet features.

Horace for his part saw his wife's damnably pretty features, as she darted at him a cowardly, and almost deceitful glance, a combination of malice and duplicity which were new there. Her blue eyes were open much wider than had once been her wont and gave to her normally placid oval features something of the look of youthful surprise which had first attracted him to her as a child at the Walkers' house in Malvern. He felt himself gulping and breathing awkwardly. It was impossible that he should not, at last, speak out. Her behaviour had been, the whole evening, outrageous. First, she had cast misery upon them all by forbidding Maudie to come to the dance. She had then appeared in *that dress*. Its swooping contours had attracted every eye in the room. Even the Platonic Master himself had cast mischievous glances towards her throat and somehow *smirked*. She had worn it for one reason, and one reason alone. She had had an expression on her face all evening which is not often seen in polite society. Horace, as the husband of her bosom, could not fail to be stirred by it, and at the same moment acutely embarrassed. He was happy to think that he had never knowingly met a courtesan, nor even seen, except in the shadows of doorways as he came home after dark in London after some very rare evening *sortie*, the sort of woman to whom the superstitious adherents of the Nazarite sect imagine a particular forgiveness has been meted out. Horace Nettleship had passed beyond the age of fascination with female depravity. He was simply chilled and revolted by it. He had noted, first with pleasure and then with distaste, that his wife seemed the youngest woman in Doctor Jenkinson's dining room, younger-seeming by far than pretty, virtuous little Mrs Ward, who was buttoned and chokered very properly, up to the chin. It was only Charlotte who glittered at the throat and whose flesh, whose bare flesh, whose freckled, pale and magnificent shoulders of *flesh* had been revealed to the vulgar gaze. It was Charlotte whose swooping necklines barely concealed her decency, Charlotte who stared at him now with the insolence of a harlot and then, the moment he met her gaze, turned away again. As if her appearance had not been enough, added to her ill-treatment of Maudie, to make her behaviour of the evening insupportable, she had felt it necessary to play the coquette with the lecherous painter, whose rendering of Doctor Jenkinson's likeness had received, as far as Horace could make out, such universal disapprobation. Glances had shot up and down the dinner table which could not be ignored. The professor was not a fool. *They* seemed to think that he was. They were happy to continue their dalliance before his very eyes. Their looks before dinner turned, when the gentlemen joined the ladies in the Master's drawing room, into conspiratorial coffee-stirring, mysteriously significant and (to Horace at that moment) inaudible exchanges of talk. Then, as if this were not sufficient to try his patience, she had had the cruelty to dance with the fellow. An expertise in volcanic lava does not necessarily guarantee light-footedness on a dance floor. Horace would have been prepared to concede that he was, during the waltz with Mrs Gutch, positively clumsy. Before the conclusion of the dance, they had retired to the chairs which were placed around the hall, hoping to rejoin their party.

'Good heavens, Mr Nettleship, while the cats are away. . . .' had laughed that good-humoured lady, indicating, with a fan, the sight of her husband pirouetting, with gaitered absurdity, Mrs Ward his partner. But all eyes had been turning to the *abandonment,* the sheer unseemly display of the lovers: little Mrs Nettleship and the painter. Already, the professor could hear the words spoken in whispers at the clubs.

The brougham was at the kerb. Mr Atwood of the Clarendon Hotel was helping Mrs Nettleship into the vehicle, her husband followed. Moonlight shone down on the faintly misty streets. It was a scene not only of romance, but of near-perfection. Perhaps they should extract from it what they could, each looking out of their separate windows as they rattled the short distance; but precedence was broken slightly earlier than he had intended. The words were coming out of his mouth almost before the horses had started.

'I hope you are satisfied with this evening's display.'

'I am satisfied with nothing.' She said it not in a clipped or angry manner, but in a melodramatic gush, as though she had been waiting her chance to speak the lines for months. There was indeed almost something exultant in her manner and he could see in the darkness of the carriage that her eyes were gleaming.

'For various reasons, chief of which was the happiness of Maud, I have said nothing to you about your behaviour in recent weeks.'

'Don't mention Maudie to me.'

'Not mention my own daughter?'

'I do not recognise your right to upbraid me, Horace. I hope that you understand that.' She had turned to him and he felt, more than saw, the intensity of her eyes upon him.

'When you took to caressing Mr Timothy Lupton in the streets of London, I could have spoken. Many husbands would.'

'I am not properly listening to you. I feel that you should be listening to me. You had no right to banish Mr Lupton from our doors. There was no reason for it. Still less had you any right to forbid me to see Mr Chatterway.'

'Do you question my ownership of The Bower? Do you question the validity of your marriage vows?' There was a little light-hearted sarcasm in his tone which was unsuited to him. It was even slightly pathetic. 'I am interested that your promise to obey and serve me can be so flippantly discarded.'

'Who made those promises?' she asked.

'I was under the impression that you did. Unless the darkness deceives me and I am sitting next to someone else. I was under the impression that you were my wife.'

Since the brougham had now drawn into the hotel yard, they both subsided into silence. After all, they had fifteen years' practice at keeping their mouths shut. They were even capable of good-humoured thanks and goodnights to Mr Atwood, and happy smiles for the night porter.

'I must go to Maudie,' said Charlotte at the top of the stairs.

'As though she were your daughter only, and not mine.'

'I was the one who ruined this evening's happiness for her,' said the mother calmly, somehow gaining ground in the argument by admitting the fault.

'I shall wait for you in your room,' said her husband.

When she returned to that room, with a pounding heart, Charlotte saw that her husband had thrown himself down in the armchair by the hearth. Opera hat and cloak lay in a heap beside him. He did not look up as she entered. She did not sit.

'The child is asleep. It looks as if she has been asleep for hours,' said Charlotte.

'Are you asking to be released from your wedding vows?' asked Horace, firmly and deliberately. Once again, he did not look up, but continued to stare at the empty grate.

'How old was I when you first met me?' She stood behind him to ask the question.

'Is the fact material?'

'Am I really the same person? I am told that over a number of years all the cells in our bodies die and are replaced by new ones. I wonder if there is any single particle standing here in this room that was present in Aunt Walker's drawing-room when you first heard me recite the mathematical tables.'

'I did not marry you when you were a child.'

'I was barely seventeen years old. I was the age that Maudie is now. Would you consider Maudie old enough for marriage?'

'The question I asked you was whether you still wished to be married to me.'

'Still? You singled out, on the way home, my promise to obey you. Someone of my name made it, I readily concede. They also promised to love you, I think. I have no memory of loving you, Horace.'

'Not ever?'

'No.'

As she said the words, she felt, as at the commencement of their dialogue, a gush of excitement which was very close to joy, but at the same time a start of fear, a knowledge that from now on, there was to be no turning back. As a child, there had been moments of ecstatic terror, during Malvern winters, when she and her cousins had dragged their toboggans to the higher slopes. She had been placed on the slatted wood, and she had held the reins fast in her hand. Then, a jolt in the small of her back and the knowledge that she was about to cascade down the snows, she knew not where. The sensation was reproduced as she said that she did not love her husband, never had loved him.

'You forget, Charlotte. You try to forget our early years.'

'I do not try to forget anything. Sometimes memories are so painful that we blot them out.'

'You are trying to break my heart.'

'I am not trying to do anything. You have already broken my heart.'

'By refusing Mr Chatterway a cup of tea?'

'Sarcasm does not suit you.'

'By expressing a concern that you should be throwing yourself at a young lecher half your age. Oh, Charlotte!'

'I refuse to reply to such a vulgar, cruel, inaccurate remark.'

'I hope you are not deceiving yourself. His sort! Why, this little dalliance of yours means nothing to him, precisely nothing. I suppose you think you love him.'

'I will not discuss it with you.'

'I am afraid you are obliged to. I insist upon it.' The veins in Horace's forehead were standing out and he turned to look up at her as she stared coolly down at his baldness.

'You? Insist?'

'I saw you, woman. I saw you, on the steps of the National Gallery in Trafalgar Square. It was quite obvious to me that you were parting as, that, shall we say, you were parting as – well, *familiars.* You can imagine how I felt. Or perhaps, again, you can not. You seem this evening impervious to ordinary decent human feelings.'

There was complete silence. In the distance somewhere a church clock or a college tower tolled the hour of two.

'If I could see you on the steps of the National Gallery, where might not the rest of London see you, the two of you – *canoodling!*'

'Please *try* not to be foolish,' she said quietly.

'Foolish! Is this a matter for levity? Is this something to which you sit so lightly that you are incapable of taking it seriously for a single instant? Oh, Charlotte, turn to me. Look at me, damn you, when I speak to you.'

'I *will* not be addressed in that tone.'

'I shall address you as I damn well please.'

'Such words don't sit upon your lips. They seem ridiculous when you say them.'

'That is all I am to you. Ridiculous.'

'Yes.'

Another clock, belatedly, took up the prompting of the first, and struck two.

'I am afraid that I insist upon knowing if you have had other lovers before Mr Lupton.'

He stood to say this and faced her. Looked down upon her, indeed, for he was six inches her superior.

'This is sheer fantasy and insult.'

'Do you deny that you love Mr Lupton?'

Suddenly, her calm features became enraged, flown with an animal hostility to him, and her voice became almost coarse and loud. She was red, and pulsating, even in the intensity of the moment, with embarrassment.

'Yes, I love him!'

'So you admit it.'

'You speak of love as if it were a crime.'

'I am speaking of adultery.'

'Oh, how *dare* you? Am I to be blamed for falling in love? You speak as if it were something over which we had any control. I wonder, had you ever loved me as you say you did, that you can speak of it in this way. Oh, Horace, believe me when I tell you that I have never been in love before in my *life*. I did not even know what the words meant, until. . . .'

'Until Lupton?'

'Yes, until I met Timothy.'

'Spare me the intimacies of your feelings, I pray. But no. Not all of them. I have a right to know where you were this evening.'

'You know perfectly well where I was this evening.'

'I saw you at dinner and I saw you at the ball.'

'Well, then.'

'Not well. Everyone else saw you too, half-naked in the man's arms, his filthy blonde hair flying about you in a passion.'

'His hair is not filthy!'

'Oh, yes we saw you. We all saw you. Your own son, Lionel, saw you. Mrs Gutch saw you.'

'It was a dance. I saw *you* dancing. What is there so shaming in that?'

'And afterwards?'

This time only the silence of the moonlight beyond the windows, unpunctuated by bells.

'You do not deny that you and Mr Lupton left the hall.'

A light breeze shook the tree outside her window. She said nothing.

'You do not deny that you left the hall and that Lupton too left the hall. I repeat the question, for much hangs on your reply. You owe me a reply.'

'I owe you nothing.'

'Did you go to his bedroom?'

'Dear God, how crude you are!'

He had advanced upon her now and seized her wrists.

'Give me a civil and honest reply, or I will. . . .'

'You will? What will you, you foolish. . . .'

With the back of a hand he slapped her cheek and said insistently, 'You will tell me what happened this evening between you and Mr Lupton.'

'Please, Horace.'

'Your tears are not credible. They are out of place.'

'Let me go.'

'You went to his bed, you slut!'

'Please, please! You are mad!'

'You gave to him what you have not given me for years, and what is my right.'

'Horace! Stop it! I shall cry out!'

'I respected you. I thought that in common with most respectable women, you did not wish, after the loss of a child. . . .'

'Let go, you are hurting me. I shall cry out.' Her words were smothered as he roughly covered her mouth with his hand. She felt a blow about her head and fell to the carpet with his lunatic weight upon her. She shut her eyes and, through her weeping, she felt all his rough petticoat-tearing and brutal trowsers-opening. Paroxysms of shame, grief, disgust, fear and horror shook her as she lay there, after his departure for his own apartments. Dawn broke upon her lying there still, shocked, sleepless, wretched and cold.

TWENTY-ONE

Brighton

Maudie Nettleship's view of the marital violence was through a multitude of hats, jaunty in their seaside variety: schoolboy caps and girlish straw bonnets; curly grey bowlers and deerstalkers on the heads of men who had never seen, still less stalked, a deer; yellow boaters, black brimless hats trimmed with wide pink ribbons: all turned in the direction of the hook-nosed marionet striking his wife with a stick. The performance took place in a crudely gilded miniature procenium whose inspiration was French Baroque. Blue curtains beneath the stage concealed the legs and feet of the puppeteer who emitted, from behind and below, the high-pitched insults and jeers, the forceful domestic vituperation which the crowds had come to enjoy. Each time Punch struck his wife, the children howled with glee and the men murmured amused approval. But the women too laughed, as though involved with a conspiracy from which the opposite sex were shut out.

Even Maudie's grandfather gazed on the scene with a modicum of delight, though it was hard to discern from the smile in his very blue eyes whether they were concentrated on the Punch and Judy show, or whether they were gazing beyond the booth to the West Pier, and the sunshine on the sea. Nor was it really possible for her to guess what the old man was thinking, for he had, as he remarked fairly often during their perambulation of the esplanade, known Brighton 'in all its glory' before the arrival of the cheap hotels and the bathing machines.

'I shall fetch a policeman!' exclaimed Mrs Punch distractedly. This made the biddies in bonnets laugh all the more riotously. The children yelped. One of the men shouted, 'Just like a woman.'

It seemed to be the human destiny to be married. Maudie therefore expected that she would come to it in the end. All the fairy stories ended with it, and the princess, having contracted it, was happy ever after. The few weddings Maudie had attended, of neighbours and relations (once as a bridesmaid) had enforced on all present a faintly plausible atmosphere of hymeneal joy. But did it come to this, to Mr and Mrs Punch, and all the grown-ups laughing, not as the children were laughing, but as initiates? Her grandfather Egg had been a widower for the duration of Maudie's life, and she had seen very little, before his demise, of her grandfather Nettleship. Her parents' marriage was therefore the one which she had been able to observe most closely at first hand. It seemed to be neither happy ever after, nor, she trusted, violent. It was simply locked up in a mystery. Maudie had begun to wonder if she would ever go back to The Bower. There was in her mother an air of unexplained determination. Maudie knew that something was on her mother's mind, that something, as she put it, was 'up'. She wished that she had Mr Chatterway beside her, rather than her grandfather, for she was sure that her dear old friend would be able to interpret for her all the baffling signs of the previous weeks.

After the Commem., which for Maudie had ended so calamitously, Mr Chatterway had vanished from view. The day after her failure to appear at the ball, he had turned up at the Clarendon, mysteriously finding a moment when both her parents were out, and left a small posy of friesias and a lot of muttered incomprehensibles about Sir Charles Dilke. He was, Chatterway, not going back to London at once. 'The country' apparently called, and there had since been some tightly scrawled communications from Mentmore which, to have been fully understood, would have required an encyclopaedic knowledge of the pedigrees of Rosebery and Rothschild. Maudie was therefore alone; without a guide or an interpreter, she found it difficult enough to interpret the events of the previous fortnight. After her evening of sobbing, and her surreptitious visit the next day from Mr Chatterway, the mystery had thickened to the point of impenetrability. Professor Nettleship and Lionel had left almost at once for London, but Mrs Nettleship had remained in the hotel with her daughter. Maudie noted her mother's changed attitude from the night before. Then, it had been strident, and unforgiving, anger. Now, it became an extraordinary blend of silent sorrow and tender solicitude. Maudie had never known her mother *pet* her so. It was so uncharacteristic as to be almost disconcerting. She had not *said* she was sorry to have prevented Maudie from going to the Ball. She had not *needed* to say. Every gesture, every unwrapped sweetmeat, every posy borne to the bedroom, had been eloquent in its air of frantic apology or, if it were not strictly speaking apology, its declaration that Charlotte wanted Maudie to love her. Catching these signals, Maudie had begun to wonder about the question. For more than sixteen years she had taken it for granted that she loved both her parents. This latest *behaviour* on her mother's part allowed her the leisure as she lay there (for she was not supposed to stir) to wonder whether she did, quite, like her mother. The question, a fortnight or so later, and in another place, remained unsolved. After the bed-confinement in the university town, mother and daughter had repaired to London, but not to St John's

Wood. Because she found it so curious their not going home, Maudie had refrained from asking her mother the reason. She was afraid that the answer would be unpleasant. Was it perhaps something Lionel had done, or said? But no. For, on their third day staying with grandpapa in Bloomsbury, Lionel had come in, very flushed and excited, from a visit to the ritualist heights of St Paul's, Knightsbridge.

How amusing grandpapa had been about it, what blushes he had summoned to poor Lionel's cheeks by asking if he had been to confession. 'So, then,' he had said to his sister through his redness, 'you are off to the sea.' And it was the first that Maudie had heard of the arrangement. Whether or no Lionel joined them seemed, still, an unresolved question. 'Will Papa ...?' she had begun to ask but something in Mama's face made the question die on Maudie's lips. At the moment – she was quick to pick up the rules of the new game – one did not *mention* Papa. Poor Papa, Maudie's heart bled for him, in a way. She imagined that he had probably tried to stick up for her and persuade Mama to let her to go the Harcourt Ball. Was that it?

Now, therefore – if there was any therefore, or anything of consequence or anything left in life which followed from another thing – they were in Brighton: she, grandpapa and Mama. They were there because Brighton was restorative, and Maudie continued to cough. She now recognised that her mother had probably been correct. She would probably have lacked the strength for a dance. She had subsided into a lethargy and, apart from very short strolls on the esplanade, she devoted most of her energy to coughing. A physician in London – a white-whiskered gentleman called Doctor Nockels – had come to Brunswick Square to pronounce the view, at the price of three guineas, that Maudie needed a change of scene. The scene – what nicer – had therefore changed to Brighton. And there she stood beside her grandfather, watching the Punch and Judy show.

Mr Severus Egg inhaled the sea air with a relish, half-closing his rather wicked old eyes as he did so. His very delicate pink face was now high-flown with the health-giving air and he looked a fine sight in his tall pale chimney-pot hat, his black frock coat and his shepherd's check trowsers, the sobriety of these garments relieved by a bright yellow waistcoat and a large yellow rose in his buttonhole. His laugh, when he let it out, was stagey and deliberate. He pointed with his cane towards the rest of the audience at the Punch and Judy show.

'Ha! ha! ha! Monsters of the deep! Hottentots! Come my darling child, you will take cold!'

'It gets boring, staying all day in the hotel.'

'You look distinctly better today.'

'Mr Chatterway wrote by the second post.'

'Darling Marvo! Ha! ha! ha! Where is 'e now, eh? Balmoral, I shouldn't wonder? What? Belvoir? Inveraray?'

'Mentmore.'

'Coming down in the world, slumming we might almost say. And I suppose we wonder how long it will be before he is sent packing with a flea in his ear.'

'Grandpapa?'

'My darling?'

'Is Marvo, I mean Mr Chatterway, is he a good man?'

'Marvo? One of the very best!'

But they returned to the hotel in silence. It was a large new building, of a vulgarity which Mr Egg, upon first surveying its potted palms and Turkey carpets, its balustrades and juvenile waiters, characterised as 'excruciating! painful!' As Charlotte Nettleship had insisted, however, it was comfortable to the point of being sybaritic. The hall porter, when they entered from the cold breeze of the esplanade, interrupted Maudie's coughing fit by presenting her with yet another envelope from her most faithful correspondent.

'The Marvellous Bore again? Open it up, let's read what he has to say!'

It was hard to know whether Mr Egg's enthusiasm to discover the contents of the letter was spontaneous, or whether he was chiefly anxious to deflect attention, above all his own, from the piteousness of Maudie as she coughed. Involuntarily, she bent double as she honked, and the redness of her face, evaporating again quickly to high-flown blotchy pallor, was in the greatest possible contrast to the even, roseate health of her grandsire. When she had recovered sufficiently, she sat herself on a little sofa by the potted palm and struggled at the envelope with a mauve-gloved thumb.

'He is always so illegible,' she pronounced, '*and* so incomprehensible when one has puzzled out the hand. I will read it later.'

'Would you like me to read it aloud to you – or are they very secret and private, your *billets-doux*?'

'They are not *billets-doux*, grandpapa.'

'But not meant for all eyes?'

'I do not mind your seeing what he writes. Only I do not always think that mother ought to see.'

'Especially not at the moment,' murmured Mr Egg.

'Especially,' Maudie agreed, with the knowing tone of the completely ignorant. 'So, yes, do! Do read Marvo's latest news!'

Affixing his pince-nez, Severus Egg held the closely written little page before his eyes, and turned it this way and that.

'Bla, bla, bla! Can't read it, oh yes, quite a pantry. No, no, quite a party. "The to-you nefarious and Pattison-slandered radical Lothario of Chelsea" – what on *earth* is all this? Dilke? Do we know a man called Dilke? Ha! ha! How he bores us with people we have never heard of. Bla, bla! "And as for the tribes of Israel, they are, as in the book no longer credited by your" can't read it, "parent, they are more in number than the sands of the sea. . . ." '

'Can't read it? He means the Jews. But what's that about my parent? Does he mean papa or mama?'

'I shouldn't. . . .'

Maudie ignored the old man's cautionary tone and snatched the little document back, in order to ponder the sentence herself. 'It says, "In the Book of Books no longer credited by the countless-times artistically" – is it "artistically"?'

'I *shall* have it back,' said her grandfather with unwonted earnestness.

'No, no! It is a word. Quite clear. Cuc*kol*ded. What on earth's that? The countless-times artistically cuc*kol*ded chronicler of craters. That must be papa! How always like a riddle Marvo's letters are.'

She prattled. For once in life she seemed oblivious to atmosphere, to all the silent signals of warning which her grandfather was urgently sending out. His face became troubled, tense, angry. His shoulders more than ever moved into a shrug of complete desperation. But it was too late. Charlotte Nettleship, pretty in blue and white stripes and looking quite young enough to be Maudie's sister, had descended the broad sweep of the stair without their spying her and now appeared, calm and composed, from behind the potted ferns. There was no knowing how long she had been there when Maudie looked up and noticed her.

'Ah, darling Mama, can you help us with our puzzle?'

'No, no, child! Let me have the letter.' Severus Egg stretched out his hand, but Maudie, all gums, seemed to think his seriousness merely added to the pleasure of the game, for she held the little piece of blue paper high above her head.

'It's mine,' she declared. And then, with persistent misemphasis of the word, she said, 'I shan't let either of you look at the letter until you tell me what cuc*kol*ded is, and why Papa has been cuc*kol*ded.'

Her voice was high and shrill. A number of heads in the hotel vestibule turned at her words, so that Maudie and her grandfather were not the only persons to see the crimson steal over Charlotte's features, or notice her large blue eyes fill with tears.

TWENTY-TWO

Father and Son

. . . I have now finished The Trial *and consider it considerably less amusing than* The Daisy Chain. *I am not supposed to go out on account of coughing, which is better whatever mother says. Oh Lionel, she is so unhappy and I don't know what to do. I know you aren't supposed to write unhappy things in letters (or so Mrs Adeney always told us, do you remember!!!) but sometimes I know she has just been in her room crying. Grandpapa is being very kind to us but it is clear he is bored to distraction. He, Mama, and I are reduced to playing whist with Mr Bacon in Mama's sitting room, so you can imagine how we want society. Please come down and stay with us, or would it be too painful leaving darling Papa? I dare not write what I am thinking and fearing, but hope that you will guess something of what is in my heart and write soon to your loving Maud.*

'Does she write of her cough?' asked Maudie's father over the wreckage of breakfast some days later.

'It seems to be improving, sir, thank you.'

'Don't thank *me*, sir, for asking about my own daughter.'

'I am sorry, Papa.'

'Does she say when she might be returning to London?'

'She rather thinks that I should join her at Brighton.'

'And leave me alone here, I suppose?'

'She did not mention you, sir.'

'Quite so.'

Horace Nettleship raised his breakfast cup to his lips. It was so large that half his face was concealed while he slurped the last of his weak tea. When he replaced this receptacle in its saucer, the professor opened and shut his mouth several times, like a fish inhaling. Lionel did not know whether his father was about to speak or whether the gesture was merely a symptom of agitation.

'I had hoped that we should all travel together to some . . . some *restorative* place,' he said at length. 'It is improper that we should be thus separated.'

'I had certainly hoped to see more of Maudie once the Long began,' said Lionel, who was trying, with as judicious a blend of truthfulness and politeness as was possible to his scrupulous nature, not to appear to assent to anything which his father was saying.

'We sup early this evening, if you recall,' said Horace.

'The Hall of Science,' sighed Lionel.

'Indeed. I am trying very hard not to hurt your feelings in this matter, Lionel. But I feel that you owe it to yourself as well as to me, to realise the sheer illogic of your position. You profess belief in a Creator who made the world in seven days out of nothing. We now know beyond question that the earth was not *made* in this way but evolved. . . .'

'But sir, we are told that a thousand ages in God's sight are but as. . . .'

'No buts. You believe in a Creator and Science has proved that there can be no such person as a creator. You believe in a Redeemer. You believe that all the moral guilt of the universe was heaped on to the shoulders of one Galilean peasant who suffered public execution in a remote province of the empire. What possible reason can there be for supposing that such a wild hypothesis could be true? So much for the father and the son. Now as for the Holy Ghost. . . .'

'I have agreed to come with you to the Hall of Science this evening, sir, and to hear Mr Bradlaugh speak. But I do not see why I should sit here and listen to you blaspheme. I will see you here at six o'clock.' And, blushing hotly, Lionel got up and left his father alone in that most melancholy dining room in London.

When the young man had gone, Horace Nettleship buried his sad bald head in his hands. Life was very hard. The pain in his bosom had grown, since we last peered into it, more sharply acute. Added to the misery of fearing that he had lost the affection of his children, the wretchedness of knowing that he had never owned the affection of his wife, there were the added torments of guilt, the fires of uninformed jealousy, the smouldering of an unquenchable rage. There was nothing he could *do*. He had consulted a solicitor in Gray's Inn the day that Charlotte had embarked for Brighton. Even the preliminary inquiries made by this outwardly respectable frock-coated personage had been horrifying in their intimate obscenity. It was quite out of the question that lawyers be brought in to solve Horace's difficulties. Besides, as the solicitor had made plain, there was really no evidence of *anything*. Mrs Nettleship had confessed to nothing. The painter, whom Nettleship assumed to be in Brighton, had likewise been totally reticent. The professor had only the evidence of his eyes on two occasions: a beautiful woman, clutching with evident passion at the sleeve of a young man on the steps of the National Gallery; and, before the gaze of everyone at the Harcourt ball, a half-naked Charlotte

dancing in Timothy Lupton's arms. The rest had been constructed in
Horace Nettleship's mind by what he thought to be reasonable
inference. She had admited that she was in love with the man! And
then. . . . The darkness of all that followed twisted Nettleship's soul
and filled him with fury and self-loathing. But she had forced him to
that ignominy, forced him to it! What else could he have done? For in
the midst of all this pain and disgrace, Horace Nettleship found that he
was more violently in love with his wife than he had ever been since
their marriage day. Now she was escaped, like a bird from the snare of
the fowler. And to punish him, she had stolen his beloved Maudie and
was doubtless teaching the little angel to hate him; to distrust her own,
her very beloved father.

There were tears on the professor's cheeks at many points during the
day. He wept so much, indeed, that he did not dare to venture as far
afield as the Athenaeum. Luncheon was sent into his study, and he did
not ask about Lionel's whereabouts in the course of the day. The
father had meant what he told the son at breakfast. He believed that
Lionel owed it to himself to discard the manacles of superstition. A
free mind, a mind which revered the truth, must always allow itself the
possibility of going where natural inquiry led it. Religion's chief sin
was its sin against truth. In providing the human mind with answers to
questions which should never have been asked in the first place, it
paralysed all intellectual freedom. It made of the most glorious and
ennobling of all human activities – free intellectual and scientific
enquiry – a forbidden pursuit. It gloried in its narrowness. It made a
sin of eating the Tree of Knowledge. For Professor Nettleship, it was
only by feasting on the fruit of this tree that men rose above the level of
their kin, the baboons, chimpanzees and orang-outangs. He could not
make Lionel love him. He was too much of a realist for that. He could
in fact do very little for the youth. But he could at least show him the
importance of *truth* and try to liberate him from the menace of
religious fanaticism which held him in its grip. The boy had been, until
the breakfast outburst, almost good-humoured about it. And he had
agreed to come along this evening to the Hall of Science in Old Street
to hear Mr Bradlaugh (a regular occurrence) speak about 'The
Necessity of Atheism'.

By six o'clock, when father and son met each other once again,
Horace would have been hard placed to explain how he had filled the
intervening hours. From time to time, he had squinted at some
fragments of stone under his microscope. For some hours, he had sat
by the empty hearth in the study and turned the pages of a learned
monograph, printed in Heidelberg, about Icelandic hot-water springs.
At some point during the day he had sent back to the kitchen a tray on

which the food had hardly been touched. He had pottered hither and thither in the shrubbery. It had been quite a mild day, and it had been a surprise to find watery sunshine of a sort in the garden. During high summer, when thick darkening deciduous foliage added to the ever-green profusions of the garden, The Bower was darker than ever, more than in winter protected from solar interference. On his shrubbery walks, the Professor had not been having thoughts, for to use a transitive verb would be to suggest that he was in control of himself. On the contrary, thoughts and impressions flooded into his mind and he was quite powerless to arrange them or to resist them. He felt that the whole of his life had been wasted. His palaeo-geological researches seemed totally pointless as he paced about. He was so wretchedly miserable that his mind could not focus on volcanoes. And where was the use of knowledge if one had a mind so disturbed by guilt and wretchedness that it would not *focus?* His inability to think, the fact that he had become a slave wholly to feeling increased his rage and grief. He felt like a cork bobbing about on the swirling tempest of his own emotions. All his married life had been passing before his gaze in a series of cruel and inescapable vignettes, all the silent hatred in Charlotte's face for so many years: and then her look of triumphant cruelty as she had said 'Yes, I love him!' There had been such enviable happiness in her face as she said the words; and such a desire to wound him; and, at the same time, such damnable beauty, such bewitching charm. Oh, she was cruel, cruel! And, even in the midst of all this churning and inescapable series of vignettes there came the other stabs and darts: Maudie's absence, Maudie's illness, Maudie's running from the dining room, weeks before, exclaiming, 'I think you're both horrid.' Yes, his unhappiness had earned him the hatred of both his children. The God who did not exist had already broken Horace Nettleship's heart at Buddleigh Salterton by withdrawing His presence and revealing, with unforgettable and irrefutable clarity, His non-existence. Now He added to the torment by inspiring Lionel to believe in Him, so that the Professor had the uncongenial task of breaking the boy's faith. For such was his duty. It was imperative. Imperative!

'Father, there you are.'

'Good evening Lionel. I have asked Aggie to put a little cold meat and some beer and cheese on the sideboard. We can have some now and, if we are still hungry, eat a little more when we return from our meeting.'

'You are sure it is happening, are you?' asked Lionel. He had come to fear and dread these interviews with his father. All naturalness, all ease between the two, if it had ever existed, had gone now, and Lionel was unavoidably reminded of the scriptural warning that a man's foes would be they of his own household. The collation was consumed gloomily. Lionel did not, in fact, object to going to the Hall of Science. He was perfectly confident that nothing could shake his convictions, not death, nor life, nor principalities, nor powers, nor Mr Charles Bradlaugh. He prayed silently that there would be no more blasphemy of the sort his father had tried to utter over the breakfast table. But, in so far as he was always hungry for new experience, and liked experiencing the art of true oratory, Lionel looked forward with positive eagerness to the Hall of Science evening. It would, at least, be an evening in which he would not feel obliged to spend three hours trying to converse with his parent.

It was at about seven that the four-wheeler collected them from the front door and conveyed them through the pinkish haze of Regents Park at evening, into the dense traffic of the Euston Road and far eastward into the City. The Hall of Science, the edifice where the atheist Bradlaugh held his weekly meetings, was in Old Street St Luke's, and the pavements were already thick with people when the Professor and his son alighted from their four-wheeler.

'Quite a crowd, you see,' said Horace with some satisfaction.

'And do they usually get such numbers, sir?'

Horace Nettleship looked at his son. An irritating smirk had passed over Lionel's features.

'Though a regular ticket holder, I do not regularly take my seat in the hall here,' said Horace, a little ruffled by the boy's smile. It was the first time that Lionel had smiled all vacation.

'Perhaps tonight there are special reasons for the crowds,' said Lionel, and he pointed to a gigantic illumination which was ablaze above the doors of the hall: FATHER CUTHBERT AND MR BRADLAUGH AT EIGHT THIS EVENING.

'You knew!' spluttered Horace.

'Father, I assure you. . . .'

'You knew that this was to be an evening when that charlatan was coming here, of all places!'

'It was you, father, you insisted that we came. I knew nothing. I assure you.'

'Now we are here,' said the Professor with prim irritation, 'we had better stay.'

'If we can get a seat.'

'I have tickets.'

Merely to enter the hall was no little effort and, although he was a regular ticket-holder, Horace could not immediately see many vacant seats, even though they were a good half hour in hand. All the galleries were filled to bursting, and most of the seats, save very few in the front row of the main body of the hall, were occupied.

Lionel could not help smiling. He felt bursting out of him a profound and holy joy, almost a sense, if it did not seem too profane to indulge it, that the Father of Lights was at play in this providential turn of events. All day, Lionel had been praying that this evening would do nothing to tempt him into uncharity towards his father, nor, on the other hand, into infidelity. He was certain of his salvation in Christ. At the same time, he knew that stronger souls than he had lost their faith. His own father had once been a believer, a devout man, regular in prayer and in his readings of Holy Scripture. But a mistaken notion of intellectual sincerity had led thousands of such people away into perdition, and Lionel, rather than face such temptation had taken the precaution of fitting himself with earplugs before they left The Bower. 'But God is faithful who will not suffer you to be tempted above that ye are able.' All unseen, the Almighty hand had chosen that both the Nettleships should come to the Hall of Science that night. As the thought formed itself into Lionel's brain, he prayed fervently that his benighted parent might be led into the Light.

The audience was oddly composed. Pale fanatical clerks rubbed shoulders with thickly bearded sages in Norfolk jackets who looked as though they had journeyed by tram from Belsize Park. It was to be assumed that the majority of the gathering were of Mr Bradlaugh's atheistic opinions, but Lionel was not sure of this when, after a few moments of expectant murmuring, they burst into rapturous applause. The principal speakers were entering from the back of the hall: Mr Bradlaugh, a tall, brash, large-headed handsome man with his hair brushed back from an enormous brow, arm in arm with the little monk. Lionel noted that, unlike the meeting organised in Oxford Town Hall by the Father himself, this one allowed women in the audience to appear bonnetless and ragged with arms and necks unblushingly bared. He wondered what the holy celibate made of that.

The chairman of the proceedings introduced himself as Mr Jacob Holyoake, who spoke for about five incoherent minutes concerning future meetings of the society. He also made, amid much throat-clearing and sipping from his water glass what seemed like an interminable reference to some committee of the society which was trying to elect new members, and reminded elected members of the committee that they were to meet on the following Tuesday. It seemed an uninspiring way for the present procedure to begin. When Mr Holyoake told them that the purpose of the present evening was to debate the question, 'Is Jesus Christ an Historical Reality?' few people in this century of theirs, he said, had taken the words of Jesus Christ at face value, forsaken all worldly comfort for the sake of following the

way of the Cross. But one man who had was Father Cuthbert, and he
would be speaking of his reasons for believing that Jesus Christ was an
Historical Reality. Mr Bradlaugh, the newly elected Member of
Parliament for Northampton needed no introduction in his own
'home territory'. There was rapturous applause and then, before the
debate began, a silence. It was broken when Father Cuthbert fell to his
knees.

'No prayers, if you please, Holy Father,' said Bradlaugh. 'They will
never give you a hearing if you begin to pray.'

'I cannot speak to you until I have spoken to my Master.'

At these words Lionel heard his father beside him give a sharp intake
of breath, but he himself was returning in his mind to the first evening
when he had heard those hypnotic, almost feminine, contralto tones.
What changes there had been in life since then, what sorrows, what
new knowledge and what clouds of mystery.

'Dear Mr Holyoake, I appeal to you,' said Father Cuthbert. 'You
have allowed me an hour to speak to you. Surely you will allow me a
few minutes out of my hour in which to address my heavenly Lord and
Master.'

The matter, for the prosaic Mr Holyoake, was evidently a pro-
cedural one, and it was put to the vote. Those in favour of allowing the
little monk to pray were asked to raise their right hand. It appeared
that, unbelievers though they were, they saw no objection to the
evangelist offering up a prayer in their midst. This he did at once, as
soon as the vote was carried, in the lilting musical manner which
Lionel found so beguiling. The prayer was no sooner finished than the
monk began to speak to his audience with the manifest aplomb of the
true orator.

'Jesus! Jesus! Who and what was this Incarnate Being, this Jesus,
whose Name has covered the earth as the waters cover the sea? That is
the question which we have come together tonight, ladies and
gentlemen, to decide. Jesus! Who was he, I ask you? And I say it would
be more proper to say who *is* he! My task is to argue rationally with
you tonight. But also to proclaim to you, as to the whole world, Jesus
who is alive. Behold the Man, the Desired of all nations, the super-
human figure towards whom the combined fingers of History and
Prophecy have pointed, backwards and forwards, from all ages and
every corner of the earth.'

There could be no doubt that the orator held in his power even those
in his audience who might be most expected to disagree with him.
There were philosophers here: Mr Spencer and Mr Huxley were in the
front row. It was perhaps the most learned audience that Father
Cuthbert had ever addressed. He seemed as confident in his speaking

to them as he had been to the strange town-hall miscellany during Lionel's first experience of him.

'And now, my friends, how were the ancient prophecies fulfilled? How was the world visited by this figure, this God-man, the Desired of all Nations? It was visited by the birth of a little Jew-baby, whose birth, its locality, object and approximate period had been whispered by every wind under heaven, ever since the Divine Gifts of Prophecy and Intelligent deduction had been breathed upon the world. Jesus, the Jew-Child of Bethlehem, was and is the living Answer to the Pantheistic Problem of the Mystic East, and the Key to the Enigma of the Polytheistic West. Oh! What a mighty rebuff to the combined anticipations of Magnificent Man, that the wheel of Supernal Destiny should so be set, that the embodiment of Omnipotence, the Consummation of the World's Vigil, was to be delegated to a stable-born Jew!'

The Reverend Father expatiated at some length upon the Jewishness of his saviour. He reiterated that the Jews were still the holy people of God, the Chosen Race and that we should honour and revere them for it. The day would dawn – oh yes, you could laugh, but it would come, for it would be the natural fulfilment of holy prophecies – when the holy people of God would once more return to their homeland. When the Lord turned again the exile of his people from Mount Sion, then would he fill their mouths with laughter and their tongues with joy, the joy of the Christian Gospel, their knowledge of the promised Messiah, born, oh yes, to the simple Jew-maiden. He could have been born a Greek. Perhaps the Master of Harcourt, who had spent so many years of his life corrupting the young by teaching them to read the hellish doctrines of Plato – would have preferred it if Our Blessed Lord had been born a Greek. Had the audience here tonight contemplated what it would be like if anybody practised the vices advocated in the *Symposium* of Plato? Father Cuthbert hoped he was not the only British man whose blood ran cold at the very thought. The pits and troughs of the Platonic teaching were worlds apart from the pure moral sweetness of our kinsmen – yes, our kinsmen the Jews. For were there not ten Lost Tribes? And had they not crossed the sea and settled in the uttermost parts of the earth, even in our own British Lands in days of yore?

All this seemed a long way from the central question of the debate, but at length, Father Cuthbert returned to his brief. Jesus the Jew-man was no myth, no historical phantom. He was true. Did anyone in that hall of science suppose that there was a shred of historical or scientific evidence which could disprove the existence of Jesus? Did they really? Was he not attested in the writings of the great Jewish historian Josephus as well as in the Holy Gospels? And did they believe that this same Jesus – yes, the same! Yesterday, today and forever, oh blessed Jesus! – did they believe that he had shed his precious blood upon the Cross, died and been buried without a resurrection of the flesh? What a story to have invented! Could not the authorities of the day, the Roman governor, the High Priests of the temple, could they not have produced this body if Jesus were indeed dead after the Third Day? How did they, those Romans and those Jews, explain the empty tomb? How did the men and women of this generation explain such a thing?

'Yes, my brethren, my dear rationalist friends! How do you explain it? You ask me is Jesus Christ an Historical Reality? I answer yes, yes! But I would want to add, He is no mere Historical Reality! He is *the* present Reality. It is in Him that all Reality takes shape, for without Him was not anything made that was made. And He is the Same, Yesterday, Today and Forever!'

Horace Nettleship felt, during this peroration, a tingling of goose-flesh all over his body, and much to his own surprise he joined in the general applause which greeted the little monk when he sat down. Bradlaugh rose to speak next. He was genial at first. 'The audience can perhaps see now why Father Cuthbert is the only man whose influence I fear for my followers.' Normally, Horace found Bradlaugh an inspiring speaker in his vulgar brash manner. Tonight, he seemed altogether flat and uninteresting. His faint Birmingham accent also added to the unpersuasiveness of his words. Horace knew it was wildly illogical to be moved by such considerations, but there had been a melody, an almost aristocratic euphony in the Reverend Father's tones which had been highly beguiling. Almost without anger, he felt that he could understand why Lionel had been so beguiled by the romance of the monk, and his passionate religious fervour.

Lionel, by his father's side, had been praying for Horace throughout Father Cuthbert's oration, but, in spite of himself, he was gripped and fascinated by Mr Bradlaugh. Here was no monster, but a handsome, honest-faced Englishman who was asking blunt questions that Lionel had never quite dared to ask himself before.

'Of course I mean no disrespect to the Reverend Father, else I shouldn't have asked him to this hall tonight, Ladies and Gentle*men*.' He stressed, for some reason, the last syllable of the word. It made him sound faintly like an auctioneer, rather than an orator, but it was an oratorical trick which held Lionel's unwilling attention. 'But I would remind you all that we are in the Hall of Science. And I am sure that you will see that it is in a scientific spirit that I make these enquiries. First, can we as men and women of the nineteenth century, knowing what we *do* now, honestly listen seriously to a story which starts out with a woman finding herself with child as a result of conversing with an angel? Yes, ladies and gentle*men*. I remind you of that. This Jesus Christ, whose historical reality you are considering, is believed by the Reverend Father and his followers to have come into existence through no human paternity, no human agency. He was conceived by the Holy Ghost. I have no experience of the Holy Ghost.'

'Evidently!' came the shrill retort of Cuthbert, who was fingering his rope girdle with long white anxious fingers.

'You have had your say, Holy Father, and I am now having mine, so no interruptions if you please.' Anger passed momentarily into Bradlaugh's pleasant features and Lionel could see that the man was a fanatic. 'It is a life, this so-called Historical Reality of the Holy Father's, which begins with a girl conceiving a child without having known a man. A fine consideration in this Hall of Science. It is a life which ends, as the Holy Father has reminded us, with an empty tomb. The Holy Father would like us to believe that Jesus Christ rose from the dead from that tomb. He would! But I can think of many and many another explanation, ladies and gentle*men*, and so can you. And so can we all. Why, the body-snatchers are out in London every night! Do we suppose that the cemeteries of London are the scenes of repeated miracles of resurrection? The empty tomb is not, however, how the story ends for the Holy Father and his disciples. For we have other stories to deal with, in this case of the most unreal Historical Reality I have ever read about. After he rose from the dead, this historical reality, this Jesus Christ is said to have risen into Heaven. To have ascended, body and soul, flesh and bone. I ask you, in this Hall of Science, to consider this question. Into Heaven, flesh and bones. Where did he go? Did he go to Mars, or to Venus or to the Moon? Since the primitive people who wrote the books of the New Testament have faded from the earth, we know more about the composition of the universe than that. A body rising up into Outer Space! Ladies and Gentle*men*, Ladies and Gen - tle - *men!*' He did not need to finish the sentence. There was a murmur of condescending agreement.

For Lionel all this was highly disturbing. Of course, he had had the experience some eight weeks before, of Jesus Christ coming into his heart. Lionel now knew Jesus as his personal saviour. But these rather more blunt and prosaic considerations had never entered his head. He regarded them as blasphemous. Even as Bradlaugh spoke, he tried to blot them out of his head. He prayed for faith to ignore the words, and to remember only the things which Father Cuthbert had said. He felt, a little unworthily, that even if Bradlaugh were right, and his faith had been in vain, he would never admit as much to his father, and allow the professor the triumph of saying, 'I told you so.'

The professor, meanwhile, attended to Bradlaugh's oration with smiles of tenderness. His thoughts were very different from those of his son. All this, he felt, may very well be true. Perhaps we do know more about the positioning of the stars and the planets than did Saint Luke. Perhaps there are many explanations for empty tombs. But there was something which Bradlaugh could not explain: the abiding presence in the world, ever since the discovery of that empty tomb, of people who were convinced that this Jesus, this Historical Reality, was alive. Why did they do so? The Professor felt an ever-deepening nostalgia for his own days of faith. He remembered the warm-glow which came to him during prayer, the sense, which had eluded him since Buddleigh Salterton, that all sorrow was endurable because 'underneath are the everlasting arms'. He tried to banish from his head the memory of a text about God choosing the foolish to confound the wise and the weak things of this world to destroy the mighty.

The applause for Bradlaugh was decidedly more muted than the clapping for Father Cuthbert had been. Lionel was astonished when his father turned to him and said, 'Do you wish to meet the speakers?'

Since they were near the front, and Professor Nettleship was on the inner committee of Mr Bradlaugh's rationalistic society, they had no difficulty in finding their way to a back room behind the stage whence emanated a steamy miasma of strong tea.

'Well, well, this is a great honour I'm *sure*,' said Bradlaugh, gripping Horace Nettleship's shoulder, and adding, 'This is the boy, this is the boy? Professor Huxley wanted to stay but he had to go home.'

Father Cuthbert himself looked as much at ease among the Norfolk-jacketed pipe-smokers and unbonneted feminists as, perhaps, he did anywhere. That is, he was staring about him with an aspect of bird-like surprise, as though startled to have alighted on that particular planet at that particular time. In his distinctive and completely idiosyncratic version of the monkish habit, his strangeness in the assembly was perhaps exaggerated. There seemed something particularly bizarre in witnessing a figure who might have stepped out of the pages of Sir Walter Scott or Bulwer Lytton stirring a cup of tea with spoon. It produced a kind of chronological shock which one would receive upon entering a drawing-room in Mayfair and meeting a Crusader armed to all points, or, the other way about, if one were to discover the brass effigy of a medieval baron smoking a cigarette. The Reverend Father had obviously, at some point in history, contrived to produce this effect of shock in the rest of the world, and succeeded, in the process, in shocking himself. The air of surprise was increased, as Lionel had noted when he last viewed the phenomenon, by Father Cuthbert's eyebrows, which were shaped in arches of almost Gothic proportions, giving to his face an expression of perpetual astonishment.

When Lionel was led up to the monk, over whom he towered by several inches, he muttered, incoherently, about having heard him preach in Oxford Town Hall eight weeks earlier.

'And I said to you then we would meet again!' beamed the monk.

This was surely a remarkable feat of memory. Lionel had spoken to the Father in a thick crush for only a few seconds after his meeting in the Town Hall. Since then, presumably, the monk had addressed countless meetings and been 'in journeyings often'. But he remembered him!

'Though myself an unbeliever, sir,' butted in Horace Nettleship, 'I feel I must congratulate you upon the manly and honest way in which you were prepared to come here tonight and speak to us.'

When his father spoke to strangers, Lionel always felt an inexplicable tingling of embarrassment. On this occasion, he felt a gush of quite irrational fury. He could cheerfully have killed his father for speaking to Father Cuthbert at all. He knew this was irrational. It was through the magnanimity of his father that he was there in the first place, face to face with his hero, his father in God. And yet this very magnanimity of Horace was intolerable. Lionel felt anger with his father that even the good things in life, which almost by definition were independent of the professor, should actually be percolated to him through the paternal medium.

'You sir, an unbeliever?' asked Father Cuthbert in what appeared to be profound amazement.

'Yes.' The professor opened and shut his mouth nervously, in the goldfish mode.

'But were you always an unbeliever?'

'No, no. The conclusions of science. . . .'

'Let me finish, my dear,' said the Father with the shrill abruptness of a sharp-tongued governess. 'Were you an unbeliever when you knelt down as a child each night and said your prayers?'

'No, as I say to you, sir, my faith, my childish faith, was shaken by the conclusions of science. When I became a man I put away my childish things.'

'Ah ha!' Father Cuthbert wagged his long snowy finger and, turning conspiratorially to Lionel he smiled, as though the argument was already won. 'And aren't we forgetting something? Aren't we forgetting that unless you be converted and become as little children you cannot enter the kingdom of heaven? And is there not perchance a person in all this that you have been forgetting, professor? Someone who would not be very impressed with your professorial arguments, eh?'

The snowy-fingered hand was replaced beneath the thick folds of the monk's scapular and he smiled with the prim satisfaction of having won the tournament 'game set and match'.

'I am afraid, sir, that I do not catch your drift,' said Horace Nettleship a trifly hotly.

'Who was it who taught you to kneel by your bedside, professor? Who was it who first taught you to lisp the Holy Name of Jesus? Who was it who taught you that you were one of the little lambs of Jesus and that *none* shall pluck thee from his hand? Ah, yes sir, your blush tells me all. Was it not your mother?'

'I would thank you, sir, to leave my mother out of this consideration.'

'But would she, professor? Would she?'

And the monk turned to Lionel with an impish expression which almost turned into a wink.

TWENTY-THREE

At Cliveden

Our old friend was a rather splendid sight in his suiting of white flannel and his large straw hat. It was this vulgarian fondness of his for the outdoors (we find him on the terrace after breakfast) which accounted for the fact that his face is yet more sunburnt than when we last met, and the touches of whisker beneath the ear yet more hoary. The rather disturbing thought occurred to him that he might be mellowing, for he had left Mentmore, the previous day, with no more excitement than could be derived from the expression on Lady Rosebery's face as he climbed into his carriage and told her that he was bound for a field full of *considerably* taller poppies than she had managed to muster with her Dilkes and her Rothschilds.

Arrangements here were certainly *ducal*, so that one would feel grand enough even without your Lord Algernon Lennoxes and your Harty-Tarties. Mr Chatterway was glad that they were not at Eaton Hall, partly because the journey to Cheshire would have been wearisome, and chiefly because he disliked its riotous Gothic modernity. The *cinquecento* elegances of Cliveden were altogether more to his taste. Indeed, standing alone on the terrace, and seeing, over the balustrade, the formal gardens still moist with dew and touched with the haze that promised a scorchingly hot July day, he felt that he could have been in Italy, in the *palazzo* of some Genoese nobleman of ancient line, or the summer residence of an American heiress, were it not for the fact that, beyond the garden's end, there stretched the unmistakable lushness – *tout à fait anglais* in its deciduous greens and almost-blues – of the Thames valley. Bright silver in the morning, the river shone in the distance. It was the sort of sight which made you glad to be in England for all the absurdities which the social routines involved. The tittle-tattle was, unquestionably, wearing a little thin. One had now got the idea. There was a limit to what could be said about the Grand Old Man's return to office, or about the marital adventures of the limited number of people whom *everyone* knew. Chatterway was grateful that his net stretched wider than that of his hostess. He had made a remark about *Mrs* Johnnie Cross to the Duchess the previous evening and discovered a stony ignorance in her face. 'George Eliot, what?' Not only did she not know 'the gentleman', but it was quite clear she had never heard of him!

Perusing the envelopes, forwarded by a faithful servant from Half Moon Street and placed in his hand that morning by one of the Duchess's footmen, Mr Chatterway reflected that he probably knew *of* just about everyone in England. He would hate to be limited to the tall poppies alone, or to the solid little foothills where such sturdy specimens as the Gutches flourished, or again to the Bohemian backwaters which were really Lupton's only stamping ground; or would be, if he carried on at the present rate!

One little letter told him of a dinner party with the Millais. He reserved the information in his head for repetition the next time he was in any sense 'in touch' with Lupton. Another card remarked upon the brilliance of a young poet called Oscar Wilde. Mr Chatterway was a while – such was the abundance of riches in his hand – before he turned to the childish little envelope with a Brighton post-mark.

I say, Marvo, this time you have properly torn it!!! Mama says I am not to write to you any more she even said she was shocked that you had been writing to me at all without her permission which isn't usually like her at all. But you must write, of course Or I shall die of boredom quite simply. She was furious of course because of your knowing about Mr Lupton. Actually he doesn't seem to come and pester us so much lately, though he is in Brighton painting what he says is a new sort of painting for him. Just a lot of smudge I think it is, Poor old sausage, he isn't really a very good painter is he.

But I don't know how I can write all this unimportant news when the two really important *things are that we are going abroad isn't it exciting and also that you will never* guess *what Lionel* has gone and done.

My news first. Well Mama thinks I am so ill (sob sob) that I really must be taken abroad. Not a very healthy time of year for travelling, according to Grandpapa, but Mama says that any-thing will be better than England and that I really must get rid of this dreadful cough. Doctor Nockells agrees with her. He has been down from London several times at untold expense.

(Next day) That is the trouble with this wretched cough. It is so tiring! I had begun to tell you that we are going abroad, Mama and I, as soon as everything may be arranged. But I had no sooner covered two sides of the paper than I found myself drifting into sleep. I am writing this wide awake. Mama has gone out so I can write in peace, but I dont know when I might post it.

I shall probably bribe *the chamber maid who is a nice girl called Fanny.*

No, it's no good really am *too tired to write properly. I* was *going to tell you* all *about our plans. We think we will go to* Venice, *what do you think. Come and see us. Come and* surprise us there! *I know Mama would be* pleased *to see you* really. *And now I haven't left room for Lionel's news but Mama thinks he is* mad, *and she has said that* Papa *must be mad to have* let *him. And isn't it funny that is the only time I have ever heard her say anything against Papa. Grandpapa says we should look on the bright side and that it is all like something in Matt Lewis.*

But I have never read The Monk *have you.*

'Yes, my pretty, and *La Réligieuse* by darling old Diderot.'

Holding his letter bundle in his right hand, loosely, he gazed across the lawns and urns in almost conscious quest of consolation. The colloquial jabber of the child had power to wound which surprised even him, who prided himself on his self-knowledge. The epistle left so little resolved, but awoke so many areas of pain. The illness was agitating. They would not be getting a doctor from London for any ordinary 'cough', and the silly little pretty would not be aware of any grave illness. On the other hand, what *was* all this: this *we* who were going abroad, this knowing about Mr Lupton? What was there, beyond what Chatterway's own speculative gossip had suggested, to know? Did the letter imply the presence of the geological professor on their tour? And who ever heard of going to Venice for their health? As if these things were not disturbing enough, she had told him that there was news of Lionel, without spelling out what it was. This was really the ultimate vexation. Nor could he, if a ban had been placed on the correspondence, write back at once and ask her to clarify, for his writing on an envelope would be recognised immediately by this new, this transmogrified and terrifying Charlotte.

He thought with sorrow of *his* Charlotte, the little one he had cherished since he first glimpsed her in her cradle and felt a pang of violent jealousy of old Egg. Perhaps it was unnatural in a man to desire parenthood with the passion of a woman. He had done so, and done so shamelessly, since consciousness of his capacity for it had dawned. What could be more mysterious, more like magic, more soberly aweful, more magnificently joyful than the knowledge that another human soul existed because of oneself? In the case of the female of the species, though he would have settled for a son, what more delightful, too, than the encasement of that soul. Mr Chatterway had a rare and unmasculine fondness for babies. Sometimes, when walking in the park, it was as much as he could do to prevent himself kidnapping one in its perambulator. He was haunted by the soft, pink, tiny screwed up hands and faces, little parcels of potential existence to be unwrapped, with what inevitably fascinating results, by the years. But although he could not pass a perambulator without peering into it and growling words of approbation to a frequently disapproving nursery-maid, he was not one of those baby-worshippers whose adoration stopped short when the object of concentration passed the age of six months. The staggering, bonneted forms of human beings on reins, learning with much trial and error to walk, filled our friend with equal emotions of wonder and tenderness. For various reasons, all these feelings, strongly marked as a generality, had been particularly concentrated in his dealings with the Eggs and the Nettleships. Charlotte's behaviour, or absence of behaviour, in his regard, throughout the months of summer, was therefore doubly hurtful. In fact, the woman was now for the first time incomprehensible to him. Perhaps she always had been. Perhaps he should have recognised her mystery much earlier on, when he had taken her reins and helped that pretty nurse (oh, Eggy could choose 'em!) to escort young Charlotte take her first steps in the gardens at Brunswick Square. He was barely one and twenty at the time. She had managed to elude him, as he now recognised, ever since; perhaps she had been making a conscious effort to do so, for females of whatever age were – he was better experienced and qualified than most to understand the fact – resistant to the notion of being *possessed*.

Vacancy absorbed him for half an hour and his face was unwontedly drawn and sad as he sat there, feeling the warmth of the day coming up, and bathing his taut cheeks, but deriving no comfort therefrom. Thus attracted, he forget the rest of his correspondence and it was only when he was about to turn back into the house that he bothered with the other envelopes. He would have discovered much earlier, had he read his letters in a different order, that he held in his hand news far more momentous than that the Nettleships were contemplating a visit to Europe. The black-smudged cheap paper and the Belgian postmark made the letter in question so uninteresting to him that he opened it at the last, after he had taken in any amount of trivia from recent hostesses and news of other house-parties going on in different parts of the country. No warning sounded in his breast. The hand was totally unfamiliar to him, but his wife's disappearance from view, now sixteen years since, was so complete that he did not associate the unfortunate with any particular corner of the globe. He heard of her from time to time. But it was one of the ironies of history that he who knew everything about everyone was almost completely ignorant of his wife's whereabouts or manner of life. He had been told enough to make him wish to blot the matter from consciousness. Belgium, had for him, other associations apart from marital ones. Had not the to him ever-genial though in general over-ambitious King Leopold referred on more than one occasion to 'that *pretty* Chatter-way'. Good enough compliment, that, from Queen Victoria's uncle no less. And it was natural that the by no means least-esteemed of the Great Duke's protegés, albeit a protégé of his dotage, should in Brussels, where Wellington held virtual court in '15, be received with no little deference and enthusiasm. Yes, a thousand curses, yes, he had read *La Religieuse*. Yes, he knew who lurked and wept and sorrowed at the Béguinage at Bruges. But he always blotted the fact out of consciousness. And since, apart from a Belgian postage stamp, there was nothing on the present communication to suggest that it came from *Bruges*, why should he mind or notice, or even bother to read it?

So, the envelope, of the cheapest and roughest quality, was bordered with a quarter of an inch of black; what of that, what? It was only on a second perusal of the object that he knew what the envelope must contain. Until that point he was in the position of the old President of Magdalen College (Routh, fine fellow) who, upon surveying a flag at half-mast had exclaimed, 'No, don't tell me, let me guess!' Mr Chatterway, when he spied that he had a letter on mourning-paper, was guessing; but not very enthusiastically. He genuinely and thoughtlessly imagined that some scarcely significant Belgian baroness, or jumped-up flower of the Ghent bourgeoisie had shuffled off this mortal coil. So what? One received the news of death all the time. It was a less miraculous, less troubling intelligence than the news of births; or anyway in Mr Chatterway's experience. Strangely, it was the unfamiliarity of the hand which prevented him at first from taking much interest in the scrubby little paper.

When, at last, he opened it, however, he knew what the news contained, for the significance of it all – Belgium, mourning, a stranger's hand – had sunk in. It was the Reverend Mother of the Order of Saint Elizabeth of Hungary who wrote to him in the French tongue. She sincerely regretted that Madame Chatterway, who had been unwell for some time, had finally passed into the hands of her merciful Saviour. She had been a most devoted Béguine, and the discovery that Madame had a husband still living rather than being, like the other Béguines, a widow, had been, for the Reverend Mother, something of a shock. However, by the time the discovery was made, Madame was mortally sick and there was nothing which could be done but nurse her in the infirmary. She had made a very good death, but asked rather than write any communication herself, that the

Reverend Mother inform Mr Chatterway when death had finally overtaken her. This had occurred at six o'clock on the morning of writing. A requiem had already been said for the repose of her soul.

'But not for mine', he said aloud to himself, with infinite sadness. 'My soul will never know repose, and nor does it deserve to.'

TWENTY-FOUR

'The most capital wheeze'

It was rather as if the capital city were a vast pan which someone had put on to simmer, and since forgotten to remove from the hob. London sweltered. It sweated and grunted. It stank. Traffic had slowed down almost to a standstill, for motion in this heat was almost impossible, and even the more energetic cab-horses became, beneath the scorching blaze of the high sun, like ambling Rosinantes. In squares, the grass and herbage were wilting, and the leaves on the trees, grown dark, dusty and cynical, had lost all memory of the enthusiasm with which they had burst upon the world three months before. The shade was scarcely cooler than the sun. In alleys, the only signs of life and motion were cats and bare-footed urchins, who hopped about because the cobblestones had grown unendurably hot on the soles. Even those who were shod might find treading the pavement a veritable ordeal by fire. At all the drinking-troughs and fountains, crowds of red-faced perspirers huddled with empty jugs and expressions of disgruntlement. The very pigeons waddled in the dusty gutters with scarcely enough energy to fly.

Any inhabitants who could do so had gone away. Many of them were being towed down to the water's edge in bathing machines in Kentish resorts or sniffing the Channel breezes in Sussex. Others, more adventurous still, had strayed far enough to get away from the heat, to rain-swept mountains and misty heaths. But London suffered and stewed, like a dogged old gentleman who had not been expecting the heat when he dressed himself that morning, but who refused to remove his top-coat for fear of revealing his braces.

If anywhere in London could have been cool, it must have been The Bower, Abbey Grove, Saint John's Wood, for no house was more skilful at keeping the elements at bay. Indeed it was only when it had tired of scorching the parasols of governesses in Regents Park, and melting the very dustbin lids in the alleys of Kentish Town that the sun thought to circle round once more and make a final assault on the residence of Professor Nettleship. To judge from the light in the drawing room, it had failed to make much impression; for everything in The Bower seemed as dark as usual. But by the clever device of a hardened practitioner of the art of siege, the sun had done a bargain with The Bower, agreeing that the house would not be pestered with light if it took double its share of heat. The Turkey carpets, velvet curtains, and abundance of lace and felts seemed as though they might smother the room altogether. It was a wonder that Horace Nettleship could stand there. It would be inaccurate in his historian to pretend that he did so coolly, or calmly. Clenching and unclenching his fist, the professor was sweating profusely: so violently in fact that trickles gushed down his sleeves like volcanic lava and poured in streams down his knuckles. Never, in forty years of interest in the volcanic surfaces of the world, had the professor felt so much sympathy with Etna and Vesuvius, nor felt so vividly what it might be like to erupt. He stood with his back to the room attempting to preserve his dignity, if the preservation of cool blood proved an impossibility.

His wife stood a long way off, so near the piano stool that if she chose she could have rested one knee upon it. But she did not choose. Charlotte was bolt upright and but for a certain glistening about the brow and the nose, you would not have guessed that she was noticing the heat. She wore a long black skirt and a striped blouse of blue and white, fastened at the throat with a large amethyst. Her poise and coolness were a little terrifying, which was perhaps why her husband turned his back so decidedly upon her. Looked at more closely, there were in fact signs of anxiety in her face. Every so often, she bit a small corner of her lip, giving her pretty mouth a twisted sneer. But her large blue eyes were calm, and as shiningly beautiful as before.

'I must know if *he* is going with you', said her husband.

'You are entitled to ask me nothing. Precisely nothing.'

'I am entitled to stop my own wife committing adultery. . . .'

'How dare you?'

'And I am furthermore entitled to protect my only daughter. What evidence is there that travel would improve Maudie's health at this juncture? Now, the Lake District, or Scotland would be another matter. But Northern Italy! In this heat!'

'You speak to me about the safety of your children.'

'Yes, I do.'

'When you have allowed Lionel to be swallowed up in the entourage of a mad monk. I find your scale of judgments to say the least perplexing.'

'Lionel has visited this monastery for at most a week.'

'Do you believe that you will ever see him again?'

'Great Scott, woman, don't be so ridiculously melodramatic. Of course, I shall see Lionel.'

He turned to say this, perhaps she thought, so that she could see his proud paternal smile. Charlotte tried not to find touching Horace's blatant desire to proclaim that he knocked along so well with his first-born.

'We shall see,' she said calmly.

'Lionel's adventures in the monastery are all under control, perfect control. This Italian scheme is altogether another matter. You perhaps do not realise that I have the power – some would say, the duty – to prevent it altogether. A woman can not simply go abroad without her husband's permission; still less can she take his child; still less, if she fails to tell him who her companions on the journey are going to be. Since you do not deny that Lupton is going with you, I have to conclude that this is your intention.'

There was a suspicion, the merest suspicion of a quiver in her statuesque poise, the hint of emotion in her voice when she said, 'You are very fortunate, husband, that you are not conducting this conversation with my father's solicitor.'

'I do not know what you mean.'

'In that case you have a very short memory.'

'You treat me as if I were a criminal.'

'No, merely an animal.'

'I ignore your abuse. It is unworthy of you. But I insist upon your telling me if Lupton is or is not going to travel with you to Italy.'

'I feel no obligation to submit to your interrogations.'

'And it is you who speak of lawyers!'

'Do you really think that the law entitles you to behave as you behaved to me . . . that night; that night after the ball?'

Once more he turned towards the window in agonised shame and silence.

'Ah!' she crowed victoriously. 'So you feel a trifle embarrassed. I am glad.'

'Charlotte, if you knew. . . .'

'I do not wish to know.'

'. . . how I have missed you, longed for you, yes. Now you blame me for Lionel going. Well, I suppose that was my fault. He will return from this monastic caper, of that I have no doubt. But in general, yes. You are of course perfectly right. He will grow away from us. He will pursue his own course. He will leave us. And now you propose to take my Maudie from me also.'

'Yes.'

'Then I shall have no one.'

'You deserve no one.'

'Does one *deserve* the members of one's family?' For a moment he had become donnish, almost detached in his interest in the generality of the question.

'I certainly never deserved you!'

'Oh, Charlotte. Remember our early days, do remember them.'

'I remember little else. If for you they are a happy memory, I am pleased. I can make no such boast myself. We are ill-matched, Horace, and always were. It was a mistake.'

'No! Do not say that.'

'I had intended to deceive you. I had intended merely to return today and pack. Tomorrow Maudie and I would have left for the continent. After a decent interval, I should have told you, through my solicitors, that I want a divorce.'

'Charlotte!'

'As it is, you force this out of me.'

'You do not know what you are saying.'

'I have considered it.'

'I should never allow it, lawyers or no lawyers. On what possible grounds could any such action proceed? I am afraid that you do not understand the law. *I* might divorce you, if I choose. But I do not choose. You are the wife of my bosom. On no possible grounds could you divorce me – your lawful husband these twenty years, the father of your children: the father of Maudie whom you propose to snatch from me. It is simple malice! I am, I repeat, Maudie's father.'

There was a very long silence in which, in the overpoweringly torrid room, they listened to one another breathe.

'I wish,' she announced with calculation, 'that I could share your confidence.'

He turned to her with a look of thunderous fury and exclaimed. 'Good God, is there no vulgarity to which you won't sink?'

'I rather thought that vulgar sinkings were *your* speciality.'

'You would be prepared to lie – to, to – *bastardise* our own daughter for the sake of this *obscene* infatuation?'

'And if it were not a lie?'

'But: she is a Nettleship to her *fingertips*.'

'It is said that even dogs grow to look like their owners. I do not know in what feature poor little Maudie resembles any of your relations.'

'But it has often been said, in your presence, that she favours me. You know that well. You would never substantiate a lie. You know that you would not.'

Charlotte blinked a little at her lord and master. She had half-expected this admittedly coarse line of conversation to throw him off his stroke. But his confidence, evidently, was unshakable. Once again, silent wilting in the heavy atmosphere of the drawing-room was broken solely by the sound of their furious exhalations. Then, as an afterthought, he burst out once more.

'Great heavens, you haven't been spinning these lies about Maudie to the painter, have you?'

'The painter?'

'You know perfectly well who I mean.'

'Why not name Timothy Lupton?'

'Because for the moment I choose not to sully my lips with his filthy name. Answer me this at least. Have you been telling *him* that I am not the father of my own children?'

She closed her eyes and sighed a little. Then she smiled, as though Horace were himself an unreasonable child with whom there was only a limited point in remonstrating.

'I think,' she said, 'that it would be a kindness to the servants if we were to shut up the house altogether for a few weeks. If Lionel is in Wales and Maudie and I are going to the continent, it would seem a little hard for Aggie and Hopkins not to be given the chance of. . . .'

'I see no reason why the servants should fail in their duty merely because everyone else in the household has taken leave of their senses.'

'Ah, so you admit that Lionel was mad to go to Wales?'

'You know my views. I merely stated that yours inclined to melodrama.'

This little skirmish came to both parties as a relief. They had charted their vessels, momentarily, into churning whirlpools. Charlotte had perhaps designed the horrifying unease which a discussion of Maudie's ancestry would certainly induce. But this did not mean that she was capable of sustaining the matter conversationally. It was not something which could possibly be talked about. Many of the things which preoccupy our most colourful thoughts are not matters which any but a mystic or a dramatist could put into words. The Nettleships, having been silent together as Trappists for fifteen years, spoke more freely, when the rule of silence was broken, than they would have done had they been more accustomed to the ordinary constraints imposed by the regular opening and shutting of mouths. But even they knew boundaries.

'Maudie and I sleep in my father's house tonight. We take boat for France in the morning.'

Her husband turned and forced his features into a different shape and pattern. She watched this facial readjustment and noticed at once that he was abandoning the offensive pose in favour of conciliation.

'Charlotte,' he said slowly, quietly, 'Charlotte.'

Charlotte Nettleship inwardly resolved that, whatever her husand did, she would be doggedly resistant.

'I have been harsh,' he said quietly as he sat on the sofa and tried to catch her gaze. But she continued to stand in the shadows and refused to look at him. She told herself that there was now nothing to stop her walking out of the room and never speaking to this – this MAN – again.

'I have behaved,' he conceded, 'with impetuous rashness. I have not recognised the difficulties which life has imposed upon you, Charlotte: my *dear*.'

This was something which she had dreaded, as the worst that could happen. She began to think that she *should* perhaps, walk out and leave him, discourteous as it would seem, in mid-sentence. Indeed, had Maudie not been above with Hopkins, packing her trunks, flight itself would have been the only way of evading the professorial endearments.

'I concede that I am fast becoming an old man, and that you still retain much of your youth.' He added, with tactless emphasis, '*Much*.'

Inwardly she prayed. For the past month she had been in dread of this meeting. She had been afraid of her husband, afraid of the embarrassment, and fearful, simply, of physical hazards and assaults. But in all the weeks apart Horace had become a conveniently odious creature, overbearing, humourless and bald. She had forgotten what it was which had held her to his side for twenty years of matrimony. She had forgotten his power to evoke pity.

> She loved me for the dangers I had passed,
> And I loved her that she did pity them.

Was it like that, all those years ago, when he had told the schoolgirl in Malvern of his journeys to the other side of the erupting earth? She had with great determination forgotten. But she was now reminded with overwhelming force that, whatever her former emotions had been, the dominant one, after a space in his company, was pity. She could not unsay the harsh things which had already passed between them. But she longed bitterly to do so. Silence, she now saw, was best, a silent watch, in which, without speaking, they at least kept one another company. But even as pity welled up in her bosom to torture her, Charlotte knew that she had gone too far. Pride could not possibly allow her to recant, and pity itself forbade her to attempt an explanation.

'Do you have nothing to say to me – nothing to the father of your children?' he whimpered.

He knew that she had nothing; he knew that he had squashed and silenced her. Even as he felt himself becoming an object of pathos, Horace Nettleship despised himself for his weakness. He should, by rights, have locked his wife in her bedroom and forbidden this hare-brained scheme of taking Maudie to Italy. Nothing good, he knew, would come of it. Was he a man or a mouse? As he removed his spectacles and rubbed his eyes despondently with sweaty knuckles he concluded that he was probably a mouse. Quite simply, he did not want Charlotte to go, and he wanted Maudie to go even less.

'I ask you no more questions,' he continued. 'I demand nothing. I ask you merely to stay with me. To stay with your husband. . . . Oh Charlotte. Please.'

It was revolting to her to see him crumple and whimper. A phrase rose to her lips in which she would have said that nothing could be gained by these exchanges. Such an observation would have belonged to an earlier phase of existence when she was still trying to leave footsteps on the sands of time. What, strictly, could be said to be gained by *any* observation? We did not say things for gain. But we were capable of saying things to console, and this she refused to do; for if she attempted by the merest word or gesture to comfort her husband in his suffering, she would be announcing her capitulation.

'I will go and see if Hopkins and Maudie have finished packing,' she said and rose to her feet. Horace Nettleship never admired his wife so much as in that moment when, with cruel majesty, she strode silently out of the drawing room. But it was a dramatic vignette, not the rounding of a story. Trunks and timetables, servants with pins and ironing boards, and above all the coughing Maudie made the cleanliness of Charlotte's cruelty impossible to sustain. Since his wife had attempted savagery in the high classical manner, he saw nothing amiss with using all weapons at his disposal.

With an obedience to convention which in the circumstances seemed both poignant and absurd, they all assembled in the dining room for luncheon, even though, as Maudie observed, it was really too hot to eat.

'Not half so hot as you will find it in Italy,' said her father.

'But it will be by the sea, Papa. You can't know how much hotter London is at this *moment* than Brighton.'

'Then why not stay in Brighton?'

'Because I am having the Grand Tour, don't you see.'

It was perfectly obvious what was going to happen next. Charlotte looked up sharply and peered with desperation at her daughter's grinning innocent expression, her staring eyes, her flush, her sticky pallor. Then she looked at the pudgy countenance of the Professor and wondered how she could have been so *naïve* as to allow the battle-ground to shift. In the drawing room Charlotte had ever been triumphant. It was the scene of her most magnificent victories. But in the tougher terrain of the dining room, Horace was a veteran campaigner. He was a master of every move, and none knew better than he how to exploit the periodic exits and entrances of servants.

'Was the salmon off, sir?' asked one of these with an inelegant sniff.

'It was delicious, thank you, Hopkins, but it is as you know very rich.'

'Two mouthfuls of salmon and I feel I could *burst,* EXPLODE!' said Maudie before collapsing into one of her barking fits.

'I am sure we shall try to do justice to the summer pudding,' said Horace.

'Thank you, sir,' said the servant and withdrew.

Charlotte looked at her husband with dread, but chiefly with self-loathing. She could not imagine how she could so gullibly have walked into the trap. He would time his remarks perfectly, when Maudie had recovered from her fit, and there would be nothing his wife could say in reply unless she chose to advertise, before her daughter, the intimate sorrows of the previous twenty years. It was the ultimate, the most triumphant blackmail.

Horace himself saw it all quite differently. Having failed, in his pre-prandial sobs and whimpers, to engage his magnificently pitiless wife's sympathies, he felt that he yet had left a daughter, and with no shame any longer at the ignominy of it all, proposed to cast himself on Maudie's surely inexhaustible mercies.

'I say!' he said as he passed his daughter her plate of quivering currants and breadcrumbs, 'I've just had the most capital wheeze.'

'Really, papa, do you have to use such slangy expressions?'

'Frightfully sorry, old girl.' Why was he grinning so inanely, so triumphantly? 'But this Italian lark. Perhaps it is not such a bad idea after all. And what I have been thinking is this. Why don't I forget about my precious volcanos book for once in my life and come along too?'

There was a moment of electric silence. Then Maudie rose with galumphing excitement from her chair and shouted, 'Oh, Papa, that's what I've been *praying* you'd say!' And rather to her mother's astonishment, Maudie flung her arms about Horace's neck and implanted a very moist kiss on the no less moist crown of his bald old pate.

TWENTY-FIVE

Kemp Town

It is questionable whether one should use the word *pain* to describe the torments of being in love. For surely, in the case of all other pains, it is of their nature that we desire to bring them to an end? An aching tooth, a scorching wound, who but the self-torturing fanatic of French fiction or the eccentric of religious enthusiasm would not attempt to salve and heal such sores? Similarly, the man who hears that he has suffered financial ruin, or that he has failed to secure the worldly advancement on which he had set his heart, would seek urgently to undo the hurt which such intelligence occasions. It is not so with the pains of love. A grieving widow positively wants, with a part of herself, to go on suffering for the loss of her husband and even feels affronted at the gradual dulling of her agony by the kind processes of time. *Ah, last regret, regret can die!* And the man who is in love, be the position ever so hopeless, luxuriates in the dreadful unhappiness which is caused by the merest thought of the girl of his dreams.

It would almost be no exaggeration to say that Mr Lupton was now Maudie-mad, for there was not a moment of any day when he was not consumed with unhappiness which he associated entirely with her, and with her beauty; particularly with her beauty. For, in truth, he had not come to know her any better in the last few months. Their talk was still on the same light, superficial level. He made her giggle, and she made him sigh. She gasped at the inadequacy of her water-colours; he assured her that they were much better than they were. She said that if she did not eat a water-ice, she would die; he rushed to procure one. She asserted that she had forgotten his need of refreshment and that she was the crudest, rudest creature in the world! He said that she must not *say* such things. And then, once more, the mysterious mother would intervene, and all serious Maudie-worship would end for another session. Thus it had gone on during drawing lessons at Brunswick Square. Thus, for a few tantalising moments it had gone on when the mother and daughter lodged alone together at the Clarendon after the ball. Thus, in the hotel at Brighton. Sometimes, on miserable, wind-blown walks at night along the esplanade (for even during this heat wave there were sea breezes at Brighton) he would ask himself how he could love someone so much of whom he knew so little? Could it not even be true that there *was* so little of Maudie to love? Most of her was yet to emerge, to develop, like a magically beautiful butterfly from a chrysalis. Who then, did he love? Not this giggling, coughing half-child? Yes, yes, a thousand times he *did* love her, even though there was nothing about her, in the ordinary course of things (had he *not* been in love with her) which he would have found interesting. Was it then merely her beauty, merely her appearance which made him love her? Perhaps it was not merely Maudie's hair, skin, teeth, eyes, voice individually which explained why he loved her. But it was the whole external phenomenon of her which made her such an object of fascination. One thing was certain. It was a thing of much greater weight than pure concupiscence. He had known the ecstasies of the baser life. He took no dualistic vision of the universe for his own, and he had no Manichean fear of the flesh. But he knew that *this*, whatever it was, was something infinitely bigger and huger and stronger than could be explained by simple animal attraction. Maudie Nettleship had transformed the whole of existence for Timothy Lupton. Before he met her, he had known what it was to be moony. He had known, furthermore, what it was to be made unhappy by a woman. But this exceeded all previous experience. Day by day in Brighton, his one object of concern was to catch a glimpse of her. At the same time, although it was the thing which he wanted more than anything in the world, he was desperately frightened by it. The longer he knew her, the less confident he became that his adoration could or would ever be acceptable to her, and he dreaded becoming one of the joke figures in her entourage of admirers. Better to have a millstone tied about his neck and be cast into the outermost depths of the ocean than to be laughingly placed in the same general category as the Reverend Field Flowers Goe. The knowledge, with all his intelligence, that no 'progress' was being made with Maudie did not prevent, in his imagination, the wildest leaps and bounds being taken. And he had no control, at night, in his few hours of sleep, over his dreams. Waking and sleeping, he found his consciousness invaded by Maudie in repeated and varied guises. If he ate or slept or drank or gazed out to sea, her countenance would stare at him, nearly always with great sadness, and her infinitely expressive voice would sound its cruel siren-music in his wearied ears. He was, in the fullest sense, *possessed*. He was full of her. But he could not endure that in the few minutes of a 'chance' encounter on the esplanade, Maudie should be in the wrong mood or humour. One day, planning his chance meeting with her with great precision, he stood afar off and watched her coming along the front on the arm of her grandfather. Her straw hat was tied beneath the chin with a ribbon, and the blue and white gingham of her skirts billowed about her black-stockinged legs. Although her face, in recent weeks, had become much thinner, there was yet a magnificent fullness about her hips and, in the glimpses which gusts of wind allowed, a shapeliness about her calves and ankles which spoke of life's fullness. Maudie was in essence, not merely in embryo, feminine. There was in her movement, her shape, the very air she gave off a feeling off fulfilment, creativity. This was surely what made women so much more mysterious than men. Though parthenogenesis be impossible, and though the race can not be multiplied without masculine co-operation, the whole growth and mystery of human life itself was hidden within the female body. A man's body, likewise, was out of joint with the stars and moon and wandered upon earth as a stranger. The female was intimately connected with the vast and mysterious planetary cycle. Her very body, like tides of the sea, and the seasons of the years, was in harmony with all moving things. When we worship a woman, therefore, we bow down unconsciously to the particle of great creating nature which she represents. And in the shape of Maudie's legs and hips, Mr Lupton caught a little of this creative mystery and was stirred therefore by a lust which felt as though it had within it something more spiritual than the highest of any previous aspirations or dreams. The wind which blew her skirts about these areas of fascination also, in harmony, swept her hair in thick tangled ropes beneath her hat of straw. It was a curious fact about Maudie's hair which he had often noticed at close quarters, that shortly after being brushed, it resumed this thick tangled appearance of raw nature so that in its abandonment, though flying beneath something so modern and demure as a sun-hat, it could have been the new-created hair of Eve in Paradise. Exposure to sunlight had, here and there, caused golden streaks to flash in its nutwoody abundance. The hair itelf, like the whole movement of the creature, was wild; a tyger, tyger burning bright, in our modest midst, in the very thick of the pleasure-loving Brighton crowds. Not to stare at such a vision would have been an impossibility. Not to follow it would have been an exercise of personal constraint of which he would have been quite incapable. The desire, therefore, to catch Maudie at precisely the right moment of day was foolhardily abandoned and he almost ran, having caught sight of her, in the direction of her and the grandfather.

'Ah!' said the urbane old voice beneath its distinguished grey top hat, 'Timothy my dear, what a perfect sea-scape for you to paint. What prevents you from sitting down here and now and beginning it? We would keep you company, wouldn't we, dear girl?'

'Oh, grandpapa, do we *have* to?' had been Maudie's swift and immediate response. And then, with immediate consciousness of how tactless she must appear, she gazed at him with large imploring hazel eyes and said, 'You see, Mr Lupton, I get so *tired*.'

The grandfather had shrugged as though there were no accounting for the vagaries of female whim.

'Anyway, my dear, I'll come out and join you. There is a little something about which I would like to *confide* in you.'

Dutifully, therefore, that day, our Timothy had set up his easel on the esplanade, attempting, with horrible absence of expedition or style, to capture the blue haze where the sky met sea, and reproduce with camel hair and turpentine, the light suggestions of cloud which occasionally wafted across the even cyaneous. An absent-minded dab into the prussian, where he meant the cobalt, blue on his palette put paid to any hopes that the sketch might improve, so that by the time old Severus Egg stood over his shoulder, the thing was really a matter for apology and excuse. In all that space, he had daubed and sploshed about without thinking of anything but, as he saw it, Maudie's snub. The thought that she might, in very truth, be tired or ill did not for a second cross his mind as a plausibility. He was simply racked with tortured ignorance of how he had offended. Had she come to weary of his affections? No one who mocked so relentlessly at the 'sweet' attentions of the acolytes and devotees at The Bower could be so innocent as not to have noticed that he had joined the band of worshippers. She *knew*, of course, and accepted his worship as a matter of course. But this did not prevent her tiring of it. No more did his Maudie-madness blind him to the fact that it was an intrusion, a telepathic or psychological equivalent of rape. Because he held her forever in his thoughts, he had come to feel, somewhat unreasonably, that she was in his possession; and with the small fraction of his rational finite mind still operative, he could see that there might be here cause for resentment or disquiet on Maudie's part. Thus, for a whole morning he had daubed and agonised, until the old man returned, and muttered in his ears information which, a twelvemonth since, would have rejoiced his heart. A mixture of motives allowed him yet, for all the manifold conturbations with which his heart was jostled, to acquiesce in the old lecher's proffered adventure.

'My dear,' he said, touching the younger man's arm later that afternoon as they met again on the red-carpeted landing of the 'house' in Kemp Town, 'Quite like times *past*. Oh death in life, the days that are no more!'

The fillies, to use Mr Egg's own noun for them, had been young enough, but of positively Georgian expertise in their chosen sphere. How he had discovered their existence Timothy Lupton did not pause to enquire, contenting himself with a morally weary relapse into the commonplace that where there's a will there's a way. To say that he had merely consented to Severus Egg's proposal of how the afternoon would be spent was on one level true and on another misleading, for there had been in his acceptance of the offer to accompany the old gentleman a very conscious pursuance of two quite separate courses. On the one hand, in all his besotted adoration of the grandchild, he had the greatest fear of losing the friendship and regard of the grandsire. It was impossible, quite impossible, for someone so experienced in the ways of the world to be ignorant of Mr Lupton's feelings about Maudie. Old Egg *knew* all right. Mr Lupton was extremely anxious to establish that, embarrassing as he found it, he did not wish to damage the quite separate regard in which he held the old poet. It did not cross his mind to inquire whether such expedients as the visit to Kemp Town were designed to clear his over-heated, passionate, fevered head. He took them in the same spirit as he would have done had Egg proposed a rubber or a walk: impolite to refuse. Meanwhile, feeling himself quite in control of his destiny, he had climbed the red stair-case with a second and quite carefully considered series of motives in his head. For in all this, he knew that there was a frenzy of madness which might easily make him, in a phrase popular to young Maudie, *burst*. If his affection for her were purely spiritual it might have been possible to endure the agony of knowing that it would always be unrequited. She awakened in him, however, not only all the great pains of unrequited affection, but also a towering and irrepressible lust, which made him no longer quite the possessor of his own body. To this poor shackle, his flesh and bones, he could at least provide refreshment, however inadequate. Perhaps for half an hour, indeed, behind the closed curtains of that Kemp Town lodging, in the inevitable and automatic ecstasy which could be provided by the allegedly French individual who was his companion, he knew something like peace. Even, in her cocknified Parisian voice observing, 'Ah, monsieur, you are a beauty', there had been matter for some moments of self-congratulatory pleasure. But the session had not stilled the aching in his breast, and nor could a thousand such interviews purge the madness which possessed him.

It was in the returning fly, as Eggy clutched his arm and chuckled with a splendid stagey suggestion of wickedness, that Timothy Lupton had first begun to suspect that there might be any particular reason for their having passed the afternoon in this comparatively agreeable manner. The scene which flitted past – white railings, ice-cream carts, babies in the arms of their grandmothers, boys with hoops and old men spreading out sandwiches on the pebbles – painted a crowded canvas by Frith at each ten-yard interval. In the sea-edge the multitudes were paddling. The large number of bare-shinned straw-bonneted females, with here and there an urchin in a boater, or a small child romping with ludicrous glee in its grandfather's bowler, blended into a shimmering silhouette against the silvery ocean which splashed about their feet. Beyond there were boats: Isle of Wight steamers perhaps. Above and behind them the Palace Pier fluttered with bunting, simmered with newly-baking doughnuts, seethed with a crowd enjoying itself. The high air, which was full of the sea (what was it about sea air, its sharpness, its hint of shellfish, its slight almost stickiness?) was penetrated with poignant shrillness, sometimes the moan of a gull, and sometimes the whoop of a reveller. From afar, it is impossible to distinguish between cries of pleasure or anguish.

'Nearly there,' said Egg, 'and before we meet the others, there is just *something.*'

'I need hardly say that I will never breathe a word of where we have been,' said Lupton.

'Of course not, my dear. But it's *Marvo,* I'm afraid. Up to his old tricks again.'

'He knows of the fillies?'

'No, no! Darling Marvo, how much he would enjoy it if he did. Though I'm not so certain any longer that that is true. One hears that he is less of a dog than he was. Time was – you are too young, of course. You never knew dear old Madame Laurent in Jermyn Street. . . . Oh, *happy* days.'

'But what, then? What tricks has Mr Chatterway been playing?'

'I wouldn't mention it if I thought it was worth bothering about,' announced Egg with a look of perplexity which matched the paradox of the utterance.

TWENTY-SIX

The City of Dreams

Whatever other vows, of poverty or chastity, the Reverend Father might have taken, it was evident that he had not placed himself beneath the constraints of a vow of silence. Lionel's journey to the valley of the Eglwys, was punctuated by an almost constant stream of words proceeding from the monk's lips. The conversational flow was sometimes interrupted by prayer and Cuthbert would ask Lionel – they travelled alone, but the two of them – to chant as best he may the psalms and suffrages which made up the Hours. The manual used for these devotional outbursts was wholly unfamiliar to Lionel, being neither the Latin Breviary (a copy of which with the air of revealing forbidden luxuries Gutch had once showed him) nor the Book of Common Prayer but a volume entitled *The Day Hours of the Church of England*. The monk explained that it had been translated from the old Latin by heretics and fiends of Hell but that it had its uses when travelling. The recitation of this office (they were fortunately alone in the carriage or the attention of fellow passengers would have embarrassed Lionel), was punctuated by a good many exclamations of trust in their Saviour and by the soulful rendering of pious ditties of the Reverend Father's own composition. But the sincerity of the monk's orisons did not prevent them from reminding him again and again of the story which he never tired of rehearsing: that is to say the drama of his own existence.

'Oh, my dear boy, the barrenness and emptiness of life without the sweet Lord Jesus!'

'Each day through your help, Father, more and more of our fellow-countrymen are banishing that barrenness and filling that emptiness.'

'So true! My destiny has been blessed indeed. But, you know, none would quite have been possible without my own election to eternal glory.'

'Yes, Father.'

'It was some years after I had already committed myself to holy religion and to building up the waste places of the monastic life on this British island of ancient lineage. Oh, yes! But though I sang the olde chaunts and wore the antique habit of the true Benedictine order, knew not the Lord Jesus. Oh, my boy, no joy, no pleasure in life can match that wondrous pleasure of knowing our Lord, can it?'

'No, Father.'

'It was when I was staying on the Isle of Wight – on the 10th Sunday after Trinity some fourteen years ago. Doctor Pusey was with me there, dear sainted man, and the Mother Abbess Priscilla, or Miss Sellon as we still called her in those days. And oh dear me, I was sad, sad! I had tried to establish my monastery in Norwich and met with nothing but persecution, diabolic malice, and misfortune. And now we had come together, the learned Doctor, the Mother Abbess and myself to see how we might possibly rebuild those old waste places. I had with me but two novices, Brother Philip and dear Brother Alban. That was all there was in those not-too-distant days in British lands of the great order of Benedict.

'Now I was alone. Doctor Pusey had taken my novices to London – with Mother Lydia, to nurse the poor sick cholera victims of Vauxhall, and I was left alone. The future seemed all uncertain. I attended the morning service at Chale Church, and then again in the afternoon, but I found no comfort therein for my weary, weary soul. If only I could then have poured out my sorrows, as you, dear boy, have poured out your sorrows to me – and as you will pour them out more and more – if only, I say, I could have poured out my sorrows to dear Doctor Pusey. But I could not. For he was not there. I returned to the house and in the oratory there I chanced to pick up a little methodistic book, a homely thing, red in colour, called *The Cottage Hymn Book* which the Lady Abbess had brought with her from her Orphans' Oratory from her abbey in Plymouth. And my eye and forefinger lighted on these words.'

Staring excitedly at Lionel, as the train rattled through the Malvern Hills, the monk wagged his long pale index as if to guarantee the maximum degree of attention, and he seemed to be speaking with as much fervour and polish as he would when addressing an audience of several thousands. Only that morning after their kipper breakfast, the Reverend Father had already recounted his conversion on the Isle of Wight, sometimes known to the faithful as the Miracle of Blackgang Chine. And it was impossible, as he eagerly repeated himself now, to know whether he thought the story so important that it had to be repeated, or whether he had in some strange way forgotten his earlier narrative. It is said that deaf persons are unable to distinguish even those sounds which proceed from their own mouths. Similarly, those who speak in monologue and allow very little conversational return from others are very often unaware of what they have just been saying, and are capable of almost ceaseless repetition. There could be small doubt that the Reverend Father had recounted the Miracle of Blackgang Chine almost as often as he had repeated the Apostle's Creed; and it was quite obvious which was the more momentous recitation. It flowed out of him, rather in the manner of those psalms in which the Hebraic poets rehearsed the deliverance of their ancestors from Egyptian bondage, or as the pre-Homeric bards must have sung the lays of Achilles and of Hector. In no case could it be expected that the audience were hearing the story for the first time. The tales indeed were valued most by those who had already heard them dozens of times. Lionel felt no resentment at hearing again how Cuthbert opened *The Cottage Hymn-Book* to be confronted with the stanza:

> 'Tis a point I long to know
> Oft it causes anxious thought
> Do I love the Lord or no?
> Am I His, or am I not?

'Oh, my boy, it needed no Daniel to interpret the burning message. It came upon me with awful realism! And as though some cruel knife had been suddenly plunged into my heart, I rushed out of the oratory and out of the house, crying aloud the bitter "No" which these mighty questions wrung from me, with a flood of self-accusation that swept all before it.

'Southlands was built upon the steep of the cliff, just half way up the Chine; and the grounds merged by a private pathway to the stretch of sand below – those sands to which I fled blindly in that hour of consummate agony.

'The contrast of the quiet scene was exquisite. So deeply are its details impressed upon my memory that I can recall them one by one, reliving them today instead of invoking mere dream pictures of fourteen years ago. I was quite alone by the seashore, and I remember how brightly the sun went down over the Needles, and how the great wet sands were flecked here and there with touches of glory from the gold-red after-glow. Slowly, and with what agony of soul I began the recitation of the Sacred Office of Compline, as our holy Rule pre-scribes. But though I chanted there upon the sands it was not till I had reached the climax of the Salve Regina that the revelation came – the Light from Heaven that once and for ever was to solve the problem of this dark world.

'I had commenced the familiar phrase which precedes the final salutation – '*Et Jesum, benedictum fructum, ventris tui, nobis post hoc exilium ostende*' – when at the final word '*ostende*' a strange and wonderful thing took place! I was what I elect to call *transported in spirit*. In my body I still stood upon the sands in the little English bay –

but in my soul I walked in Jerusalem, not the Jerusalem of wreck and ruin, but in God's city. The sunset was blotted out and I had been translated by an unseen Hand to that glorious place. Yet though I was set down in unfamiliar surroundings they were all inexpressibly familiar to me. I was in the City of my dreams!

'And in the midst of that city was set a temple, in whose courts I wandered. And there I encountered an elderly man of unpretending appearance who carried two white doves and a fair young girl bearing in her arms a babe. And in an instant as I looked upon Her Child I knew it to be Jesus! And as the old man took that Child in his arms I knew that his withered fingers closed over a most Precious Burden. He had received Jesus.

'Oh that I might have received such a privilege! "Give Him to me also," I cried – at which the mother of Mercy turned to me and said, "Jesus is for you, as much as for Simeon." And then the ancient Israelite approached me and laid the Holy Child upon my breast. Oh, I dare not dwell upon the rapture of that Divine contact, that breathless moment of incarnate communion in which the conversion of my soul was accomplished.

'It was a vision! For an instant it had faded, I was pacing as before on dull grey sands. The glory of the sunset had sunk behind the rocks – and my hands were empty, save for the shabby red hymn book, which I still almost unconsciously held. Nevertheless I was a new man, the happy possessor of a Personal Saviour, redeemed by an all-atoning and finished Redemption, and it was with an overpowering flood of joy and thanksgiving that I concluded the interrupted salutation of that miraculous hymn of praise. To Her, from whose Virgin Arms I had received the unspeakable gift of Salvation, how gratefully, how confidently, could I now offer my soul's tribute *O clemens, O pia, O dulcis Virgo Maria. . . .*'

At the climax of this narrative, the monk's natural contralto reached almost a treble pitch and his cheeks were moist with tears. He seemed blessed with an extraordinary ability, even when the glory had gone down behind the rocks, to neglect, as it were, the grey sands, and inhabit still a world of red and gold, the City of his dreams. To the physical embodiment of those dreams, to the monastery he had built in the Black Mountains of Breconshire, the travellers were now directing their steps, and Lionel felt, at every stage of the journey, an increased elation. It was as if they travelled not merely westward, but into the numinous, where temporal and physical things had been visited, penetrated and transformed by the heavenly, and where old forgotten far-off things were brought near and where ancient mysteries had all the reality of the modern empire. Perhaps this visionary way of looking at things came about because he was viewing things so purely through the monk's eyes. But Lionel seemed to recall in after days when the vision had been clouded, that there was nonetheless something of old magic in the very landscape itself. How intensely green everything was when, having changed trains at Hereford, they wound their way through rolling lands and reached Abergavenny. The violent brightness of the emerald fields, hills and trees was emphasised by the almost savage glare of the sun which sometimes, catching a cottage window as they rattled by, gleamed with blinding diamond effulgence and which exaggerated everything including the thick flat blue of the July sky. At Abergavenny, a governor's cart awaited them, driven by a rubicund, round-faced middle-aged man whom the monk addressed in Welsh.

'You see here,' said Cuthbert as Lionel clambered aboard the cart with his meagre luggage, 'we speak the ancient British tongue, just as we keep the ancient British faith.'

While he lapsed into what sounded like a fairly primitive rendering of this language – Lionel hearing the word Rhydychen concluded that his own residence at Oxford was being explained to the driver – the nag conveyed them up a winding hill road to the north of the pretty little town. Lionel began for the first time on his journey to be a little anxious concerning the fact that he was about to enter, albeit as a mere visitor, the walls of a Benedictine monastery. Was there not something about the very word monastery which sent an instinctive shudder down the spine of any Englishman? It was something which spoke of the imprisoning of the human spirit, the treading down of much which was manly, free-hearted and good. It spoke of dark secrets and the resurrection of spiritual tyrannies which all English boys are taught to believe were swept away by the Reformation. Lionel suddenly began to be afraid. In London, the oratory of the little monk's words had been all persuasive. It had been nothing short of miraculous that Father Cuthbert was talking to the Hall of Science on the very week that Lionel was taken there to be convinced of atheism by his father. The professor's acquiescence in Lionel's going for a week or two's sojourn in the walls of the revived priory of Llangenedd was also, in the circumstances, truly remarkable, though Lionel was fully aware that his father had preoccupations which made him crave solitude. All, in some mysterious manner, was not well at The Bower. And with his usual diffidence, the professor could not explain to his son what the nature of the trouble was. In a fashion not entirely flattering to himself, Lionel supposed, his absence fitted in with the professor's plans. There had been too, an unmistakable softening. A change was in the air. Could it be that Lionel, whose parent had been lost to perdition after that fatal visit to Buddleigh Salterton, should become the instrument of his father's salvation, by praying for him at the monastery.

The monastery! The chilly word summoned up a picture of long grey shadowy aisles in which the rows and rows of hooded monks wandered with downcast eyes and sandalled feet, seeming in their marshalled austerity to have taken leave of physical existence altogether and become some new order of things, halfway between men and angels. Lionel's heart thumped as if he were to be introduced to an abbey full of ghosts. Indeed, as the cart wobbled and creaked along the valley pass, he felt – city, railway, inn, town all left behind him, – as if he had taken leave of the modern world, abandoned the universe of time and lost thereby the greater part of liberty. The higher the hills loomed on every side, and the thicker the greenwood, the further Lionel felt that he was being led to some sort of imprisonment, some involvement which might threaten or encage. The very sky appeared to close upon them like a cowl. At length, when they had journeyed perhaps ten increasingly tortuous miles, a bend in the road revealed over the hedges a range of ruined Gothic buildings halfway up a gently sloping hill to their right. Framed with mature elms and oaks in full leaf, the medieval abbey was the very embodiment of all that an earlier generation would have regarded as picturesque.

'There is old Llangenedd,' said Lionel's companion, 'which fell into secular hands at the time of the despoiling of our own holy order's lands in Henry's reign.' He spoke, it seemed to Lionel, as if Henry VIII were a monarch who had existed in very recent memory, and from what he went on to say it half-appeared as though the bluff Tudor despot were mingled in the monk's mind with the present owners of the site.

'Landors own it now, unworthy tribe of impenitent heretics. Some twenty years since, dear boy, I tried to buy these hallowed fields and bare ruined quires.'

'What for?' asked middle-class mercantile Lionel with a sudden pecuniary interest in the value of the 'property.'

'Why, for the eternal praise of the Precious Blood of our Saviour – for Jesus only! But the wicked man who owned these lands, that infidel Walter Savage Landor, would neither sell nor discuss a sale. I cursed him and called down upon him anathema according to the rules of our most holy mother the Church. Had he not stolen those lands from the monks? Had he not filched them, Kirkrapine? Was it not his sacred duty to undo auncient wronges and to restore them to us, their rightful owners? But he had not the praise of God before his eyes.'

The rubicund driver turned to Father Cuthbert as they left the ruined abbey behind them and made an observation in the olde British language which had to be translated for Lionel's benefit.

'About a mile hence we must needs stop,' said the monk, 'and continue on foot to my own cloister.' And he proposed that for the remaining part of the journey they say the rosary together. This form of devotion being very strange to Lionel, its repetitions and slightly blasphemous-seeming refrain were sufficient to beguile the remaining quarter of an hour in the cart as they made their way deeper and deeper into the Eglwys valley. The sky which had been blue in Abergavenny had filled with dramatic clouds – some large, puffy and white, one black and threatening. The sunshine fell with dramatic force on to one side of the valley, revealing a barren, rocky and mountainous wilderness, while all to their left on the north side was completely shadowy. It was to this, the valley of the shadow, that they turned when they reached the tiny hamlet of Glan-yr-afon and, since the track had all but petered out, and at the same time become almost unassailably steep, the two travellers left their luggage with the carter, who was given instructions to follow with it on a hand cart, while the monk and the young man made their way towards the monastery on foot. It was with scriptural appropriateness that they trod the stony and narrow path which led through the pretty little dingle into the Abbot's Meadow, a large hay-field, bordered on one side with a ramshackle vegetable garden, where, picturesquely enough, a tonsured figure in a black habit was stooping among the flowering bean poles. In the meadow itself, two men similarly attired were sitting on a pile of dried grass surrounded by an ill-assorted tribe of little urchins, aged between eight years old and fourteen and laughing in what seemed to Lionel a highly unmonkish fashion. Behind them, at the top of the field there was a tall Gothic church, brand new, and an imposing Gothic house of grey stone, the two linked together with a corrugated iron cloister, painted a somewhat garish green.

'Dear boy! Stand with me but a little while and take in this *holy* scene!' said the monk, with a look of rapturous intensity which exceeded any that Lionel had seen on that frequently rapturous countenance. 'See there, the great abbey church – and there the mother house of the order. The green cloister shields our holy anchoresses and nuns. Ah Lionel!' and he gulped with emotion as he spoke and moisture spurted from his gleaming eyes. 'I was *glad* when they said unto me, we will go unto the house of the Lord!' The last word could barely be enunciated, so profound was the monk's emotion at approaching the City of his dreams.

Afterwards, Lionel was not so certain as to be able to vouch for the fact, but he thought he had seen one of the monks in the field furtively remove a cigarette from between his lips and rub it beneath the sole of his sandal. The little group who had been gathered about him hastily, and somewhat unconvincingly, scampered into a semi-plausible agricultural activity at the abbot's approach, clutching handfuls or forkfuls of dried grass and arranging them into disorderly bundles at irregular intervals about the meadow. One of their number, however, a lad of about twelve, ran to greet them and surprised Lionel by falling on one knee and kissing Father Cuthbert's hand.

'I greet you Brother Caedmon of the Sacred Heart,' said the abbot in solemnly fruity tones, 'and introduce you to Mr Nettleship who has come to visit us from the auncient Priorye foundacioun of Harcourt in Oxenfoorde which we of the British race call Rhydychen.'

Lionel felt that it would have been pure pedantry to point out that Harcourt was not, in fact, a monastic foundation.

'Now under the grip of the hell-fiend Plato,' added Cuthbert to the baffled youth who stood before them, in an irresistible reference to Doctor Jenkinson.

Still less was it worth mentioning that they had travelled not from Oxford but from Paddington Station. It was obvious that Brother Caedmon of the Sacred Heart had more exciting news to communicate – in tones of a surprisingly cocknified vernacular.

'Gor 'blimey, dear Father, you'd never guess what Brother Hyacinth's been and done.'

'Brother Hyacinth of the Garden of Gethsemane?'

'Yeah, E's orf and 'opped it wiv one of the girls in the village, Siân Pritchard it were: says as 'ow 'e couldn't stomach no more 'ere, dear Father, and pinched a tea caddy full of tanners from Brother Almoner's cupboard too. Makes yer sick, dunnit dear Father, I mean *really,* makes yer want to spit.'

'Dear Brother Caedmon, this is grave news. You must lead me at once to your elders.'

The little boy scampered ahead into the field, Father Cuthbert and Lionel following. As they made their short progress towards the other monks, Lionel felt his whole being swirl with revulsion and disappointment. He longed not to be there, but he felt trapped. Suddenly, more vividly than ever before in life, he missed home; he missed his bald, gloomy father; he missed his sister and his beautiful mother. He missed them with all the tenderly irrational emotions of a child. But he was also conscious in his longing of a need for the normal, the quotidian, the mundane. He wanted a drawing room crowded with modern furniture, he wanted newspapers borne into breakfast on a tray by starch-capped maids, he wanted the everyday world to which the postman and the baker's boy called, a world untouched by fancy. He wanted a city of trams not a city of dreams.

Even as he approached the other members of Father Cuthbert's community, Lionel was aware that all his own illusions and dreams about the monastic life were about to be rudely shaken. There were fewer than a dozen monks, and only a couple of them were men rather than boys. The man who had been surreptitiously smoking a cigarette presented a surprisingly roguish appearance. For all his shaven head and monastic habit he might have been a tinker or some hardened practitioner of petty crime. It was a face, though it was here seen in open daylight, which seemed to glint at you from the darkness of an alley. The other man's face was as pale as an oyster and looked no less robust. If his roguish companion gave one a start of fear because he seemed so rough, this other man was uncanny because it seemed as if he might be quite idiotic, his lips were wreathed in an ineradicable grin and his dull eyes stared through Lionel at his approach, as though focussing on something infinitely far away.

'Good day, my dear brethren,' piped Father Cuthbert, receiving in reply a kindergarten chorus of rhythmic chanting, 'Good-day-ver-y-dear-Fa-ther.'

The juveniles – they ranged in age from about eight to about fifteen – who gave this greeting were a strange mixture, some being very evidently the children of poverty, but others whose soft hands and skin and genteel treble tones suggested either a particular desire to imitate the mannerisms of Father Cuthbert, or a personal history of some comfort and education. But where – Lionel still found himself asking the question – were the proper monks, the others? Where were the hooded ranks of human crows processing to Ye Divine Office? Could it be that the much-vaunted order of Saint Benedict, revived in British lands and modern times, was no more than this human ragbag, this miscellaneous collection of urchins and ragamuffins? Lionel could not believe that it was the case, and forced himself to grin as he was introduced to the community, and as the narrative of Brother Hyacinth's absconding was repeated by the *louche* tinker-monk whose name, it seemed, was Brother Columba of Our Ladye's Seven Dolours. From this, and subsequent accounts of the matter, Lionel learnt that Brother Hyacinth had been a merchant seaman, nineteen years old, Jo Wiggins by name, who had attended one of the Reverend Father's rallies some nine months previous in Liverpool and been converted to the true faith in Our Lord and Saviour. It was not altogether clear whether Jo had been a deserter from the Merchant Navy, nor whether there was truth in Brother Columba's hint that Wiggins was a housebreaker on the run from the police. Wiggins, almost as soon as he arrived at the monastery, had found himself being 'professed' as Brother Hyacinth of the Garden of Gethsemane, and although he was said to make frequent protestations against the austerity of the life, Father Cuthbert had, whenever he returned to the valley for his periodic visits during his great tours, declared that Hyacinth was a 'model novice'. Father Cuthbert saw good in all his *confrères,* but only the good he wanted to see. Perhaps Wiggins had been a good enough lad, but the Reverend Father wanted him to be a good novice. Everyone else knew of his surreptitious valley-visits, his collusion with Siân, the wench of the nearby smallholding, his scapular upliftings, his habit-removals, his barn-writhings in beds of straw, since, after the Greater Silence began in the dormitories, Brother Hyacinth would fill the minds of his younger brethren with impure thoughts as he described, his tongue as vivid in its coarse way as the brush of many a renaissance minor master, the naked contours of his paramour and the fleshy exploits, which he, with his knowledge of the bordellos, had been able to teach her. Everyone else knew, but Father Cuthbert was visibly astonished when he heard of the young blade's elopement.

Fishing beneath his scapular, not without visible enjoyment of its dramatic effect, Brother Columba produced a letter which the unfortunate Wiggins had left for his father Abbot. Even the briefest survey of this document effected a remarkable change on Father Cuthbert's countenance. His eyebrows, ever surprised, now shot up in an excess of astonishment towards the crown of his head, and his complexion darkened with fury.

'This,' he spluttered, 'is not to be believed.'

Lionel, at that stage knowing no more of Brother Hyacinth than a few minutes' incoherent narrative had been able to enflesh, could have no feelings about the justice of Father Cuthbert's expression of surprise. But he was very considerable struck by the monk's anger. It was rage that was so exaggerated as to appear comical and it was some little while before Lionel understood that it was perfectly genuine.

'This is . . . apostasy . . . of the blackest dye! It is the work of the devil! Oh yes, in this nineteenth century of ours, my brethren, the devil is very active, as here we see! Brothers, we must go at once into ye Vespers, without delay!'

And without any domestic reassurances – no offer of refreshment, no showing to his bedroom – Lionel was left, in a bewildered way, to struggle behind the group which filed into the chapel. Two further monks whom he had not seen – perhaps one was he who played the harmonium at the first occasion of Lionel's seeing the Father – were prostrate in adoration before the large Gothic tabernacle which gleamed on the high altar. One of the brethren tolled the bell at the back of the church. Another, with quivering taper, lit a multitude of candles, not only on the altar, but also a glowing line at the front of the stalls. The chapel, apart from all these little oases of fire, was black as night. There was a feeling of mystery, almost of terror in it, so powerful that all previous temptations to scorn the revived order of St Benedict were forgotten in awestruck contemplation. After the tolling of the bell, complete silence. And then after the silence, the great west door opened and the Infant Samuel, youngest of nine-year-old novices and adopted child of the Abbot, proceeded up the aisle, arrayed in his habit and a lace collar, and carrying a large missal or bible. Cuthbert followed him, weighed down by a thick cope of black velvet trimmed with gold, and wearing on his head a plain white funereal mitre. When he turned and looked at his monks from the chancel steps he was terrible-eyed. No figure of fun, he, as with bell, book and candle he enunciated in the most solemn tones the everlasting curse of God upon the errant merchant seaman who for a few misguided months had attempted, or pretended, to live up to Cuthbert's idea of the perfect Benedictine novice.

After the sombre ceremonies of excommunicating poor Brother Hyacinth had been completed, the abbot was escorted to his stall by the Infant Samuel who assisted in divesting him of his cope and mitre. Then he warbled *O God make speed to save us,* and Vespers took its course, a strange *pot pourri* of a service with little bits of Latin woven round a mutilated version of the Prayer Book Evensong. The familiarity of so many of the words, the unfamiliarity of chants and settings, once more tugged at Lionel's heartstrings and made him doleful for St John's Wood. But after the ceremonies were complete there was a novice to show him to a well-scrubbed apartment, and to lead him in due time to the refectory where he shared in the ample vegetable stew prepared by Brother Samson of the Holy Child. Exhausted by his journey, he almost dozed off during Compline, and he had not read far into his chapter of *John Inglesant,* as he lay for his first night under the monastic roof, before he had fallen asleep.

Father Cuthbert, it should be said, did not share in the monastic refection, but ate some lamb chops in the religious solitude of his abbatial cell, waited upon by the Infant Samuel. This taciturn child was attendant upon the Father at all hours and slept in a little truckle at the end of Cuthbert's own more commodious bed, like a spaniel at the feet of a crusader. Lionel, in consequence, did not see either of them again until their appearance, at the very shriek of dawn, next day in the chapel, where they presided over the somewhat bleary chanting of Lauds. This office complete, the Father delivered them a sermon about the importance of loyalty and obedience to Jesus only and to their abbot as the Viceroy of Jesus in their lives.

'Oh Brother, dear Brothers, how unlike *certain* reprobates who

have wounded the Sacred Heart of our dear Lord, how unlike these is
the dear Infant Samuel! And shall I tell you how he is going to show his
love of the Lord Jesus this morning? Not long ago I asked him whether
or not we should be sorry for our sins before we come to Holy
Communion. "Yes, very, dear Father," was the child's reply. "But," I
said, "how can we tell you what you really are?" "I don't know, but
you can tell," was his reply, "and Jesus knows, doesn't he, my father?"
"Yes," I said, "but should you not like to prove to us too that you were
sorry for grieving blessed Jesus by taking a good caning before your
communion and another after, and without crying for the pain? I think
that would prove to us that you were really sorry." And I want you
now, dearest boy, to reply in face of all this congregation what you
have already said to me in reply.'

The lad's voice was weak, quiet with excitement, as he said, 'May I
have the beating, dear Father, for blessed Jesus's sake.'

The little child knelt down, having said these words, and crouched
on the chancel steps. The abbot went to his stall where it appeared a
lithe cane was kept, and proceeded to thrash the child with careful
thoroughness. The crumpled little figure, protruding his buttocks to be
castigated, emitted no sound during all this purgation. Then the cane
was offered to his mouth and child kissed it. It was put down on the
chancel steps, and assisted by two acolytes, Father Cuthbert then had a
humeral veil draped round his shoulders, and advanced to the
tabernacle. When he opened it and produced the ciborium containing
the most holy sacrament, he fell on his face in worship, and then,
carrying the sacred vessel toward the Infant Samuel, he placed the
most holy host on the child's tongue. Then the Sacrament was once
more replaced in its shrine, the door of the cupboard locked, the
curtain drawn, the boy once more knelt down and raised his buttocks
for the second thrashing. When this had been performed the monks in
chorus chanted *Let us adore forever the most holy sacrament.*

Their devotions however were not quite complete. For Brother
Angelus, the thin rather saintly-looking man who had accompanied
Father Cuthbert on his Oxford mission, was the first out of his stall
and went to lie across the open doorway at the west end of the Chapel.

One by one, the dozen or so boys and monks then passed out of the
building. None did so without treading on Brother Angelus, as if he
were a piece of coconut matting. Brother Bernard of the Annunciation,
a whimsical youth of some thirteen years, actually crouched over his
elder and managed to fart directly in his face. Others contented
themselves with kicking the unfortunate Angelus, and spitting in his
face.

When Lionel's turn came, he tried to step over the pathetic and abject figure of this etiolated monk. But Father Cuthbert, following behind, called out, 'Dear boy, each day one of my monks takes it in turn to be humiliated. It is part of our holy rule and discipline – you must abuse him somehow. Spit upon him! Kick him in the vitals! Do!'

Out of politeness Lionel prodded Brother Angelus in the ribs with the rim of his toe. He never forgot the look of pleasure on the man's face. Perhaps he was thirty-five years old, but he was grinning with the innocent delight of a baby in a cradle.

TWENTY-SEVEN

The Europeans

For Maudie, the sorrow's crown of sorrows was that Lionel was to be left behind. She had realised that her mother's 'We take boat for France in the morning' had been an exaggeration, and that these things could not be done overnight. The sentence had spilled out of childhood reading, as Maudie had, not without condescension, decided. Only her parents would have behaved in this way. Only the Nettleships would be so acrimoniously silent with one another that they were unable to discuss arrangements for the summer until the last moment. But more characteristic than that, only the Nettleships would be able to make the last moment endure for three weeks. Even the tedium of Brighton, Maudie opined, was to be preferred to this sweltering, this standing at counters in shops, this purchase of new hats and bonnets, shawls and gowns, picknicking baskets, paintboxes, butterfly nets, writing desks, parasols, larger trunks and cases, boots, boot-hooks, medicine boxes, bathing dressses ('quite different standards obtain at Mentone' had been her father's piece of unconvincingly assumed sagacity), travelling rugs, maps, gazetteers and guides. Oh those maps, and these railway time tables, spread out in the heat of the dining room!

The initial plan, once the professor himself had taken over the arrangements, was that they should attempt to see everything that could be seen. A dozen or more complicated itineraries had been drawn up and discarded. At one point they had even contemplated 'taking in' Spain.

'The child must see Toledo!'

'You seem to forget we are going for her health.'

It was Charlotte who said it. Maudie thought that both her parents forgot this most of the time, which was just as well since it was not true. Her health, by which they meant her cough, would probably go away in its own annoying time. She had suspected it of getting very slightly better while they were in Brighton, but of course the London air had brought it on again. If they would only leave her *be*, she would be better. But instead there was this ceaselessly disconcerting combination of fuss and neglect which she began to see had been a feature of 'their' treatment of 'their' children. Mrs Nettleship and her husband had become for the first time in the eyes of their daughter 'them'. It was a marital achievement of a kind. Since (and Maudie *had* noticed, it was queer) the parents had begun to speak to one another they had doubled in annoyingness. The child! And why should she be always referred to in the third person as though she was not present in the room when they had these discussions? When the idea of abroad had been raised with her mother's own abruptness, Maudie had known clearly enough that the tour was to be the three of them, herself, Charlotte Nettleship and Mr Lupton. When for the first time in his daughter's observation the professor had shown courage and said that he too was of the party, Maudie had rejoiced not merely that life began to take on a semblance of the familial normalities, but more, that it was assumed, merely, that she would be going to Europe with Lionel. To see Paris with her beloved brother was a very different thing to hours in the Louvre with Mr Lupton. It was, in fact, about a week before she fully grasped her parents' plans. Or rather, surely, absence of plans? It could not be – *could* it – that either of her parents wanted Lionel to be walled up in a monastery surrounded by rank on rank of ancient medieval-looking friars? It was quite simply incredible: Professor Nettleship was insistent that Lionel should be man enough to live with his decision! If this was what men had to do, Maudie rejoiced that she was turning into a woman. Lionel besides had not made a decision. Papa, most unaccountably, had taken him to see a performing crackpot whom he himself described as 'singularly impressive' and he had further allowed Lionel, a week or so later, to go down to the monastery – 'for a spell'. That at any rate was how he had first described the arrangement. 'For a few weeks' was how Charlotte had furiously repeated it, but then, as Maudie had come to observe, Charlotte got everything wrong. But everything. On another occasion, sawing their way through cold duck, the professor had said Lionel had gone to the monastery 'to see how he liked it' which suggested residence among the fanatics of an indefinite period. 'He had made his bed,' said the father, 'and he must lie on it.'

Poor, poor Lionel, they were simply punishing him for his religion. Truly it was harsher than the cruellest excesses of Diocletian or Nero, about whom Mr Goe had once (with the air of telling tales about the crustier of his parishioners) informed her. She had written to Lionel, of course, imploring him to run away: suggesting that she could not escape the conclusion that he was being trapped, put away, persecuted. But she had not yet had a reply, and she was not wholly certain that she had put the correct address on the envelope. Everything had too hideously gone wrong since the dear boy wrote from Oxford to say he wanted to be ————. She grew like Papa, she could hardly bring herself to say the word without feeling an explosion of rage erupt in her skull. Why had her parents not *concentrated* upon the importance of this news, as they would have done had they been human beings with any brains rather than donkeys with none? Marvo had seen the significance of *everything* at once. Marvo did see. Moreover he did not merely see (grandpapa *saw* and much good it ever did anyone) but he cared, Marvo.

Never in a thousand years would Maudie, whose sixteen of the wretched things began to feel pretty long and weary, have been ingenious enough to correspond *via* the servants. Never in a thousand would she have thought of bribing Hopkins. But grave of countenance and betraying *nothing*, that maid now brought her Marvo-messages almost daily while she dressed. It transpired, from his scrawl, that he had 'fixed' this individual with a number of sovereigns, the supply of which would increase were discretion guaranteed, but dry up altogether if the slightest evidence were adduced of clumsiness, or curiosity, or envelopes steamed open with kettles, or tittle-tattle to her mistress. Thus Maudie managed to keep open her lifeline to the world while her father planned and readjusted and altered the farcically ambitious itinerary. The plans to revisit Etna (for of course *that* old interest was soon enough reactivated) had been sadly abandoned. 'They' began to wonder whether there would be time for the Rhineland and the Italian Lakes if they were also to see the Châteaux of the Loire and the paintings in the Uffizi. They were quietly settling to the position of thinking, after a week in Paris, that they would get on a train to Saint Moritz and stay there for a couple of months or until it was time to come home. Venice, the grand end of their journey in the original conception, had not been mentioned for days.

And they were days. Days and days of sultry coughing. Fräulein Schwartz – Maudie tried to be thankful for the few small mercies of life – was in Scotland, brushing up or as she self-confidently phrased it, dressing down the German of her *other* young family. But in spite of all the promise of a surname which constantly suggested departure, Mr Goe stayed and mornings were taken up with the *Odyssey*. It was after one such scarcely endurable hour of Homer and Mr Goe between them bla-ing on about Calypso of the braided tresses that Maudie strode out of the house, without saying where she was going, and paced purposefully towards Regents Park. Let them shriek over their banisters if they wanted to find her. Why *should* she always tell them her plans and doings? Her hurried pace had little or nothing to do with a letter, delivered under the very nose of her Greek tutor by the adorable Hopkins, to suggest that her admirer would be strolling near the bandstand, if she could get away, towards noon, but that she was not to trouble her pretty head if it were tempted by metal more attractive.

Shimmering in the sunlight, tubas and horns and trumpets had been laid down, for she approached in the interval and missed – though she had heard them from afar as she drifted along, twirling her parasol behind her bonneted locks, between the herbaceous borders – the medley of tunes from *Pinafore*. She was even slow to catch his drift as *in medias res* his drawling voice began, behind her, and before she had seen or greeted him.

'Dull stuff, what, Sullivan's music, though I was with the Edinburghs two nights ago and the Duke who likes in every literal sense to play second fiddle to Sir Arthur was reminding me that the Prince of Wales would travel the length of the Kingdom to hear Mrs Fanny Ronalds sing 'The Lost Chord'. Haven't I myself heard her sing it in no less than six ducal houses this summer, often with little Sullivan seated at the keyboard, if not at that stage of evening at anything which might be called an organ.'

'Marvo, I don't know what you are talking about.'

Unwontedly, she had held his head for a second between her palms and kissed a cheek, an action which required her to stand prettily a-tiptoe.

'You must know that Mrs Ronalds and Sir Arthur are coupled in a more than musical score?'

'I know nothing, and the more *you* move in the world the less comprehensible you become.'

'Sullivan is hardly the world – a bandmaster's son. But you are right of course. There reaches a point, when you have climbed sufficiently high up a moutain, when you can only yodel to make yourself heard. I've done a good deal of yodelling lately. I have moved among those who can *only* yodel to those on other peaks, sufficiently exalted, and who have forgotten – ah! how to talk.'

'You will never forget how to talk. Look here, we've only a week before They take me off to St Moritz and I don't know I can quite endure it.'

'Peaks and yodelling there, if you like, though not quite of the sort I was describing. I expect they're taking you there for the cough. Mountain breezes, what? Hardly the most stimulating society in Europe – the Duke of Connaught and a few other mountain goats. Now why not Vienna where instead of Sullivanning your young ears with twaddle you could be listening to the music of my own darling Brahms of whom I am so fond. . . .'

'But. . . .'

'You will say it and it will make me blush.'

'It's true. It has become true.'

'Ah! Anything can become true, most things do, more's the pity.'

'But I really shall miss you.'

'Which might be further reason why your parents – eh? In their wisdom? Spotted postman-Hopkins surreptitiously delivering the letters under the crumpet cover, what?'

'I shall miss you simply because I shall have no one else to talk to.'

'You can be Wordsworthian and talk to the mountains.'

'In fact. . . .'

'Now that is absurd.'

Instinct made them move away from the bandstand as the uniformed figures resumed their instruments of brass, and to potter across the lawn to the airs of Rossini.

'I gather,' he resumed, 'that your part in *Nausicaa and her maidens* is as unforgettable as it is unmistakable.'

'What has Goe. . . .'

'Gone and done? I am not speaking of Mr Goe. Let Goe.'

'I would do no such thing.'

'Let Goe be bygone, I'm talking of Lupton's canvas – a real return to the manner of his old master. A most unusual study not least because of the naked Odysseus among so many clad or almost clad maidens. . . .'

She tittered and interrupted, 'I suppose you are going to say Odysseus looks like Mr Goe.'

'You forget I haven't seen the canvas myself.'

'I hope never to see it.'

'Which is more than one can suppose Mrs Nettleship hopes.'

'Mama is ridiculous. You know! As if we needed two hat boxes, but we are taking four. Four hatboxes for a holiday in the mountins. She keeps quizzing me about vests and bodices. It is too. . . .'

'Don't laugh at your mother.'

'But she. . . .'

'There, you've made yourself cough and you may choke to death.'

'Beast!'

'Your grandfather is the last of the romantic poets, and your mother is the last romantic heroine. No poems nowadays, what – you don't call Gravy Browning and Maud Tennis-Elbow poets, I hope –'

'I shall scream if you say you don't like *Love in a Valley*.'

'Oh – Merry-death, well. Maybe. But no Byrons, what? No Shelleys. No, we have to make the poetry these days out of our own lives. I'm stuck on about Canto one hundred and fifty – and you are still only halfway through your Prologue. But your mother. . . . Put it another

way, we are all walking about and spinning about ourselves not
cocoons – we aren't caterpillars – but yarns – self-pictures – three-
volume shockers, perhaps. We're living in the stories of our own
composing, what?'

'I feel I'm living in a very dull tale.'

'No you don't – you have the whole thing written out in your head –
right up to the point where Lothario – Lupton chases you to the
continent and you elope together. Then you'll die of consumption I
shouldn't wonder – in his arms, what?'

'That's not the story. . . .'

'Oh, so you'll live, eh? A touch of the long unlovely street about it –
dear Elizabeth. Now she couldn't write poetry any more than her
gravy Boatman husband but she was a *pet*.'

'I have no desire to emulate the Brownings. That's not the tale I have
written. I would rather you didn't distress me, yes it is distressing to
speak in this way.'

'Mama's silliness?'

'That and *all*. It's not a matter for jest, you know it. Sometimes I
think you are a sort of monster, you are so mean. I almost fear you.'

There were really a tolerably unmonstrous pair making their
northern toddle across Regent's Park beneath the strengthened August
sun, seeming from afar – as Mr Lupton, the subject of their discourse,
watched them – to have little of London about them. The pale loose
grey of Mr Chatterway's coat and the wide-brimmed white hat
suggested a light-soaked French canvas. And as for Maudie, whose
hair burst beneath her straw bonnet and wrapped her gingham
shoulders in a little cape now flecked with sunshine and gold!. . . as for
Maudie. Mr Lupton turned aside and, after a sweaty stroll, plunged
into the deadened catacombs of the Circle Line. Oblivious to his
presence the couple, who somehow most ostentatiously and unambiguously *made* a couple, shortened the distance between themselves
and the swooping elms of the suburb which in thick summer seemed
unwhimsically named St John's Wood.

'I wish I could make you *see*,' said Mr Chatterway. 'And then again I
am glad you can't.'

'About the three-volume shockers?'

'Yes.'

'Lionel has written a shocker for himself all right. How *can* mama
and papa take me off to the Continent without him?'

'You've never seen the little monk, I suppose? Father who's-it, I
mean, not Padre Lionello.'

'The whole thought makes my flesh shudder.'

'So provincial, *si anglais*. In my various necks of the woods it is perfectly common for people to find themselves shut up in cloisters. Not bad places some of them – Solemnes, what? And as for that dear man, the Abbot of Monte Cassino. . . . But in your pretty little English way you think anyone is a monster who doesn't want a suburban villa and a bank balance and a vote.'

'That's mean. You realise too well that in a much prettier and even more English way I don't think at all.'

'Not bad, not bad!' He smiled at the speed of her *riposte* as though a poodle, after weeks of coercion, was starting to leap through hoops of flame. 'But little Father What's-he-called; he's a romantic. Completely –' Mr Chatterway touched the side of his hat and made screwy gestures with his forefinger.

'Mad?'

'Not as mad as your Miss Adeney. Cracked. But with one of the most highly developed, well printed, lavishly bound three-volume shockers on sale today, in which he takes the principal and most glittering role. He will never leave its pages for the distasteful columns of what you or I might in our prosaic way call real life. He isn't a villain. Augusta Stanley says he's the most saintly little being on earth, and *she's* a judge of character. No question he's genuine. The real thing. But a story-teller on the grand scale. Lionel will come to no harm. For a while he will walk into the pages of the little Father's romance and then once more he will step out of them.'

'And Mama, what of her three-volume shocker?'

'Oh, that *is* a shocker.'

'Truly a shocker? Is that what you *hear*, or is it the shocker you have been writing all along?'

'I know your mother so *well*. It isn't gentle, it isn't *proper* to talk about her.'

'But you have – all summer – talked about her to me. Sometimes I think we have spoken of nothing whatever except her and . . . that *man*.'

'And I have never been sure whether you were more jealous of him or of her.'

'I wasn't *jealous* of either. I do, most seriously, wish you had never brought him to our house. Not for the reason you think either.'

'And is there a reason I think?'

'You think I'm just cross because of Mama and Mr Lupton. It's much more than that. It is *you* that I am worried about – you and your penny shockers. I don't want simply to be written into a melodrama and then discarded when you go back to your darling princes, your sweet abbots, your divine duchesses. . . .'

'This is raving.'

'Is it? What part would I have to play with them?'

'You?'

'Me. I can't yodel, can I? I can't make myself heard. . . .' but it was only a short coughing fit and she resumed, 'above the mountain peaks.'

'And darling pretty Maudie, do you want to?'

She turned and stared at his face. She didn't know why she felt great waves of fear make her stomach heave or why she felt such jabs of disappointment. It had something to do – she could get no closer to the mystery than this – with his being grown-up and her, so maddeningly not *quite*. For he looked amiable enough: never more benign but yes, that was it, avuncular. Or so it seemed, adding to the poignancy of their optical exchange, so he was *trying* to look.

'I'm not clever enough for you.'

She gave him a moment or two to mull over the last two words and then mollified it with a *bourgeoise* dismissal. 'And I don't know *anyone*.'

'It makes us in some sense of the words a pair.' And so it was her turn to mull over his final phrase. It silenced them both, and they walked on until a bench came in sight.

'Anyway,' he abruptly enquired, 'how about the professor? He's not going to enjoy St Moritz. Long time since anything much there erupted, what?'

'Papa said he wanted a holiday from volcanoes – said' – she giggled with gummy disloyalty and for a moment it was like the childish moments of their earlier conferences – 'that it would be a capital wheeze.'

'So it might be. Thought you said he wanted to go to Etna. There's a good novella – he could fall in like that johnnie written about by Mary Ward's Uncle Matt.'

'Empedocles.'

'That's the cove.'

'Papa's really only interested in extinct volcanoes.'

'That's what I call self-obsession.'

'Anyway, we *aren't* going to Etna. Nor, as I am aware, to Vesuvius. Nor anywhere else volcanic.'

'Used to be volcanoes in the Auvergne I expect. Before my time.' He chuckled and said, 'I like to think of the professor in St Moritz.'

'I can't *bear* it when you are rude about papa.'

'You look well enough on it to me.'

A dreadful honk was all the reply this deserved.

'And the professor, for all his projected self-interest in spent fires and empty craters, is probably the only one of us who is writing a shocker about people other than himself. So you are right to rebuke me.'

'There! You are learning.'

'Well, right and wrong. After all, it is about *ourselves* that we should be writing the shocker. The others. . . .'

'Don't you care at *all* about the others . . .?'

'Ah, but too much.'

'Papa cares, poor darling. He cares in his way about all of us.'

'*Minding* isn't the same as caring.'

'He *cares*, which is better than romancing. It really is you, I declare, who is writing the romance, and it frightens me more than a little to be in it.'

'No – you're wrong. You see, I can't sustain my romances beyond five minutes. Evanescence is my essential *métier*. I haven't got the scrambling, galloping *endurance*, the pure energy of your three-volume papa.'

She took his arm, for they neared the conclusion of their tryst at the northern perimeter of the park.

'I'm not allowed to tease mama. . . .'

'I never said anything about teasing Carlotta. I said you mustn't mock her to *me*.'

'And yet you mock papa perpetually.'

The grumbling noise emitted suggested that, where the professor was concerned, mockery was more inevitable; and that, besides, things were more complicated than that.

'Marvo please. I have a request and it has waited till now because I don't know how to frame it.'

'Is it a request for information, or are you asking a favour?'

Her little mauve mittens took his stubby white gloves between them.

'Neither – don't always pose false alternatives.'

'Hoity-toity.'

'You see, I think you're much nicer when you aren't having to yodel to duchesses, and in spite of everything mama really really does like you. In fact she adores you, and you know it and, well, I think you ought to come with us to St Moritz.'

Again the emission of grumblings as though, used as he was to conversing in several tongues, he had a variety of languages rumbling and quarrelling beneath his larynx; and asking to be released.

'You wouldn't have to speak to the Duchess of Connaught or whoever is there.'

'Nothing would give me greater pleasure than speaking to the Duchess.'

'Then you wouldn't have to present *me* to her.'

He laughed at her ridiculousness but his eyes were troubled as he said, 'Run along, you little adventuress.'

'But you will consider coming with us?'

'I thought I was meant to have come *back* from Europe.'

'Just a visit.'

'You're making yourself late for Hopkins's veal and ham pie, what.'

And with a shrug, he accepted her kiss and by the turning of a corner vanished. A brisk walk, pausing only once to lean against a lamp post and cough, managed to convey Maudie to The Bower with twenty minutes 'in hand' before the last-named domestic's dispensation of eatables. The professor was in the hall moving small piles of books from one side of the staircase to the other. Books on the right were volumes which he was definitely taking to Europe, books on the left were ones which he regretted having to leave behind. Every twenty minutes or so he emerged from his library and moved another handful from one side to the other. Evidently, he intended to spend much of the summer reading.

'Maudie *darling* love,' was his exclamation when her silhouette appeared against the front door – a huge fuzz of hair, temptress shaking a bonnet, a tightly waisted fairy-emanation. 'We were in despair.'

'I went to post a letter.'

'Shouldn't you give letters to a servant to post – in this heat?'

'Oh, papa, don't fuss.'

Momentarily, the professor paused midway between his two piles. He had forgotten whether Froude's history of the English in Ireland was a book which he wanted to take to read in the train or to leave behind. Scrutiny of the books he was definitely taking did not really help. Having vowed that he would take nothing that could remotely be thought of as 'work' he wondered why George Lewes's *Physiology of Common Life* was on the pile. He had meant to pack the *Life of Goethe*. And what was this? *Leonard Morris* – some novel Lionel had been reading. He sighed, not so much because he disapproved of novels but because he could not see the *point* of them. Now, Sir John Herschel's *Essays*. He tapped it with the air of greeting an old friend. There was a book.

'I hope you will be using the journey as an opportunity for improving your mind,' he said, still humming and hawing between the two piles, and deciding at length to start a *third* pile – of books he was not quite sure why he had got down from the shelf in the first place.

'I have that pretty little Lamartine which grandpapa gave to me, and *Rookwood*, which is the most thrilling thing you have ever read in your life.'

'The journey will, I suppose, give you the chance to improve your French and German. It would be perhaps a good idea if you were to take along your German grammar so as to be able to practise your irregulars.'

Horace beamed at his daughter with adoration, and with concern. He was so very glad that things were at last, and thanks to his tactful management, working together for good, and that the little family was more harmonious than at any stage in its history.

TWENTY-EIGHT

Nausicaa

Leaving Hopkins, even for an hour and a half of London sunshine, had become for Charlotte an adventure which required a certain steeling of herself, a plucking-up of courage. Not that she had ever, previously, been much addicted to the old servant's company. But in recent weeks Hopkins had been the only woman to whom Charlotte had been able to turn. We need hardly say that she had not told Hopkins all there was to be told. That would have been out of the question. Charlotte had not needed, or wanted, a confidante. She had wanted a bosom to cry on, and the bosom of Hopkins was amply reassuring.

Charlotte felt guilty to be dragging Hopkins off to the Continent. No protest had been uttered. The old servant had done little more than raise her eyebrows at the original, ambitious itinerary. 'Italy, is it?' had been one question and, 'Spain is it now?' another. The fact that they were to 'settle for' France and Switzerland was a matter of indifference to Hopkins who had never crossed the seas and who regarded foreign parts with suspicion.

'I need a friend to go with me,' Charlotte had stated simply. Hopkins had acquiesced in this. At the precise period we are speaking of, she was Charlotte's only friend in the world. Charlotte could not turn to any of Horace's 'friends', not possibly to the 'friends' who had occasionally attended the dreary little dinners at The Bower. More distant, or far-flung acquaintances, such as those on whom she had called at Oxford, were even less plausible comforters. Anything told to Mrs Pattison would be broadcast to the world by the end of the week. Besides, as Charlotte kept telling herself, she wanted comfort, not advice. Doubtless, there were courses of action which she should or should not be taking. But she felt altogether too miserable to be working them out in her mind.

She had seriously supposed that it would all be easy. Painful, yes, she had told herself that it would be painful. There would be a 'scene' or two. Words would have to pass between herself and Horace which neither would ever forget and both would wish had not been spoken. But then it would be over. After these initial distasteful preliminaries, she would retire to her father's house and leave the rest in the hands of her solicitors. Fond hope! She knew that she was feeble in the matter. But with no ally, how could she proceed? Calling on a solicitor by herself, with no introduction from anyone and nothing but the (highly shocking and surprising) opposition of her father required a degree of emotional energy which she did not at that stage possess. It was all so astonishing to her, that Horace had refused her request, brushed it aside as a childish impossibility, not to be contemplated. Oh, she would have defied him. She should have threatened a scandal! But it was not in her nature to do so. She felt entirely crushed by the force not merely of her husband, but of her family and of The Bower itself. She had planned an elopement to Italy, taking only her daughter and her beloved Timothy. Within a twinkling of an eye it had become a thing of hunting for the Professor's butterfly net and organising servants for a full-scale family exodus. She could not resist. Therein lay the worst of it. She was powerless, utterly swamped by misery and despair.

In such circumstances, the old bosom of Hopkins had been the only thing available to weep upon, and its starch had been well-drenched, in the past fortnight, with tears. For, it was much more than a domestic defeat. The reversal compelled Charlotte to recognise that all had not been quite as in dizzier moments she had envisaged; all, that is to say, with Mr Lupton. One of the things which made Charlotte weep was that she did not know whether he had made a fool of her or whether she had made a fool of herself. A fool, however, she had unquestion-ably been made, and a fool she remained: foolishly, rapturously and now despondently in love. She was (the passing day, and now weeks, made her recognise this) in love with a man who did not, as she supposed, love her in return. The humiliation of this was bitter and infuriating. She tried to look back over the whole summer, to remem-ber the first moment of his coming into her house and into her life. It was all a blur. It had seemed to her perfectly obvious from an early stage that he was flirting with her. Either somebody was being unimaginably stupid, or someone else was being unimaginably treacherous and cruel. Charlotte could not make out which. She did not feel that at any juncture she had been stupid. She could not believe, even now, that her darling would be as cruel as *that,* even though she knew he did not love her. Perhaps it was God who was being cruel.

Her composure, her costume, her facial stillness were all somehow too perfect as she made her stately little walk to Fitzroy Square in the blaze of a hot afternoon. A tiny black veil came down from her *toque,* disguising some of the trouble in her brow, and some of the pinkness about the eyes. The very pale blue of her dress was glacial and stiff. It looked, and was, rigid with an armour beneath of belts and bodices and corsets. The parasol which she held above her head was pushed forward at an aggressive angle to suggest that she was keeping off more than the rays of the sun. A previous letter, proposing some meetings, had not been answered. That was the reason for her pilgrimage. She was brave enough, still for that. She could not allow herself to be treated in this manner. She knew him to be in town. Her father, sheepishly, had revealed as much. It was, in any case, the sort of thing which instinct tells the tormented heart. There was no excuse for the sudden drying-up of response. In Brighton, he had hovered about their party all the time, frequently making excuses to play whist with her and her father even if it meant the irritating presence of Maudie with her cough who would *chatter* through rubbers. He had been content enough, she now furiously told herself, to sponge meals off her, while he daubed his representations of the sea. But since the return, and the crisis, there had been the most eerie silence from Mr Lupton.

Her first sense of betrayal had come, the day after her 'scene' with Horace in which she had scribbled off a note to Timothy.

> *My Husband has been told of our attachment. I have asked him for a divorce which at present he is unwilling to grant. I must see you soon to discuss this matter. C.*

These, or something like them, had been her scribbled Monday morning sentences demanding, in common courtesy, a reply, if not by the afternoon post, at least by next day. A longer letter, fuller of endearments, had been therefore posted, expressing fears for his health, and trying – she knew despicably – to explain that the wretched Maudie's cough had somehow made it impossible to deny the child the presence of her father on a continental journey. It might – who knew – be a cough to be fearful of. Hopkins had said she didn't like Maudie's *flush*. And all these trivia had intruded themselves into what Charlotte had intended as a letter of pure passion. Timothy could not, as a bachelor, have been expected to understand the way in which families and their various demands can swoop upon us and destroy everything in our lives, even romance. But if they had the power to intrude, and to dominate they could never, ever, kill her love. That had been the burden of her second communication. And that, too, had been greeted with silence from a man who was *known* on the very afternoon of its delivery, to be drinking Madeira at Pratts.

Was he disowning her, purely because she had a daughter with a cough? Was he impatient, or merely fickle in his affections? Charlotte had tormented herself by supposing that there had probably been many other flirtations in his life; perhaps, indeed, they 'meant' very little to him. He could have no conception of the trail of miserable women he left behind him. But although this line of thought was good enough to work herself into a rage of tears, she could not entirely believe it. She knew that what had been between herself and Timothy was something larger than that, something grander and more impossible to ignore. It was the great thing, which comes to most lives not at all, to those few it visits, but once.

She now recognised that for a very long period, perhaps since early childhood, and certainly from a date which preceded her disastrous association with Horace, she had known herself to be a person marked out for tragedy. Almost, as she paced towards Fitzroy Square in the afternoon heat, there was in her head a swirling accompaniment of operatic music, as though she were a heroine about to step on to the boards of an Italian theatre for the tempestuous dénouement. The fear which possessed her, however, was something much more than social 'stage fright' or an anxiety that she would not remember her lines. She was (it was for this reason that she missed, even for an hour, the reassurance of Hopkins to cry upon), she was afraid of Timothy, as she was also afraid of Horace. The men had all the power. As far as Charlotte could see, they always would, even if the likes of that heroic Mrs Bodichon got their way. She moved and trembled in fear of Timothy for his simple power to hurt her. Almost anything he said or did not say, did or did not do, had from now onwards the power to send her swooning further down into the tunnels of pain.

She was too frightened to knock on the door with any vigour. As she tried to rap, she found her knuckles somehow ceased to exist. It was like the experience, when dreaming, of finding herself to have imperfect or transient physical existence; of running but having no legs to carry her over distance; of crying out for help, but having no voice. On this occasion, her fingers curved themselves into a girlish little fist, but she was too flustered to make contact with the sheer woodenness of the door. A voice above rescued her from her perplexity.

'I saw you crossing the square,' he said humorously. 'Come on up!'

He was leaning over an open-cast balcony above her head. His shirtsleeves damp in the warmth of afternoon, his brow glistening, his trowsers tight against his thighs. His grin itself was cruel for he must have known how agonisingly she found the apparition beautiful.

A gentle staircase swooped up to the first floor where she stepped into the large high-ceilinged studio, whose polished boards and carefully arranged draperies surprised her by its elegance. It was light, but for all its adventurous letting-in of the day, the room was cool, almost chilly, for she slightly shivered as he took her parasol and directed her to sit upon the upholstered day-bed.

There had been an attempt, as she could see, to recreate a little of the fantasy of the Alma-Tadema studios from which he had sprung; for at one end the marbles and ferns were arranged for a tableau. The other end of the studio, as if a separate compartment of Timothy's life, was evidently reserved, with its half-finished uniformed dignitary on the easel, for his essays in portraiture.

'Well,' he said, good-humouredly. 'What can I do for you?'

'I simply felt that we were going away for so long . . .'

'We?'

'Maudie, me. . . .'

'The whole household in fact?'

'Lionel remains.'

'Ah, but Professor Nettleship is going with you.' After a pause she was left to fathom out the significance of his adding, 'Good.'

It seemed a kind of disloyalty if she allowed herself to mention Horace in Timothy's company; not a disloyalty to her husband, but to her own romantic visions.

'And you are still thinking of Italy? That was the wheeze last time we met in Brighton.'

She winced at his using the very vulgarism that had fallen from Horace's lips to describe their European adventure.

'Our plans have been very much curtailed. We are making our way to Switzerland, and then – probably coming home, if the child's chest improves.'

Mr Lupton mused a little space, like Lancelot in the poem, and decided that it would be impossible to improve on Maudie's chest, however long they remained at a Swiss resort. The more recent written communications he had received from Maudie's mother had been so alarming that at first he supposed she had been, perhaps, a little mad. Doubtless, at Jenkinson's dinner, wine had flown, dances had been danced, cheeks had been flushed. Perhaps – he could not remember the evening with sufficient accuracy – fingers had lightly encircled one another on college lawns, or strayed with a little too much frequency to Mrs N's fascinating little waist. But that this should be used as an occasion to draw her into an unravelling of the murkier marital intimacies was really unendurable. Divorce? Women like Mrs Nettleship did not get divorced, and if they wished to do so they did not tell men like him about it. He had heard of cases of self-delusion; he knew, too, of low women who used their skills to trap rich men with wiles and lies. But this was not, as he could very evidently see, Mrs Nettleship's style. Not that he did not appreciate, to the very fullest, her attractions. Even as she sat there, so prim on the sofa, he could imagine the pleasures of untying and unbuttoning, and all which would so languidly follow. There was, undoubtedly, something *there*. Even the faint brindling of that fine hair, only sprigs of which were visible at the sides of her rather overwhelming hat, had beauty in itself. He had long seen that her hair was quite 'something,' a delight to be appreciated quite independently of the daughter's *chatain foncé*. But he had been so *slow* to see Mrs Nettleship's game. Now that he did so, he took refuge, as on all occasions of potential embarrassment, in simple good humour. It was, he concluded, the only way. He did not wish to be ungentle. She was an intelligent woman. If the light had not yet dawned, it soon enough would, and he thought to release her as gently as possible from any of her previous rashnesses and outbursts.

His own misconceptions had, after all, been sufficiently glaring. He wondered how he could ever have supposed that the mother was quite deliberately loosing the daughter to him; deliberately encouraging him to love the divine Maudie, as though encouragement were necessary! He could not, as he searched his mind to call back their initial conversations, his and Mrs Nettleship's, recollect what had been *said* which conveyed this highly misleading impression. There was something decidedly humiliating in the thought. Mrs Nettleship's misapprehensions were perhaps perfectly understandable compared with this. Men after all did pursue beautiful married women. This was known. Respectable mothers did not sell their daughters into slavery? Well, no. That too had been known. Little remained of either fantasy, his or Mrs Nettleship's, beyond what art could salvage. On the other hand, dinner tables who had not heard of either of them might be told in Chatterway's unpunctuated drawl of the unsuitable attachment 'old Egg's daughter' had formed for a – how would he phrase it? Lupton could not do the puns. There would be a kind of art in whatever Chatterway chose to make of it. For his own part, the painter had 'Nausicaa and the maidens.'

He could see Mrs Nettleship's eye drifting to the unguarded canvas which stood on the large easel down at the marbly end; and since conversation had become desultory (they had begun to make allusion to the heat for the second time within five minutes' space), he admitted, 'Yes, that is my new Homeric scene.'

While she rose and walked over to the painting, she said, 'There have been several?'

'As I was saying at Brighton, I had planned a whole Odyssey. It just got resolved into a few sketches; of girls, mainly!'

'So' – an arm indicated the neatly stacked walls – 'I see.' Did she see that she was in a room which was simply *populated* with images of her daughter? As she approached the canvas most prominently on display, was it obvious to her that Nausicaa, her shift slipping from a shoulder to reveal, with what shadowy smoothness, a body more marbly than the steps leading down to the water where her maidens, some more scantily clad, did the laundry, was really the little beauty of St John's Wood? Was it equally obvious that the naked wanderer from Ithaca, with golden locks and eyes ablaze, was himself scarcely transmogrified? She let out no indication of *what* she saw. She merely repeated, 'I see.' And then she added, 'Your style is much more confident when you do this studio work.'

'Than when I was trying the seascapes?' he laughed to conceal the wound. He was, decidedly, never going to be a Whistler, still less Manet or Turner.

'Light is all that a painter ought to mind about,' he said, with a slightly pompous caressing of his beard.

'But this one is – well, charming! You must let me – us – if we ever do return, that is!'

'Not buy it?' he asked a little too eagerly.

How else could her sentence have ended, but sensitive to the awkwardness of the moment, she simpered, 'Oh no, of course not?'

And so they stood and gazed at the figures he had depicted. It had to be confessed that his draughtsmanship did not bear a very close scrutiny. The maidens, the trees, the marble and the surface of the water carried – at this stage of composition at least – the marks of being done not in a hurry, so much as according to a formula. If it were possible to make women, like culinary 'shapes', in a mould, then these women were they. They did not wobble, like something in aspic. But they were undeniably ready-made. The marble was all right. He could paint any amount of marble. The ostrich fan he could have painted in his sleep; possibly he really had done so; the trees and potted palms still required attention and the laundry-basket would need repainting. The scene however made up in brightness what it lacked in vividness. With a nice enough frame, it would look perfectly decent on someone's wall. The most obvious thing about it, well! She reserved those speculations for later. It was, in fact, so extraordinary that she blushed to behold it.

'Timothy,' she braved – looking away from him and speaking with suddenness. 'I know that you are after all not coming to Europe. I came to say that, really. And I suppose that when we return, whenever that may be, things will be different.'

'Clearer?'

'Things' – her eyes strayed towards the canvas once more and opened wider in incredulity – 'things could hardly be clearer,' she said.

'I suppose they couldn't, in a way.'

'What I said to you in my last letter – in all my letters – has been true.'

'Could it have been otherwise?'

'I realise it was perhaps wrong of me to write quite so specifically, so brutally.'

'I say, I quite understand, you know?'

'Yes, yes. I suppose you do. You know, when you are married, it is like living in a house where almost all the cupboards and rooms are locked up for ever.'

'A Gothic castle designed by Mrs Radcliffe?'

'Precisely like that; for only the most intrepid or innocent person would ever try to unlock the cupboards, or prise open the doors. It is a *tacit* thing, you understand. You know, both of you. . . .'

'You mean both of *you*.'

Her blush deepened. 'You know not to open the cupboards without any verbal agreement. Speaking about them would be tantamount to opening them. And then some innocent, or, as I say, intrepid person, bursts into the house who does not know any of the rules, and flings open the cupboard doors. They weren't locked after all! And demons fly out of the rooms; and skeletons are seen to lurk in the cupboards. And yet, oh – and yet.'

'Are they real demons or skeletons? Or are they merely what the young heroine of Mrs Radcliffe's story thought were supernatural hauntings?'

'Oh no,' said the thirty-nine-year-old Emily from the chasms of Udolpho, with an appropriate tremor in her voice. 'They are real.'

'Now do you know?'

'And do you realise that when my father brought you to tea that day, you inadvertently flung open some cupboard doors? Of course, you must realise it, or we would not be having this conversation, we would not have had. . . .'

He tried to interpose a joking inquiry. Was he an innocent, or merely intrepid? But the inevitable and horrid gulp told him that it was too late for pleasantness to work its obviously cowardly effects.

'We would not have had this whole summer,' was the gist of a sob which burst from her. She was rushing at him now, her poor unwanted head was shaking on his embarrassed shoulders, her mittened hands were clutching childishly at the bones beneath the shirt.

'We can't,' he tried to say.

'I know, I know.' This was a wail. But still she held to him and moaned in a long agony.

He did not know how long she stood like that moaning and pawing. He should perhaps have thrown her aside roughly, but it was not in his nature to do so.

'Don't make it worse for yourself than it really is,' he murmured, sensing the faint absurdity of their contrasted states of mind; for she – God knew what she was allowing to pass through her tormented mind! And he was trying to keep the situation dignified, for her sake, and at the same time trying to ignore that little feather which arose from the hatted head on his shoulder, and darted across his face with each throb of the tormented breast, threatening now to poke him in the eye and now to tickle his nose.

That was it, he realised as the feather jabbed and bobbed, almost as though it possessed a life of its own. He had never for a moment taken Mrs Nettleship seriously. Further, she was not even quite real to him. *The Mysteries of Udolpho* had considerably more reality than the mysteries which she had concocted around her mundane and tiny suburban dreams. Poor thing, he despised her if the truth were told. She too uncomfortably awoke in him a picture of how spiritually unbecoming naked passion really is. Something nightmarish and ugly was making her cry and rage and half-blind him with her damned feather. And was it the same thing which made him weak at the very mention of Maudie? Surely, it couldn't be, it wasn't; a rum thought, though. He loved Maudie with a holy worship; she had made him mad with love. But there was none of this slobbering about it, was there? Perhaps there was.

'Please, please try not to be unhappy,' he said, pushing the form of Mrs Nettleship away from him.

'Have you never. . . .' Her question was drowned in the shaking misery of her moan. But she resurfaced, determined, it would seem, to derive the greatest possible degree of unhappiness from the exchange. 'Have you never loved me?'

'I think you ought to go home,' he smiled.

'Oh, Timothy, please, please.'

'To your husband.'

Fishing in a reticule, she found a handkerchief and performed the ignominious necessities in the region of eye and nostril.

'It really would,' he feared to provoke another flood of grief, but he wanted to make his point, 'it would be better.'

'Do you hate me?' she asked quietly.

She turned and was gone. Going to the balcony moments later, when he had listened patiently to her pat-a-pat of footsteps on the stairs, and her opening and shutting of the door, he could lean out and watch her scurry across Fitzroy Square, carrying her tragedy briskly, poignantly brave. He mused thus over the sunny scene a full hour, until another, altogether more slatternly figure made her bonneted progress towards his steps, a pale redhead of muddy complexion who had come, as she regularly did, to pose. For if the face and the hair and the look (as Mr Lupton saw it) of irresistible pathos in Nausicaa's face were all derived from his concentrated adoration of Maudie, the rest was paid for. The shoulders and breasts which had been turned out of a shape and preserved in aspic were Ethel's, who had now arrived and was undressing behind the screen. He stood and watched this screen, pleased at the ribboned, lacy garments which were being chaotically tossed or hung over its edges. A man, this was the cruel thing, had his consolations; the sort which Mrs Nettleship could never know. Maudie might fill his dreams, but Ethel would do all right.

Oh Christ, as she came round from behind the screen with a hairbrush and her mouth full of grips, she certainly would *do*.

'I'm assuming as how you'd want me 'air loose like in the pitchers as normal,' she half-articulated through motionless, thin lips. Removing the metal grips from her mouth she was able to speak openly. 'Shall I go and assume that startled expression what we was practising by the potted palm?'

She did so, walking slowly because of the heat, her red hair falling loosely over her very white rounded shoulders and nestling somewhere in the freckled small of her back. It was when she turned that all her glory was revealed. And the startled expression (though not so very startled) came easily enough to her snub-nosed features as, trowserless and awkward with desire, the bearded Odysseus ran to pay his court to the noble daughter of Alcinous.

TWENTY-NINE

The Apparition

It was in Father Cuthbert's absence that Lionel began to form impressions of the man. The outlines of his nature were so sharply drawn, he so approached to self-caricature, that in his presence, one was merely overwhelmingly aware of him without being able to disentangle, precisely, what made his presence so distinctive. It was not unlike the experience of eating a strongly flavoured dish of curry: only after the actual consumption of it had taken place and the taste buds were recovering was it possible to take note of the taste at all. When, therefore, the little monk left the monastery – Lionel had been there perhaps a fortnight – for yet another money-raising lecture tour, his character pervaded the cloister and garth more appreciably than at any moment in the previous two weeks.

Father Cuthbert was infinitely the most remarkable, the most distinctive person whom Lionel had ever met. In the two public performances which the young man had witnessed, the monk had been so wholly plausible that it never seemed for a moment that anything he said could possibly be untrue. He plainly was intimately and beautifully in touch with his Divine Saviour; he equally clearly enjoyed a mystic sweet communion with the Mother of God. Single-handed, moreover, who could doubt it, he had built up the monastic orders of England and undone, by perhaps a dozen years of labour and money-raising, the whole wicked work of the Reformation. Nothing could match, therefore, Lionel's horrified disillusionment when he had arrived at the 'monastery' to discover that the place seemed to exist more fully in the imagination of the good Father than in very truth. Sure enough, there were individuals in the household with shaven heads who trooped into the church and sang the divine office, who fell to one knee at the Father's approach and who accepted, at his command, the most ignominious forms of discipline. But it hardly constituted what Lionel had been led to expect.

Perhaps it was simply that he had been living out the romance which was inside his own head, and failing to appreciate the romance in Father Cuthbert's. For the power of the abbot was not merely self-delusory, nor merely persuasive. Lionel discovered, as the days passed

on the mountainside, that there was a very distinct and spiritual power
in Father Cuthbert which did actually transform the world about him.
When Lionel had first seen the raffish 'monastery boys', and the few
stray wild-eyed men who made up Cuthbert's reformed order of
Benedict, he had felt himself cheated. Furious disappointment, and
fear had mingled in his breast with a desire immediately to escape. He
would go to Gutch in London. He would work among the poor in
Holborn. Anything to be away! These feelings had emended themselves further, in the days which immediately followed, into a sense of
such utter disillusionment with religion itself that he felt he never
wanted to go near a church or hear a bell or breathe the scent of
incense ever again. The scales, as he felt them to be, had fallen from his
eyes completely. He felt nothing but flat and agonised disappointment.

How could this have happened so quickly? When he set out with
Father Cuthbert on the train, he had been so full of spiritual happiness
that he was half-afraid that nothing could dissuade him from joining
the order as soon as he arrived at the abbey. In rather less than a week,
however, he had felt all his dreams and delusions fade away. He was
only conscious of a macabre gallery of semi-lunatic individuals,
cooped up in a house together on a remote mountainside in Wales and
– the Nettleship in him rose sensibly and defiantly to the surface of his
mind – 'making each other worse'. His feeling of personal salvation
vanished. He felt indeed rather bleakly ashamed of himself for having
indulged in such unmanly and hideous displays of emotion. There had
surely been something unhealthy about them? And the more he
witnessed the antics of the monks, and the more he heard Father
Cuthbert's opinions, the more vividly he felt that perhaps he did not
believe in God at all.

For, let it be understood, the good Father was not merely the
restorer of monkery in British lands. He was also a sort of Arthurian
revival, called back from the vasty deep of time to remind the British
people of their ancient roots; and these roots, superficially Celtic as
they might have seemed, were really to be found in the pages of the
most holy scriptures. Oh yes! The lost tribes of Israel had crossed the
sea in boats, it would appear, and chosen to settle in Britain. How they
were navigated, Lionel had not been informed; certainly not with
compasses, for all the cosmography that had ever been taught in
schools had been shewn by the holy Father's wisdom to be 'quite
hideously unsound'. Night after night in the cloister at recreation, the
little man, his black eyes gleaming, would assure the community that
the world was a flat disc; an opinion he claimed to derive from his
study of the Pentateuch.

If Father Cuthbert were the true primitive Christian which so many great men and women appeared to recognise, did it not follow that true primitive Christianity was, to say the least, hollow and improbable? Lionel would like his questions on these matters answered. He had even thought that, during these conferences at recreation, he might be able to pipe up and *ask:* 'Oh, please Father Cuthbert, *explain* why Plato is a hell-cat comparable in wickedness with Darwin and Doctor Jenkinson!' But his smile, and the attention of the 'monks', made any such intervention impossible. It was quite obvious that he only saw what he wanted to see.

This was evident enough in his attitude to the other monks. Although he pronounced the most abominable curses and anathemas upon the heads of his spiritual enemies like Voltaire or the former Bishop of Norwich, and though he poured out abuse when remembering members of his community who had deserted him, there was something fundamentally sweet-natured in the monk which made these outbursts seem purely childish. Of those near to him, he was completely incapable of seeing any ill at all. However disreputable a lad or a man might be, Father Cuthbert seemed to see in them only budding saints, so that it was only when he was gone that Lionel was able really to take their measure. For one thing, when the abbot was in residence, the discipline was extremely strict. Talking, except during the hours of recreation, was absolutely forbidden; the hours of prayer were rigorous and long; the life was harsh; the beds uncomfortable, the food inadequate.

Moreover, the chiaroscuro of the place was oppressively disturbing. Since the abbey was on the south side of the valley, no sunshine reached the buildings at any hour of the day, though a little reached, by some mercy, the lower patch of ground by the Abbot's Meadow. The days had been, in fact, quite bright and clear. Beyond the Tyrddu, the little stream at the bottom of the valley, mountains and hills rose up, a multitude of colour in the light of the sun. But none of the light ever percolated to the gloomy house perched on the side of the rock, or to the hanger or coppice which shrouded it. There was a sense of inhabiting the shadows and gazing out towards the light, which brought to Lionel's tired heart variations of the Platonic cave myth from *The Republic*. For he felt himself living in the shadows and gazing upon shadows, and without the emotional stamina to escape them.

When the Father disappeared, however, for a three-day visit to Manchester, Lionel was appreciably struck by the quality of his *confrères*. It is true that they relaxed somewhat the 'silence rule', and that the occasional cigarette got surreptitiously passed round the little group who huddled in the sunless garth. But they were not, as he supposed, purely hypocritical. They wished to keep up, even in Father Cuthbert's absence, the diurnal routines of the monastery.

Once this fact had dawned on Lionel, he began to wonder why he had supposed them hypocrites in the first place. After all, the meanest workhouse in the poorest of our cities would have provided more luxurious accommodation than the abbey of Father Cuthbert. These strange ashen-faced creatures had not merely come there, as Lionel had so loftily supposed, because they wished to 'feather their own nests'. Some feathers! They too were drawn, as he had been, by the rhetoric and the vision of Cuthbert to seek among the mountain heights the City of his dreams. Some of the boys, ill-spoken and dishonest as they might appear, had been there for as long as two and a half years.

Their talk, in the abbot's absence, if they happened to encounter Lionel, was a curious and rather shocking blend of piety and impropriety. The caucus, as it seemed, were a group of three lads ranging in age from nine to fifteen. These boys, Thomas Foord (11), Daniel Maguire (15) and Joseph Chalkey (9), were all figures that Father Cuthbert had 'found' among his city-peregrinations. Daniel Maguire had certainly, before he fell in with the father, led a semi-criminal existence in Wapping, and he was not above, even now, offering to show the others trinkets he had surreptitiously removed from visitors to the abbey: a clergyman called Mr Kilvert's pocket watch; a silk handkerchief belonging to the Father's uncle; a small engagement book which had 'falled' from the pocket of some unnamed visitor who had 'the tallest 'at you ever saw'.

These things, in the safety of the coppice behind the house, could be taken out and shewn to the other boys as evidences of Daniel Maguire's ability to gain a march on the rest of the world. Lionel, as a mere visitor, but one sufficiently boyish to be privy to their councils, had once come upon them there behind the house and been shewn the trophies. They had also titteringly informed him that the Infant Samuel – the nine-year-old who danced attendance on the Reverend Father – 'piddled his drawers'. This allegation gave the group considerable confidence in facing the world.

As Lionel got to know 'the monastery boys' a little better, he came to discern how bitterly they all disliked the Infant Samuel. He, for some reason best known to the Father Abbot himself, had been set apart for the Lord's service and had already taken something very like monastic vows. They, however, who had laboured under the heat of the day in the monastic vineyard, were still ignominiously 'the monastery boys'. It was partly in their longing to steal a march – spiritually speaking – on the over-privileged 'Sam' as they insisted on calling him – that

Lionel smelt out a little of Cuthbert's extraordinary power. Here were
three very humble little urchins whose greatest aspiration was to be
accepted into the monastic life by their abbot. That was surely the
impressive thing about the man. In his absence, Lionel felt less inclined
to dismiss his dreamings and his fantasising. It was something to
persuade anyone, even Daniel Maguire, to leave their own city and to
make their way to the delectable mountains of another man's
imaginings.

One morning, Cuthbert having been away for perhaps three days,
Lionel was making his way towards the potting shed in the yard
behind the house. Time not spent in church hung heavy on his hands
and he had asked Brother Columba of Our Ladye's Seven Dolours
whether there were not some menial task he could perform, 'to make
himself useful'. He had been answered that hoe-ing the path could
possibly effect this transformation, and he had therefore made his way
towards the wooden edifice as speedily as possible. It was evident as
soon as he approached the door that a conference was in progress, and
Lionel feared at first, with a jolt of near-nausea, that he was about to
come upon something unspeakably hideous. He could recognise
Daniel Maguire's voice above the others, but when he flung open the
door he was a little surprised to be addressed by the nine-year-old
Joseph Chalkey in terms which suggested a nonchalant familiarity
with vice.

''Ard cheese Mister Lionel!' he smiled impudently. 'Wrong day!'

'Chalkey! I don't quite follow your drift.'

'It's Tuesdays and Thursdays little Sambo's in here letting Brother
Angelus ****** him.'

A word was used which was quite unfamiliar to Lionel but which, in
its gross simplicity, conveyed to him abysses of horror which he had
not known existed. He was about to splutter some words of protest at
so vile a calumny being uttered about any human being, and to suggest
that Chalkey's perception of the Infant Samuel's character was
pathetically distorted, when Daniel Maguire intervened.

'Shut yer marf, Chalks.'

'If we told the Father what you said,' said a third child, Thomas
Foord, 'you would have to do such *wicked* penances. Like the time
you had to roll in the nettle patch stark naked and then spend the rest
of the day in church reciting the whole psalter.'

'Not that again, Thomas, *please*.'

'Well, ven.'

'I came for a hoe,' said Lionel. 'To hoe the path.'

As Thomas Foord handed him the implement, he said to Lionel,
'You won't say as how you saw us, Mister Lionel will yer?'

There was a look of pale, intense emaciated fear in the little creature's face which excited pity, even before he added, 'It's only 'ow the Farver's allus favourin' the little Samuel and 'e don't seem to notice 'arf the time how we sez our rosaries and keeps clean and don't swear.'

'Let Brother jes try it wiv me,' said Chalkey spitting a fist. 'Jes' let 'im *try* it.'

'No, well 'e 'asn't as he?' asked Maguire, somewhat mercilessly.

'Anyway, Mister Lionel, you know as 'ow the Farver's coming back tomorrer?'

'Chalkey!' said the others. And Maguire added, 'Put a bleedin' sock in it, will yer?'

Any conspiracy, however trivial, excites curiosity, and as he hoed and trimmed Lionel wished that he had heard more of the whispered exchanges in the potting shed.

The day was overcast – the far hills beyond the valley being hung with densely black cloud which turned, in the course of the afternoon to a Scotch mist, bathing everything in a moist haze. The rain stopped some time after Vespers and Lionel from a bedroom window could see all the boys, except the Infant Samuel, playing a rudimentary sort of rounders in the meadow in front of the house. He saw Daniel Maguire toss a ball to another child – not one of the conspirators – it looked an easy enough ball to hit, but the boy dropped his bat and stared above him in amazement into the sky, as though a remarkable bird had just flown over and distracted him from the game. He was calling out to the others, Maguire, Chalkey, Foord and the rest, who ran to where the batsman stood and they too peered upwards. Then he heard Chalkey cry out: 'Oi'll 'it it. Oi'll 'it it wiv the bat if you won't!' and grabbing the bat he waved it defiantly, and somewhat madly to the sky.

They seemed, most ostentatiously, to be creating a 'commotion'. Soon enough, the unfortunate Brother Angelus had materialised to see what the fuss was about. Brother Columba had come out of the house and stood looking over the hedge into the meadow. By the time Lionel had gone down, irresistibly drawn to the cluster of excited figures, all the members of the community had assembled and were all jabbering at once.

'Oi told yer Oi'd 'it it wiv me bat.'

'It was like a great bird.'

'It were more like a flash of light.'

'Or a lady.'

'Yeah, it were. It were like a lady. It was like as if our Blessed Lady herself flew over our 'eds as we prayed and played, like.'

'It was our Lady!' Brother Angelus's effusive tones now rose above the starling-twitter of the boys. 'Who can doubt it?'

'Our Blessed Lady,' added Maguire, "as come down into our very midst! And to fink the Infant Samuel was tucked up in bed and missed it, and dear Farver was away.'

In later life, when he looked back on the entire episode, it was hard for Lionel to summon up the extraordinary and potent atmosphere of the abbey after this curious evening. There was an air of expectancy about the place. There was a feeling, suddenly, of seriousness. Maguire seemed to have taken on a special dignity, a dignity which increased when, after a day or two, he fell ill and complained of blinding pains in the head. Among all the community, it was generally understood that the boys at play that Monday after Vespers had been granted a vision of Our Ladye.

Father Cuthbert returned a few days later on an appallingly wet afternoon to discover a community of people behaving like his own celebrated monkish romances: each afternoon and evening, in spite of the fact that rain had now been falling without cessation for half the week, a little group of the boys gathered in the Abbot's Meadow and knelt on the muddy turf, reciting and singing Ave Marias in a rhythmic, almost hysterical chant. The chapel services, likewise, had become completely dominated by the vision of Chalkey and his little friends, with Father Cuthbert's elaborate hymns to Our Ladye being sung instead of the usual introits and propers. Meals had become a thing of memory. Dry bread and water were consumed in the morning and last thing at night, but it was surely felt – Brother Angelus had perhaps suggested it – that should the heavenly visitant design to pass by their monastic domain once more they should receive her fasting and praying. The group Father Cuthbert found therefore were ashen-faced, wide-eyed, and red-nosed, for a cold was as they say 'going round' the community and the long hours kneeling out in the rain did little to improve it. But Father Cuthbert liked all that he saw.

'Oh my dear brethren!' he exclaimed, 'watch for we know not in what hour she cometh – not the Bridegroom of the heavenly banquet but his spouse and bride, his celestial and spotless mother, even our British cousin the Jew-maiden, our most Blessed Ladye!'

Lionel's feelings, during the period which had elapsed since Chalkey and Maguire's 'vision', had undergone more than one transformation. A significant factor in his mood change had been the reception of a bundle of letters from Maudie which had obviously been stuck for some days – perhaps longer – at Abergavenny and which were brought up by a rain-sodden farm hand from the village a day or so after the apparition occurred.

The outpourings of sisterly affection on the small, closely written pages tugged Lionel this way and that with feelings that were new to him. Hitherto he had felt nothing but spontaneous and uncontrollable love for Maudie. A whisper from her that she was in distress would have torn at his heart-strings; the suggestion that she was about to be whisked abroad would have brought him at once to her side. Now he felt merely a polite sensation of guilt not to be with her, which was not the same sort of emotion at all. It was what he felt whenever he remembered his father, and the recognition that, since the beginning of the summer, he had lost that keen innocent Maudie-adoration made him feel that he had lost the greater part of himself. The little bundle of letters made it clearer to him than anything – he had moved *on;* whither he knew not, whence he regretted with the homesickness of a boy.

Maudie had a distinctive literary gift, for she could jabber on paper; she could lay bare her tortured little soul, she could gossip and muse, she could laugh and suffer all in the same tiny space, some four inches by five. They were going abroad – well he knew that, but, oh *no,* Lionel, you can't guess the muddle and fuss there has been, and Papa keeps saying he is to forget vulcanology for a season but then proposing expeditions to look at bits of glacial lava. And Hopkins says she'll starve rather than eat any foreign food and you should just see poor Mama's unhappy face. Oh darling Lionel, what has gone wrong with Mama? At the beginning of the expedition it was to be all light, fun, art and joy: moonlight was to shine over gondolas; Umbria was to be visited, and the Pitti Palace and Fiesole and the Bay of Naples: and now! St Moritz, and have we remembered smelling salts and moth-balls. What had happened to the original vision? Was the losing of it or the making of it the reason that Mama was so sad?

Oh, and Lioney *dar.* Mr Chatterway's coming too, I *know* he is, and if he's there who *knows* what will happen or who will nod to us in the hotel: for half the crowned heads in Europe nod to Mr Chatterway. Think, *think* of it, Lioney darling, all those crowns and coronets bobbing and nodding to *us.*

These little thoughts were poured out, as we have indicated, in several communications and they all equally did or did not desire an answer. She had evidently been scribbling them ever since he left London. They came to him now as an infinitely distant babbling like some hardly-heard cascade in the next valley or the chatter of a foreign tongue. The world of The Bower, of the professor, of Mr Chatterway, even the world of Maudie seemed, in the mountain-fastness of his monastic seclusion to be like a half-forgotten dream buried in Lionel's mind. It was not – the effect of reading the letters was cumulative – it was not an unpleasant memory. He was not like the prince in the play who, being awake, despised his dream. He had simply had other dreams since which had overlaid the very impulses which he might have guessed, in other circumstances, to be instinctive: the ties of family and of fraternal love. The expedition of his sister and his parents to St Moritz seemed so trivial a matter that he was half-cross with her, in some moods, for drawing his attention to it. He knew, after all, that they were going; and whether or not Mr Chatterway accompanied them was of singularly little consequence. His perceptions were entirely dominated by other things which seemed to be beyond and outside himself. For his initial reactions of hostility, scepticism and disillusionment with the monastery had been entirely subsumed, in the last week, by the much closer and more dominant sensation of being there. He was aware, as never before, of the *place:* of the high crags above the house and the slope of the meadow in front of it; of the valley brooding below beneath tree-tops which were grey-blue in the rainy haze; thick with their late-August, full outburst, dark foliage in all its moist maturity. And beyond the tree-tops in the blackened clouds was the other side of the valley; the sharp outline of its mountainous edge dulled now with cloud and rain though still or fixed. For sometimes the rain would slightly lessen and the clouds rise up in the sky; and then, though the monastery remained swathed in darkness, the valley opposite would become streaked of a sudden with white or gold, or one field in a grey sodden mass would flashingly grow green. And all this while, they ate less and less – three days perhaps they fasted or nibbled only bread – and Lionel was not alone in suffering from the cold. Daniel Maguire's 'headache' threatened to become influenza. The other boys in his dormitory said that at night he cried out in his delirium and pain and kept them all awake. Lionel himself was not ill, and was not going to become ill. He found some inner reassurance to that effect. But his perception of the sodden misty world was through a haze of his own dripping and streaming catarrh. His nose and ears were blocked, and when he slept he awoke to find his eyelids almost stuck together with the thickness of his cold.

But neither the dripping within or the pouring without, nor the chill, nor the damp, nor the sodden trowser-knees nor the leaking boots were for Lionel the dominant emotions during those days. And he knew that he was not alone. They were all of them – the novices and the brethren and the monastery boys – in a state of expectation for a visitant. The Reverend Father himself was not noticeably controlling this atmosphere though in latter days Lionel came to believe that it had been a case of – among many another mystery not to be plumbed in this life – a group of people controlled by the vision of a single man. Strangest of all strange features of those days was their silence. Even Cuthbert himself was quiet for much of the time, though those who passed by his rooms could hear his excited *contralto* discoursing to the Infant Samuel. Most of their time, everyone's time, was spent in the chapel or in the meadow. And it was after three days of such raining, and soaking, and praying and waiting and sneezing and hoping that the three boys came running from the bushes at the edge of the vegetable gardens. Daniel Maguire, for all his illness, insisted on the most extravagant devotional rigours, and every evening he and his friends led the others to the place where they had caught their last glimpse of the brooding form who had initially disturbed their play.

'Look, look!' Daniel's croaking laryngitic voice could be heard again. 'Down by the bush!'

Lionel was at this point in his bedroom. He could only see a limited amount, for the light was falling; it was evening, and the rain continued to pour. But he quickly came downstairs and found the others assembled – Father Cuthbert under an umbrella and two of the nuns from his sisterhood who had come briefly to sojourn in the corrugated iron cloister at the back of the house.

'The light is in the bush!' called Chalkey. 'Very dear Farver, the light's in the bush!'

They all followed the monk, squelching through the mud and the dark to where the three boys knelt, reciting the rosary in their curious croaky little voices. There was, it seemed to Lionel, a curious lifting in the clouds, a brightness not so much in the sky as in the air. Daniel Maguire cried out once more, 'Look, look!' but though this was what he asked them to do, Lionel found in his recollections that he had been unable to look, only to feel – and more than to feel, to be certain – that they had all been in the presence of some extraordinary power, terrifying in its purity, vast in its benignity, huge in its strangeness. Those who looked at Daniel Maguire as he spoke said that the child glowed, and Brother Angelus saw a light above the boy's head which seemed to be an angel. They knelt there, all of them, in the dark and the rain until ten o'clock at night, and the next morning Maguire explained the vision. For as he, and Foord and Chalkey followed the light which they had seen, and as they recited their rosaries, the form of the light hardened. It seemed as though they saw the still and infinitely beautiful form of a woman advancing over the meadow and with her head and face covered with a veil.

Hail Mary, full of grace, the Lord is with thee; blessed art thou among women, and blessed is the fruit of thy womb, Jesus. And when they came to these words, *Blessed is the fruit of thy womb, Jesus,* the light which glowed in the bushes behind the Ladye appeared in the form of a naked man, clad only in a loin cloth, whose hands were stretched out towards the Ladye. And as he advanced upon her, she and he both vanished. But at the moment of their vanishing, the pain and illness from which Maguire had been suffering left him instantly. It was noticed that, in spite of all the rain and mist and dew, the ground in front of the bush where the boys had knelt was dry and warm.

Over the next few days, several other boys, nuns or novices had flashes of vision. Lionel did not. But he felt stunned and absorbed and awe-struck by what was going on, and not a little afraid. He had supposed himself so fully in control of his faculties. He had felt so confident, until this week, that he knew, in the little phrase, what was what. But this assertion of knowledge presupposed some certainty about our criterion for knowledge which had completely deserted him. Lionel did not know what was what. He did not even know what he meant by know. Now we see through a glass darkly, now through a cloud, and now we pass out of seeing into experience. Waking the day after Daniel Maguire's vision, Lionel looked out through the sodden valley and felt that this itself was miraculous enough – those mountains, this rain, this visible creation in which mankind felt himself to be so fully sentient, so knowing and so vigorously in control: so superior in his perceptions to the animals, so certain that he was alone in being able to discern and catalogue experience, so sure that vehicles such as eyesight, touch, smell or *thought* were reliable witnesses to experience!

Oh, he had learnt his lesson and there was no doubt now where his duty lay. He must wend his way back to Dover. He must be with his sister. He must even, perhaps, spend the rest of the summer on other mountains, and swan about in St Moritz with foolish old Chatterway and the melancholic mater. It was twenty-five years later that he turned the pages, published by Methuen and Co., and read the printed chronicle of what had happened in that day or so before he took his leave of Father Cuthbert.

We had sung the last Vespers of the Blessed Virgin. By eight o'clock it was very dark. Heavy clouds and rain falling fast. By the Reverend Father's order, we all assembled at the Monastery porch to watch. The mountains looked black in the darkness, and all around was stormy night. A gentleman from Oxford was with us, a Mr N. from Harcourt College. The Reverend Father told us to sing the 'Ave Maria' three times in honour of the Holy Trinity. Directly we began to sing, we observed outlines of bright forms flashing about in all directions, just outlines of light, here, there and everywhere in the Abbot's Meadow, monastery ground and farm garden. We must have been fully quarter of an hour singing the three 'Aves' for we paused between each, and in awed whispers commented on what we were seeing. *Then,* we could

not imagine the meaning of what we saw, but afterwards we concluded that a cohort of Angels were assembling to welcome Blessed
Mary, the Mother of their Lord, the Queen of Angels. The Reverend
Father then said, 'Now sing an "Ave" in honour of the Blessed Virgin
Herself.' We had no sooner begun it, than the whole heavens and
mountains broke forth in bulging circles of light, circles pushing out
from circles – the light poured upon our faces and the buildings where
we stood, and in the central circle stood a most Majestic Heavenly
Form, robed in flowing drapery. The Form was gigantic, but seemed to
be reduced to human size as it approached. The Figure stood sideways,
facing the Holy Bush. The Vision was most distinct, and the details
were very clear; but it was in the 'twinkling of an eye'. These are the
witnesses of this mighty and glorious Vision – the Reverend Father
Cuthbert, Brother Dunstan (now an Anglican priest), Brother George
(now George Swaine of Wisbeach) and Sister Janet (Janet Owen). This
latter person was kneeling in the meadow at the time. A few moments
after this, Mr N. from Oxford and one of the boys saw the shadowy
Form of the Blessed Virgin in light, by the Enclosure gates, with
uplifted hands. This is the last of the Visions vouchsafed by God's
mercy to us. May His Holy Name be praised for this Confirmation of
the Christian Faith in this age of unbelief!

THIRTY

Place of Victory

It was strange how the old scriptural phrases remained in one's head. But it was perhaps, even stranger that they no longer represented a source of torment. Horace Nettleship heard them like the distant melody of much-loved old airs. They stimulated memory, but they no longer awakened awkwardness, anger or regret. *We know that all things work together for good.* That was the old tune, playing in his head in those last few days before they took ship.

Life was at last benign, after what seemed like decades of anguish and torment. Life was smiling. The future was gilded. All things were working together for good. And the crown of all his achievement was this morning's letter from his son. Horace had taken it out to read in the shrubbery after breakfast. The heat of the day in all its strength had not yet begun to assail the laurels and the lawns, or the somewhat dried-out mossy pathway which led between the two. There was still a hint of dewy moisture on the over-burdened peony bushes, and cool in the shadows cast on the gravel by long-dead laburnum. Hollyhock and mallow pierced through the verdant clusters of Virginia creeper by the arbour, and beyond, in the dark green walk, the box and yew provided a yet thicker shade where he could let his eyes play joyfully over the words from Lionel.

The boy wrote in the eager copperplate of any educated man of his age, but there was always something in it of childish urgency: the way the sentences swooped upwards like lamb's tails! And he was leaving the monastery: after, what? Only three weeks? Less, perhaps. Not a month. Horace felt it was very hard not to congratulate himself on the way that he had handled this delicate matter. It would have been easy to be heavy-handed, to play the role of the *paterfamilias,* and forget that Lionel was, as well as a son, a fellow-creature, a man in all things like himself. (Oh, the old tunes, how they returned, how they returned!) Horace did not have much doubt that, had he put up a strong opposition to Lionel's visiting the monastery, the boy would by now have shaven his head and taken life vows! As it was, his attitude of – what did they call it, the economists? – *laissez-faire!* It had paid off! Charlotte had been, well, Horace did not like to use the word hysterical. He did not even, of his own dear Charlotte, the wife of his bosom, like to use the word shrill. He did not even choose to think that she had allowed the matter to get grossly out of proportion. But, try as he could to prevent them, these words and judgments and verdicts came jostling into his strangely cuboid bald head. It was hardly his fault if they chose to remain there. And if the further outrageous phrase *silly little woman* knocked on the door and pleaded admission, who was he to turn it away again? Oh *laissez-faire!* Poor Charlotte, she had never learnt to take things calmly. She had been all for taking out affidavits, paying an attorney, hiring a *chaise,* calling up the runners, sounding the alarm! So like a woman! So like again, the phrase was irresistible touching! *So like a mother.*

Bless her soul, the dear little mother of his children, his Nettleships. How she had fretted. How she had been unable to let things be! But he had known that all things were working together for good! Now, again, this madcap scheme of hers for going abroad with Maudie for the sake of the child's little cough (a thing of no consequence, the father all too clearly saw, but tiresome, certainly). A cough was something which, speaking quite personally, the professor felt able to take in his stride. It was not, when measured scientifically, in quite the same explosive category as a volcano. The professor could not pretend to any expertise in the matter of the cough. He did not approach his daughter's cough with the knowing spirit that he would have been able to come to metaphorical grips with Popocatepetl or Ixtaccihuatl. He approached it with something surer, however; sounder and safer. He approached it with common sense. And he approached it, nay, he heard it, with the well-informed love of a father. And from this very considerable epistemological vantage-point, it was possible to conclude that the cough was simply a cough. There was nothing sinister about it, and nothing dangerous, no matter for foreign travel or expensive physicians! However, and this was his point, the cough would have no chance of improvement at all – none whatsoever! – were the little woman be allowed to take it – yea, and the possessor of the cough also, little Maudie herself – to, of all places Venice! Venice, yes, ladies and gentlemen – for almost, inwardly, he found himself as he paced the laurel walk giving a small public lecture on the subject – Venice with its notoriously foetid lagoons and its infested canals. Was that, he asked himself, a place for a cough!

Horace Nettleship smiled at the 'little woman's' incompetence. She had really tried to organise a small continental expedition on her own initiative. It was highly droll. That was how it appeared to him. A light-headedness, almost a feeling of drunkenness had taken possession of him: a feeling of triumph, since the dark clouds of melancholy had lifted from him. The little one, who was once again the wife of his bosom, his own dear Charlotte, had let him take control? He felt that he knew a few things about travel. He had – it almost made him snigger to think upon the modesty of the sarcastic phrase which had bubbled out of his lips one day at luncheon – he had a smattering! When little Charlotte was still a little child, staggering about on reins with her Walker aunts in Malvern or being cooped up so unsuitably with a blackamoor butler in Bloomsbury – he, Horace Nettleship, had travelled. He had seen the smouldering Mexican peaks, and watched the bubbling surfaces of Icelandic geysers. The volcanic shores of the Mediterranean had known his footsteps and though he had not visited them, he had read accounts of the far-flung volcanic islands of the Pacific Ocean. So, oh dear yes, he had a smattering! A napkin had been pressed into service against his whiskers to disguise his amusement at the little woman's naïveté! He knew the mysteries of luggage, the occult business of bag and baggage, the rules of nets – mosquito, butterfly or, as Maudie had impertinently interjected, shrimping. The thing had been done properly. Maps had been taken out and spread on the table. Decisions had been made. Itineraries had been devised and revised according to later contingencies. And he had finally settled, with a judiciousness on which it was impossible not to congratulate himself, on St Moritz.

They were to be there two months.

Now, as he read again, or at least, *got the flavour of,* his son's letter, Horace Nettleship felt proud. '*It would be impossible to describe in a page of two what has been happening . . . there are occasions when words do actually fail. . . . I will be returning to London . . . the rest of the vacation perhaps with Gutch . . . and to see you before you go. Perhaps we can all spend a few days together in Dover before you sail. . . .*'

This was what came of simple, parental common sense. The boy was coming *back*. And he intended to pass a few days with his family in Dover before they sailed. What could be better, or more pleasant? Arrangements had been made. By the end of the week, they would be there in the hotel, living proof, the four of them, that all things were working together for good. Little Maudie was already on the way to recovery and he had no doubt that the excitement of a continental tour followed by some eight weeks of mountain air would put an end to any of that notorious cough! Her rebellious brother had come to heel nicely: no coercion, notice, no bullying, no rant. In the initial stages of the trouble, when the first disturbing signs had manifested themselves, the father of course had a duty to send some fairly stiff letters to the young puppy in Oxford; to complain, indeed, to Doctor Jenkinson at

allowing such excesses of superstitious claptrap to flourish in a
modern seat of learning. But things had settled. And when he had
actually heard the little monk for himself, Professor Nettleship had
been compelled to admit that there was something obviously impressive about the man. So, once again *laissez-faire* came into its own. He
had known when to be strict. He knew now when to hold back – to let
the puppy off the leash, certain that after an hour or two chasing
rabbits, it would return pretty gratefully to its kennel.

As for the boy's mother. Oh, Charlotte! It was wonderful, truly, the
way that particular crater had, after an aeon's cooling, been found to
re-erupt. Horace's mind discovered that it was unable to concentrate
on every detail of the marital summer. Scenes from it which should, by
any ordinary canon, have been unforgettable, were swathed in a
tactful cloud of oblivion or incomprehension. Unforgettable things
had been said and for that reason had he forgotten them. Unforgettable blows had been delivered, but he found that he was unbruised
and unbloodied. He and Charlotte had been through the fire and they
had emerged. The rest of it – the nonchalant parental competence, the
sheer brilliance of the itinerary – were nothing, compared with this,
this triumph. Now that he looked back on their period of awkwardness, he wondered truly at his tolerance, forbearing. It had not been,
really, as much of a virtue as he had thought. The little woman had
been sulking for nigh on fifteen years! Fifteen years? And he had let
her. He had sat there patiently in the breakfast room and watched her
stare at her plate, as demurely as a novice, as coldly as a statue! He had
put up with the insolence of it, in his own house, because it seemed,
like the whole cloud of miseries with which it was associated, as if it
were necessary. He had believed, all those years, that he had no option
but to suffer. When she added to these unspoken insolences the
flagrant suggestions with which the painter's name were associated,
Horace had felt all but broken. Something, indeed, had broken within
him, and he had believed at first that it was his heart. But he had been
wrong. It was not his heart but – he smirked now at the happy choice
of phrase – it was the camel's back which had been broken. Poor little
Charlotte made an unconvincing slut, with her proud sudden outbursts, and her talk of divorce. The scalding humiliation of it all had
stirred his manhood, however. And now she was *his* once more, for all
her shoving of chests of drawers against her bedroom door, and for all
her struggling as he had dragged her into his dressing room. It was
something which he should have done long since. Politeness was a
curse in this primeval area of things. She, too, like his children had
come to heel, and he was master once more in his own house.

Folding his Lionel's letter and replacing it in his pocket, Horace

Nettleship made his way from the shrubbery back towards the house. The sun was now rising higher in the sky. His thick eyebrows gave to his face a mangy sort of stupidity which made him seem like some predatory beast as he strode back, hatless, towards the open French window.

Charlotte stared up at him, with a face much aged and an expression in which contempt and fear were fighting for predominance. Mr Goe, roaring hilariously at his own jokes, had just been given his hat in the hall. Maudie had seen the last of her tutor until the autumn and had now come into the room where her mother stared despondently at the open trunk and the little piles of things.

'If those are travelling rugs,' said her lord and master, 'they shouldn't be *in* the trunk.'

'The travelling rugs are in the hall,' Maudie intervened.

'Let your mother answer for herself,' said the professor.

'Maudie is right. These rugs' – she made a weary gesture towards the trunk – 'are to replace the others should they become lost or dirty.'

'Then we are we provided for. Excellent, excellent!'

'Though whether we should need rugs,' Maudie piped up, 'on the way to Dover!' Her sentence dissolved in giggles.

'August is always unsettled,' her mother said quietly.

'Why do we have to stay in Dover,' the child persisted, 'at all? Why can't we stay here, and then perhaps have one night in Dover before we go to Switzerland?'

'We are going to France first,' her father reminded her in the sage tone of the man who had discovered that you can not make an omelette without breaking eggs. He added, with apparent irrelevance, 'Besides, Lionel is joining us there.'

'But he could as easily join us here. And oh, papa, I so wish he was coming too with you and mama and Hopkins and all. It seems so bleak that he alone should be left behind.'

'You speak as if half London were to accompany us,' said her father, speaking, it seemed to Maudie, more truly than he knew.

'He will be company for grandpapa.'

'It is very kind of Mr Egg to accommodate him,' said Horace, 'very kind indeed.'

'He is our *grandfather*.'

'Does that make it any less kind of him to have you in his house?'

'Yes, of course it does. It might even suggest that he wanted to see us.'

'The quiet of that household will be conducive to study,' glossed her father. 'Lionel has had his mountain-holiday for this year.'

'I still think we should persuade him to come too,' said the sister.

'He has made his decision,' said Horace with weird and not quite plausible firmness.

As father and daughter settled this almost flirtatious and wholly absorbing altercation, Charlotte quietly drifted from the room. She looked perfectly brisk and what the servants would have called 'normal', but inside, it felt almost as if she were sleepwalking. She moved beneath a heavy cloud of despair. The past weeks, so raw and so recent, had destroyed something within her. Their dramas had been enacted too lately for her to be able to understand what had happened, or what had not happened, beyond the generalised knowledge that she had broken her heart. In stories, women died of this. And only a few months before, when her love for Timothy was full of such hopes and expectations, she would have thought it probable that the denial of her desires would kill her. At the very least, if her heart did not crack and her life shatter, she would be tempted to take desperate remedies. So she would have surmised when she still nursed all those foolish hopes. But now that the hopes were gone and she nestled beneath the black shade of unutterable gloom, she found that she had lost her will. She could not kill herself because it would have involved forming a decision, and decisions, at the moment, were the hardest thing of all. The hammer-blows of her husband's mockery about travel rugs, the light cruel way in which Maudie discussed the question, made her reel with agony. She had spent a whole afternoon, the previous day, trying to decide the matter. Of *course* (she found that she was crying) they would not *need* travel rugs on the Dover road; but how could Maudie have been so simply callous as to say so? The sudden forming of the alliance of daughter and father against her was one of Charlotte's worst griefs. It mingled hopelessly with the greatest grief of all, with her lost demi-god and her lost dignity.

Through all the tears and the sleeplessness and the exhaustion and the dull desperate thuds of her own heart-beat Charlotte felt quivering rage against Timothy Lupton. He had, quite simply, played fast and loose. He had made her foolish. He had toyed with her for his own evil pleasures. And he had, most humiliating of all, prised out of her revelations of her own astonishing innocence. Only innocents commit adultery; of all sins it is the one which suggests the most optimistic capacity to alter the *status quo*. She had thought that her life could be *improved!* She had weakened. She had lifted a corner of the coverlet, and shown to Timothy the torments which lay beneath, the agonies, which for fifteen or twenty years she had kept so bravely and sensibly concealed. And he had done no more than cuddle her like a sick child and send her away sobbing: after all their wildly overt public lovemaking, their partings on street-corners, their Harcourt-dancing, their glance-exchanges! She wondered now whether there were not something defective in the manhood of such a creature. Could he not be one of those men one had heard about? Could that be the explanation?

If the question formed itself in her head, its interrogatory mode did not suggest any line of rational inquiry. She was no longer seeking an answer. Any stick, within her flinty little bosom, was good enough now to beat the monster with, or to prod him through the bars. Horace, in a strange way, hardly concerned her. He was merely the prison she had hoped to escape. She liked its dungeons, chains and slimy walls no better than before. But it had not been the stinking old prison walls which were to blame, as she was being let down from them by rope, if Mr Timothy Lupton cut that lifeline and handed her back to the warder. It was he who had delivered her back to the house of death, the house of slow death which we so wrongly call life, the house of disappointed lodgings and thwarted hopes.

The next few weeks or months would be horrible, but she saw no particular reason to dread them, more than any other weeks. The house of death was itself horrible, and if her sentence was cruel, she might not yet be more than halfway through it. She could hardly rouse herself to the great decisions of what clothes to pack and what to wear. It was not to be wondered at that she flinched from the trivial ones – where they were going, and who with. When Horace had decreed that they should continue to close The Bower for the summer, and dispatch Lionel to her father's house in Brunswick Square, she had acquiesced. It should have been interesting to her, the whereabouts and future of her son, but it was not. Maudie's cough was a more immediate concern, but even *that*, infuriating as its sea-lion insistence was, got forgotten. In three days, they would all be in Dover and another stage of the journey would be complete.

Charlotte looked about her. She had, apparently, come upstairs and she was in the little morning room. She did not know what she was doing there, or whether she had gone to that room for a purpose. More and more, now, she found that she had moved from one part of the house to another with an apparently purposeful movement, and more and more she found that she did not have any purposes to justify the feeling. But what *was* it that she had come upstairs for? There was *something*. The failure to remember again made her feel that she might be about to cry. Life is real, she tried to remind herself, biting her lips, and life is earnest. But next door, Maudie had started to thump the piano and sing 'The Lost Chord' in her weak but haunting soprano. The words were only half-heard by the mother as they came through the thickness of the walls, and crept over the thicknesses of carpet.

It may be that Death's bright angel
Will play me that chord again,
It may be only in Heaven,
I'll hear that great . . .

but, before she reached the great 'Amen' the song was interrupted by the everlastingly irritating cough.

Maudie herself, perched on the piano stool, muttered in her Marvo voice, 'Dull stuff, what, Sullivan's music,' and smiled to think of her victory. For she *had* persuaded the old wanderer to stray from Half Moon Street once more and 'to come with them as far as Paris'. This was, to Maudie's way of looking at things, more than half the battle won. Her heart was very light at the vision of herself strolling with Mr Chatterway in the Elysian Fields or carousing with him in the Field of Mars. Paris did not need to be transformed in her imagination into a city of dreams. It mythologised itself. Who could ever get excited by the thought of London, by its hideously unpoetic Hyde Park, Piccadilly, Pall Mall, or Strand? Where were *its* places of Victory and Concord, or its fields of Elysium?

THIRTY-ONE

Love in a Mist

But Lionel had *not* seen the Virgin Mary floating towards him on the clouds. He had not seen what Father Cuthbert and the monastery boys said that they had seen. As the days had passed since the visions faded, the mountain community were granted a clearer and sharper impression of what they had seen. The narratives became hardened. They became capable of chronicling at what moment the lights had turned into shapes, and shapes into unmistakable forms of Our Ladye Herself and of the Christ Child. For Lionel, over the same period of reassessment, the over-emotional rain-sodden days and evenings became, in retrospect, impossible to focus. There had been a feeling, certainly, a presence, perhaps. But he could not say that he had seen what the others had seen, and his inability to do so shook the foundations of his life.

Little Cuthbert received the news of his departure without acrimony. After all, Lionel had not promised he would stay, he had taken no vows. There was even a suggestion, which he did not choose to deny, that he would return; but as the cart wove its way through the valley to Abergavenny, he knew that he could not return. A change had taken place within himself; some buried aspect of his character was left on the dark side of the Tyrddu valley, some outgrown childishness, some raw lack of control which he now found it painful to contemplate. In later years, when, by the standards of the good Father Cuthbert, Lionel had been 'corrupted', he would recall his first moment of stepping out of the shadows and into the light. A similar sensation of clearing would come to him after the conclusion of some painful liaison. Somewhat differently, and more terrifyingly, there was something of the same feeling, not of thrill, but of having moved on, when he read, as a crusty figure in late middle-age, that the arch-duke had been assassinated; and it gradually dawned on him, a hideous relief mingled with his fear, that Europe itself was to change, that one chapter of existence was finished and the next pregnantly, excitingly unwritten.

So the Cuthbert era ended, in Lionel's life, with decisive absence of complication. It was a bright, hot day when he left, a fact which emphasised the transition: the visions, and the emotions that had gone with them, were left behind among the hilly celtic vapours. There was a wonderful sense of freedom about saying goodbye to it all, an enormous relief as he carried his bag to the little station, bought the ticket, and made his journey eastwards through violently emerald hill country and into the parched hopfields of Herefordshire. At Hereford itself, he changed trains, and occupied an hour or two by wandering about the old town in sunshine which was almost hispanic in its power. He saw the chained library in the north aisle of the cathedral. A decrepit sexton allowed him to finger the pages of the old folios and quartos, and to gaze on the brightly-illuminated medieval gospel book. How vividly, it seemed to Lionel at that moment, he had romanticised the past. The very word *monastery* had been, for him, synonymous with order, beauty, wisdom. It was the monks and the monks alone who had saved Europe from barbarism by copying such books as these; by preserving such codices in their libraries, just as, in their great gothic churches, they preserved the faith once delivered to the saints. Impersonal guardians, Lionel had thought of them until now. Nothing made him suppose that there was anyone in the middle ages quite as remarkable as Father Cuthbert: and he was to learn enough about the history of monasticism to recognise that the Holy Father's version of the religious life bore about as much resemblance to the rule of St Benedict as it did to the statutes of the Stock Exchange. But monks were, well, people, and that was now something of a shock. A human hand had penned the book offered for his perusal, and, with tiny delicate brush-srokes, adorned each capital with a fantastical bestiary. A human eye had overseen it. Obvious thought, but it came to him late, and its import was so disturbing that he almost forgot to offer a shilling to the scarlet-nosed verger who said, what with seemed surprising percipience, that he supposed that Lionel was a gentleman from Oxford. The verger's voice was old. Beyond its English burr was a mysterious Welsh lilt, so that hearing him speak was something like looking back into the past, or gazing across the fields of Herefordshire towards the marches and the mountains of Brecknockshire beyond. A stroll in the cloister, a walk up and down the picturesque streets of the place, a luncheon which he felt too hot to relish, at the Green Dragon: cold chops, a good salad of potatoes and radishes, a slab of cold gooseberry pie and some slightly cheesy, but excellent cream.

Throughout this accumulation of sensations, Lionel felt an increase of his sense of expectation, and his mind – not merely his mind, but his whole being – churned and churned about. He seemed to have pinned so much on improbabilities, to have accepted so much, and so soon, and so readily, and so without question. And now, with the fading of a vision he had never had, he felt bereft, he felt that he had made a fool of himself. It was nothing so crude as a fear of returning to his father and admitting that the older man had been right. Besides, Lionel did not believe that his father was right – about the great issues or about the small – or, necessarily, about anything in the universe. He was more egotistically concerned with his own impressions and sensations.

There had been such momentary *certainty*, when he first heard Father Cuthbert preach: certainty of a *presence*, certainty, suddenly, of the truth! But the truth now no longer seemed to him capable of apprehension in a single gulp. Like a glimmering canvas by Turner, it had bright patches, and darks, its moments where perception seemed merely a smudge, its carefully drawn outlines where what was seen or felt was unmistakable. It couldn't be *reduced*. This, he decided, was what he had tried to do. He had tried to bottle it up for himself as something contained, and possessed, and now, in his non-experience of a vision, his experience of the truth had burst out like the genie in the fairy tale. There was not *enough* mystery in the city of Father Cuthbert's dreams: that was its lack. Some would imagine that there was too much, but they would be mistaken. Father Cuthbert looked at his rhubarb patch in the rain and saw there a vision of the heavenly Mother. Lionel did not deny that the others had seen this vision. But he felt that they had been so busy looking for the miracle of Mary in the rhubarb that they had never stopped to consider the equally stupendous miracle of rhubarb itself. They had been so intent upon seeing an apparition in the clouds that they had not sufficiently fallen silent and awestruck at the apparition of clouds themselves. There was nothing ordinary about this world. There was nothing ordinary at all in the swirling vapours which surrounded it, or in the plants that grew on its surface. The consciously pious mind seemed only capable of ignoring the wonders of the natural in its myopic quest for the supernatural; just as the allegedly scientific mind was so focussed on a pedantic analysis of details that it could not see into the life of things. And so they struggled between each other: the scientists condemning the religious as obscurantist, and the religious condemning the scientists as heretical. And all the while the most mysterious and inexplicable miracles were being enacted before our very gaze. For instance, the sun shone. The darkness and cold of night was transformed, every dawn, by a miracle. Lionel, as he made his way back through the strong midday sun, to collect his luggage at the station, felt almost choked by its strangeness, and young as he was, he heard some words echo in his head from the old play, 'O I have ta'en too little care of this.'

Too little care, as the train trundled eastward towards the sombre blue of the Malvern hills, rising like giants' gravemounds against the horizon. Too little care of the intense oddness of existence itself: the fact that we breathe, the fact that we *move;* the fact, that breathing and moving, like other animals, we yet exist chiefly in our own imagined lives, our inner vision of ourselves, determined in part by heredity and education, in part by the simple and mundane fact that we inhabit this particular body, rather than another. Lionel knew now that he had been too young, simply, to take care of this. He only began now, at twenty, to sense a glimmering of the mystery and he knew that it would be a mystery which deepened rather than becoming clearer. If he lived for a hundred years, he would still come no closer to understanding it: the fact that he sat in a railway carriage, rattling through Worcester, and *saw* the houses, and fields, the cricket pavilion, the cathedral tower splendid by the Severn. All these impressions, thoughts, sights! The wonder was that so many corresponded, even slightly, with the thoughts and impressions of others: corresponded enough, that is, for language to be possible, and the illusion of communication with other human minds to be sustained. How do I know, however, that the cathedral I saw is the same as the cathedral others saw? Was there anything outside ourselves, or was it all contained within our collection of sense-impressions?

The mind could not approach it, but sense could: that is, both physical and common sense. For there it all was, outside the window of the railway carriage! The world! Little Cotswold towns, grey lichen-covered stone lazy beneath the heavy afternoon sun; haystacks in fields; bonneted women spreading out check tablecloths under the dappled shadow of sycamores; red-faced, collarless men, their leggings tied up with string, rubbing sweaty brows; children chasing with hoops on village greens; a clergyman in a hard black straw hat riding a penny-farthing bicycle; a startled herd of deer running up a bank into the Wychwood; low flats of meadow-land and lines of poplars; harsh new suburbs intruding into emerald fields; the spire of the new church, so unmedieval in its perfect medievalism in the Woodstock Road: Oxford. There it all was, having its own reality in the baking late summer heat. Lionel knew that, however false our impressions of this reality, it would be lunacy to pretend that there was no such reality, or that there was nothing external to ourselves. He was tempted, more, in his present frame of mind, to feel that it was he himself – at least as a sentient being – who lacked substance, and that the solid world would go on happily without him, whether he observed it or not, whether he existed or not.

At Oxford, he changed trains once more, and an impulse led him to wander through the town. His young brain was teeming with a desire to pour out its torrent of mingled excitement and disappointment, and he felt that there was one old brain, should it still be resident at this deep stage of the Long, into which the outpouring could be made.

The streets, as he wound his way on foot towards Harcourt, were almost unimaginably empty. It was half-possible, from their appearance, that a state of plague had been declared and all the inhabitants had vanished.

No undergraduates were there, and almost certainly the majority of the dons were abroad on reading parties. The Jenker himself was much more likely to have been hobnobbing with Mr Chatterway and his duchesses in some Scottish baronial *schloss* than pottering in the gardens of Harcourt. But Lionel thought it was worth trying to see if the great man was there. He was not one of those undergraduates who had built up a close intimacy with Jenkinson. But he revered him, and felt himself, in the regular interviews with the Master which were a part of weekly life at Harcourt, a sympathy beneath the silences and beneath the asperity of his shrill, bird-like utterances. It was therefore a great relief to Lionel, pushing open the wrought-iron gate which led into Harcourt's walled garden, to see the little figure of the Master perambulating the gravel walks, an austere shovel-hatted shape of black and white against the splash of herbaceous colour in the border – the profuse love-in-a-mist which still flowered in the front of the bed bright in its blues and greens.

Jenkinson showed absolutely no surprise at seeing Lionel. He waved at him indeed with the air of a man who had been expecting a guest, but was perfectly tolerant about his being a few moments late.

'The hour of the sandwich is not altogether past, nor the time of tea,' he said. 'But let us walk in the garden first'. There were no trivialities in the Master's conversation, unless one regarded the private lives of the aristocracy as trivial. Since Lionel knew no marchionesses, it was inevitable that he should plunge straight into the inner debate which had been tormenting his soul ever since the Welsh 'apparitions' began. In a narrative flow which seemed somehow much more possible because they were walking, and not sitting down, Lionel began to tell Doctor Jenkinson all that he had seen and heard of Father Cuthbert. Callow youth, he did not even omit the detail that Father Cuthbert considered Doctor Jenkinson himself one of the most fiendish purveyors of error since Plato.

With each new development of the story, the Jenker let out a higher squeak, whether of anguish or amusement it was not entirely possible to know.

'Not, of course,' he was saying when Lionel's chronicle had run its course, 'that the coenobitic ideal is wholly inimical to me. But I feel, don't you, that Plotinus would have felt more at home in the Common

Room at Harcourt than in the cloisters of this, this – mummer!'

'But *sir!*' said Lionel, 'if I have lost my *faith*, what am I to do?!'

The master turned to him with pursed lips. His round cherubic face was very pink, and his high winged collar and bow tie were very white.

'The simple answer to *that*, Nettleship, is that you must find it again by the time you come back to Harcourt next term. You're not *allowed* to lose your faith. It is against the statutes of the University.'

They walked for a while in silence and listened to their heels crunching on the hot gravel. Pausing to stare at the flower-bed, the Master blurted out – 'Nigella! Love-in-a-mist!' and then they walked some more without saying anything. Then, as if Lionel had been so talkative that it was hard to get in a word, the Master blurted out, 'But you *know* all that anyway. Love-in-a-mist. Now we know in *part*. I do not think you have lost your faith. I think you are only just beginning to understand what it is. It isn't *faith* which makes people believe they have seen miracles. I happen to believe that the age of miracles is over. But if I were proved wrong, the existence of the miracle would not alter faith, which is the substance of things hoped for and the evidence of things *not seen*. We are called upon to worship the Deity in Spirit and in *Truth*.' There was another silence and then he added, 'Love-in-a-mist'.

'But were they real experiences?' Lionel asked him. 'When I felt myself being converted, changed, suddenly taken over? And again, when I heard Father Cuthbert speak in London. And in the monastery, there was this sense of a presence. There really was. But if I couldn't see what they could see, it must mean that they were wrong, doesn't it? That they were deluding themselves? Or that I was too sinful to see? But if I wasn't wrong. . . . Oh, I can't really say what I mean.'

'Learning to say what one means is not merely a scholarly fad. It is the first requirement of politeness,' snapped Jenkinson. 'One can at least be grammatical even when logic fails'.

Duly reproached, Lionel sank into silence once more. Then he was brave enough to speak out. '*You* say I must find faith, or that I am only just beginning to have it. And you would dismiss Father Cuthbert as a superstitious crack-pot.'

'This would be a fair summary of my position.'

'But Father Cuthbert would say that you didn't have any faith, and that you were a heretic.'

'If I disputed with him, it would not be to call him a liar, but to call in question his definition of faith. You might think it was a definition of purely philological concern. But this is not the case. What we understand by the meaning of the word *faith* determines our understanding of this world. A false understanding of religion leads to a false understanding of life. We only possess the impressions of our own senses and faculties. We can only see what our eyes will (often so misleadingly) *let* us see. We can only touch what our hands will reach. You understand the point?'

'I think so, sir.'

'And you would agree, would you not, that true knowledge must be universal knowledge.'

'What do you mean by universal?'

'I mean that it is of very little interest to say that I believe that there is a statue of Mercury in the middle of the quad at Christ Church if I am alone in this belief, or if my belief is only shared by a small number of enthusiasts.'

'You mean, it is only knowledge because we have all agreed to say that Mercury is there?'

'No, that is *not* what I mean. But it is our knowledge because we have agreed to share our individual impressions. The number of impressions which conspire to make me believe I have seen Mercury in Christ Church overlap with the impression of others. All this belongs to the region of knowledge. And because life is brief and scepticism in all areas of knowledge would be intolerable, we shorten life by taking most forms of knowledge on trust. You do not have to find out for *yourself* that the Persians were vanquished at Marathon. You take it on trust from the reliable witness of historians.'

'But if I were writing a history, I would have to doubt all the earliest testimonies about Marathon, wouldn't I?'

'Oh yes. I am not suggesting a return to blind acceptance of untruth of the sort your friend Father Cuthbert might advocate. All truth must be *tested*.'

'But not all truth can be tested.'

'Precisely, and there is a point, even in areas of material knowledge where truth must be taken on trust, or *pistis* or faith. Not to retain this quality of faith is to deny ourselves the possibility of knowledge. This is true in the fields of natural science or history and philology. I am equally convinced that it is true in the area of theology, where we can only ever hope, according to the Apostle, to know in *part* and prophesy in *part*.'

'So faith is taking things on trust which we fear might actually be untrue.'

'Very sharp, but no! Faith is not that. That is what you still want to make it. You are still spiritually at one with Father Cuthbert. You want to reduce faith to the level of what can be seen and touched and tasted. My point is that it is of its essence that it cannot contain knowledge.'

'But knowledge is impossible without it?'

'Yes. Almost all knowledge is impossible without it.'

'And so, sir, what have we said that faith is?'

'You thought that faith was the capacity to believe improbabilities.'

'I did, but then I changed my mind.'

'And then you swung to the sillier extreme of thinking that faith was merely the capacity to be awestruck by mysteries.'

'I think I still think that.'

'The capacity to be awestruck is not to be despised. Shelley, the greatest poet of this University, and in my view of this century, manages to make his greatest effects through this capacity. But faith is a different thing. As the philologists would want to remind us, it contains the quality of *trust*.'

'Isn't that just the same as believing improbabilities because we want to be loyal to someone or something that propounded them?'

'You mean that we are only Christians because the Church tells us to be?'

'Precisely.'

'I always say to people the precise opposite. Believe in God in *spite* of what the clergymen may tell you.'

'In what, then, does this quality of trust consist?'

'It consists,' said the Master of Harcourt, 'in recognising that we cannot derive our impression of the world entirely from the evidence of our own senses. We might get things very wrong if that was all we did!'

'So, we have to accept what others tell us on trust? It comes back to that.'

'It is not *all* that I am saying. I am saying that just as knowledge can not be achieved without *pistis* or trust or faith, nor can our apprehension of moral truth, nor our sense of beauty, nor our vision of the Godhead. But this faith is not something we take on trust from *others*.'

'Then from whom?'

'Faith is not taken on trust from others. It is what we give on trust to ourselves. Without nourishing it we turn in on ourselves completely. Solipsism is the ultimate lunacy.'

'For if we only know ourselves we can't be said to know anything else?'

'Precisely. We don't want to get into Bishop Berkeley before tea. But it really is, you see, why so many of the ancient philosophers have something to teach us even when they made so many mistakes. They believed in a reality outside themselves.'

'And this belief that there is something outside ourselves, that is faith?'

'It is the beginning of faith.'

'So without faith, we can't live.'

'Oh, you can live!' His voice rose to a falsetto squeak. 'But you can only live like a pig.'

And taking Lionel's arm, he led him into the study, where cucumber sandwiches were waiting, and a cherry cake, and ginger bread and a dish of watercress. Over the consumption of these delicacies, the Master fell silent. Lionel had never known him talk so much, and he did not really expect him to talk any more. When the last ginger biscuit had been offered and refused, the young man rose to go.

'It was clumsy of me to intrude on you in the middle of the Long,' he blusteringly began. 'I simply felt I had to talk to someone, and the train had stopped at Oxford anyway. I mean, having come all that way, I felt I should call just in case. . . . But I am sorry. . . . I feel you probably wanted to spend the afternoon. . . .'

'Dear boy,' said the Master as he rang for his butler to show Lionel the door, 'never apologise, never explain.'

THIRTY-TWO

Wherefore to Dover

Mr Chatterway had almost made his decision, but it still remained merely a matter of *almost*. Events, or their lack, had forced his hand, and it was this, more than any other consideration, which gave him pause. For he liked to picture himself as the governor not only of his own destiny, but of others'. Nevertheless, the sense of having gone too deep, and into the wrong pools, troubled him. It awoke so much pity, and so many old memories: of little Charlotte herself growing into womanhood. There had been a particular moment in Brunswick Square in the old days: old Eggy and his daughter were strolling there beneath the planes in spring sunshine, and Chatterway, back from – where was it that time – (Vienna?) – had alighted from his victoria and surveyed them through the railings. Nothing more than that. A vignette, of his handsome old friend, and the daughter. Chatterway had approached, and bowed to Charlotte. She was hardly fourteen years old at the time. But they had all *known*. The laughter was as brittle as before, the talk was as pointless, the social boasting as stupendous, the cynicism as hard. But from that moment, perhaps a quarter of a century before, they had all shared the secret. Charlotte was his woman. It was one of those things decreed by the fates.

The summer squabble had complicated his sense of it. Her uncharacteristic petulance and pomposity had affronted him. Who was little Nettleship to deny entry to a gentleman of Chatterway's standing? There was something more than preposterous in a jumped-up usher, some groveller in volcanic ash, some scribbler of scientific bosh, thinking to govern the exits and entrances of a man who was on terms with the Duke of Connaught; a man, moreover, who had eaten, nay dined, with the ever-maligned Marchioness of Lorne; and who had been described by their dumpily diminutive but majestically matriarchal monarch as 'that odious Mr Chatterway'. Worse than any of this was the knowledge that darling Charlotte had put up with the prof's embargo! So unlike her to be obedient. Marriage was the deuce. One stared at it from the outside, just as, all those years ago, he had stared at her through the railings of Brunswick Square. What was going *on* behind the railings, one would never know. It was necessary to conclude, painful as the acknowledgement became, that Charlotte was fundamentally happy with her lot. Mr Chatterway had received many blows to his pride over the years but he found it hard to bear this. That Charlotte loved the professor! Still, after a score of wretched years watching him blow his fat nose over the breakfast-porringer, poor little Lottie must love the bald ass!

It hurt to know this. It was simply hurt, nothing more devious, which enabled him to accept his exile from The Bower. In what he sometimes found himself calling normal circumstances (but what circumstances, particularly in his life, were ever normal?) he would have battered at her door and disregarded the ban. Now he believed that much distress would have been avoided had he done so. A little good-natured teasing would have put a finish to the Lupton escapade. Silly fool, why did she have to go and squirm on sofas with a bearded puppy, infecting herself with God knew what whore-diseases that he might carry around in his surely fairly unspectacular though easily stimulated loins? Now all London knew that she had been the painter's whore. If they hadn't known already from her flagrant parading of the fact in Brighton, they knew now. He had told them. He wasn't cross with Lupton. Charming fellow. It was Charlotte who had stooped. There was always something intolerable about a woman stepping out of her class. She wasn't some vulgar Duchess from Kentucky, nor some Jewess pawed by Bertie's Hanoverian little hands. Nor was she a shameless slut. So why behave like one? The inescapably bourgeoise quality of her marital position made it ridiculous for her to behave as she had done.

The hurt had perhaps led, in the initial stages of the flirtation, to a deliberate alienation of Charlotte's daughter's affections. But the thing quickly developed its own momentum. Perhaps if Maudie had been thrown less upon her own society, Mr Chatterway would have lacked, simply, the time or the opportunity to see her. Perhaps if young Lionel had not happened to choose this summer, of all summers, to receive a visitation from on high, his besotted younger sister would have been able to claim his undivided attention and company, as she had done for all previous summers and vacations. This element in the story almost made it seem, to old Chatterway's open-minded way of seeing things, as though his attachment to Maudie had been meant. Not meant, perhaps, by the selfsame celestial father who had called Lionel out of darkness and into light, but by whatever muses of tragedy or comedy inspired the governing daemon of Mr Chatterway's destiny, for we choose, he was sure of it, our own destinies, and it is thereafter they who hover about us, whether we altogether like it or not. They had hovered, all right, and determined that from the very first zoo-encounter, Maudie should have had him in her power. From thence he began, so foolishly, to enjoy with Maudie what he had enjoyed with her mother so intensely a quarter of a century before. It made the mistake of Charlotte's marriage to the professor almost redeemable. At last life seemed to be offering him a reward for his patience. Quickly enough, the child had come to haunt him, so that her voice and face possessed his consciousness throughout the season and were with him in all his downsittings and uprisings at the dining tables of the rich. Maudie, Maudie, Maudie, Maudie. The little witch had even drawn out of him a certain disloyal *tone* when discussing Charlotte, which was entirely new. It fanned the flames. He began to hope. And he became aware, in the destructive way that hope brings awareness, that she too was becoming entangled in her own web. What had they been *doing* all summer except, quite simply, falling in love with each other? The question led on to others, some trivial, some not. In his confusion of heart, it was not always possible to disentangle these questions or to arrange them in order of triviality. Did, for instance, a gentleman who had already wasted three score of his allotted years *allow* a young girl of sixteen to fall in love with him? That was the question. But he did not know whether it was more important than considerations of happiness: hers, his? What if there really were, as in a romantic monogamist's theory of the universe, one person and one person only in this world who can 'make us happy'? What if one meets this person and they appear to think that, as far as they are concerned, one would do pretty nicely oneself? Dashed awkward, what? What if life were not all some tinkling banality by that whiskery little fornicator Sullivan, but contained some of the dramas and mystery of Brahms? Where, in other words, did politeness yield to romance? Where, on the other hand, did common sense and common kindness modify simple lust? Yes, dammit, lust again at his age.

Supposing, supposing he married her. Supposing, even, she made the loyal little wife that her mother had made to her eggheaded papa, and that this subjugation brought her a glimmer of security? Wasn't marriage itself a mistake? Didn't it take the gilt off the in this case far more golden than gingerbread? Charlotte might have thought she was happy with the professor. But her very eyes had gone flat, her hair brindled, her mouth pinched and tight. Once, in Brunswick Square, she had had all the exuberance, the sheer vivacity, the untamed and untapped wells of joy which one saw shining in Maudie's satirical face. Now, did a man want to go and snuff out the lights of that joy by doing a selfish thing like marrying her; marrying her before she had the chance to *know*. . . . It seemed like the idea of capturing a sprightly pony and making it pull a tram-car.

So, in the mind of our old friend, the dilemma churned and churned about. He had all but made up his mind to cut loose. Exile could be *managed*. He had done it for the last twenty years or so, and he could do it again. London wasn't everything. Even as he said it, he felt the city tugging at his heart strings like a woman. He thought of all the things while abroad he had missed; all the aspects of London to which on his return from exile he had been looking forward with such eagerness to enjoying: the grey dawn of a winter morning on the Thames, the crowds, shuffling and clip-clopping through dank fog over the bridges; or Carlton House Terrace in the bright gold of autumn, and the view of Westminster, and Pugin and Barry's deuced nonsense giving the thing a spindly Gothic air of fantasy. He thought of the squares of Bloomsbury, each different, each so stately, and yet so unpretentious. It didn't give itself airs, this place, in the way that Paris did. He thought of cobbled streets beyond Clerkenwell, of criers grinding knives or selling lavender; of shirt-sleeved boys pushing barrows of fruit; of glimpses from the hill there of the City, and the dome of St Paul's. He thought of the whole city and all it had meant to him. He thought of how he had missed it, lying awake in hotel bedrooms in some other European capital, missed it yet despised it, like a lofty younger son who could not forbear from teasing his mother. He thought of his own recent Mayfair perambulations, the pleasure it gave him, brushed and made ready by his valet, to set out from Half Moon Street, and to walk down Piccadilly. He was aware that he cut a figure. He did so today, with his tall grey hat perched at a rakish angle on his silver-haired sunburnt head, his immaculate morning coat, his trowsers, his spats, his gleaming shoes. It was impossible to resist this masterpiece as it passed by. Not bad, old Chatterway, he thought to himself, not bad, *what?*

Meanwhile, in another part of London, less salubrious than Mayfair and thicker with the turmoil of humans, Lionel was walking to visit his friend Gutch. He had slept the night at his grandfather's house and, by an afternoon train, he was to arrive at Dover. But now, having risen early, he had walked the short distance from Brunswick Square to the ritualist church in Baldwin's Gardens where Gutch was spending the long vacation.

Though Lionel had very often visited his grandfather in Bloomsbury, he had never in his life been any further east, so that the crossing of the Gray's Inn Road constituted something of a spiritual adventure in itself. On the one side of this thoroughfare, running in an almost straight line from High Holborn to King's Cross, were the leafy, spacious courts of Gray's Inn, rather grander in its trees and quadrangles than one of the Oxford colleges, for it bore its beauty less coyly and with more metropolitan self-confidence. Often, as a child, Lionel had walked there with his grandfather, who had remembered walking there with Charles Dickens, during the 'thirties. They had admired together the fine old Tudor hall where some of Shakespeare's comedies had received their first performance, the splendid seventeenth-century chapel – its fittings more or less unchanged since the days of Archbishop Laud, himself a member of the Inn. In the gatehouse, Severus Egg had pointed out to Lionel the spot where old Jacob Tonson, the bookseller, had his shop; it was he who had published *Paradise Lost* for the first time, and many of the works of Dryden, though some fool had lately covered over the old brickwork with thick coatings of cement.

The place, in other words, seemed (like the whole of London when one was in Grandfather Egg's company) redolent of a multi-layered and largely benign and quietly vanishing civilisation. Beyond, only a few yards on the opposite side of Gray's Inn Road, the old man had been content to suggest, was where the barbarian proletariats lived and moved and had their being. Eggy's grasp of what it was like there seemed, and probably was, as hazy as that of the grandson. He mentioned airily that Fulke Greville, the biographer of Sir Philip Sidney, had a 'little *palazzo*' there, as though this Elizabethan gentleman had only lately quit the London scene, and as though a gentleman nowadays would not concern himself with the sordid three hundred years which had elapsed since his departure.

But it was into this place of dread, this land beyond the road, that Gutch had chosen to penetrate. Lionel's heart was beating with fear as he wove his way between the heavy traffic of Gray's Inn Road, the horse-drawn omnibuses, the cabs, victorias and broughams, which made the air hazy with pinkish dust as they rattled to and fro on their way.

What greeted his gaze as he turned into Baldwin's Gardens was a species of habitation which he had never seen at close quarters before and in which it was scarcely believable that human beings were expected to exist. These habitations were of wood. It would hardly be a fair use of language to say that they were built of wood, or constructed of wood or made of wood, for it looked more as if they had been thrown together out of those pieces of wood too rotten or too lice-infested to be of much use in any other capacity. Indeed, they might very well, for all Lionel could discover, have been the original woodpile of the proverb and he might have been about to meet the famous negroid inhabitant of that concatenation. The idea of the woodpile itself was frightening enough. The thought that the nigger might at any moment spring out at him from these rotting boards and beams, added further terror to his penetration of the dusty little street.

If the nigger was at home today, he was keeping himself well-concealed in the woodpile. There were however plenty of other human beings there, whether white or black it was not easy to determine since none of them seemed, from their appearance, much addicted to the purchase of soap. There was something particularly quaint about the fact that this sordid little street was called Baldwin's Gardens. It was hoped that Baldwin, whoever he might have been, did not hope for any cabbages, or for that matter, cabbage roses that summer from his gardens, for the flower-beds there had been somewhat neglected. It was very much to be hoped that he was not relying on a good crop of pears or apples from the orchard. Even if he had been merely setting his heart on a stroll across the lawn, old Baldwin was going to be sorely disappointed. For there was not a blade of grass left in Baldwin's Gardens, not a roof, not a leaf, not a twig, not a petal. It was the most barren garden you could hope to see in your life. In fact, you could say without unfairness to his character, that unless it had been his intention to grow stunted, squint-eyed little barefoot urchins, and slatternly women of twenty-five who looked fifty as they hung out of upper-storey casements, and a dwarf, no taller than three feet, standing in the gutter and shouting furious abuse at no one in particular, and a drunkard vomiting into the stret, and another urinating out of a window, and old people in doorways with looks of infinite sadness and decreptitude in their worn, tired old faces; yes, it could be said that if Baldwin had not meant to grow these in his Gardens, then he was not very much of a gardener.

The squalid tenements were so close together – with gables jutting so precariously that people on either side of the street could almost have reached out and taken each other by the hand – or, as seemed more likely in this not wholly amiable environment, shaken each other by the throats. A pathetic sort of bunting hung across the street, obscuring the sky, strings from which very ill-washed garments depended – shirts, stockings and vesture of a more indeterminate character, seeming at first glance as if they might be human beings who had given up hope and hanged themselves, and provoking, on second glance, the thought that it was probably these washing lines them-selves which held the street together. It you had cut them with a pair of scissors all the houses would very probably have collapsed.

Lionel's nameless fears were fully justified as he entered this hellish place, for the first welcome afforded by one of the more public-spirited of the inhabitants was a raw potato, sprouting somewhat and going slightly rotten, which was directed with some speed and precision at his hat, sending this item flying from his head into the gutters where other vegetables and their peelings provided, as they mingled with the ordure of dogs, horses and humans a feast for the flies in the warm morning sunshine. Whoops of merriment from either side indicated to Lionel, as he stooped towards the gutter to retrieve his hat, that the accuracy with which he had been divested of it was a matter of no little pride to the potato-hurler and his or her friends. The sense that a lot of other people were laughing at him inspired unpleasant memories of school. But this was much more frightening. At school, the worst that could happen to you was that you might be given a drubbing. Here you might be murdered. Indeed, the thought had no sooner occurred to him, as he stooped forward to pick up his hat, than a sharp kick in the small of the back sent him sprawling forward on his face, grazing the palms of his hands and giving excruciating pain to his nose. The caterwauling of the amused spectators grew louder as Lionel felt someone kneeling on his back and saying, in the coarsest tones, 'Let's be 'avin' yer.'

Expert hands ruffled through the trowser pockets and removed a handful of coins, and they were just feeling their way round to the front, when the same voice said, 'Let's scarper'. Lionel was suddenly abandoned. He did not care to turn or look up for fear his assailants might pull a knife on him. But he then heard a gentleman's voice, perfectly well-educated with a little in it of the military, saying sharply, 'This is disgraceful! And you needn't think I can't see you, young Martin, just because you've gone into your mother's house, hiding behind her apron strings.'

'Same as I say, Farver,' said another voice which (if Lionel's ears did not receive him had, only a moment or two before, been baying for his blood), 'it's a disgrace the way that Martin Chivvers behaves, a bloomin' disgrace if you'd pardon my language, Farver.'

Lionel turned and saw a clergyman in a cassock looking down at him. He was strikingly handsome and manly, even though his dark hair and olive skin gave him a slightly foreign air, which was increased by the cut of his soutane, and by the biretta which was perched on the back of his head.

'Are you all right?' he asked Lionel.

'I think so.'

'Which is more than can be said for your hat I'm afraid. I apologise for the raucous behaviour of my friends here. They are not as rough as you would expect.'

'I was making my way to the church,' said Lionel. He was feeling shattered and frightened. He was even afraid that he might burst into tears, and he wanted to cling to this priest for protection.

'Well, there it is,' said the clergyman. 'Always open.'

The church of St Alban towered above these horrible wooden tenements in its new-built brick, and spawned various other large buildings which were attached to it: a parish hall, a school chapel and, on the other side of the street, a charming little Gothic school.

'A friend of mine is living in the clergy-house – Everard Gutch.'

'Gutch. You must be Nettleship,' said the priest with a bit of a smile. 'We heard you had gone off to stay with Father Cuthbert.'

'Well, I left.'

'They all do.' Lionel found it hard to define the smile. It established at once that he thought Father Cuthbert a little fantastical. But there was nothing in it of satire or malice.

'Do you not approve of Father Cuthbert, then?' he asked.

'Good heavens, man, it isn't our calling as Christians to approve or disapprove. I am forgetting my manners by the way. I happen to know your name because your fame travelled before you. My name is Stanton.'

So this was the legendary Father Stanton, the curate who had stood by Mackonochie throughout all the riots and prosecutions, and the throwing of stones, and the invasion by mobs.

'You've been knocked up. You must come back to the clergy-house and recover yourself.'

At these words of kindness, Lionel did actually crack, and found himself snivelling like a junior. The priest merely said, 'Come on, old man, you're not as hurt as all that. We'll cut through the church. It's the quickest way.'

They approached the porch which bore the legend FREE FOR EVER TO CHRIST'S POOR THIS CHURCH IS BUILT AND ENDOWED IN THANKFUL ACKNOWLEDGEMENT OF HIS MERCIES BY A HUMBLE STEWARD OF GOD'S BOUNTY.

Coming inside from the sunlight, one had the immediate impression of intense blackness. Even after a minute or two of blinking, the interior presented a mysterious darkness, lit here and there by distant twinklings, of hanging lamps and candles. Far at the east end, a golden reredos glowed numinously, its gilded figures as the eye followed them up and up being gradually lost in shadows, in the high rafters of the roof. It was, indeed, one of the tallest churches Lionel had ever seen as well as being undoubtedly one of the 'highest', in the ecclesiastical sense of the word. Here, as in Father Cuthbert's monastery, there was a sense of a Presence which you could not define. But the Presence here seemed all the more mysterious, for it was not hidden high among the ethereal and mist-enfolding mountains, but in the very midst of squalor, poverty, crowds and pain.

'Let's kneel for two minutes,' said the Priest, 'and thank Our Blessed Lord for all the benefits he has bestowed upon us by giving us the birth and bearing of gentlemen; and let us ask him to forgive the poor boy who attacked you just now, and bring us all and each to his everlasting kingdom.'

He said these words quite naturally, without any of Father Cuthbert's histrionic tones. There was no waving about of arms, no swirling of the eyes. He spoke simply and with conviction and, having said the words, sunk quietly to his knees.

Lionel, pressing his grazed palms together, was glad of the chance to collect himself. He could not focus his mind on prayer, but he felt great strength from the silent praying figure beside him. After a very short while, Father Stanton arose and led him through the other side of the church, and out into a little courtyard where there was an almost life-size Calvary, with the figure of Christ on the cross.

'I have a little iodine and some lint if you need them for those cuts on your face,' said the priest as he put the key in his front door. 'There's a bathroom upstairs and at the far end of the corridor on your left. Go and wash yourself and assess the damage.'

When he had brushed the worst of the dust and the filth off his clothes, and washed his face, Lionel could see that the cuts were not very serious, and he came downstairs, where Gutch was waiting for him.

'Father Stanton's sorry,' he said, 'he's been called out again to a woman whose baby's dying. I must go soon myself, because Father Walker – that's another of the curates – is taking me on his rounds. We're going round the tenements at the other side of Brooke's Market and taking some blankets to an old woman there who feels cold in spite of all this heat. What did you think of Stanton, by the way?'

'Very impressive.'

'I thought he might have reminded you of my cousin Freddie. They are distantly related and everyone sees the resemblance.'

'I haven't met your cousin Freddie.'

Gutch did not seem to think this was a very adequate answer. He grinned as though Lionel had said something foolish and went on to say, 'What did you think of the church. D'you like the big six?'

'Six?'

'The six candlesticks on the high altar. The bishop's issued so many court orders to have them removed that I think he is bored with trying. It's got quite a "feel", hasn't it, this place. My father thinks it's idolatrous to put a modern statue *in*, but vandalous to tear a medieval statue *out*. What do you think? We couldn't very well have medieval statues here, the church has only been built for about twenty years.'

'It's – it's the poverty,' said Lionel incoherently, 'and the dirt.'

'Stanton said I'm to give you a cup of tea if you want one. Then we can perhaps have a walk back through the parish. They threw a potato at you or something? I won't go out unaccompanied yet. But they are all right if you go in twos and they won't throw things if you wear a cassock. Funny that, isn't it? But they all respect the clergy here.'

'Perhaps the clergy have earned their respect.'

Over tea, and the subsequent walk, Lionel discovered that in spite of his superficial immutabilities, young Gutch had changed. There was still the same unstoppable flow of unconnected observations about church furnishings, and there was still the unshaken expectation that one should have devoted all one's spare time and energy to a study of the Gutch genealogical tree to its last twigs and interstices. But beneath this superficial exterior, Lionel was aware of something else.

'I shall try to become a curate in this place if they'll have me,' said Gutch as their nostrils reminded them that they were outside again and among the parishioners. 'Or somewhere like it.'

One did not want to ask him why. It was so obvious that he simply wanted to clothe the naked, feed the hungry, visit the sick and the old, the prisoners and the dying. Moreover, it was obvious that he was not doing these things purely out of a sense of duty (though that must have come into it) but because he enjoyed it. Not it, but them. He enjoyed the people with whom he worked. He was full of stories, and this time they were not all about his relations. They were about an old woman who believed that it was unsafe to do knitting during a thunderstorm for fear that lightning would be 'conduced darn me needles'. Of an old man, bedridden and incontinent, who had fought at Waterloo and who complained if the clergy visited him too often. 'Moi naiboursull say uz oi'm doi-in, vich oi baint.' Of children in the Sunday school which Gutch helped to run; how he had asked them the name of the mother of Christ and received the answer 'Victoria' ('my father would have liked that. . . .')

It was all so obvious that Gutch had immersed himself, like the curates at St Alban's, in the lives of the poor.

'D'you think I could come here and work too?' asked Lionel.

'Well the vicar's away, but you could ask Stanton, I suppose. It would be very amusing for me to have a companion. I'd enjoy it and I think you would.'

'You see I've been talking to the Jenker.'

'Hmmph!' Gutch made a strange noise with his mouth which was something between a high-pitched snort and a suppressed guffaw. After this outburst, it was less easy to say what Lionel had wanted to say: how he felt rather a clot, agonisingly wondering about his visions and lack of visions, as though these had anything at all to do with the Christian religion. He was trying to articulate a thought, but it would not quite form itself in his mind. It was something to do with the *practice* of religion, rather than its theory. What is the point, he had begun to ask himself, in saying that we believe Christianity to be true if we do not intend to do anything about it? What conceivable virtue could there be in contorting one's mind to believe in the Resurrection if one has no intention of living chastely, or of accepting violence without thought of revenge, or of taking no thought for the morrow, or of refusing to hoard up wealth in this life, or of living simply and helping those in need? Christ had not promised, and nor had His Virgin Mother, that He would be found in visions, or in mountain tops, in 'mystical experiences' or in exalted practices of the 'spiritual life'. He had promised to be with his people in the breaking of bread. And He had said that in so far as we had not recognised Him in 'the least of these my brethren' we had not recognised him at all. That was all. And here was a church, and a group of men entirely dedicated to the worship of Christ in the breaking of bread, and the service of Christ in the least of his brethren. It all made Lionel feel a little choked and for the second time in a short space, he feared he might blub.

'I shouldn't come at once,' Gutch advised. 'You've got to go to Dover and see your people off to the continent, haven't you? And then I should think your grandfather would be a trifle lonely if you didn't spent the summer with him. His house is only ten minutes' walk away – you can always drop in again, if you don't mind being pelted with rotten vegetables.'

And it was, so incredibly, only ten minutes' walk away, or at most, quarter of an hour. As he made the journey in reverse, Lionel could hardly believe the contrast between the violence, the odours, the crowds, the noise, the absolute repulsiveness of the world he now left behind him, and the symmetry, the elegance, the cleanliness and the quiet of the gated streets he crossed to get to Coram Fields, until he arrived at his grandfather's door.

'My dear,' said the old gentleman. 'What have you done to your face? You look as though you've been scratched by a cat – or a tart more likely.' And with a low laugh he sent Bacon to his dressing table to get young Mister Lionel some powder. 'We can't lunch in the club with you bleeding like a young Prussian duellist. And when Darling Bacon has patched you up we really *must* go.'

Mr Lupton, their lunching companion, had hardly dressed himself by the time Lionel was having his cheeks powdered by the attentive, long chocolatey fingers of Mr Bacon. Lupton's morning uprisings became, with the wearisome unfolding of time, more and more of an effort. Sometimes, in the very blackest moment of the night, he would wake for the space of some half an hour and ask himself, Why? Why am I living like this? What is it all for? Where is it all going? The mind at that hour, as it clears itself from the immediate and merciful numbing of alcohol, has a cruel sharpness. It sees life with more despondent clarity than daylight hours, and the various distractions of noise and company would allow. At such moments, Lupton saw himself coldly and ruthlessly. You are, he would tell himself, a tenth-rate artist. You are fast becoming a slave to drink, which you consume partly to conceal from yourself your slavery to erotic pleasures. But you can not forget it. Drink won't undo the deed. You did it. If you heard of another doing it, you would despise them for it. But it was not another. It was *you* who had that ignominious union with the model by the potted palm; it was *you* who found that wretched girl on your homeward journey from last night's debauch and who, after the exchange of a few shillings, possessed her in an alley; it was you, you, you. And so, at that hour, the whole series of sordid coitions passed through his brain and reminded him of what he was and what he had done. He seemed on such occasions not so much bestial as semi-existent. It was as though he merely inhabited the rampant body which needed to be satisfied in this way; the more he gave his body up to its erotomania, the less, in any discernible sense, he existed to himself. Memory of these base encounters only stretched back a month or twain. For long periods before that, he knew that there had been girls, many of them, but he was not always capable of summoning back their faces or voices.

And how long could any of this continue? The more enslaved he became to it all, the less possible it seemed that he could defile such a beauty as Maudie by *marrying* her! And yet it was, in part, the little witch's fault that his mad pursuit of gratification had, of late, got so wildly beyond control. Herein lay the feature of his own behaviour that he most despised. He paid these creatures in alleys, these girls in his studios, because with all his beauty, he was unconfident that any woman whom *he* adored might want him in the same, free animal manner that he wanted them. No satisfaction could really be derived from Maudie accepting him, in the grudging way he *knew* most modern wives accepted their husbands. He did not want to be 'accepted'. He wanted to be hungered for, worshipped, devoured. He wanted Maudie to be screaming with desire for him, to be clawing at his legs, and tossing her tangled tresses about his loins in agonies of despair. The fact that in life she merely wanted to snigger at him was clearer than ever in those dark night-watches.

There was little left of self-esteem at that hour, little that he would want his old surgeon father to know about. And he added to these feelings of self-reproach a terrible questioning. Was there a single person in London at that moment who lay awake and called him to mind? He was not now demanding that he be loved, as he so passionately and impossibly loved Maudie Nettleship. He was lowering his sights. He wanted merely to know whether anyone was thinking about him. He knew that they weren't, unless one counted Maudie's mother; and this attention, paradoxically, was so hateful to him now that he had discerned its full nature, that he blotted it out and would not think of it. On the one hand, he hungered for worship. But he loathed and despised the worship of Charlotte because it was completely unwanted. He would have preferred, it seemed when he was merciless enough with himself to think about it, the worship of anyone to this. But apart from her, who? Was there anyone who, after a fortnight or three weeks, had said to themselves, 'I haven't seen much of Lupton lately?' Was there anyone in the world who would very much grieve (the little Nettleship woman excepted) if he were to be discovered mangled beneath a train? And, as the despondent negative sounded in his brain, he would sink into the profoundest sleep of the night, which became deeper and deeper – or so it felt – as the morning approached. By the time nine or ten o'clock had been reached, he was almost so deeply asleep as to be comatose. And it was strange that when waking, the night-despair was left behind on the pillows and he assumed the carapace as readily as he clambered into his unclean breeks. Things and questions once more became manageable. He asked himself not, What is the purpose of my life? but, Will I, this week, finish painting the Lord Lieutenant of the county of Kent? He asked not, Am I gradually destroying my soul by my slavery to carnality? but, Do I have this headache because I am ill or because I consumed half a decanter of whisky six or seven hours ago? His waking, normal self was as incurious as it had to be. He did not ask himself, passing the first water of the day – or rather, he only half-realised that he *might* ask himself – whether he suffered from a stinging sensation which was unusual or whether it did not always feel a little like that?

By the time half an hour had passed, in the Charlotte Street bedchamber which we now know rather well, his figure was ready for the day. His head still ached a little, but the consumption of some coffee in a nearby chop-house would soon banish that inconvenience. The collar he had selected was a clean one, the silken cravat only greasy if illuminated by a more searching light than ever penetrated his club. The coat and trowsers and spats and shoes had all been, in his phrase, licked into shape, and the wide-brimmed hat, a slightly French affair, was the better for being faintly spotted. Oh yes, he would finish that portrait by the end of the week. And then, surely, he owed it to Art that he should attempt another scene from the Odyssey. For in daylight hours, he still aspired: he had not written himself off as a failure; he thought that if he daubed and daubed with sufficient persistence the masterpiece would one day appear, as if by magic, on the canvas.

So, the horizontal figure in a nightshirt, suffering from a hideous sense of his own nothingness, worthlessness, and a terrifying vision of life's emptiness became once more the comparatively sunny vertical bearded figure known and liked in his own circle as Timothy Lupton, and this collection of churning limbs and organs, the circulating blood, the gurgling stomach, the affronted liver, the bladder gradually refilling with urine, encased in its faintly hairy skin, encased in its bones, nails, hair, teeth, and covered up once more with the clothes in which it felt comfortable, transported itself with the familiar human movements which were so habitual that the brain merely sent out messages to the feet without thinking, telling them to walk downstairs, along the pavement, and on its way. The pause to buy a newspaper at the vendor on the corner, the entry to the chop-house, the decision, formed in the brain's spongy tissue, to stay the stomach, late as it was, with some thick slices of the dead body of a pig hotly fried in some of the pig's fat, to mash these small lengths of flesh with the slightly odorous molars, and to convey them with a gulp of coffee to the moist red area where the acids of the stomach were so anxious to consume something that they were starting to consume themselves: all this happened without thought. Nor did Mr Timothy Lupton think, as he finished breakfast and made his way to the club, by foot, and passed hundreds of these human beings, these strange collections of mobile offal held together by skin and bones, how odd it was, how rum, that they were invested with thoughts, feelings and desires which were almost entirely dominated by the state of their physique, and that, for instance, those with toothache or acute arthritis would be scarcely capable of enjoying the fact that the sun was shining, whereas for those who had, the previous evening, eaten a wholesome dinner and slept well, had probably woken to think that London was the most beautiful city in the world. Lupton merely observed that the world seemed a better place with some coffee and bacon inside him.

When about an hour later he reached the club, he found that there were four of them at Egg's table: old Chatterway, himself, Egg and the old boy's grandson, who bore enough resemblance to Maudie to make it painful to be in his company. His features alluded to hers in an almost insulting fashion, since he was not in the least beautiful. And yet the dark eyes, and the flare of the nostrils and the shape of the chin were not merely similar, but almost identical – even though the rest of the face was different. Chatterway was, as ever (or so it seemed), in mid-sentence and saying something which would have only been completely comprehensible to those present if they had been in close touch with all his thought-processes over the previous week, with the contents of his engagement book and, if one had open copies to hand, of Debrett and Crockford's clerical directory, not to mention the Army List and *Who's Who*.

'. . . whose erstwhile mistress is now none other than the young duke's in every sense *belle* – (though not always so chaste as her uncle, the free-from-all-vice-admiral) *soeur*. I remember her so well wetting her drawers, no less than twenty years since, when a bridesmaid at the wedding of Lord and Lady Bayswater, a union unblessed by progeny for seven lean but hardly (on his lordship's part) restrained years, a fact attributed by some to his inability to distinguish one orifice from another and by others to her ladyship's notorious fondness for very hot baths, a taste which she has in common, Padre Lionello, with your father's vulcanalogical rival Herr Schülken. . . .'

'Marvo, you crashing bore, stop gassing your head off and tell me what you are eating,' said Egg, whose pencil was poised on his pad.

Lionel had never lunched before at a gentlemen's club, and was a little surprised to discover that one ordered meals not by giving directions to a waiter by word of mouth, but by writing the names of dishes on a small piece of paper. His grandfather wrote slowly and beautifully, and they decided for simplicity's sake that would all eat the same modest meal of turtle soup, some poached bream, saddle of mutton with caper sauce, new potatoes and broad beans, a slice of Guards cake, and, to conclude, Scotch woodcock, the whole accompanied by a Chateau Lafite '51.

Although he spoke for most of the time in riddles, Mr Chatterway had something of the effect of champagne on his company. They were not necessarily any more witty or more talkative because of his presence. But they *felt* that they were. Lionel lost his shyness and felt able to catch up with a notion of conversation which was the precise opposite of his normal practice. He had come to assume that one should use the gift of speech to say things which were important, and which came up from the depths of his soul, and which were hard to put into words. Chatterway's rule – his practice anyway – seemed to be only to put things into words which could not, properly speaking, be felt at all. The paradox was that, by keeping conversation purely on the level of surfaces, he enabled everyone to speak of what in other settings they would have described as being on their minds.

Those minds, those consciousnesses which floated independently around the luncheon table in the long beautiful coffee room, occasionally overlapping in sympathy, but which were more often possessed in their own inner secrecy, all felt something like repose, not stimulation, as the words shot to and fro.

'Is that the Lady Bayswater,' asked Lupton, resuming the thread of Chatterway's gossip, 'who was painted by Millais in last year's Summer Exhibition at the Academy?'

His attitude to Chatterway had changed since it had become apparent that the older man had 'a way' with Maudie Nettleship, and since Lupton had taken to spying on their walks together in Regents Park. But it was not a matter of straight jealousy, and it could not prevent him from seeing Chatterway; partly because seeing Chatterway, if one were out and about, was an inevitability, also because part of his very fascination was that he was likely, at any moment, to come out with some Nettleship-disclosure.

'. . . and he made her look, as he makes all women look, like his charming lady wife whom I still think of as poor little Mrs Ruskin. . . .'

'Ah, poor darling mad Ruskin,' piped in Eggy.

'Lord Bayswater's up at the House,' Lionel heard himself saying.

'If up,' glossed Chatterway, 'is the right term for a man who has not only been rusticated twice for riding to hounds on the very day of his Divvers, but could also be said, given his fondness (which he shares with you, Lupton) for the tangles and tresses of the young ladies, to have been running with the hair.'

'Our age loves hair more than any in history,' said Egg. 'Or I should say your age: for I am out of it now.'

'Nonsense,' said Lupton.

'What do you say, *monsignore* Lionel? Does your dear, and herself well-tressed, mother love hair?'

'I have never thought of it.'

'Herr Professor not well-endowed, what?'

'Bald,' agreed Lionel.

'What we'd call it, if it weren't for the presence of your grandsire, an egg-head, what? what?'

'Very funny, Marvo dear,' said the old man whose eyes creased with the weariness of a man whose name had been the subject of jokes for nearly three quarters of a century. 'In the days of the wig, of course . . . I can remember when all the bishops wore wigs. Howley wore a wig at the coronation. Very restful, I should say. Did I ever tell you the story, which I heard from the lips of Mrs Piozzi herself, about the Great

Cham coming to the door of his house in Gough Square without a wig?'

'Many times,' they all chorused to much merriment.

'And now,' added the grandfather unperturbed, 'they are all off to the continent of Europe. Darling Netty, and beloved Charlotte and a thousand times darling Maudie.'

'She'll miss you especially, sir,' said Lionel to Mr Chatterway.

'How so?'

As soon as he had made this observation, which came flying out of his lips for no particular reason, Lionel regretted it. But he heard himself, having had another sip of the admirable claret, charging on into the conversational undergrowth.

'She has a particular fancy for you, sir.'

'My little secret out, what?'

'Marvo, you old fraud, nothing you ever do is a secret from anyone. Now please put that fork down and let the poor waiter bring forth the mutton.'

'I still don't know why you are not going with your family to the continent,' said Lupton.

'Because,' said Lionel, 'the main thing is Maudie's cough, and they planned the whole expedition thinking I should be in Wales.'

'Besides,' said Egg, 'he is staying to keep me company, aren't you, dear boy?'

'Yes, grandpapa. But Mr Chatterway, you really are a *particular* favourite of Maudie's. She writes about you endlessly. And I've noticed that she has started to adopt your phrases.'

'Lord save us!' exclaimed old Egg.

'That's the reverend Lionel's department,' growled Chatterway.

'I shouldn't be in the least surprised if this sudden departure of yours from London doesn't have something to do with my little family's vacation,' added Egg.

'Sudden departure?'

'You know quite well. Bacon was told by your valet that you are leaving us for a couple of months. He seemed to think you were going to Paris. But he'll find out soon enough. It is only by living a life of *complete* poverty and having nothing to do with servants that one could hope to keep one's life a secret in London!'

'Can this be *true?*' Lupton's face was tense, almost thunderous. 'But they are going at the end of the week.'

'Set off a nasty train of associations there, Lionel old boy,' said Chatterway. 'Never ask about a man's movements, what. I say, Eggy, this mutton's uncommon good. Not, as I once heard an American say, "half bad". Rum phrase, very. Speaking of whom, by which I mean our rebellious colonists on the opposite side of an ocean which seems wholly devoid of any of the legendary qualities of Atlantis, has anyone ever come across this bearded scribbler called James?'

'A friend, surely, of darling Tourgenieff's?' asked Eggy.

'Who spoke enthusiastically of him to me,' added Chatterway, 'when last met at Baden Baden. But I mean, the little fella's at every deuced house you go to. Thought he was the butler when I dined at the Dilkes' – of which *more* later – and then, when I went out to the Countess of Dufferin, blow me: there he was again. Lodges not far from me, as well. Bolton Street. We shared a cab one evening coming out from the Rothschilds' in the rain.'

Lionel had noticed that this unwonted excursion into narrative was Mr Chatterway's manner of deflecting attention from his continental journeyings. He could not, surely, be intending to *accompany* the Nettleships on their pilgrimage to the Swiss mountains? The professor would not stand for it. Unless, unless. . . . It was unthinkable. Completely unthinkable. But Lionel thought it. He gazed from the face of Chatterway to that of his grandfather, and back again. Hard, worldly faces, but full of charm, and still bright with a certain brittle beauty.

'I know I'm too old for him,' said his grandfather, still harping on the new American writer, 'I'm too old for almost *everything*. I found myself re-reading darling Walter Scott the other day. Now there is a proper writer. He is so funny, and so simple, and so *clear*. Is it my ears and eyes growing old, or is all art nowadays diffuse and somehow *smudged?*'

'You're thinking of the French painters,' said Lupton.

'This other Yankee-doodle, Whistler, can be smudgy too,' added Chatterway.

'Oh they *all* smudge, the good ones,' said Egg.

'Alma-Tad?'

'The *good* ones. I can tell their merit, but I can't *discern* it. The music doesn't seem to have any melody – just swirling. And the pictures don't have all that glorious clarity that one got in a canvas by Etty or a watercolour by Cotman – that sense of the world just being *there* and our accepting it clearly and joyfully. Why do they have to smudge it? I can see that they *do* have to. and then, you see, the novelists. . . .'

'Nothing smudgy about Trollope, what?'

'I was thinking of that Welsh monster poor darling Peacock's daughter married.'

'Meredith?'

'Or Merédith. One or the other. It's clever, I can see that. But it's all

so opaque. Like these last poems of Browning's. Can't make them out.
Everything getting misty and *difficult* of a sudden. Where's the virtue
in difficulty? They say that Prussian you're so fond of, Marvo. . . .'

'Brahms.'

'Or whatever he's called. But I mean, it isn't Mozart is it? However
good it is, there's no clarity there. Can't even *hear* the tunes in it
myself. I'm too old. The whole world seems swathed in *mist*.'

'The effect of your excellent claret.'

'No, no. These younger ones, Marvo. They know what I mean.'

'I think I do,' said Lupton. 'Is it a sense that we mustn't do what our
fathers and forefathers did?'

'You'd paint like Sir Joshua if you *could*,' Egg insisted.

The wine was drunk, the food was gobbled down. The physical
beings that absorbed them, the varying pulsating bits of live meat
beneath the gentlemen's waistcoats, their stomachs and their livers,
sent back contented messages to their brains. In those brains, three of
them flashed intermittent and disturbed visions of Maudie Nettleship,
while her grandfather prosed on about the old days and asked them if
they had heard his conversation with Northcote recalling the practices
of Sir Joshua Reynolds.

When the meal was ended, the vision of Maudie was stronger in the
minds of the three others, not weaker. Lionel could hardly believe that
his grandfather could remain so calm, when Mr Chatterway had made
it clear that he intended, in effect, to *kidnap* the girl! Why were they all
sitting there like friends, when they knew that, as soon as the party
reached Paris, Maudie and Mr Chatterway would mysteriously meet
up and run away into the crowds?

The intensity of the brother's feelings did not specifically communicate itself to the others. But perhaps the very fact that he was
concentrating so vividly on Maudie made the others have their own
thoughts about her. Timothy Lupton added to his usual feelings of
abandonment and lust a revival of his hopeless spiritual adoration. He
saw her in his mind's eye as a naked nymph; and in his ears, while her
grandfather carefully, and claret-inebriated, enunciated the words
Mrs Piozzi so as not to slur the sibilants, Lupton heard the voice of
Maudie. He heard the way she made even the word *hello* into a little
tune: first, a downward note, a high-pitch descending to contralto and
sounding a little like *hurl*. And then an abrupt little *o* which sounded
faintly impatient with life. She was laughing in this daydream. Laughing at him. And yet, in her rather flagrant nakedness, she was
stretching out to him, all teeth, hair, breasts, and waist calling to him
and promising that if he could only reach her, he would achieve the
absolute abandonment which seemed to be suggested by the very

prompting of lust. For *it* began so crudely and so simply. *It* seemed so
easy to satisfy. How was it, that the longing still remained, after the
sordid mechanism of the thing had been so easily repeated? The girl in
the studio, the girl in the alley, the dozen other girls with whom he
could achieve the satisfaction which the body *appeared* to be demanding, truly satisfied nothing. If anything, appetitite in that area was
increased by what it fed on. And the more appetite increased and was
fed, the less the *longing* was diminished. The longing had in it all the
ingredients of lust. But it was a much bigger thing. Perhaps it was an
illusion that Maudie could satisfy this longing, as much an illusion as
the thought that he could assuage it by taking (as he put it on those
baser occasions) comfort where it was offered. If so, it was an illusion
which could only be tested by chasing the will o' the wisp to its furthest
limits.

To hear Chatterway talk of her, inflamed Lupton's bosom with such
sudden waves of jealousy and desire that he felt his very heart might
crack with the grief of it. Maudie's pathetic mother had said it, those
months before, at their first embarrassing and by him wholly
unwanted tryst: *This could but have happened once.* With an irrational certainty, he felt that if he could not capture Maudie before she
set sail for France, he would never capture her. And yet, how could he
possibly do so? For she was in an hotel surrounded by her family, her
nursemaid, her brother, . . . this wretched cough seemed, to his
inflamed imagination, less an affliction from which she suffered than
another obstacle put in *his* way. He had a sense that nothing else
would matter in his life, except this. This girl. These bright eyes. This
abundant mane of dark hair. These pale shoulders. If he could have
them, hold them in his arms, press to his own lips her pouting cherry-
mouth and feel her fluttering little white breast against his own shaggy
bosom, then nothing else in life need be accounted as a failure. And
yet, he knew, as the phantom-Maudie spoke to him again in his inner
daydream with her almost insolent *Hurl . . . lo!* that she never would
be his and that he was condemning himself to despair.

Chatterway who, like Lupton, also thought on Maudie as her
grandfather spoke, fashioned his thoughts along lines which suggested
that he was still in *control,* though in control of *what* it would have
been no easy task to specify. He would take this action, he would take
that. He would cut *loose.* He would disengage his valet in Half Moon
Street. But then, what if he were to return? Against the intoxicating
excitement provided by the knowledge that he could at last perform
the ultimate outrage, that he had it in his power, there lurked the
safeguards of loneliness and snobbery. Supposing he did it, and
snatched the little creature away from the bosom of her minerologi-

cally minded, not to say stone-hearted and rock-brained professorial papa? He had once read, in the memoirs of M. de Montgolfier, the inventor of the hot-air ballon (Chatterway's patron saint, a sharp-tongued *marquise*, once remarked, in English, in some *salon* of the Faubourg St Honoré) of the delights of suddenly realising that there was nothing between oneself and the ground. The pure *bonheur* of floating up into the clouds had its reflexion in the social scene. He had perhaps been trying it ever since he grew to manhood. But if the balloon never came down to earth again? If he was left floating forever with little Maudie turning into a scolding middle-aged Maudie, up there in the basket, what? Any fun? No more invitations to dinner after that. He would be condemned forever to shamble about in European cafés, and to stare across drizzly, pigeon-infested squares with terrible loneliness in his eyes. For the first time in his life, he knew that he had found love: the sort the poets write about, the 'real thing'. And it had come at a stage when love was not the thing he most wanted in the world. Love, one of the most impeccably medieval of wallpaper-designers had remarked in a ditty which caught Chatterway's fancy, *Love is enough*. He felt now like rising from the table and penning a short epistle to W. Morris Esq., to the brief effect that it wasn't. And the fact that it wasn't enough was why the world went buzzing on the course that had so amused and delighted Chatterway for the last forty years: the jabbering gossip, the surreptitious erotic liaisons, the thrust of professional ambition, the vainglorious furnishings and gilded interiors (so little to Mr Morris's taste), the carriages and carriage drives, the advantageous marriages, the witty books, the adventurous travels, the gallant imperial expansion into Africa, the continued efficient subjugation of India, the dominance of the seas, the conquest of knowledge, the establishment of colleges for women at Oxford and Cambridge, the perpetual founding of clubs to which gentlemen in London seemed addicted, the belching of factories, the rumbling of railways, the decline of the poor into wretchedness, the high-minded desire of the good to rescue them. . . . No, no, Mr Morris. So long as these activities possessed and interested gentlemen and ladies, we could be sure that, in England at least, love was very far from being enough.

They shuffled now, the four of them, across the thick turkey carpet of the coffee room and on to the landing. A rubber was proposed in one of the drawing rooms. Old Egg posed a notional question – he had asked it at that spot of the landing for decades. 'Now, where shall we sit ourselves?'

There was a little table by the window, with four chairs at it, where Mr Severus Egg had sat since the days of Talleyrand and Castlereagh.

He sat there today, and cards were called for, and Lionel was to deal.

Mr Chatterway wondered, if he left for Paris directly, as soon as this game of whist was over, whether he would even need to make explanations. A few little walks and talks, a few *billets-doux* left at Maudie's hotel as they passed through on their way to the ever-to-be-regretted St Moritz, and then, when she left and said *au revoir,* he need not say the word *adieu* aloud.

'What's trumps?' he asked, in his shortest recorded sentence of the afternoon.

'Hearts,' snapped old Egg. ''Sblood, Marvo, concentrate for *God*'s sake. We always start with hearts.'

'So we do,' said Marvo.

And as Lionel dealt the cards to Mr Chatterway, to his grandfather and to Timothy Lupton, old Severus gazed with a smile down the long saloon and exclaimed valiantly in his high-pitched voice, 'I'll wager no one could tell me when the last game of *ombre* was played in this room!'

THIRTY-THREE

'It's coming in'

His mother was waiting for him in the vestibule when he reached the hotel at Dover: or so it appeared, for she was looking about her with the unmistakable air of one who momently expected an arrival. She was pale, hollow-eyed; even, in the nervous wringing of her mittened hands, a little terrible. She did not see him at first – but when she at last recognised Lionel, the most she rose to, while allowing herself to be kissed, was – 'I thought you would have travelled down with Dr Nockels.'

'The doctor?'

With a few more stabs at normal comprehension, Charlotte elucidated that she had sent a telegram to Brunswick Square urging that Lionel bring the family physician to Dover with all speed.

'But we were lunching at the club.'

'A fine time for the club.'

'One must lunch somewhere, I take it.'

'And too well by the smell of you. Truly, papa goes too far.'

There was a moment of silent confusion, for sometimes 'papa' on her lips meant her own father, and sometimes Lionel's – though more usually she referred to Horace as 'your father'.

'But Mama – Dr Nockels – why do we need him – it isn't' – the horror dawned at last and with overwhelming sharpness penetrated the sleepiness induced by the last half-bottle of madeira and the two hours in a train – 'isn't Maudie?'

'Maudie?'

'Her cough.'

And then Charlotte threw herself into her son's arms and he clasped her, and for the first time in his life he recognised that she was a woman.

'Can nothing ever proceed smoothly in our family?' she asked through sniffs.

'It would seem not.'

'Darling, forgive me for being so foolish.'

'It's not foolish.'

'Let us sit and wait for Dr Nockels.'

'But if I haven't told him?'

'I sent a telegram to him also.'

'And if it isn't Maudie? Good heavens, mother – you're not'—

'I told you in the – but of course you must have left the house before you received it. It's your father. He has had an accident.'

'Serious?'

'No, no.' It was her turn to pat his hand as they sat down. Though the dinner hour was close upon them, the waiter suggested tea, a proposal in which they acquiesced.

'But is there no doctor in Dover? – and what sort of accident, and why were you waiting here to warn me?'

'He fell down those stairs this morning' – she said – indicating the scene of the calamity with a small sideways gesture of the head. 'We got a local doctor here, of course. He says your father has broken his ankle.'

"Then that's *that,* I suppose?'

'That?' she asked.

'That puts paid to any idea of the Pater going off to St Moritz.'

'He believes Nockels can patch him up.'

'Oh hoor-ay.' Maudie's scream drowned the *sotto voce* in which mother and son had been conversing. Lionel looked up at her. Because he was sitting and she was standing, she seemed to have grown in the very short period since he had last seen her. She seemed almost large, and bursting with mirth and vivacity. 'Our knight in armour – I say, though, poor papa – fancy though: a butterfly net! I told him not to bring the stupid thing – and he got tangled up in it the moment we arrived. Dr Nockels is with him now, I suppose.'

'He hasn't come yet,' said Charlotte.

'Lionel, you perfect clot.'

'He didn't get our telegram' – but there was no chance for the boring rehearsal on which Charlotte had set her heart, of things which had *not* happened. Maudie was too full of things which might happen.

'We shall just have to leave poor Papa behind and take you instead, darling –'

'But I have no luggage, no passport.'

'You can use Papa's. . . .'

'It is all much more difficult.'

'And besides Mama will need an *escort* in Paris,' Maudie sniggered. In her glee and her health, all the touches of homeliness in her appearance – for instance, the pallor and the freckles – seemed to be worn with majesty, even *hauteur.* She was magnificent as she tossed back her thick chestnut tresses and laughed with her dark, knowing, slightly mandarin eyes.

'You are not proposing to go about Paris unaccompanied yourself, I take it?'

'You know perfectly well,' said the sister. 'Oh poor Papa, it is the end, simply the *end!*'

'You were so anxious for your father to come with us,' said Charlotte, as she thanked the tea-waiter. 'Before, that is. . . .'

'Before whom or what?' asked Lionel.

'Before the butterfly net,' sniggered Maudie. 'Of course it is all impossibly sad for Papa but we needn't go for so long, need we? And he'll be all right, won't he, with his books and his volcanic samples.'

'More all right than any of us perhaps,' said Lionel, joining in the laughter for it all seemed, of a sudden, funny.

'You seem to forget we have closed the house – sent all the servants away.'

'Oh *Mama*. there is Hopkins.'

'She *must* stay with me,' said Charlotte quickly.

'Well, can't Papa stay at the Athenaeum?'

'With a broken leg?' said mother and son simultaneously, a gabble which provoked – for some reason – more squeals of hilarity from Maudie, picked up by Lionel.

'Anyone would think,' said Charlotte, 'that you were *pleased* that your father has fallen downstairs. Think if it had been his neck that he had broken.'

They thought for a moment while their mother fussed with a cream jug and sugar tongs.

'We will probably,' Charlotte said, 'find ourselves not going abroad after all. We must make our pleasures at home. There is plenty to *see*, heaven knows, in England.'

'We weren't going to Paris to *see* things, Mama.'

'Really, Maudie, I thought you *were*. Think of the list we made – Le Brun's *Magdalene* in the Louvre, and the *Colonne de Juliet* which my father watched being built, and. . . .'

But her list could continue no further, for, black-coated and salmon-gilled, Dr Nockels was making his enquiries of the clerk encaged in the confessional at the door.

'. . . I must,' she said, and rose, leaving the young people to themselves.

'See the *bounce* in poor mama's walk,' said Maudie. 'A real spring in her step, so suddenly.'

'I don't see it, truly,' said Lionel.

'We all see what we want to see, apparently.'

'We see what our faculties will *let* us see, which is sometimes quite different.'

'Don't be clever, I pray you.'

'I'm not, only. . . .'

'Let it be only. Darling Lionel, it's so nice to see you. It's almost as if they've been trying to keep us apart all summer.'

'They?'

'They! You know.'

'Look,' he said – for their mother had already escorted Dr Nockels up the swooping iron tracery of the staircase towards the bed of suffering. 'Let's go and look at the sea. Do let's.'

The afternoon had by now become early evening. Not much horse traffic, few people. Walking against the stiff breeze, and leaping down into the steep shingle of the beach, they soon were able to feel themselves alone, and walk for a good while in happy silent communion. Being together by the sea brought back, for brother and sister, any number of shared walks and childhood explorations – times of shrimping nets, moments of unrolling stockings and plunging pale little feet into rock pools or feeling, simply, the delicious freedom which came from knowing that there was sand beneath the toes. But this was a new beach: they had not been here before; and it was not sand but shingle beneath their well-shod and grown-up feet. So suddenly it had all happened. They were, in surveying the parents, no longer quite children. Charlotte and Horace were inescapably hedged by the past. The future – if that was anyone's possession – it was Maudie's and Lionel's, these two young persons whose almost grown forms made such enormous shadows on the shingle.

Lionel, although drowsy with a good luncheon when he arrived in Dover, had been so full of impressions which he meant to convey to Maudie and to his mother. There was the whole story of the monastery – one day that would be told (though strangely enough, it was not for another forty years, when he and Maudie sat in Brunswick Square, smoking cigarettes one evening and drinking tea a half-brother had brought back from India). There was all that had happened since – the long conversation with Dr Jenkinson, the coming and going and return of faith – the encounter with the legendary Father Stanton, the change in Gutch. So much Lionel had to say. But it was all subsumed in the farce of a broken ankle. Much he had to give, too, in the way of pompous warnings to Maudie concerning a certain old gentleman about to embark for Paris, and yet, who was Lionel to give his sister a talking-to about prudence? Thus he argued with himself as they scrunched and slithered along in silence. There was nothing, surely, improper in her fondness for an old man with whom – that very day, dammit! – Lionel had himself played a rubber.

'Lioney,' she asked him with sudden intensity. They had been silent

for about half an hour now, and in order to emphasise the importance
of the moment, Maudie stopped walking. The Channel churned and
swirled – the heaving green of the sea thickening into white foam as it
crashed on to the shingle. They stared at it – at all its surging and
relentless energy.

'Just as well you're not sailing tomorrow at least if it's going to be
like this.'

'But *Lioney*.'

'Yes?'

'Do you think Mama once loved Mr Chatterway?'

'Old Chatterbox?' For a moment, the boy echoed his grandfather. It
wasn't the sort of thing to talk about. 'Shouldn't think so. You ask
some rum questions.'

'Look at that huge wave?'

It was indeed, a vast towering, thing. Maudie, who imagined herself
in it, taking a dip, shuddered at its immensity, for it was many times
taller than she. It seemed so furious, so insistent, so destructive. But
Lionel, who loved its fury, gazed at it with awe, and licked the salt
from his upper lip.

'Do you realise Mama was only a year older than me when she got
married?' she asked.

'And Papa was about three times older than you when he got
married.'

'Aren't they *funny?*'

'Mama and Papa?' Lionel had never seen his parents in a comic
light. He was, besides, just at that moment, caught up with the beauty
of the sea. Both were mesmerised by it, for they took one another's
hand and gingerly approached the foaming waters' edge.

'Is the tide in or out?' asked Maudie. 'Oh this air! Haven't you
noticed I haven't coughed once!'

'I can't tell – about the tide. I mean.'

'Because if it's coming *in,* and we continue to stand here,' she began
with the mock gravity, suddenly, of her old governess, Miss Adeney.

'We're going to get out feet wet, aren't we?' echoed Lionel, with a
burst of laughter, and playfully he refused to let go of her hand, but
held her firmly where they stood, just at the border of the tide. Another
wave decided it – a small one this time, but a wave none the less which,
even though they were staring at the sea, took them by surprise and
soaked them completely – shoes, stockings, skirts, trowsers. Both
squealed with childish merriment.

'It's coming in!' laughed Maudie.

'Watch out!' called her brother – as hand in hand, they scampered
from the next wave which advanced the inflowing of the ocean several

feet into the shore.

'It's got yards to come in yet!' added Maudie with her taste for exaggeration. 'If we were still standing where we were before we'd be in up to our necks?'

And they ran along, no longer minding if they were wet or dry, still hand in hand, and still laughing.